The
Handmaiden's
Necklace

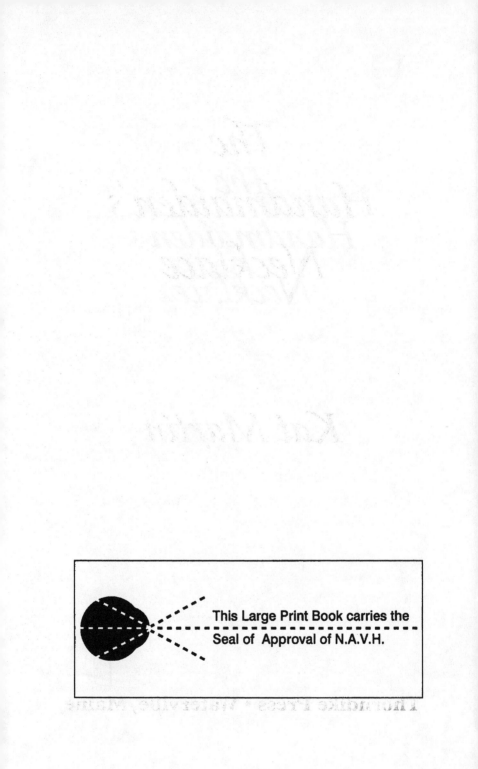

This Large Print Book carries the Seal of Approval of N.A.V.H.

The Handmaiden's Necklace

Kat Martin

Thorndike Press • Waterville, Maine

Published in 2006 by arrangement with Harlequin Books S.A.

Thorndike Press® Large Print Romance.

The tree indicium is a trademark of Thorndike Press.

The text of this Large Print edition is unabridged.
Other aspects of the book may vary from the original edition.

Set in 16 pt. Plantin by Carleen Stearns.

Printed in the United States on permanent paper.

Library of Congress Cataloging-in-Publication Data

Martin, Kat.
    The handmaiden's necklace / by Kat Martin.
        p. cm. — (Thorndike Press large print romance)
    ISBN 0-7862-8686-5 (lg. print : hc : alk. paper)
    1. Large type books.   I. Title.   II. Series: Thorndike
Press large print romance series.
    PS3563.A7246H36 2006
    813'.54—dc22   2006010377

To my husband, Larry.
My true life hero.

One

" 'Tis a shame, is what it is." Cornelia Thorne, Lady Brookfield, stood near the center of the ballroom. "Just look at him out there dancing . . . so completely bored. Him a duke and her such a mousy little thing, completely terrified of the man, I'll wager."

The Duchess of Sheffield, Miriam Saunders, raised her quizzing glass to peer at her son, Rafael, Duke of Sheffield. Miriam and her sister, Cornelia, were attending a charity ball along with Rafael and his betrothed, Lady Mary Rose Montague. The evening, a benefit for the London Widows and Orphans Society, was being held in the magnificent ballroom of the Chesterfield Hotel.

"The girl is actually quite lovely," the duchess defended, "so blond and petite, just a bit shy, is all." Unlike her son, the duke, who was tall and dark, with eyes even bluer than her own. And there was Rafe, himself,

7

a strong, incredibly handsome man whose powerful presence seemed to overshadow the young woman he had chosen to be his future bride.

"I'll grant, she is pretty," Cornelia said, "in a rather whitewashed sort of way. Still, it seems a shame."

"Rafael is finally doing his duty. It is past time he took a wife. Perhaps they don't suit as well as I would have liked, but the girl is young and strong, and she will bear him healthy sons." And yet, as her sister had said, Miriam couldn't miss the bland, bored expression on her son's very handsome face.

"Rafael was always so dashing," Cornelia said a bit wistfully. "Do you not remember the way he was before? So full of fire, so passionate about life in those days. Now . . . well, he is always so restrained. I do miss the vibrant young man he used to be."

"People change, Cornelia. Rafe learned the hard way where those sorts of emotions can lead."

Cornelia grunted. "You're talking about The Scandal." Thin and gray-haired, she was older than the duchess by nearly six years. "How could anyone forget Danielle . . . ? Now, there was a woman Rafael's equal. 'Tis a shame she turned out to be such a disappointment."

8

The duchess cast her sister a glance, not wanting a reminder of the terrible scandal they had suffered because of Rafe's former betrothed, Danielle Duval.

The dance ended and the couples began dispersing from the dance floor. "Hush," Miriam warned. "Rafe and Mary Rose are coming this way." The girl was nearly a foot shorter than the duke, blond, blue-eyed and fair, the perfect picture of English femininity. She was also the daughter of an earl, with a very sizable dowry. Miriam prayed her son would find at least some measure of happiness with the girl.

Rafe made a polite, formal bow. "Good evening, Mother. Aunt Cornelia."

Miriam smiled. "You're both looking quite splendid tonight." And they did. Rafe in dove-gray breeches and a navy-blue tailcoat that set off the blue of his eyes, and Mary Rose in a gown of white silk trimmed with delicate pink roses.

"Thank you, Your Grace," said the girl, with a very proper curtsy.

Miriam frowned. Was her hand trembling where it rested on the sleeve of Rafe's coat? Dear God, the child would soon be a duchess. Miriam fervently prayed she would manage to infuse a bit of backbone into her spine as the months went along.

9

"Would you care to dance, Mother?" Rafe asked politely.

"Later, perhaps."

"Aunt Cornelia?"

But Cornelia was staring at the doorway, her mind a thousand miles away. Miriam followed her gaze, as did Rafael and his betrothed.

"Speak of the devil . . ." Cornelia whispered beneath her breath.

Miriam's eyes widened and her heartbeat quickened, turned wildly erratic. She recognized the short, plump little woman entering the ballroom, Flora Chamberlain, Dowager Countess Wycombe. And she also knew the tall, slender, red-haired woman who was the countess's niece.

Miriam's mouth thinned into a hostile line. A few feet away, her son's expression shifted from incredulity to anger, deepening the slight cleft in his chin.

Cornelia continued to stare. "Of all the nerve!"

A muscle tightened along Rafe's jaw, but he didn't say a word.

"Who is that?" asked Mary Rose.

Rafe ignored her. His gaze remained locked on the elegant creature entering the ballroom behind her aunt. Danielle Duval had been living in the country for the past five years. After The Scandal, she had been banished, shamed into leaving the city. Since her father was dead and her mother had disowned her for what she had done, she had moved in with her aunt, Flora Duval Chamberlain. Until tonight, she had remained in the country.

The duchess couldn't imagine what Danielle was doing back in London, or what had possessed her to come to a place where she was so obviously not welcome.

"Rafael . . . ?" Lady Mary Rose looked up at him with a worried expression. "What is it?"

Rafe's gaze never wavered. Something flashed in his intense blue eyes, something hot and wild Miriam hadn't seen there in nearly five years. Anger tightened the skin across his cheekbones. He took a steadying breath and fought to bring himself under control.

Looking down at Mary Rose, he managed a smile. "Nothing to be concerned about, sweeting. Nothing at all." He took her gloved hand and rested it once more on the sleeve of his coat. "I believe they are playing a rondele. Shall we dance?"

He led her away without waiting for an answer. Miriam imagined it would always be that way — Rafe commanding, Mary Rose obeying like a good little girl.

The duchess turned back to Danielle Duval, watched her moving along behind her rotund, silver-haired aunt, head held high, ignoring the whispers, the stares, walking with the grace of the duchess she should have been.

Thank heaven the girl's true nature had come out before Rafael had married her.

Before he fell even more in love with her.

The duchess looked again at petite Mary Rose, thought of the biddable sort of wife she would make, nothing at all like Danielle Duval, and suddenly she felt grateful.

Crystal chandeliers gleamed down from the lavish, inlaid ceilings of the magnificent ballroom, casting a soft glow over the polished parquet floors. Huge vases of yellow roses and white chrysanthemums sat on pedestals along the wall. The elite of London's elite filled the room, dancing to the music of a ten-piece orchestra in pale blue livery, members of the *ton* attending the gala in support of the London Widows and Orphans Society.

At the edge of the dance floor, Cord Easton, Earl of Brant, and Ethan Sharpe, Marquess of Belford, stood next to their wives, Victoria and Grace, watching the couples moving around the floor.

"Do you see what I see?" Cord drawled, his gaze turning away from the dancers to the pair of women walking along the far wall of the room. "I swear my eyes must be deceiving me." Cord was a big man, powerfully built, with dark brown hair and golden brown eyes. He and Ethan were the duke's best friends.

"What are you looking at so intently?" His wife, Victoria, followed the line of his vision.

"Danielle Duval," Ethan answered, surprised. "I can't believe she has the nerve to come here." Ethan was as tall as the duke, lean and broad-shouldered, with black hair and very light blue eyes.

"Why, she's beautiful. . . ." Grace Sharpe stared in awe at the tall, slender redhead. "No wonder Rafe fell in love with her."

"Mary Rose is beautiful, too," Victoria defended. "Yes, of course she is. But there is something about Miss Duval . . . can you not see?"

"There is something about her, all right," Cord growled. "She's a treacherous little baggage with the heart of a snake and not the least bit of conscience. Half of London knows what she did to Rafe. She isn't welcome here, I can tell you."

Cord's gaze found the duke, who was concentrating on his petite blond dancing

13

partner with an interest he had never shown in her before. "Rafe must have seen her. Damnation — why did Danielle have to come back to London?"

"What do you think Rafe will do?" Victoria asked.

"Ignore her. Rafe won't stoop to her level. He has too much self-control for that."

Danielle Duval fixed her gaze straight ahead and continued walking behind her aunt. They were headed for a spot at the back of the room, a place where Dani could remain for the most part out of sight.

From the corner of her eye, she saw a woman turn abruptly away from her, giving Danielle her back. She could hear people whispering, talking about The Scandal. Dear God, how could she have let her aunt convince her to come?

But Flora Duval Chamberlain had a way of convincing people to her will.

"This charity means everything to me, dearest," she had said. "You have been instrumental in all the good work we have accomplished and received not a single word of thanks. I refuse to go without you. Please say you will agree to your aunt's one small request."

"You know what it will be like for me,

Aunt Flora. No one will speak to me. They will talk about me behind my back. I don't think I can bear to go through that again."

"You have to come out of hiding sooner or later. It has already been five years! You never did anything to deserve being treated the way you have been. It is high time you reclaimed your place in the world."

Knowing how much the ball meant to her aunt, Danielle had reluctantly agreed. Besides, Aunt Flora was right. It was time she came out of hiding and reclaimed her life. And she would only be in London for the next two weeks. After that, she was sailing for America, embarking on the new life she intended to make for herself there.

Dani had accepted a proposal of marriage from a man named Richard Clemens, whom she had met in the country, a wealthy American businessman, a widower with two young children. As Richard's wife, Danielle would have the husband and family she had long ago given up hope of ever having. With her new life on the horizon, coming to the ball at her aunt's request seemed a small-enough price to pay.

Now that she was there, however, Dani wished with all her heart that she were somewhere — anywhere — besides where she was.

15

They reached the back of the elegant ballroom and she settled herself on a small gold velvet chair against the wall behind one of the urns overflowing with flowers. A few feet away Aunt Flora, undeterred by the hostile glares being cast in their direction, made her way over to the punch bowl and returned a few minutes later with crystal cups filled to the brim with fruit punch.

"Here, dearest, drink this." She winked. "I put a splash of something in there to help you relax."

Danielle opened her mouth to say she didn't need alcoholic spirits to get through the evening, caught another hostile glare and took a big drink of the punch.

"As co-chairman of the event," her aunt explained, "I shall be expected to give a brief speech a bit later on. I shall ask for a generous donation from those in attendance, express my gratitude to all for their past support, and then we shall leave."

It couldn't happen soon enough for Dani. Though she had known what to expect — the scorn she read in people's faces; the acquaintances, once her friends, who would not even look her way — hurt even worse than she had imagined.

And then there was Rafael.

Dear God, she had prayed he wouldn't be

here. Aunt Flora had assured her he would simply send a hefty donation as he had done every other year. Instead, here he was, taller, even more handsome than she remembered, exuding every ounce of his powerful presence and aristocratic bearing.

The man who had ruined her.

The man she hated more than anyone on earth.

"Oh, dear." Aunt Flora waved her painted fan in front of her round, powdered face. "Apparently I was wrong. It appears His Grace, the Duke of Sheffield, is here."

For an instant, Dani's back teeth ground together. "Yes . . . so it would seem." And Rafe had seen her walk in, Danielle knew. For an instant their eyes had met and held, hers as green as his were blue. She had seen the flash of anger before his gaze became shuttered, then the bland expression he had been wearing before he saw her fell back into place.

Her own temper climbed. She had never seen that look on his face before, so calm, so completely unruffled, almost serene. It made her want to hit him. To slap the smug, condescending look off his too-handsome face.

Instead, she sat in her chair against the wall, ignored by old friends, whispered about by people she didn't even know, wishing her

17

aunt would finish her speech and they could go home.

Rafael handed his betrothed, Lady Mary Rose Montague, back into the care of her mother and father, the Earl and Countess of Throckmorton.

"Perhaps you will save another dance for me later," Rafe said to the little blonde, bowing over her hand.

"Of course, Your Grace."

He nodded, turned away.

"They will be playing a waltz a bit later," said Mary Rose. "Perhaps you would . . ."

But Rafe was already walking away, his mind on another woman far different from the one he intended to wed. *Danielle Duval.* Just the sound of her name, whispering through the back of his mind, was enough to make his temper shoot to dangerous levels. It had taken him years to learn to control his volatile nature, to bring his emotions under control. These days, he rarely shouted, rarely lost his temper. Rarely allowed his passionate nature to get out of hand.

Not since Danielle.

Loving Danielle Duval had taught him a valuable lesson — the terrible cost of letting one's emotions rule one's head and heart. Love was a disease that could unman a man.

It had nearly destroyed Rafael.

He glanced toward the rear of the ballroom, catching a flash of Danielle's bright hair. She was here. He could scarcely believe it. How dare she show her face after what she had done!

Determined to ignore her, Rafe went to join his friends at the edge of the dance floor. The instant he walked up, he knew the group had spotted Danielle.

He took a glass of champagne off the silver tray of a passing waiter. "So . . . from the astonished looks on your faces, I gather you have seen her."

Cord shook his head. "I can't believe she had the nerve to come here."

"The woman has unmitigated gall," Ethan added darkly. Rafe flicked a glance at Grace, who studied him over the rim of her glass of champagne.

"She is quite beautiful," Grace said. "I can see why you fell in love with her."

His jaw tightened. "I fell in love with the woman because I was an idiot. Believe me, I paid the price for my folly, and I assure you it won't happen again."

Victoria's head came up. She was the shorter of the women, with heavy brown hair as opposed to Grace's rich auburn curls. "Surely you don't mean you will never

19

again fall in love," she said.

"That is precisely what I mean."

"But what about Mary Rose? Surely you love her at least a little."

"I care for the girl. I wouldn't marry her if I didn't. She's a lovely young woman with a pleasant, biddable nature, and a very fine pedigree."

Ethan rolled his pale blue eyes. "Need I remind you, my friend, we're discussing a woman here, not a horse?"

Cord stared off toward the redhead at the far end of the ballroom. "You're doing a splendid job of ignoring her. I don't know if I could be quite so magnanimous."

Rafe scoffed. "It isn't all that hard. The woman means nothing to me — not anymore."

But his gaze strayed again across the dance floor. He caught a glimpse of the deep red curls on top of Danielle's head and felt a rush of angry heat to the back of his neck. He itched to stride across the floor and wrap his hands around her throat, to squeeze the very life from her. It was a feeling he hadn't known since the day he'd last seen her — five years ago.

The memory returned with shocking force . . . the weeklong house party at the country estate of his friend Oliver Randall.

The excitement he felt, knowing Danielle, her mother and aunt would be among the guests. Ollie Randall was the third son of the Marquess of Caverly, and the family estate, Woodhaven, was palatial.

The weeklong visit was magical, at least for Rafe. Long, lazy afternoons spent with Danielle, evenings of dancing and the chance for them to steal a few moments alone. Then, two nights before week's end, Rafe had stumbled upon a note, a brief message signed by Danielle. It was addressed to Oliver, had obviously been read and tossed away, and in it Dani invited Ollie to her room that night.

I must see you, Oliver. Only you can save me from making a terrible mistake. Please, I beg you, come to my room at midnight. I will be waiting.

Yours, Danielle

Rafe felt torn between anger and disbelief. He was in love with Danielle and he had believed she loved him.

It was only a few minutes after midnight that Rafe knocked, then turned the knob on Danielle's door. When the door swung open, he saw his friend lying in bed with his betrothed.

Lying naked beside the woman he loved.

He could still remember the wave of nausea that had rolled through his stomach, the awful, terrible feeling of betrayal.

It rose again now as the music in the ballroom reached a crescendo. Rafe fixed his gaze on the orchestra, determined to dispel the unwanted memories, to bury them as he had done five years ago.

He spent the next hour dancing with the wives of his friends, then danced again with Mary Rose. A brief speech was made by one of the co-chairwomen of the fund-raising event, and recognizing Flora Duval Chamberlain, he understood why Danielle had come.

Or at least part of the reason.

If there were others, he would never know. After the brief speeches ended and the dancing resumed, Rafe looked again across the ballroom.

Danielle Duval was no longer there.

Two

"Did you see the way he looked at her?" Smoothing back a curl of her heavy chestnut hair, Victoria Easton, Countess of Brant, sat on the brocade sofa in the Blue Drawing Room of the town house she shared with her husband and ten-month-old son. Her blond, elegantly lovely sister, Claire, Lady Percival Chezwick, and her best friend, Grace Sharpe, Marchioness of Belford, sat just a few feet away.

"It was really quite something," Grace said. "There was fire in that man's eyes. I have never seen quite that expression on his face."

"He was probably just angry she had come," Claire reasoned. "I wish I had been there to see it."

Tory had ordered tea but the butler had not yet arrived with the cart, though she could hear the wheels rattling down the marble-floored corridor on the other side of the door. "You weren't there because you were home with Percy doing something far more fun than attending a benefit ball."

Claire giggled. She was the youngest of the women and, even after her marriage, still the most naive. "We had a wonderful night. Percy is so romantic. Still, I should have enjoyed seeing a truly scarlet woman."

"I felt sorry for Rafael," Grace said. "Rafe must have truly loved her. He tried to hide it, but he was furious, even after all these years."

"Yes, and Rafe rarely loses his temper," Tory said. She sighed. "It's terrible what she did to him. I'm surprised she fooled him so completely. Rafe is usually a very good judge of character."

"So exactly what did she do?" Claire asked, leaning forward in her chair.

"According to Cord, Danielle invited a friend of Rafe's into her bed — with Rafe and a number of guests just down the hall. He caught them and that was the end of their betrothal. It was all very public. The scandal followed him for years."

Grace smoothed a faint wrinkle in the skirt of her high-waisted apricot muslin skirt. "Danielle Duval is the reason Rafe is determined to marry without love." A week ago, her little boy, Andrew Ethan, had just turned six months old, but Grace's lithe figure had already returned.

Timmons knocked just then and Tory

24

beckoned the short, stout butler into the room. The tea cart rattled over to the Oriental carpet and stopped in front of the sofa, then the small man silently left the drawing room.

"All is not yet lost," Tory said to Grace, leaning forward to pour the steaming brew into three gold-rimmed porcelain cups. "You gave Rafael the necklace, so there is still a ray of hope."

Rafe had been instrumental in saving Grace's life and that of her newborn baby. She had wanted her friend to find the happiness she had found with Ethan, so she had given the duke a very special gift. The Bride's Necklace, an ancient piece of jewelry made in the thirteenth century for the bride of the Lord of Fallon. The necklace, it was said, carried a curse — it could bring great joy or terrible tragedy, depending on whether or not its owner's heart was pure.

"I suppose you're right," Grace agreed. "Rafe has the necklace, so there is yet a chance for him to find happiness."

Claire toyed with the handle on her teacup. "What if all the things that happened to you and Tory were just strange coincidences and nothing at all to do with the necklace? It could be, you know."

Tory sighed, knowing her sister might be right. "It's possible, I guess, but . . ." But Tory couldn't help thinking of the time the necklace had belonged to her, of the wonderful man she had married and their beautiful infant son, Jeremy Cordell, who was asleep in the nursery upstairs.

She couldn't help remembering that she had given the necklace to Grace, who had met Ethan and saved him from the darkness that surrounded him. Grace, who now also had a wonderful husband and son.

And there was her stepfather, Miles Whiting, Baron Harwood, an evil man who had owned the necklace and now lay moldering in his grave.

Tory shivered, shoving away the unwanted thought. "We know Rafe has a good heart. We can only hope the necklace will work."

Claire looked up from studying the leaves in the bottom of her teacup. "Maybe the duke will fall in love with Mary Rose. That would be the perfect solution."

Tory cast Grace a look and tried not to grin when Grace rolled her eyes. "That is a very good notion, Claire. Perhaps he will."

But when she thought of the searing glance Rafe had tossed at Danielle Duval, she couldn't make herself believe it.

"Please, Aunt Flora. I simply cannot do it. How can you even think of asking me to go through that again?"

They were standing in Danielle's bedchamber, in their elegant suite at the Chesterfield Hotel, a lovely room done in shades of gold and dark green. Aunt Flora had let the rooms for the next two weeks, until their ship set sail for America.

"Come, now, dearest. This is an entirely different sort of affair. To begin with, this is an afternoon tea, not a ball, and a number of the children will be there. You know how you love children, and you are always so good with them."

Dani toyed with the sash on her blue quilted wrapper. It was not yet noon. The benefit tea would begin in a little over an hour. "The affair may be different, but I will be shunned, just as I was before. You saw how people treated me."

"Yes, I did, and I was proud of the way you conducted yourself. You made it clear you had every right to be there. I thought you handled the situation beautifully."

"I was miserable, every single moment."

Aunt Flora sighed dramatically. "Yes, well, I am truly sorry about the duke." She looked up at Dani from beneath a set of finely plucked, silver-gray eyebrows. "At least the man didn't cause you any trouble."

Dani didn't mention the angry look he had tossed her, or the furious expression he couldn't quite hide. "He would have been sorry if he had said even one word."

"Well, he won't be there this time, I promise you."

She glanced down at her aunt, who was a good eight inches shorter and quite a few stone heavier. "How can you be so certain?"

"It was merely a fluke the last time. An afternoon tea is hardly the sort of affair that would interest a duke. Besides, I wouldn't ask you to go if I were feeling up to snuff. Lately I've been a bit under the weather." She coughed lightly for effect, hoping to make Dani feel guilty.

Instead, Danielle saw it as a last thin ray of hope. "Perhaps, since you are ill, it would be best if you stayed home, as well. We can have some nice hot tea and fresh scones sent up and —"

Aunt Flora stopped her words. "As co-chairwoman of the society, I have duties, responsibilities. As long as you are with me, I shall be fine."

Dani's shoulders sagged. How did her aunt always manage to get her way? Then again, Aunt Flora had agreed to accompany

28

her on the difficult journey to America. She would be there for Dani's wedding and remain until she was settled with her husband in her new home. Surely she could buck up enough to make it through this last fundraising event before they departed.

And, as Aunt Flora had said, the children would be there. There would be at least a few friendly faces to get her through the afternoon affair.

A knock at the door drew her attention. An instant later, the door swung open and her lady's maid, Caroline Loon, walked in.

Caro smiled widely. "Lady Wycombe sent for me. Shall I help you pick out something to wear?"

Dani rolled her eyes, thinking that she hadn't had a chance from the start.

"Well, then I shall leave you to dress," Aunt Flora said, making her way out the door. "You may join me as soon as you are ready."

Giving in to her fate, Dani made a resigned nod of her head, and as soon as the door was closed, Caro hurried over to the armoire against the wall. At six-and-twenty, a year older than Dani, Caroline Loon was taller and more slenderly built, a blond woman, attractive in a different sort of way, with an incredibly sweet disposition.

29

Caro was a gently reared young lady whose parents had died unexpectedly of a fever. Penniless and orphaned, she had arrived at Wycombe Park nearly five years ago, desperate for any sort of employment.

Aunt Flora had immediately hired her as Danielle's lady's maid, but over the years, the two of them had become far more than mistress and maid. Caroline Loon, a vicar's daughter likely destined for spinsterhood, had become her best friend.

Caro opened the door of the armoire. Though most of Dani's clothes were packed away in heavy leather trunks in preparation for her journey, a modest assortment of gowns hung inside.

"What about the saffron muslin embroidered with roses?" Caro asked, dragging out one of Dani's favorite gowns.

"I suppose the saffron gown will do well enough." If she had to go to the blasted tea, she intended to look as good as she possibly could, and wearing the bright yellow muslin always made her feel pretty.

"Sit down and I'll do up your hair," Caro instructed. "Lady Wycombe will have my head if you make her late for her tea."

Danielle sighed. "I swear, between the two of you, I am surprised I ever get to make a decision."

Caro just laughed. "She loves you. She is determined you return to society. She wants you to be happy."

"I'll be happy — once I'm on my way to America." Dani reached over and took hold of Caro's slim, long-boned hand. "I am only grateful that you have agreed to go with us."

"I am glad to be going along." Caro managed a smile. "Perhaps we will both find a new life in the Colonies."

Dani smiled, as well. "Yes, perhaps we will." Danielle certainly hoped so. She was tired of her nonexistent life, tired of being hidden away in the country with few friends and only an occasional visit from the children in the orphanage to look forward to. She was eager for the chance to make a new life in America, where no one had ever heard of The Scandal.

In the meantime, she had to find the courage to get through her aunt's miserable tea.

Rafael slipped a forest-green tailcoat on over his beige piqué waistcoat. His valet, a short, slight, balding man who had been in his service for years, reached up to straighten the knot on his stock.

"There you are, Your Grace."

"Thank you, Petersen."

31

"Will there be anything more, sir?"

"Not until my return, which should be sometime late this afternoon." He didn't intend to stay at the affair very long, just drop by and pay his respects, and of course leave a sizable bank draft for the orphans. After all, it was his civic duty.

He told himself it had nothing to do with the notion Danielle Duval might also be in attendance, convinced himself that if she were, he would ignore her as he had done before.

He wouldn't say any of the things he had longed to say five years ago, wouldn't let her know how badly her betrayal had hurt him. He wouldn't give her the satisfaction of knowing how devastated he had been, that for weeks after it had happened he had barely been able to function. Instead, he would make clear his disdain for her without a single word.

His coach-and-four waited in front of the house, a lavish three-story structure in Hanover Square that his father had built for his mother, who now lived in a separate, smaller, but no-less-elegant apartment on the east side of the mansion.

A footman pulled open the carriage door. Rafe mounted the steps and settled himself against the red velvet squabs, and the coach rumbled off down the cobbled street. The afternoon tea was being held in the gardens of the Mayfair residence of the Marquess of Denby, whose wife was deeply involved in the charity for London's widows and orphans.

The mansion, in Breton Street, wasn't that far away. The carriage rolled up in front and a footman opened the door. Rafe departed the coach and made his way up the front porch steps past two liveried footmen, who ushered him through the entry out to the garden at the rear of the house.

Most of the guests had already arrived, just as he had hoped, and they clustered here and there on the terrace, or walked the gravel paths through the leafy foliage of the garden. A group of children, plainly dressed but clean, their hair neatly combed, played at the base of a stone fountain on the right side of the garden.

The charity organized by Lady Denby was a good one. There weren't enough orphanages in the city to care for the needy and many homeless children who wound up in infant poorhouses, workhouses, apprenticed as chimney sweeps, or grew up as vagrants and beggars, living hand-to-mouth on the streets.

Most orphans were taken care of by local

parishes, often abominable excuses for homes. Foundlings brought into their care rarely lived to reach their first year. Rafe had heard of a parish in Westminster that had received five hundred bastards in a single year — and raised only one of them past five years of age.

But the London Society funded several large orphan homes of a very high caliber.

"Your Grace!" Lady Denby hurried toward him, a big-bosomed woman with glossy black hair cut short and curling around her face. "How good of you to come."

"I'm afraid I can't stay long. I just stopped by to present you with a bank draft for the orphanage." He dragged the folded piece of paper from his pocket and handed it over, all the while scanning the guests to see who might also be there.

"Why, this is quite wonderful, Your Grace — especially since you made such a generous donation at the ball."

He shrugged his shoulders. He could certainly afford it and he had always liked children. Having a family of his own was the main reason he had recently decided to take a wife. That and the fact his mother and aunt hounded him incessantly about living up to his responsibilities as duke.

He needed an heir, they said. And a spare. He needed a son to carry on the Sheffield title and manage the vast fortune entailed to it so that his family would always be taken care of.

"Tea is being served on the terrace." Lady Denby took his arm and began to guide him in that direction. "Of course, we have something a bit stronger for the men."

Smiling, she moved him off toward a table covered with silver trays laden with cakes and cookies of every sort, and tiny finger sandwiches so small it would take a dozen to fill him up. A silver tea service sat in the middle of the linen draped table, along with a crystal punch bowl.

"Shall I have one of the servants bring you a brandy, Your Grace?"

"Yes, I'd like that. Thank you." It might help him make it through the next half hour, which was all he intended to stay.

The brandy arrived and he sipped it slowly, searching for a friendly face, seeing his mother and Aunt Cornelia in conversation with a group of other women, glancing past them to the round, powdered face of Flora Duval Chamberlain. His gaze lit on the woman to her left, a woman with flame-red hair and the face of a goddess. Rafe's stomach contracted as if he had suffered a powerful blow.

His expression instantly hardened. He told himself he hadn't come because of her, but seeing her now, he recognized the lie for what it was. For an instant, Danielle's eyes met his and widened in shock. Rafe felt a shot of satisfaction as the color drained from her lovely, treacherous face.

He didn't glance away, certain that she would.

Instead her chin shot up and she gave him a look meant to burn right through him. He clenched his jaw. Long seconds passed and neither of them looked away. Then Danielle rose slowly from her chair, flicked him a last seething glance and walked off toward the rear of the garden.

Fury engulfed him. Where was the humility he had expected? Where was the embarrassment he had been certain he would see in her face?

Instead, she walked the gravel path with her head held high, ignoring him as if he weren't there, making her way over to where a group of the children played at the back of the garden.

Inwardly shaking, Dani fixed her gaze on the children playing tag near the gazebo, determined not to let her unnerving encounter with Rafael Saunders show in any way. She had taught herself that after The Scandal, how to take rigid control of her emotions. Never let them know the power they held, how badly they could hurt you.

"Miss Dani!" Maida Ann, a little blond girl with pigtails, rushed toward her. "Tag! You're it!"

Danielle laughed and felt a breath of relief. She had played the game with the children whenever they came for a visit to Wycombe Park. They expected her to play with them now. At the moment, she was glad for the distraction.

"All right. It looks as if you have tagged me. Now . . . let me see . . . which of you is going to be next? Robbie? Or maybe you, Peter?" She knew some of the children's names, not all. None of them had living parents, or if they did, the parents refused to claim them. Dani's heart went out to them. She was happy that her aunt was a patroness of the charity, which gave her a chance to spend time with the children.

Giggling, Maida Ann darted past her, just out of reach. Dani adored the feisty little five-year-old with the big blue eyes. She loved children, had hoped one day to have a family of her own.

A family with Rafe.

The thought made her angry all over again.

And sad.

It wasn't going to happen. Not with Rafe or any other man. Not after the accident, the terrible fall she had suffered five years ago. Dani shook her head, pushing the bitter memory away.

She fixed her gaze on a boy named Terrance, a red-haired child about eight years old. Terry ran past her, just out of reach, each child rushing forward then darting away, secretly hoping she would direct her attention to him, even if she tagged him and he or she would be *it*.

She played the game for a while, dancing away, bolting forward and finally tagging young Terry. Waving at the children, she gave them a last warm smile and made her way deeper into the garden.

She didn't hear the footfalls approaching behind her until it was too late. She knew who it was before she turned. Still, she couldn't help the gasp of surprise as she stared up into Rafe's handsome face.

"Good afternoon, Danielle."

Her heartbeat thundered. Anger made rosy circles appear in her cheeks. She turned away, rudely ignored him, caught the look of shock that appeared on his face, and simply started walking.

But the Duke of Sheffield wasn't used to being ignored, and she felt the pressure of his fingers as they wrapped around her arm. His grip was firm enough to stop her forward motion and turn her around to face him.

"I said good afternoon. I expect at least a civil reply."

She clamped down on her temper, told herself not to let him bait her. "Excuse me. I believe my aunt is calling."

But he didn't let go of her arm. "I think your aunt is otherwise engaged at the moment. Which means you have time to greet an old friend."

Her fine thread of control stretched to the breaking point and then completely snapped. "You are no friend of mine, Rafe Saunders. You are, in fact, the last man on earth I would think to call a friend."

Rafe's jaw hardened. "Is that so? If not a friend, then how, may I ask, should I think of you?"

She lifted her chin, the knot of anger in her stomach almost painful. "You may think of me as the biggest fool you have ever met. A woman foolish enough to trust a man like you. Stupid enough to fall in love with you, Rafael."

She started walking, but Rafe's tall figure stepped into the path of her escape. His jaw was set, his intense blue eyes diamond hard.

"I believe it was you, my dear, I found with one of my closest friends. You who invited Oliver Randall into your bed, under my very nose."

"And it was you who was eager to believe your friend's lies instead of the truth!"

"You betrayed me, Danielle. Or perhaps you have forgot."

Dani looked up at him, her eyes snapping with fire. "No, Rafael. It was you who betrayed me. If you had loved me, trusted me, you would have known I was telling you the truth." She gave him a thin, bitter smile. "On second thought, as I think of it, certainly it is you who are the fool."

Rafe's whole body vibrated with anger.

Good, she thought. She hated the bland, uninteresting man he had become, so cool and unaffected. The sort of man she wouldn't have found the least bit attractive.

"You have the nerve to stand there and claim you are innocent of the affair?"

"I told you that the moment you stepped into my bedchamber. The events of that night have not changed."

"You were in bed with the man!"

"I didn't even know he was there — as I

40

told you that night! Now, get out of my way, Rafael."

Fury burned in his cold blue eyes but she didn't care. She started walking again and this time Rafe made no move to stop her.

She was surprised he had approached her in the first place. They hadn't spoken since the night he had walked into her bedchamber five years ago and found Oliver Randall lying naked in her bed.

She had tried then to tell him that Oliver was playing some kind of cruel, terrible joke, that nothing had happened between them, that she had been sleeping until Rafe had walked into the room and startled her awake.

But for reasons she still didn't understand, Oliver had set out to destroy the love Rafael had felt for her — or at least said he felt — and the man had brutally succeeded.

Rafe hadn't listened to her that night, nor responded to any of the dozen letters she sent him, begging him to hear her side of the story, pleading with him to believe she was telling him the truth.

As word of the scandal began to leak out, he never once defended her, never once paid the slightest attention to her version of events. Instead, he had abruptly ended their betrothal, confirming what the gossip-mongers said.

Telling the world that Danielle Duval was not the innocent she pretended, but a scarlet woman who had conducted herself shamelessly, and with blatant disregard for her intended. She'd been shunned in society, banished to the country. Even her own mother had believed the tale.

Dani's vision blurred as she made her way through the garden. She rarely thought of Rafael and those awful days back then. But now she was here in London and Rafe was tossing the entire affair back in her face.

She sniffed and fought back the tears she refused to let fall. She wouldn't cry for Rafe, not again. She had wept more than enough for the man she had loved five years ago and she would never weep for him again.

Three

Rafe stood in the garden, angry and oddly disturbed as he watched Danielle's elegant figure moving along the gravel path until she disappeared inside the house.

He didn't know what had possessed him to seek her out. Perhaps it was keeping his silence for all of these years. Whatever it was, instead of the satisfaction he was certain he would feel once he had confronted her, he was more troubled than ever.

As she had done that night, Danielle had professed her innocence. He hadn't believed her then and he didn't believe her now. He'd read the note, after all, and he had two eyes in his head. Oliver had accepted Danielle's invitation and he was there in her room, lying naked beside her in bed.

Rafe had called the bastard out, of course. Ollie was supposed to be his friend.

"I won't meet you, Rafe," Oliver had said. "I won't fight you no matter what you do to me. We've been friends since we were boys, and there is no denying the fault is mine entirely."

"Why, Ollie? How could you do it?"

"I love her, Rafael. I've always loved her. You know that better than anyone. When she asked me to come to her room, I found it impossible to refuse her invitation."

Rafael had known for years that his friend was in love with Danielle, had been in love with her since he was a youth in his teens. But Dani had never loved Ollie.

Or so Rafe had thought. He had stupidly believed that Danielle loved him and not Oliver Randall, though Ollie had for years pursued her. After that night, he had come to believe she had accepted Rafe's offer of marriage simply to become a duchess. It was wealth and power she wanted, not him.

As he walked out of the garden, he reminded himself of all those things, told himself that just as before, nothing Danielle said was the truth.

But he was older now, not insane with jealousy, not blinded by love as he had been in those days, not furious and aching with pain.

And because he was a different man than he had been back then, he couldn't get the image out of his head. He couldn't forget the way Danielle had looked at him there in the garden.

Without a shred of remorse, without the

slightest hint of embarrassment. She had looked at him with all of the hatred that Rafe had felt for her.

No, Rafael. It was you who betrayed me. If you had loved me . . . you would have known I was telling you the truth.

The words nagged at him, gnawed at his insides all the way back to Sheffield House. Was it possible? Was there the slightest chance?

First thing the following morning, he sent a note to Jonas McPhee, the Bow Street runner he and his friends had used over the years whenever they needed information. McPhee was discreet and extremely good at his job, and he promptly arrived at Sheffield House at two o'clock that afternoon.

"Good day, Jonas. Thank you for coming."

"I am happy to assist you, Your Grace, in any way I can." The runner was short and balding, and wore small, wire rimmed spectacles. He was an unimpressive man whose muscular shoulders and knotted hands were the only indication of the sort of work he did.

Rafe stepped back from the doorway, allowing McPhee into his study, then turned and led the man over to his desk and indicated that he should take a seat in one of the dark green leather chairs in front.

"I'd like to hire you, Jonas." Rafe sat down behind his massive rosewood desk. The room was two stories high, with book-lined walls and an elegant molded ceiling. A long mahogany table sat in the middle of the room, lit by green glass lamps that hung down from above, and surrounded by a dozen carved, high-backed chairs. "I'd like you to investigate an incident that happened five years ago."

"Five years is quite a while, Your Grace."

"Yes, it is, and I realize it won't be easy." He settled back in his chair. "The incident involved a woman named Danielle Duval and a man named Oliver Randall. Miss Duval is the daughter of the late Viscount Drummond, who passed away some years back. Lady Drummond died just last year. Oliver Randall is the third son of the Marquess of Caverly."

"I'll need to make some notes, Your Grace."

Rafe held up a sheet of foolscap. "I have all the information written down for you right here."

"Excellent."

Rafe set the paper down on his desk. "At one time, Miss Duval and I were betrothed. That ended five years ago."

46

Rafe went on to tell the ugly story of what had happened the evening he found the note Danielle had sent to Oliver. He explained how at midnight he had gone into Danielle's room and found the two of them together. As the tale unfolded, Rafe did his best to relay the information without revealing any of the emotions he had felt back then.

"Is there any chance you kept the note?" Jonas asked.

Rafe had anticipated the question. "Oddly enough, I did, though I can't begin to tell you why." Opening the bottom drawer of his desk, he moved the pistol he kept there aside and pulled out a small metal box, then fished out a key he kept on a ring in another drawer to open it. The note inside was yellowed and faded, the creases where it had been folded wearing thin. Still, it had the power to make a knot form in his stomach.

He handed the note to McPhee. "As I said, I have no idea why I kept it. Perhaps as a reminder never to be so ridiculously trusting again."

McPhee took the note from his hand and Rafe handed him the list he had made of places and names, people somehow involved in The Scandal, however remotely.

"This may take some time," McPhee said.

Rafe stood up from his chair. "I've waited five years. I don't suppose a few more weeks will matter." And yet he was strangely anxious to know what McPhee would find. Perhaps he merely wanted the affair resolved, as it never really had been.

Perhaps he was thinking of the future, of his upcoming marriage. Perhaps he merely wanted the past dead and buried — once and for all.

With Caro's help, Danielle packed the last of her belongings into her traveling bags, taking special care with the garments she would need on board the ship during the two-month voyage to America.

Dani couldn't wait to leave.

"It looks as if we are done," Caro said, always cheerful. "Are you ready to go?"

"More than ready. How about you?"

Caro laughed, a joyous sound. "I have been packed and ready for days."

"What about Aunt Flora? Is she completely packed?"

Dani's robust aunt bustled into the room just then, strands of silver hair, loose from its pins, floating around her pudgy face. "I am ready to leave whenever you are, my dears."

Like Dani, Aunt Flora considered Caroline Loon almost a member of the family. At one time, Danielle had suggested Caro no longer needed to work as her lady's maid, but could continue instead as Dani's companion.

Caro had been mortified. "I don't want your charity, Danielle. I never have. I am happy to work for whatever I receive. Besides, you and Lady Wycombe have always been extremely kind and generous to me."

Dani had never brought up the subject again. Caro was happy to earn her way and Dani was happy for their friendship.

"Well, then, if all of us are ready," Aunt Flora said, "I will send down for the carriage." Which would take them to the dock, then head back to Wycombe Park. Lady Wycombe would eventually be returning to England, but Dani and Caro would be staying in America, making their home with Dani's future husband, Richard Clemens.

"Oh, this is all so exciting!" Flora bustled off to make the final arrangements and Dani looked over at Caro, who also looked excited.

"Well, I guess we're on our way," Dani said.

Caro grinned. "Just think — soon you will be a married woman."

Danielle just nodded. She couldn't help

thinking of the last man she was supposed to wed and his terrible betrayal.

Richard is different, she told herself.

And Dani prayed that she was right.

The ship prepared to set sail with the tide the following morning, a big, square-rigged passenger ship, the *Wyndham,* with the most modern accommodations available. The captain had personally greeted the women and promised he would look out for their well-being during the journey, since they were traveling without the protection of a man.

Dani tried to imagine a man who had ever protected her from anything. Certainly not her father, who had died when she was so young. Not her cousin, Nathaniel, who had made lecherous advances when she was only twelve years old.

Definitely not Rafael, the man who was to be her husband, the man she had loved with all her heart.

She wondered about Richard Clemens, but thought that it really didn't matter. She had learned to take care of herself and she would continue to do so, even after they were wed.

Danielle stood between Aunt Flora and Caro at the rail, looking out over the water as the ship prepared to sail. A late May wind chilled the air and whipped Dani's pelisse around her shoulders.

"I can scarcely believe it," Caro said as they watched the London dock disappear in the distance. "We are truly on our way to America!"

"What an adventure we are going to have!" Aunt Flora said brightly.

Though Dani was nearly as excited as they, she wished she could be more certain she was doing the right thing. She barely knew Richard Clemens. And after Rafael, she was far more wary of men. Still, Richard was giving her the chance at happiness she had given up ever having.

She leaned over and hugged each of the women, her dearest friends in all the world. "I am just so glad the two of you are coming with me."

But she knew the women wouldn't have it any other way. They were family. The only real family she'd ever had.

Now a new family awaited her in America. Richard and his son and daughter, children she wouldn't have if she had never met him. She tried to remember his face, got an image of a man with thick blond hair and brown eyes. An attractive man, intelligent and generous.

They had met at Wycombe Park. Richard was in the textile manufacturing business and had come to England hoping to increase his accounts. He was a guest of Squire Donner, one of Aunt Flora's friends who lived nearby. The squire and his wife, Prudence, along with their houseguest, Mr. Clemens, had been invited to dinner at Wycombe Park.

That night, after an evening of cards and pleasant conversation, along with an hour of Dani and Prudence entertaining on the pianoforte, Richard had asked if he might call on her again. Dani had surprised herself by saying yes.

In the days that followed, they hadn't spent a great deal of time together, yet they seemed to get on very well. And even after she had told him about The Scandal, Richard had wanted to marry her.

Unlike Rafael, he had actually believed her when she told him she was innocent of any wrongdoing in the affair.

Standing on the deck of the *Wyndham*, Dani felt the wind in her face as her gaze moved farther out to sea. She was lucky. So very lucky. God had given her a second chance at happiness and she intended to grab hold of it and hang on with both hands.

Four

Ten days passed with only a few brief communications with Jonas McPhee. As Rafe waited for answers, he conducted his life as he had before, attending the usual soirées and house parties, spending most of his evenings at White's, his gentlemen's club, making an occasional stop of a more private nature, at Madame Fontaneau's House of Pleasure.

In the old days, his best friends, Ethan Sharpe and Cord Easton, would have accompanied him, drinking and gaming, paying a visit to the ladies, though Cord had usually preferred the company of his mistress.

But Ethan and Cord were married now, happily so, each of them devoted husbands, and each with a son. Rafe intended his future would be the same. Though his marriage to Mary Rose wouldn't be a love match, it was imperative that Rafe produce an heir. The Sheffield fortune was large, its land and holdings vast and complex.

Since he had no brothers, if he died

without a son to carry on the name, the fortune and title would pass to his cousin, Arthur Bartholomew. Artie was a wastrel of the very worst sort, a dedicated rake whose main objective in life was to spend every guinea that passed into his hands. He whored, drank and gambled in excess, and seemed determined to debauch his way into an early grave.

Arthur was the reason Rafe's mother had been so persistent in her efforts to see her son wed, and in truth, he couldn't blame her. Like his aunts and cousins, his mother was dependent on an income from the vast Sheffield fortune to take care of her and the rest of the family. It was Rafe's responsibility to see that the fortune passed into hands that would insure its existence for present and future generations.

To make sure that happened, Rafe was determined to marry and set up his nursery. He needed sons — more than one — to fulfill his duty. Beyond that, he looked forward to having a family of his own. He was ready for that to happen. Had been ready, he supposed, since his betrothal to Danielle, though after her betrayal, for a number of years the notion had been nearly abhorrent.

The memory sent his mind in that direction. He was still thinking of Danielle an hour later when he received a message from Jonas McPhee requesting a meeting that evening. From the tone of the note, Rafe believed he had uncovered important information.

It was almost nine o'clock when the butler showed McPhee into the study, where Rafe prowled impatiently in front of his big rosewood desk.

"Good evening, Your Grace. I had hoped to come earlier, but there were some last-minute details I needed to verify before I presented my information."

"That's quite all right, Jonas. I appreciate your being so thorough. I presume, then, that you have brought news."

"I'm afraid so, Your Grace."

At the words, Rafe's stomach constricted. From the look on the runner's face, he wasn't going to like what Jonas had to say. He motioned for McPhee to sit down in one of the leather chairs in front of his desk, then took his usual place across from him.

"All right, let's have it."

"To put it simply, sir, on the evening in question five years ago, it appears you were duped."

The words drew the knot in his stomach even tighter. "In what way?"

"This acquaintance of yours, Oliver

Randall, who was involved in the events that transpired, had apparently been harboring a secret animosity against you for years."

"*Animosity* is a very strong word. We were friends. Never all that close, but I never sensed any blatant dislike on his part."

"Were you aware of his feelings for your betrothed?"

"Yes. I knew he was in love with Danielle, that he had been for years. Mostly I felt sorry for him."

"Until you saw them together that night."

"That is correct. I found them in Danielle's bedchamber. I found him naked in her bed."

"There is no question he was there. A number of the guests who were attending the weeklong house party verified the events of the evening . . . as far as they knew. A number of them heard the commotion and ran down the hall to Miss Duval's bedchamber. They saw you there, saw Oliver Randall in Miss Duval's bed. All of them, including you yourself, came to the same conclusion."

"You seem to be suggesting that all of us were wrong."

"Tell me again how it was you found the note."

Rafe allowed his memory to return to the

56

painful events of that night. "One of the footmen brought it to me after supper. He said he had found it on the floor of Lord Oliver's study. He said that he knew Miss Duval and I were betrothed and he didn't believe what was going on between Miss Duval and Lord Oliver was right."

"Do you recall the name of the footman?"

"No, only that I rewarded him handsomely for his honesty and vowed to keep his involvement in the affair a secret."

"The footman's name was Willard Coote. He was also paid quite handsomely by Lord Oliver, who instructed him to bring you the note."

Rafe frowned. "That doesn't make sense. Why would Oliver wish to be caught with Danielle?"

"It makes sense if you understand how determined Lord Oliver was to insure you and Danielle Duval never wed. I believe he hoped that eventually he might win her for himself but, of course, that never happened. Mostly, I think he wanted to hurt you as badly as he possibly could."

Rafe mulled that over, his mind spinning, trying to fit the pieces together. "I'm afraid I still don't understand. Why would Oliver wish to hurt me?"

"There is no doubt he was jealous. But

that appears to be only one of the reasons for his animosity toward you. In time, I should be able to discover the balance of his motivations."

Rafe straightened in his chair, his mind swarming with images of Oliver and Danielle together that night. "That won't be necessary, at least not at present. For the moment, what I need to know is if you are certain — without the slightest doubt — that Danielle Duval was innocent of the accusations made against her that night."

In answer, McPhee dug into the pocket of his rumpled, slightly frayed tailcoat. "There is a final bit of evidence I can give you." He laid the note Rafe had given him out on the desk. "This is the message the footman gave you that evening."

"Yes."

McPhee unfolded a piece of foolscap and set it down next to the note. "And here is a letter written by Miss Duval. I believe it provides the final proof." Jonas leaned over the papers. "As you can see, Your Grace, the handwriting is similar, but if you look closely, you will notice it is not exactly the same."

Rafe followed each line, assessing the similarities and differences between the letter and the note. There was no denying the handwriting, though close, was not quite the same.

"Note the signature."

Again Rafe compared the two. The signature was definitely a better forgery, the letters practiced more often, perhaps, but again, there were slight differences in the script.

"I don't believe Miss Duval wrote the note to Oliver Randall," Jonas said. "I believe Lord Oliver wrote it himself, wadded it up to look as if it had been read and discarded, then ordered his footman to bring the note to you later that evening."

Rafe's hand shook as he picked up the letter McPhee had brought. It was from Dani, addressed to her aunt. In it, she described the awful events of that night and begged her aunt to believe she was innocent of the accusations made against her.

"Where did you get this?"

"I paid a visit to Miss Duval's aunt, Lady Wycombe. The countess wished to cooperate fully in the matter of proving her niece's innocence. She arranged for several samples of her niece's handwriting to be brought to me from Wycombe Park."

Rafe set the letter down next to the note. "Danielle wrote to me again and again, but I never . . . I never opened any of her letters. I was so sure, so certain of what I had seen."

"Considering how well the events of that night had been planned, that is understandable, Your Grace."

Rafe clamped down on his jaw so hard an ache throbbed in the back of his neck. He shoved back his chair and stood up. "Where is he?"

McPhee stood up, as well. "Lord Oliver is currently in residence at the town house of his father, Lord Caverly. He is in London for the season."

Rafe rounded the desk, his pulse racing, his anger building moment by moment. He bit down hard on his temper.

"Thank you, Jonas. You've done your usual fine job of uncovering the facts. I'm only sorry I didn't know you five years ago. Perhaps if I had hired you back then, my life would have turned out far differently."

"I am sorry, Your Grace."

"No one could be sorrier than I." Rafe walked McPhee to the door of his study. "Have your bill sent to my accountant."

McPhee simply nodded. "Perhaps it is not too late to mend the damage, Your Grace."

A fresh jolt of anger tore through him, his rage becoming so strong he feared it would spin out of control. "Five years is a very long time," he said with deadly menace. "But of one thing you may be certain — it will soon be too late for Oliver Randall."

The knock came early on Oliver's door. At the firm, insistent pounding, he dragged himself from sleep, silently cursing whoever roused him at such an ungodly hour. He was surprised when his valet walked in, a terrified look on his face.

"What is it, Burgess? And whatever it is, it had better be important. I was sleeping like a babe until you started banging on the door."

"There are three men downstairs, my lord. They insist on seeing you. Jennings told them it was too early for callers. He tried to turn them away, but they refused to leave. They said the matter could not wait. Jennings came to me and asked that I awaken you." The small, black-haired valet held up a green silk dressing gown for Oliver to put on.

"Don't be an idiot. I can hardly speak to them in *that*. I'll have to dress. Whoever it is will simply have to wait."

"The men said if you don't come down in the next five minutes, they are going to come up and get you."

"What? They dare to threaten me? What matter could be of such import these men have arrived at my home at such an indecent hour demanding to see me? Did Jennings give you their names?"

"Yes, my lord. The Duke of Sheffield, the Marquess of Belford, and the Earl of Brant."

A shiver of alarm went through him. Sheffield was here. And with him two of London's most powerful men. The reason for their visit didn't bear thinking about. Better to wait and see.

Burgess held out the robe again and this time Oliver stuck his arm through the sleeve. "Well, get down there and tell them I am on my way. Show them into the drawing room."

"Yes, my lord."

They were there waiting when the butler pulled open the tall double doors and Oliver walked in, trying to maintain some semblance of dignity while wearing his dressing gown and slippers. It unnerved him a good bit more to see that the three men were standing, not sitting, as he walked into the drawing room.

"Good morning, Your Grace, my lords."

"*Ollie,*" the duke said, an unmistakable edge to his voice.

"I assume your business is a matter of some urgency, since you have appeared on my doorstep at such a disreputable hour."

Sheffield stepped forward. Oliver hadn't seen Rafael Saunders in years, had made it a point, in fact, to keep his distance. Now he was here in his house, a man several inches taller and more powerfully built. A handsome man of wealth and power beyond anything Oliver would ever know.

"I've come in regard to a personal matter," the duke said. "A matter that should have been resolved five years ago. I believe you know to which matter I refer."

Oliver frowned. None of this was making any sense. "I thought what happened was all in the past. Surely you are not here to resurrect old infamies, not after all of these years."

"Actually, I am here to defend Danielle Duval's honor, as I should have done five years ago. You see, I made the mistake of believing you and not her. It is a mistake I mean to rectify — once and for all."

"W-what are you talking about?"

Instead of answering, Rafe pulled a white cotton glove out of the inside pocket of his morning coat. He slapped the glove hard across Oliver's cheeks, first one and then the other. "Danielle Duval was innocent of any wrongdoing the night I found the two of you together, but you, sir, were not. Now you will pay for the damage you've done and the lives you have ruined. You have the choice of weapons."

"I don't . . . I don't know what you are talking about."

"Actually, you do. As you are the one who forged the note I received and paid the footman, Willard Coote, to see it delivered, you know exactly what I mean. I'll expect you to meet me tomorrow at dawn on the knoll at Green Park. These men will act as my seconds. If you refuse, as you did before, I will find you and shoot you where you stand. Now choose your weapon."

So . . . the truth had finally come out. Oliver had begun to believe it never would, begun to think he had won the game completely. Now, five years later, he wondered if the price he would pay for the revenge he had attained would be worth it.

"Pistols," he said finally. "You may count on my arrival at Green Park at dawn."

"One last question . . . *Ollie.* Why did you do it? What did I do to you to deserve such a cruel form of punishment?"

A corner of Oliver's mouth twisted up. "You were simply you, Rafael. From the time we were children, you were taller and smarter and better looking. You were heir to a dukedom that included a fabulous fortune. You were a better athlete, a more charming guest, a better lover. Every woman wanted to marry you. When Danielle fell under your spell, I was determined you would never have her." His smile turned harsh. "And so I destroyed any chance for you to have the one thing you truly wanted."

The duke exploded, grabbing the lapels of Oliver's robe and hauling him up on his toes. "I'm going to kill you, Oliver. You may have accomplished what you set out to, but you are going to pay for what you have done."

Both the earl and marquess rushed forward.

"Let him go, Rafael," Brant said, his golden eyes burning into the cold blue eyes that belonged to his friend. "You'll have your vengeance in the morning."

"Give him time to ponder his fate," said the black-haired Marquess of Belford, as if he knew the sort of fear time could breed.

The strong fingers squeezing his robe together beneath his chin slowly loosened.

"Time to go," Belford said to the duke. "By now the servants have probably called a watchman. As Cord says, tomorrow is another day."

Sheffield released him, shoving him away

so hard he crashed into the mantel on the fireplace, sending a jolt of pain up his arm. But Oliver's fear was slowly fading, replaced by an iron resolve. He had prepared himself for this day. Perhaps fate had given him a final chance to win the game.

"We'll see who winds up dead," Oliver taunted as the three men started for the door. "I'm not the same weak man I was five years ago."

The men ignored him, just continued out of the drawing room, Belford limping slightly, an old wound perhaps. Oliver wasn't acquainted with him well enough to know.

The door closed in the entry as the men left the house, and Oliver sank down on the brocade sofa. So he would face the Duke of Sheffield at last. There was a time he'd been sure this day would come. He had bought a set of dueling pistols and practiced with them daily, until he had become a very skillful marksman.

For the past few years, he had begun to think he wouldn't need the weapons. Now it appeared that he would.

Oliver almost smiled. Rafael wanted vengeance. Oliver knew the feeling well. In a way, he was glad Rafe knew what had happened that night. It would make his victory all the sweeter. Tomorrow, if he got lucky, he would see his nemesis dead.

A thin fog hung over the knoll. The grass was deep and wet, forming beads of dew on the men's leather boots. The first thin rays of dawn spread over the horizon, enough to outline the two black carriages parked at the edge of the grassy field below.

Ethan stood next to Cord beneath a tall sycamore tree, next to the two men who had accompanied Lord Oliver Randall. In the open space at the top of the knoll, his best friend, Rafael Saunders, Duke of Sheffield, stood back to back with the man who had ruined his life, Oliver Randall, third son of the Marquess of Caverly.

Randall was perhaps two inches shorter than Rafe, with a slightly leaner build, auburn hair and brown eyes. He had nothing of the power and command that Rafe always seemed to have, and yet Ethan hoped his friend hadn't underestimated his enemy.

Word was, Oliver Randall was a very skillful marksman, one of the best in London.

Then again, so was Rafe.

The countdown began, Cord calling out the numbers, the men taking long strides away from each other as the steps were counted off. "Five. Six. Seven. Eight. Nine. Ten."

Both men turned at exactly the same instant, casting their bodies into profile. They lifted their long-barreled, silver-etched dueling pistols and fired.

Two distinct shots rang out, echoing over the knoll. For several seconds neither man moved, then Oliver Randall swayed on his feet and went down, crumpling into the wet grass on the knoll.

His seconds ran forward, two faint shadows in the purple rays of dawn, along with the surgeon, Neil McCauley, a friend who had agreed to come along. Both Cord and Ethan started toward the men, Ethan's blood still pumping, though some of his worry began to fade as he saw Rafe standing there, apparently unharmed.

Then he spotted the bright patch of blood that appeared on Rafael's sleeve, though Rafe didn't seem to notice. Instead he strode toward Oliver Randall.

Bent over the injured man, Dr. McCauley looked up at the duke. "It's bad. I'm not sure he'll make it."

"Do the best you can," Rafe said. Turning, he strode toward Ethan, who caught up with him at the edge of the knoll.

"How badly are you injured?" Ethan asked, shoving back a strand of wavy black hair that fell across his forehead.

For the first time, Rafe seemed to realize he had been shot. "Nothing too serious, I don't think. Hurts a bit, not too badly."

Cord walked up just then. "My house is closest, and the women are there. Let's get you home and get that arm taken care of." Cord glanced toward the knoll. "Looks like McCauley has his hands full with Randall, but my wife is a fairly good nurse."

Rafe just nodded. His jaw clenched with pain several times as they moved over the grass toward the carriage, but his mind seemed miles away.

Oliver Randall had been dealt with. Still, there were other matters of honor that would need to be mended. Danielle's name would have to be cleared, Ethan knew, her innocence made known to society.

Ethan wondered what steps Rafe next intended to take.

Five

Rafe leaned back in the chair behind his desk. A mild June sun streamed through the mullioned windows, warming the room, but it didn't improve his mood. His arm was throbbing, yet the wound, thankfully, had proved to be minor. The lead ball had gone through the fleshy part of his arm without hitting bone and passed out the opposite side.

Oliver Randall had not been so lucky. The ball had hit a rib beneath his heart, glanced off and lodged in an area near his spine. Neil McCauley had successfully removed the ball but the damage had already been done. Assuming the wound escaped putrefaction, Oliver Randall would live, but the man would never walk again.

Rafe felt no remorse. Oliver Randall had cruelly and deliberately destroyed two people's lives for no other reason than jealousy. He had plotted and planned, lied and duped the entire town of London and especially Rafael. Now, in return, Oliver's own life had been destroyed.

"You reap what you sow," Rafe's father had said when Rafe was a boy. The late duke had been fair and just. He would have seen justice in the outcome of the duel.

Still, Oliver wasn't the only man at fault. In the days since the duel, Rafe had set out to mend some of the damage he, himself, had caused. He meant to clear Danielle's name of any wrongdoing in the scandal that had ended their betrothal, but he wanted to speak to Dani first. In that regard, his efforts had failed.

Rafe swore softly. Frustrated and out of sorts, he was thinking of Danielle when a knock at the door drew his attention. His butler, Jonathan Wooster, silver-haired with a narrow face and watery blue eyes, stood in the doorway.

"I'm sorry to bother you, Your Grace, but Lord and Lady Belford are here to see you."

He had wondered when his friends would arrive. "Show them in." They were worried about him, he knew. He'd been holed up since the duel and hadn't left the house. Though justice had been served, he felt defeated. He hadn't left the house because he couldn't find the will.

Ethan ushered Grace into the room, a lovely young woman with heavy auburn hair and jewel-green eyes and dressed in a fashionable, high-waisted gown a paler shade of green. Grace and Rafe had long been friends, but never anything more. Rafe believed that Grace had been destined from the start to become Ethan's bride, the one person who could dispel the darkness his friend had carried inside him.

"How are you feeling?" Ethan asked, a worried look on his face. He was as tall as Rafe, leaner, darker, his features more sculpted, the sort of man women were drawn to. Even more so now that his demons were gone.

"The wound was never that serious." Rafe strode toward them across the room. "And the arm seems to be healing very well."

"That's very good news." Grace's pretty face lit with a smile. "Perhaps you feel well enough to accompany us to luncheon. It's such a lovely day."

Rafe glanced away. His body was mending, but his mind lingered in the past. The day after the duel, he had summoned Jonas McPhee to discover the whereabouts of Lady Wycombe and her niece, Danielle Duval. Since Rafe hadn't seen her since the afternoon tea and neither had his mother, he thought that perhaps she and her aunt had returned to Wycombe Park.

Instead, according to McPhee, Danielle

and her aunt had left the country.

"I can tell by the grim look on your face that you have discovered Danielle is gone," Ethan said.

Rafe frowned. "How did you know?"

"Victoria told us," Grace said. "She seems to have an invisible connection to every servant in the city. She was looking for information about Danielle. I suppose she thought you would probably wish to see her."

Rafe bit back a sigh of frustration. "Unfortunately, Jonas McPhee informed me three days ago that Danielle and her aunt have sailed for America, gone off to the city of Philadelphia. I had hoped to speak to her, to apologize and somehow try to make amends. I don't suppose that is going to happen now."

"Certainly not right away," Ethan agreed.

Rafe looked at his friend. "Did Victoria also tell you that Danielle has accepted a proposal of marriage from an American named Richard Clemens?"

"No. I don't think she knew."

Rafe stared past the couple, out the window into the garden. The sun was shining as it hadn't in days, and a pair of sparrows sat on the branch of a sycamore tree beside the house.

He turned back to his friends. "Danielle has given up her home, been forced to leave her own country to try to find some kind of happiness for herself. She has sailed thousands of miles to escape the terrible things that were said about her — none of which were true — and the fault is entirely mine."

Grace reached over and touched his arm. "That is not so. Your actions undoubtedly played a part, but Oliver Randall is the man responsible. He planned to end your betrothal to Danielle and destroy your feelings for each other — and he succeeded."

Rafe's hand unconsciously fisted. "Randall accomplished exactly what he set out to do. He destroyed any chance for happiness Danielle and I might have had. Unless, of course, she finds some measure of contentment with the man she intends to marry."

Grace's fingers pulled on the sleeve of his coat. "Are you willing to take that chance, Rafael?"

"What are you talking about?"

"Danielle's marriage might make her life even more unhappy than it's been for the past five years. Are you willing to take that risk?"

His chest tightened. The thought had occurred to him more than once in the past few days. He remembered the Dani he had fallen in love with, so sweet and innocent yet filled with such passionate fire.

Who was this man she intended to marry? Did she love him? Would he take care of her, treat her the way she deserved?

Ethan's voice filled the silence that had fallen in the study. "Grace believes there is yet a chance for you and Danielle — if you are brave enough to take it. My wife believes that you are still in love with the woman. She is convinced that you've never stopped loving her. She believes you should go after her and bring her home."

Rafe cast a hard look at Grace. "I realize you have always been an incurable romantic, sweeting, but this time I think you may have gone completely over the mark. Dani is marrying another man. She is probably in love with him. And I . . . I am betrothed to Mary Rose."

"Are you still in love with Danielle?" Grace pressed.

Rafe took a steadying breath. Was he still in love with Dani? It was a question he had never allowed himself to ask. "It's been five years, Grace. I don't even know the lady anymore."

"You have to find out, Rafael. You have to go after her. You have to discover if you still love her — and if she still loves you."

Rafe snorted. "The woman loathes the very sight of me."

"Perhaps she does. Perhaps she only thinks she does. Once I convinced myself that I hated Ethan. I blamed him for everything that had happened to me. But the day he showed up on my doorstep, I realized that the feelings I once held for him were still there, hovering just below the surface. At the time, I wished it weren't so. Now . . ."

She turned, slid her arms around her husband's waist and leaned into his embrace. "Now I am only grateful that he came for me, grateful that he has come to love me the way I love him, grateful for the son he has given me."

Ethan bent his dark head and pressed his lips against his wife's auburn curls.

"What about Mary Rose?" Rafe asked. "We are betrothed, in case you have forgot."

"You don't love her," Ethan answered, surprising him. "And I don't believe she loves you. I don't think you want her to."

No, he didn't want Mary Rose to love him. Because he knew he could never return that love.

"Ask her to wait," Grace urged. "Surely a little more time before the wedding wouldn't be too much to ask."

Rafe made no reply. His chest was

76

squeezing. The questions Grace posed had been hovering at the edge of his mind since McPhee had discovered the truth about that night. The list had only grown since the duel. They were questions that needed to be answered.

There were words that needed to be spoken, a past that needed to be resolved.

"I'll think about what you've both said. I want you and Ethan to know that no matter what happens, I appreciate your friendship. You will never know how much."

Grace's pretty eyes filled with tears. "We just want you to be happy."

Rafe only nodded. He had given up that hope five years ago. Now, hearing his best friend's words, the thought burned inside him again. Was it possible? He didn't know, but he knew he had to find out.

Tomorrow morning, he would book passage for himself on a ship bound for America.

"If you decide to go," Ethan said as if he had read Rafe's mind, "Belford Shipping has a vessel sailing for America three days hence. The owner's cabin is yours. The *Triumph* can sail you straight up the Delaware River to Philadelphia, and she's a fast ship, Rafael. With good weather, she'll cut at least a week off the time Danielle has ahead of you."

Rafe looked up at him. Inside his chest, his heart was squeezing as if it were locked in a fist.

"Make the arrangements" was all he said.

Six

Needing a moment alone, Danielle stood at the window, staring into the darkness of the city they had reached just two weeks ago. Tonight she and her aunt were attending a small house party being given by close friends of Richard's in honor of their engagement. It seemed there were always more people to meet, and though they were friendly, sometimes it was a bit overwhelming.

Dani gazed into the quiet outside the house. With its narrow cobbled streets and redbrick buildings, tall white church steeples and large, open green parks, Philadelphia was charming, if nothing at all like London.

Though America and England had once been connected, it was as if the American colonists had done everything in their power to carve out a new identity all their own. Their speech was less clipped, less formal. Their clothes followed English fashion, yet, with the distance between the two countries, even the most lavish costumes seemed slightly out of vogue.

Still, the people here had a strong, rugged independence that Danielle admired and respected. They were their own people, these Americans. She had never met anyone quite like them.

Danielle turned away from the window and walked over to join her aunt, who stood next to the cut-crystal punch bowl. During the two weeks since her arrival, Dani had settled comfortably into the narrow brick row house Aunt Flora had let for her stay in America. At present, Dani and Caro resided there with her in the charming, colonial-style home.

After Dani's wedding, three weeks hence, she and Caro would move into Richard's home on Society Hill, and once they were settled, Aunt Flora would return to England, accompanied by a companion she hired for the journey.

Dani would remain with her husband in Philadelphia, a completely new and different world. She was grateful Caro would be staying, as well.

She took a sip from the cup of punch Aunt Flora slid into her hand.

"Here comes Richard," her aunt whispered, smiling at the blond man who approached from across the parlor, what the

Americans called a drawing room. "He is certainly a handsome man."

She cast Danielle a sideways glance, trying to read her emotions where Richard was concerned, but Dani kept her features carefully blank.

She liked Richard Clemens enough to accept his proposal, but she wasn't in love with him. And she didn't think Richard was more than moderately enamored of her. He was a successful, practical man who needed a wife to replace the one who had died in childbirth and a mother for his two children. Over time, Dani hoped, their affection would grow deeper.

"Ah, Danielle — there you are." He smiled and she returned it.

"I saw you talking to Mr. Wentz," she said. "Since you and he both own textile manufacturing companies, I imagined the two of you were talking business."

He reached down and caught her hand, gave it a squeeze. "Very astute. I sensed that from our first meeting. A man with a wife who understands her role can be a tremendous asset to her husband's business."

Dani continued to smile. She wasn't exactly certain what role Richard expected her to play, but in time she supposed she would figure it out.

"Actually Jacob Wentz is in the dye manufacturing business. His plant is in Easton, not far from Clemens's Textiles." Richard turned for a moment to speak to Aunt Flora, and as the pair made polite conversation, Dani studied the man she was to wed.

Richard stood slightly above average in height, and he was attractive, his hair a deep golden blond and his eyes a mixture of brown and green, turning more one color than the other, depending upon his mood.

She had only begun to know him during his time in England. He'd been attentive and interesting, an intelligent man, successful in his business endeavors, a widower who seemed to find her attractive. Here he was different, more driven. Here, business always came first. At times it seemed to consume him.

"If you will excuse us for a moment, Lady Wycombe," Richard said, "there is a gentleman I would like Danielle to meet."

"Of course." Aunt Flora gave him a last warm smile, turned her attention to the matron standing next to her and they began to pleasantly chatter.

Dani let Richard guide her across the parlor, a well-designed room with molded ceilings, Aubusson carpets and Chippendale furniture. Even the furniture in the houses she had visited seemed decidedly American, mostly mahogany, with smooth lines and graceful curves, pretty lace doilies and high-backed Windsor chairs.

Richard covered her hand where it rested on the sleeve of his tailcoat as they wove their way among the guests, stopping for a greeting here and there. It was obvious by the way people deferred to him that her fiancé held a high place in Philadelphia society. In fact, there were times he seemed overly concerned with it, but perhaps she was mistaken.

He stopped in front of a tall, burly, gray-haired man with mutton-chop sideburns. "Senator Gaines, it's good to see you."

"You, as well, Richard."

"Senator, I'd like you to meet my fiancée, Danielle Duval."

Gaines made a very polite bow over her hand. "Miss Duval, you are every bit as lovely as Richard has said."

"Thank you, Senator."

"Senator Gaines was once ambassador to England," Richard told Dani. To the senator he said, "Danielle's father was the Viscount Drummond. Perhaps you met him while you were abroad."

One of the senator's thick gray eyebrows went up. "I'm afraid I never had the privilege." He tossed Richard a look. "So you've caught yourself the daughter of a viscount. Quite a feather in your cap, old boy, if I do say so myself. Congratulations."

Richard beamed. "Thank you, Senator."

"When's the wedding? I presume I'll be invited."

"Of course. We'd be very disappointed if you couldn't attend."

They spoke a moment more, then Richard said a polite farewell and so did Dani. She tried to ignore the uneasy feeling the conversation had stirred. Richard seemed so concerned with her background, so impressed that she was a member of the English aristocracy. It seemed to come up at every party they had attended since her arrival.

"Richard! Do bring your lovely bride-to-be over here for a moment. We've a guest tonight I would like the two of you to meet."

Dani recognized their rotund little host for the evening, Marcus Whitman, a wealthy farmer Richard had introduced her to at a musical affair they had attended last week. Since her arrival, her fiancé had insisted on attending one affair after another.

"I want you to have a chance to get acquainted with my friends," Richard had explained.

Dani had hoped they would have more

84

time to themselves, a chance to get to know each other better before the wedding. So far, she had only met his children once and then only briefly.

"Good evening, Marcus." Richard smiled. "It's been a lovely party. Thank you so much for hosting the affair."

"My wife and I were pleased to do it. Before he died, your father and I were friends for nearly twenty years."

Richard politely nodded. His father was often mentioned at these events. Apparently he had been quite a respected man in the community. "You said there was someone you wanted us to meet?"

"Yes, yes . . . indeed." He turned and touched the coat sleeve of a tall man standing behind him, drawing the man's attention.

"Richard, I would like to introduce you to an acquaintance from London, a friend of a friend, if you know what I mean. Rafael Saunders is the Duke of Sheffield. He's here in Philadelphia on business."

Shock ricocheted through Dani. She felt as if the floor had just tipped sideways. She could feel the blood slowly draining from her face.

Whitman continued the introduction. "Duke, meet Richard Clemens and his fiancée, Miss Duval. She's a countryman of yours. Perhaps the two of you are acquainted."

Dani stared into the bluest eyes she had ever seen, eyes she would never forget. Her chest tightened almost painfully.

"Mr. Clemens," Rafael said, making Richard a very formal bow. "Miss Duval." His eyes fixed on hers and for an instant she couldn't look away.

Dani couldn't talk, couldn't form a single word. She just kept staring, her hand trembling on Richard's sleeve. When he turned to look at her, he must have seen the pallor of her face.

"Darling, are you all right?"

Dani wet her lips, her mouth gone completely dry. "I am . . . I am happy to make your acquaintance," she said to Rafael, silently thanking God she had never told Richard the name of the man who had once been her betrothed. The man who had ruined her.

Rafe's eyes remained on hers. "The pleasure is mine, I assure you, Miss Duval."

She dragged her gaze away, ignored the wild beating of her heart, and glanced frantically around the room in search of an avenue of escape. "I — I'm terribly sorry. I'm afraid I am feeling overly warm. I think I could use a breath of fresh air."

Richard slid an arm around her waist. "Here, let me escort you. A moment on the terrace and I'm sure you'll be right as rain." Guiding her toward the French doors leading out into the garden, Richard led her across the room. Several people glanced their way, but Dani barely saw them. Her mind was spinning, her stomach tied into a knot.

Rafael had followed her. She couldn't think of any other explanation. Why had he come? What did he want?

Did he hate her so much that he had come to ruin her chance for a new life with Richard?

Dani clamped down on a moment of fear and prayed there was some other reason Rafael had traveled all the way to America.

Rafe watched Danielle leave the parlor and wished he had handled things differently. She looked so pale, so shaken. Then again, what had he expected?

Not that he'd had any choice.

Before he'd set sail, he had done his best to discover any information that might help him find her, but there simply wasn't enough time. He knew the name of her ship, the *Wyndham*, and that she had sailed to

Philadelphia, where her fiancé, a wealthy manufacturer, apparently had a home.

Beyond that, he didn't know exactly where to look for her. Instead, he had arrived in the city with letters of introduction engineered by Howard Pendleton, a close family friend. Letters from men of influence in London with friends in Philadelphia who might be able to help him find Danielle.

Howard Pendleton, an army colonel who worked in the British War Office, had helped Cord and Rafe bring Ethan home from France, where he had been imprisoned. Through Ethan, Pendleton had heard of Rafe's intended journey and come to him with an offer of assistance — but there was a favor he wanted in return.

"Rumors have been surfacing," the colonel had said, "whispers that a venture may be in the making between the Americans and the French. A deal that would be of great benefit to Napoléon. We need your help, Your Grace. If you agree, you won't be on your own. You'll have Max Bradley to assist you."

Rafe knew Bradley well, knew how good he was, and that he was a man to count on. England had been fighting the French for years. Thousands of British lives had been lost.

Rafe agreed to help in any way he could and received the colonel's assistance in return, which included the letters of introduction. When Rafe set sail aboard the *Triumph*, one of the newest ships in the Belford shipping fleet, Max Bradley sailed with him, a man who worked undercover for the War Office — a polite way of saying that Max was a British spy. In the days since their arrival, Bradley had gone underground in search of information, and Rafe had used the letters to find someone who could lead him to Dani. He had been introduced to Marcus Whitman, a close friend of Richard Clemens, and secured an invitation to the house party Whitman was holding in honor of the bride and groom.

Rafe stared off toward the terrace, his chest feeling heavy. In her gold brocade gown, with her glorious red hair swept up, Danielle looked even more beautiful tonight than she had the last time he had seen her.

Still, as he had watched her moving around the room on the arm of the man she was to marry, there wasn't a spark of joy in her lovely green eyes, not the least hint of passion. Perhaps, like himself, she had merely learned a greater degree of self-control.

As he watched her disappear out of sight

into the garden, he wished he could have found a better way to proceed. But he had wanted to meet Richard Clemens, to discover as much about the man as he could, and with the wedding just three weeks away, there wasn't much time.

Rafe made conversation with Whitman and his dark-haired, likable little wife, all the while watching the terrace door, hoping for another glimpse of Dani.

"If it isn't His Grace, the duke." Flora Chamberlain appeared beside him, a round-faced little woman with keen blue eyes. "One never knows whom one might encounter, even all these miles from home." She studied him from beneath thick gray lashes, her gaze coolly assessing. "It never occurred to me that you might actually come."

Rafe's gaze met hers. "Did it not? You knew I would discover the truth when you gave Jonas McPhee that letter. Did you really believe I would let the matter rest without speaking to Danielle?"

"You could have discovered the truth five years ago if you had made the effort."

"I was younger then, and extremely hot-headed. I was insanely jealous of Dani. And I was a fool."

"I see . . . You're older now, not so wildly passionate."

"Exactly. When I last saw Danielle and she continued to profess her innocence after all of these years, I decided to investigate the matter and discovered, to my everlasting regret, that I had wronged your niece."

"Quite a surprise, I'm sure. Still, it was a goodly distance to travel."

"I would have gone to any lengths to find her."

"I'll admit I hoped you might come. I believe Danielle deserves an apology from you — even if you had to sail nearly four thousand miles to make it."

"Is that the only reason?"

She glanced away, out toward the terrace. "For the present . . . yes."

"I need to speak to her, Lady Wycombe. When can that be arranged?"

The countess continued to stare off toward the garden, then she turned back to Rafe. "Come to my house tomorrow morning — 221 Arch Street. Ten o'clock. Richard isn't due to arrive until noon."

Rafe reached down and captured the lady's white-gloved hand. He lifted her fingers to his lips. "Thank you, Lady Wycombe. You have ever been a good friend to Dani."

"Whatever you do, do not make me regret my involvement in this affair. Promise me you will do nothing more to hurt her."

Rafe looked down at the stout little gray-haired woman who had been far more loyal to Danielle than he ever had been. "I give you my solemn word."

Wearing only her chemise and a light silk wrapper, since the night was warm even at this late hour, Danielle sat on a petit-point stool in front of the dressing table in her room. Caroline Loon sat on the edge of the four-poster canopied bed across from her.

"He was there at the party, Caro. I still can't believe it. He came all the way from England. What could he possibly want?"

"Perhaps it isn't what you think. Perhaps the man who introduced you is right and the duke is simply here on business. You told me the duke is quite wealthy. Perhaps he has financial concerns in America as well as England."

Dani felt a glimmer of hope. "Do you really think it's possible?"

"I think it's entirely possible."

"Perhaps he has come to see Richard, to warn him against the sort of woman he believes me to be."

"Your fiancé knows the truth. There is nothing the duke can tell him that you haven't already told him yourself. What

Sheffield might say won't make any difference."

"I'm not so sure. Richard is extremely concerned with appearances. He might believe in my innocence, but he would be highly concerned should others hear the story."

Caro tapped the silver-backed hairbrush she held in one hand. "You said the duke pretended not to know you last night. Perhaps he will keep his silence."

Dani shook her head. "Rafael hates me. He ruined my life once before. How can I believe he will not try to do it again?"

"Maybe you should talk to him, find out what he is thinking."

An odd feeling stirred to life in Dani's chest. She couldn't imagine what it was. "Yes, perhaps I should. At least I will know where I stand."

Caro got up from the bed, taller and thinner than Dani, wearing a mobcap over a thatch of pale blond curls. "It's getting late. Turn round and let me brush out your hair, then you should try to get some sleep. Tomorrow we can make some sort of plan."

Dani nodded. She turned on the stool and Caro deftly pulled the pins from her hair, letting the heavy strands fall loose down her back. The bristle brush followed, stroking through the thick mass of curls. Caro was right. Tomorrow she would make plans to confront Rafael.

Her stomach tightened.

In the meantime, it was highly unlikely that she would be able to sleep.

Danielle was up early . . . at least by London standards. Americans didn't seem to enjoy the same ungodly hours as the *ton,* whose members stayed out half the night, then wasted most of the next day in bed preparing to repeat their indulgence again the next evening. The people in this country might enjoy a late night on occasion, but it didn't seem to be the norm. The Americans she had met were hard workers and extremely ambitious.

Richard was certainly one of them.

Still, today he had promised they would spend the afternoon with his children and share an intimate supper with his mother and a couple of family friends before he left for his factory in Easton, a small town fifty miles away where he would be working for the next few days.

"Dani! Dani!" Caro burst through the doorway, her blue eyes wide as saucers. "He's here! He's downstairs in the parlor!"

"Slow down, Caro. *Who* is downstairs in the parlor?"

"The duke! He says he wishes to speak to you. He says it is a matter of extreme importance."

A wave of nausea hit her and her hands started to tremble. Dani took a calming breath and tried to slow her wildly beating heart.

This was what she wanted — wasn't it?

She needed to talk to him, discover his intentions.

Dani made a quick survey of her reflection in the tall, cheval glass mirror, turning to assess the back of her pale blue muslin day dress, straightening the slim skirt, adjusting the high-waisted bodice.

The gown looked presentable and Caro had pulled back her hair on the sides and fastened it with tortoiseshell combs, but a heavy mass of curls fell down her back.

"You look fine," Caro said, tugging her toward the door. "You wanted to talk to him. Now go find out why he is here."

Dani took another deep breath and raised her chin. She squeezed her hands together until they stopped shaking, then headed for the stairs. As she entered the parlor, a comfortable room done in shades of white and soft rose, she spotted Rafael's tall figure seated on the sofa. He came to his feet the instant she walked through the door.

"Thank you for seeing me," he said very gallantly.

"Did I really have a choice?" She knew Rafael. If he wanted to speak to her, aside from shooting him, there was no way to keep him away.

"No, I don't suppose you did." He motioned toward the sofa. "Join me?"

"I would prefer to stand, thank you."

Rafael released a breath. He was six years older than she, which meant he would be thirty-one by now. Fine lines crinkled beside those blue, blue eyes, and there was a weariness in his features that hadn't been there when he was younger. Still, he was handsome. One of the handsomest men she had ever seen.

She felt those intense blue eyes on her face. "I have traveled thousands of miles to see you, Danielle. I understand your animosity toward me — no one could understand it more — but I would appreciate it if you would sit down so that we might have this chance to speak."

Dani blew out a breath. Knowing it was useless to argue, she went over and sat down on the rose velvet sofa and Rafe walked over and closed the parlor doors. She was surprised when he settled himself beside her a barely respectable distance away.

"Shall I call for tea?" she asked. "Since we are suddenly being so civilized."

"Tea isn't necessary, only your attention. I came here to apologize, Danielle."

Her eyes widened. "What?"

"You heard me correctly. I am here because everything you said was true. That night five years ago, I am the one who betrayed you, not the other way around."

She swallowed, suddenly feeling light-headed. She was glad she had agreed to sit down. "I'm afraid I don't . . . don't understand."

Rafe turned more fully toward her. "Oliver Randall lied about what happened that night — just as you always claimed. He engineered everything, right down to the note I received, which was the reason I went to your room that night."

Rafe explained the events of the evening and the reason he had been so convinced she was having an affair with Oliver Randall. The story was so incredible that the words began swimming round in her head.

"Why . . . ?" she asked softly. "Why would Oliver do such a thing? I tried to figure it out, but it never made any sense."

"He did it because he wanted you for himself. He was in love with you, Danielle, but he couldn't have you. And he was insanely jealous of me."

Dani leaned back on the sofa, her heart beating oddly, a tight feeling inside her chest. Rafe got up and walked over to the sideboard. Pouring a dollop of brandy into a crystal snifter, he returned to where she sat and pressed the brandy glass into her hand.

"Drink this. It'll make you feel better."

When she made no effort to raise the glass, he wrapped his fingers around hers and lifted the snifter to her lips. Dani took a tentative swallow, felt the warm burn, and took another. In truth, she did feel somewhat better.

She looked up at Rafael, still unable to believe he stood there in the parlor. "How did you find all of this out?"

"I hired an investigator, a Bow Street runner, a man I had used on a number of occasions before."

Danielle shook her head. "I still can't believe it."

"What is it you don't believe?"

"That you would travel thousands of miles simply to tell me you were wrong."

"And also to tell you that Oliver Randall paid the highest price for his treachery."

Dani came up off the sofa so swiftly

brandy sloshed against the sides of her crystal glass. "You killed him?"

Rafe took the snifter from her unsteady hands and set it down on the table. "I challenged him to a duel, as I did before, only this time I forced him to accept. My shot bounced off a rib and lodged in an area around his spine. Oliver Randall will never walk again."

She tried to feel something, tried to make herself abhor what Rafael had done. But she knew the code of honor a highborn Englishman lived by. Knew that if Rafe ever discovered the truth, he would make Oliver pay.

"I'm sorry," she said finally.

"For Randall? Don't be."

"For all of us. For the years we lost. For the damage that was done."

"Randall destroyed our lives, Danielle. Mine as well as yours. You might not believe it, but it's true."

"Well, now he has paid, so it's over. Thank you for telling me. I was afraid . . ."

"You were afraid of what, Danielle?"

Her chin went up. "I was afraid you had come to destroy my plans for the future. My chance of finding happiness with Richard."

"You believed I would go that far, that I hated you that much?"

"Didn't you?"

"I never spoke a word to anyone about that night. Not once in all of these years."

"But you never denied the rumors. You cried off two days after it happened. By breaking our betrothal that way, you made it clear that I was guilty."

Something moved across his features. She thought it might be regret. "There is no denying my role in what happened. If I could change things . . . if I could do it over, I would."

"But we can't do that, can we, Rafael?"

"No. We can't undo the past."

Danielle rose from the sofa. "Goodbye, Rafael." She started walking toward the door, her heart still beating fiercely, fighting an urge to weep.

"Do you love him?" Rafe called suddenly.

Danielle just kept walking, out through the parlor doors into the entry. Lifting her skirt up out of the way, she concentrated on climbing the stairs, one by one, up to her room.

Seven

Rafe sat on the horsehair sofa in the parlor of his suite at the William Penn Hotel. Thinking of his meeting with Danielle, he propped his elbows on his knees and rested his head in his hands.

"That bad, was it?" Emerging from the bedroom, Max Bradley strolled up beside him as silent as a wraith. He always seemed to appear without warning. Rafe still wasn't used to it.

"Worse," he said, leaning back against the sofa, stretching his long legs out in front of him. "I'll never forget the look on her face when I told her I had finally discovered her innocence in the affair. My God, if she hated me before, she loathes me completely now."

"Are you certain? Or do you just hate yourself?"

Rafe sighed, knowing it was true. "There's no denying the guilt I feel for not believing her that night. I wish there were something I could do to make it up to her."

Max walked over and poured himself a brandy. He was nearly as tall as Rafe, several years older, and thin to the point of gaunt. His face was weathered and hard, the deep lines hinting at the sort of life he led. Thick black hair, always a little too long, curled over the back of his plain brown tailcoat.

Max poured a glass of brandy for Rafe, walked over and handed him the drink. "You look like you could use this."

For the first time Rafe realized that Max was speaking with an American accent. In France, he'd spoken French like a country-man. He was a man who stayed mostly in shadow and he never slipped out of what-ever role he played. In Max's line of work, such talents were invaluable.

Rafe took a swallow of brandy, grateful for its inner warmth. "Thank you."

"You said Danielle came here to be mar-ried."

"That's right."

"Have you met the man?"

"Briefly. From what I've been able to find out, he's a very successful businessman, a widower with a daughter and a son."

"Is your lady in love with him?"

One of Rafe's dark eyebrows went up. "Danielle is no longer my lady, and I have no idea. She wouldn't tell me."

"Interesting . . . ." Max took a long draw on his brandy. "In that case, I suppose it's something you need to find out."

He scoffed. "Why? Lots of people marry for reasons other than love."

"You said you wished there was something you could do to make up for what happened in the past."

"I said that. As far as I can see there isn't a damn thing I can do."

"If the lady doesn't love the man she is going to wed, then you might consider wedding her yourself. She could return to England, to her aunt and her family. More important, marrying her would end the gossip, set the wagging tongues to rest and make your lady's innocence clear once and for all."

Rafe's chest squeezed. There was a time he had wanted to marry Danielle above all things. That time was long past — wasn't it?

Or had the thought been brewing in his head ever since he had found out the truth of her innocence? Was that the true reason he had gone to see the Earl of Throckmorton in regard to his betrothal to Mary Rose?

He had asked the earl that the wedding be postponed and was surprised — and secretly relieved — when the earl suggested the betrothal be ended completely.

"I believe I have made a mistake where my daughter is concerned," the earl had said.

"Mary Rose is so young, so innocent. A worldly man like you . . . a man so much older. It's obvious you're a virile man of very strong appetites . . . to put it bluntly, Your Grace, my daughter is completely intimidated by you, and particularly frightened of sharing a bed with you. I don't believe, even over time, that is going to change."

Rafe could hardly believe his ears. The man was giving up the chance to wed his daughter to a duke. It simply did not happen in the world of the *ton.*

"Are you certain ending the betrothal is what Mary Rose wants? I would be patient with her . . . give her a chance to get used to me."

"I'm certain you would, Rafael. I hope you understand I am doing what I believe is best for my daughter."

It was surprising, and Rafe gave high marks to the earl. "I understand completely. And I respect you greatly for putting your daughter's best interests first. I'm grateful for your honesty and I wish Mary Rose every happiness."

Though he should have been depressed, should have been angry that his plans for the future had been ruined for the second time in his life, Rafe had left the house feeling as if a great burden had been lifted from his shoulders. He didn't understand it. He had imagined a future, a family, with Mary Rose.

He looked up at Max Bradley, sipping brandy in the parlor of his suite. "Though I admit the notion of marrying Danielle has merit, there is the small matter of her dislike of me. If I asked for her hand, she would most certainly refuse."

"I suppose that's for you to find out. And of course, there is the not so small matter of whether or not you still care for the girl."

Did he care? Today he had looked at Dani and seen her as he had five years ago, seen her without the taint of his hatred, a beautiful young woman, intelligent and caring. A woman innocent of the betrayal he had so ruthlessly accused her of committing.

"I want Danielle to be happy. I owe her that much and I am determined to see that it happens — one way or another."

Max clapped him on the shoulder. "Well, then, good luck, my friend. It sounds like you're going to need it." Max took a final sip of his brandy and set the glass down on the mahogany table in front of the sofa. "In the meantime, I've got a number of things to do. If my information proves correct, I may need your help."

Rafe had told Colonel Pendleton he

would help in any way he could. "Just let me know what you need me to do."

Max simply nodded. Seconds later he was gone from the room, disappearing as quietly as he had arrived, and Rafe's thoughts returned to Danielle.

He owed her the chance at happiness that he had stolen from her. To do that, he needed to know more about the man she was to wed.

Rafe smiled grimly.

Rising from the sofa, he walked over to the silver salver sitting on the Sheraton table in the entry. He picked up the folded piece of paper he had received that morning, an invitation from Mrs. William Clemens to a small dinner party at her home that evening.

Sometimes it paid to be a duke.

Rafe had already sent word that he would be delighted to attend.

The intimate supper with Richard's family, Danielle discovered, would be dinner with twenty people, all formally dressed, arriving in expensive carriages at Richard's mother's elegant brick residence in Society Hill.

Richard had his own, slightly smaller but no less elegant home just a few blocks away, as well as a cottage in Easton that he used whenever he was there working, which apparently happened quite often.

Dani had spent the afternoon with Richard's mother; Richard's son, William Jr.; and his daughter, Sophie — their first real time together. Richard had been with them for a while, but the children seemed to prey on his nerves and he made an excuse to leave.

Dani almost didn't blame him. William and Sophie had argued and fought and thrown tantrums through most of the day. They were still arguing when Dani prepared to return to Aunt Flora's house on Arch Street so that she could change out of her day dress and into a more elaborate gown for the evening.

They were still at it when she and Aunt Flora returned at seven o'clock to join the first of the supper guests.

"Give me back my horse!" William Jr. was seven years old, Sophie only six. Both were blond, William with brown eyes and Sophie with green. Both looked a good deal like their father.

"It's my horse," Sophie argued. "You gave it to me."

"I didn't give it to you — I only let you play with it!"

"Children, please . . ." Dani hurried toward them, hoping she could stop this latest row before more of the guests arrived. Earlier in the day, their grandmother had tried to placate them with gifts, a toy horse for William, a new doll for Sophie, though the bedchamber they used when they came for a visit overflowed with toys she had given them before.

"Your grandmother's guests have begun to arrive. You don't want them thinking you are ill-mannered."

William whirled on her viciously. "We don't have to do anything you say! We don't like you!"

They didn't seem to like anyone, at least not anyone who tried to control them. Of course, neither Richard's mother nor Richard himself bothered to try.

Dani sighed. She couldn't help thinking of the little girl, Maida Ann, and the little boy, Terrance, from the orphanage. They were happy with the tiniest trinket, the least bit of affection. Terrance would have treasured the carved wooden horse Mrs. Clemens had given to William. Maida Ann would have loved the doll Sophie had tossed into a corner.

Dani looked down at the two blond heads in front of her. Getting the children to accept her as their mother was going to be a

Herculean task. She would do it — even though she suspected that neither Richard nor his mother, or even the children themselves really cared if she succeeded.

Mrs. Clemens bustled toward her, a large woman as tall as Dani with blond hair going gray. "Richard's driver is here to pick up William and Sophie and take them home. Their nurse will be waiting when they get there."

Dani turned to the children, still bickering over the little carved horse. William tugged the toy from Sophie's small hands and she started to cry.

"It's all right, sweetheart," Dani said. She hurried over and retrieved Sophie's toy from where she had tossed it, then returned and knelt in front of the little girl. "Here's your new doll. You can take her home with you if you like."

Sophie took the doll and slammed the porcelain head against the wall, smashing it into a dozen pieces that rained down on the carpet. "I don't want a silly old doll. I want a horse!"

Mrs. Clemens took hold of Sophie's hand. "You mustn't fret, dear. Grandma will get you a horse the next time you come over." The look she cast Dani told her not to argue. Both mother and son seemed to believe that the way to make William and Sophie behave was to give them anything they wanted.

Dani hoped that in time she would be able to convince Richard that what he and his mother were doing was not in the children's best interest.

She turned at the sound of her fiancé's voice as he walked up behind her. "I'm sorry I had to leave, darling. In my business, sometimes these things happen."

He had said he had forgotten an important business meeting and had no choice but to leave, but Dani smelled the faint aroma of liquor on his breath. He had stopped by his house and changed into his evening clothes, dark blue breeches and a light gray tailcoat over a silver waistcoat, and as always, looked extremely handsome.

And the way he was looking at her, his hazel eyes moving over her high-waisted green silk gown, said he was pleased with her appearance, too.

He tipped his head toward William and Sophie, who were ignoring him as if he weren't there. "The trials of being a parent. It'll be such a comfort to know you'll be there to take care of the children."

"Will I, Richard? Will I actually be taking care of them, or will I simply be their nurse-maid?"

"What are you talking about?"

"I'm just not sure we are going to agree on how much William and Sophie ought to be indulged."

Though the smile remained on his face, Richard's features subtly tightened. "I'm sure we can work something out — as long as you keep in mind that these are *my* children. Where they are concerned, I am the one who will make the decisions."

Angry heat rushed into her cheeks. She'd been afraid that was the position Richard would take. She opened her mouth to argue, but guests had started pouring into the house and this was obviously not the time or place.

Richard's smile softened. "Let's not fight tonight, darling. We'll discuss all of this tomorrow, work everything out. In the meantime, I've got a surprise for you."

He turned a little, revealing the presence of a tall man watching them from a few feet away. "When I told Mother you had a fellow countryman — a duke, no less — visiting here in the city, she invited him to join us." Richard stepped back, allowing her to see the man behind him, but Dani had already spotted Rafael.

Her chest constricted and her heart began a too-rapid beat. Dear God, why was Rafe torturing her this way? Surely he knew how uncomfortable his presence made her. She had loved him once. Didn't he know that looking at him now reminded her of times long past? Reminded her of what might have been?

"Miss Duval," Rafe said, capturing her gloved hand, making a formal bow as he brought her fingers to his lips. "A pleasure to see you again."

Dani ignored the little tremor that ran up her arm. She didn't know why he had come. She only wished he would leave.

It wasn't going to happen, she realized as he conversed with Richard, made polite conversation with Aunt Flora and Mrs. Clemens, then accompanied the group in to supper.

Rafael was seated at the head of the table, as he would have been back home, but Mrs. Clemens sat to his right and Jacob Wentz to his left. The remainder of the guests took their places.

Dani sat next to Richard, farther down the table, Aunt Flora across from them. Rafael made polite conversation with his hostess and spoke often to Richard and several of the other men, but even as Dani stumbled through the lavish meal, she could feel his eyes on her.

She did everything in her power not to

look at him, but dear God, time and again her gaze searched for his and she seemed unable to look away. There was something in those intense blue eyes, something hot and fierce that shouldn't have been there. Something that stirred old memories of the way the two of them once had been.

She remembered the day nearly five years ago that they had walked together in the apple orchard behind Rafe's country estate, Sheffield Hall.

Laughing at something she said, he had lifted her into the swing that hung down from the branches, then bent his dark head and kissed her, softly at first, but with such barely leashed passion she could still recall the feel of his lips moving over hers, remember the masculine taste of him.

The kiss had grown hot and wild, and Dani hadn't stopped him when his hand found her breast. She remembered his soft caresses and the sensual tug of heat that flowed through her body, the way her nipples hardened beneath the bodice of her blue muslin gown.

The way they were hard even now.

Dani flushed.

"Darling, you weren't paying attention," Richard scolded. "Did you hear what I just said?"

Her face was burning. She prayed that in the flickering light of the candles in the silver candelabra on the table, Richard wouldn't be able to see the color creeping into her cheeks.

"I'm sorry. My mind must have wandered. What were you saying?"

"I said that the duke has agreed to join our bird hunting party next week."

She managed to smile, but it wasn't easy. "That is . . . that is wonderful. I'm sure he'll enjoy himself."

"I was thinking that we would make a weekend of it. Jacob's country house is quite large and he has invited all of the ladies to join the men."

Her stomach squeezed into a knot. More time with Rafael. What in God's name did he want? "That sounds . . . very . . . pleasant."

Obviously pleased with himself, Richard turned back to the conversation he was having with the duke and the other men, and Dani concentrated on her food. Why was Rafael intruding in their lives this way?

Danielle didn't know, but she intended to find out.

Rafael endured the seemingly endless evening, determined to discover as much as he could about the man Danielle intended to marry. It was midnight by the time he returned to his suite at the William Penn Hotel. When he got there, he found Max Bradley waiting.

Sitting in the darkness, Max rose as Rafe reached over to light one of the whale-oil lamps, and Rafe swore a soft curse.

"I wish you would stop doing that. It's extremely disconcerting."

Max chuckled. "Sorry. How was your evening?"

"Tedious."

"You spoke to Clemens?"

He nodded. "I'm doing my best to like the man, but so far I'm having a devil of a time. There is something about him. . . . I can't quite put my finger on it. I've managed an invitation to join Richard's hunting party." Rafe smiled faintly. "Danielle will be traveling to the country, as well."

"When is it?"

"The end of the week."

"That shouldn't be a problem."

"What do mean?"

"I may be on to something. If I'm right, I may need your help."

Rafe moved across the room toward Max. "You've confirmed the Americans are making a deal with France?"

"It looks that way. So far I've only heard rumors . . . something to do with a schooner called a Baltimore Clipper."

"Indeed?"

"I've got a lead I need to follow up on. I'm not sure how long I'll be gone."

"You'll let me know if there is anything I can do." According to Max, a man of Rafe's social standing would be better able to move in upper-class circles, thereby gaining access to the men who were privy to the needed information.

"I'll let you know if I need you. In the meantime, you look like you could use some sleep."

Rafe nodded, more weary than he should have been. "Good luck, Max." Rafe headed for his bedroom, leaving Max to disappear as he usually did.

As Rafe undressed, his mind returned to the earlier hours of the evening and the unsettling events he had seen.

His arrival at Mrs. Clemens's home had been early enough to see Danielle with Richard's children. They were spoiled little wretches, raised without manners, and mostly left to run out of control. Worse yet, from what Richard had said to Dani, he didn't intend to allow her the slightest say in their upbringing.

Rafe believed the children would be far better off if Danielle took a hand. She had always been good with youngsters. They had planned to have a large family of their own. At the afternoon tea he had attended, he had watched her with several of the orphans, who seemed to adore her, as he could have guessed they would.

But Richard seemed too dictatorial to see the good she could do his offspring. It made Rafe wonder . . . what else would he be unbending about?

Rafe slid beneath the sheets trying to imagine what sort of future Dani would have with Richard Clemens.

Rafe wanted her to be happy.

He had to be certain marrying Richard Clemens would bring her the happiness she deserved.

Eight

Dani heard nothing from Rafael. Determined to discover the reason he continued to interfere in her life and hoping she could dissuade him from accompanying them to the country, she had sent a note to where he was staying at the William Penn Hotel. She had requested a meeting, but received no reply and wondered if perhaps he had gone out of town.

Dani hoped so.

As she awaited the arrival of Richard's carriage that Friday morning, she prayed Rafe had changed his mind and would not be joining them, now or any time in the future.

Aunt Flora had declined to make the trip, but a number of married women would be in attendance so there was no need for a chaperone, and Caro was accompanying her, acting as her lady's maid but actually there for support. Since Dani had only just met the other women and she barely knew Richard, it was good to have a friend along.

Richard's carriage finally arrived for the

journey to Jacob Wentz's country house, nearly twenty miles away. The three-hour ride, Danielle hoped, would give her the chance for a bit of conversation with her fiancé.

Unfortunately, once they were on the road, Richard slept most of the way.

They reached the house in the early afternoon, a large stone residence surrounded by acres of rolling green fields and patches of dense green forest.

"It's lovely," she said, staring through the carriage window at the countryside that reminded her a little of home.

Richard smiled from the seat beside her. "We'll have to consider buying a place like this for ourselves. Would you like that, darling?"

She turned to look at him. "I've always loved the country."

"And it would be good for the children, as well."

"Yes, I think it might be." Anything to get them away from their overindulgent grandmother. Perhaps they would have the chance to be a family after all. The family she never thought to have.

Her spirits lifted. They went into the residence, a large house with low, beamed ceilings in the main rooms and plaster fireplaces tall enough for her to walk into. There were hooked rugs on the wood-planked floors, and each of the guest rooms had a lovely four-poster bed. When she went upstairs, she found Caro pulling a trundle out from beneath the bed in the room the two of them would share.

"It's very nice." Caro smiled as she glanced round the bedchamber. As she walked over to the open window, a breeze blew fine blond curls loose from their pins and fluffed them around her narrow face. "There's a lovely view of the garden and the hills at the edge of the valley."

Dani walked over to see them. Instead, as she peered out the window, her gaze snagged on the tall man riding up the lane, mounted on a lean gray horse. She couldn't see his face, but she knew who it was, recognized the confident way he sat his mount, the width and straightness of his shoulders.

"Rafael is here," she said softly, drawing Caro's attention.

"The man on the dappled gray horse?"

She swallowed. "Yes."

Though Dani had told her friend a good deal about him, Caro had never seen Rafael. He drew closer, his face coming partially into view.

"Oh, my . . ."

"Exactly," Dani said. There wasn't a woman alive who wouldn't be impressed by Rafael. Aside from his dark good looks and impressive, broad-shouldered physique, there was simply something about him, the way he carried himself, the way he looked at a woman, giving her his complete attention as if she were the only female in the room. Dani watched him continue down the lane until he disappeared behind the high hedge surrounding the garden, riding toward the front of the house.

"Well, he is here," Caro said practically. "You will simply have to accept the fact." She turned away from the window and a bright smile bloomed on her face. "On the good side, you wished to speak to him, discover his intentions, whatever they may be. Perhaps you will now have the chance."

Dani dragged her gaze away from the window. "I suppose you are right. He has played the gentleman so far. Since my presence seems to have no effect on him, I shall simply behave the same way." Still, she wished he hadn't come, wished that he would turn round and go back to England where he belonged.

It was late in the afternoon. Danielle was wandering the pathways through the garden, meandering along, in no real hurry to get back to the house when she spotted the duke striding toward her, a determined look on his face. It deepened the faint cleft in his chin, made his eyes look a deeper shade of blue. Her heart stuttered, set up an erratic clatter.

"I apologize," he said, stopping on the path directly in front of her. "I'm afraid I didn't get your note until late last night. Apparently, the desk clerk put it into the wrong box."

"I thought that perhaps you were out of town on business."

Rafe's smile softened, lifting the edges of his full, sensuous mouth. It was the sort of smile she hadn't seen since before that awful night five years ago and it made her heart kick into a higher gear.

"I may have a matter to deal with while I am here, but that isn't the reason I came. The business I came for, Dani, is you."

The use of her nickname, said in that deep, resonant voice roughened with a hint of affection, made her tremble.

"If I am the reason you are here, you needn't remain. You've done what you came for. You've set matters straight, which is more than most men would have done. Go home, Rafael. I don't want you here. Surely you can understand why."

The smile slid from his face. "I want you to be happy, Danielle. I owe you that. Once I'm certain you will be, I promise to be on my way. Until then, I am staying."

Her temper inched up. "You don't owe me anything. I'm marrying Richard Clemens. I don't need your approval — I don't care what you think. Leave me in peace, Rafael. Let me get on with my life."

She started to turn away, but Rafe caught her arm.

"I asked you before — do you love him?"

Her chin shot up. "That is none of your concern."

"I'm making it my concern. *Do you love him?*"

Jerking free of his hold, she ignored the fierce scowl on his face, turned and started walking, her temper still high.

She was marrying Richard Clemens. Her decision had been made. Whatever Rafael thought was unimportant. Her own thoughts needed to focus on Richard, not Rafael.

But as she made her way out of the garden she could still see his tall image in the back of her mind, feel his intense blue eyes burning into her. She remembered the smoky look she had glimpsed in those eyes the instant before she had turned away, and keeping her thoughts on Richard wasn't all that easy to do.

Rafael joined the men for the hunt the following morning, riding out on horseback, Rafe on the saddle horse he had hired in town, an exceptionally fine gray mount that belonged to the man who owned the stable. The well-trained gelding was well worth the extra money he had paid for its use, he thought as they rode across the open fields.

The countryside was beautiful, rolling hills crisscrossed with low rock walls, interspersed with forested knolls, bisected with occasional rippling streams. Meadows sprinkled with white-and-yellow daisies stretched across the landscape in front of them.

They reached their destination and dismounted, leaving the horses to graze on the lush grass sprouting up between their legs. There were five men in the hunting party: Richard Clemens, Jacob Wentz, a wealthy merchant named Edmund Steigler, Judge Otto Bookman and Rafael, along with a pack of blue-speckled and rusty-red hunting hounds, brought to search out woodcock and quail.

As the dogs fanned out with the young man who was their handler, Richard

Clemens walked next to Rafe across the field, a smoothbore long gun with a silver-engraved flintlock gripped in one hand.

"Nice-looking piece," Rafe said, the long gun Richard had loaned him resting comfortably in the crook of his arm.

"My father's," Richard said proudly. "It's English, extremely well crafted." Richard held the gun out for Rafe to examine more closely.

Pausing for a moment, he leaned his own weapon against the trunk of a tree and took the gun from Richard's hand. He snapped the piece up against his shoulder, lowered it and turned it over to look at the maker's initials.

"I know the gunsmith, Peter Wells. Wells is still making very fine weapons."

Clemens beamed. "My father was always proud of this gun."

"He had reason to be."

They talked a little longer, building a sort of camaraderie, though Rafe yet remained wary. He wasn't quite sure why.

"So how are you enjoying our country so far?" Richard asked. "Had the chance to meet anyone interesting?"

"I've enjoyed meeting you and your friends, of course." Rafe looked up at him. "Are you talking about a woman?"

Richard shrugged. "You've been here for several weeks. A man has needs. I thought perhaps I might be of help, if you're interested."

"Then you're suggesting an evening of pleasure."

"There's a place in the city I enjoy on occasion. I think you might find it entertaining."

"And you would accompany me?"

He smiled. "I have a lady friend there . . . a very talented lady friend. We're quite well acquainted."

"You're getting married in less than two weeks."

Richard just smiled. "Getting married hardly precludes a man from taking his pleasure. I don't imagine it is any different in your country."

Rafe couldn't argue with that. In fact, had he wed Mary Rose, he would surely have turned to the company of other women. "A number of married men keep mistresses or pay an occasional visit to a brothel such as the one you mentioned."

But it wouldn't have been so with Dani, and the thought of her new husband intending to live such a life made his stomach start to churn.

"Your fiancée," he said, "seems to be a

126

very lovely young woman. Perhaps her attentions will be enough."

Richard just laughed. "I'm definitely looking forward to the marriage bed, but with my factory in Easton, I'm gone from the city quite often. I keep a mistress in the country. I don't intend for that to change."

Rafe said nothing more. He had vowed to see Danielle happy. She would never be happy with a man who planned from the start to be unfaithful.

"Look there!" Richard pointed toward a ditch running along the side of the field. "The dogs have flushed up a covey of quail!"

Richard and the other men swung their guns into position. Rafe slammed the stock of his flintlock against his shoulder and pulled the trigger. A pair of birds went down. If the rest of the day went as well, they would be having quail for supper.

Unfortunately, Rafe's mind was no longer on the hunt. He was thinking of Danielle. He had the answers he had been seeking, but he couldn't break a confidence and tell her.

The question arose, what should he do?

Nine

Caroline Loon sat at a long wooden table in the basement kitchen of the Wentz house, talking to the serving women and sipping a cup of tea. It was one of the advantages of being a lady's maid. She could cross without a problem from the world above stairs into the one below.

"How 'bout a nice slice o' pie, dear, to go with your tea?" The buxom cook, Emma Wyatt, waddled toward her, a warm smile on her face. "It's just out of the oven. Picked the apples meself — right off the tree outside the back door."

"It looks delicious, Emma, but I'm not really hungry."

"Are ye sure? A girl needs to eat."

"I'm fine."

The sound of footsteps rang on the stone floor behind her. Caro turned to see the shadowy figure of a man appear in the open doorway.

"You had better do as Emma says. You look like you could use a little meat on your bones." His gaze ran over her. "Though they are very lovely bones, indeed."

Caro blinked at the sudden commotion in the kitchen — one of the kitchen maids giggling, Mrs. Wyatt grinning like a schoolgirl.

"Leave her be, Robert." Emma waved her spatula in his direction. "Ye'll embarrass the poor lass." The cook turned to Caro. "Pay him no mind, dear. Robert's a terrible flirt. Why, the man could charm the sparrows right out of the trees."

He just smiled. Setting the knee-high black leather boots he carried down beside the door, he walked over to the long wooden table and sat down on the bench across from her. The visitor, a man in his thirties with thick brown hair and a very nice smile, was handsome as sin, and a wicked glint appeared for a moment in his warm brown eyes. They assessed her from top to bottom, paused for a moment on her not particularly substantial breasts, then returned to her face.

"I'll have a piece of that pie, Emma." He winked at Caro. "If you've never tasted Emma's pie, you don't know what you're missing. By the way, my name is Robert McKay. It's a pleasure to meet you, Miss . . . ?"

"Loon. Caroline Loon. I work for Miss Duval. She's one of Mr. Wentz's houseguests."

"Ah, that explains it."

"Explains what?"

"You're from England. I haven't heard those particular speech patterns for quite some time."

He was referring to her polished manner of speaking. Regardless of her family's lack of finances, Caro had received a solid education and spoke with the crisp, clipped tones of the British upper classes.

It occurred to her that Robert's resonant speech held the same upper-class intonations. "But you're English, as well."

"I was. I'm American now, though not exactly by choice."

Emma set a large piece of pie down in front of Robert McKay and the delicious aroma made Caro's stomach growl.

"I knew it!" Robert grinned. "Emma — bring a slice of this marvelous pie for Miss Loon."

Emma laughed and waddled over a few minutes later with a slightly smaller piece of pie, which she set down in front of Caro along with a fork for each of them.

Robert waited politely for her to begin, then attacked his food like a man who hadn't eaten in a week, which, with his well-muscled frame, Caro highly doubted.

As he had promised, the pie was delicious,

the apple-cinnamon aroma filling every square inch of the overly warm, low-ceilinged kitchen, yet with the handsome man seated across from her it was difficult to concentrate on her food.

"Do you work for Mr. Wentz?" she asked, interrupting his last bite of pie.

McKay shook his head and swallowed. "I'm here with Edmund Steigler. I'm his *manservant.*" He said the word with such repugnance Caro's blond eyebrows went up. "At least I will be for the next four years."

"You don't like your work?"

He laughed, but there was no humor in it. "I'm indentured to Steigler. He bought seven years of my life. I've only paid back three."

"I see." But she didn't really see at all. Why would an educated man, as McKay appeared to be, sell himself into the service of another man?

"Why?" she asked, the word popping out before she could stop it.

McKay studied her with renewed interest. "You're the first person who's ever asked me that."

She glanced down at her half-empty plate, wishing she had kept silent. "You don't have to answer. It's really none of my business." She looked up at him. "I just . . . you seem an independent sort of man, not the kind to sell yourself into bondage."

McKay studied her a moment more, then glanced around the kitchen. Emma was busy kneading bread, her helper determinedly scrubbing pots and pans.

"If you want to know the truth, the constables were after me. They were trying to arrest me for a crime I didn't commit. I had to leave the country in a hurry. I hadn't the money to book passage on a ship. I saw an ad in the London *Chronicle* advertising for indentured servants to travel to America. The advertisement was placed by a man named Edmund Steigler and his ship was set to sail the following morning. I went to see him. He didn't ask questions. I signed the papers and Steigler brought me here."

Caro knew her blue eyes must be round as saucers. "You're not afraid to be telling me this?"

Robert shrugged. He was taller than average, but not overly so, with shoulders that filled out his full-sleeved homespun shirt. "What would you do? Tell Steigler? He would hardly be concerned. Besides, I'm wanted in England, not America."

"But if you are innocent, you must go back. You must find a way to clear your name."

McKay's laugh was harsh. "You are certainly a dreamer, love. I still haven't got the money. And I owe Steigler four more years." At the troubled look on her face, he reached out and touched her cheek. "I think you must be a very nice person, Caroline Loon. I believe I like you."

Caro didn't tell him that she liked him, too. Or that she believed his story. She was a very good judge of people and she knew instinctively that Robert McKay was telling the truth.

He shoved his empty pie plate away and came up from the bench. "It was nice meeting you, Miss Loon."

"You as well, Mr. McKay."

He started walking toward the door. Caro noticed the muscles in his legs and the trim fit of his breeches, and a hint of warmth rose in her cheeks.

At the door, McKay stopped and turned. "Do you like horses, Miss Loon?"

"I'm afraid I am a dismal rider, but I like horses very much."

"In that case, there's a new foal you might enjoy seeing. Perhaps you could meet me in the stable after supper."

Caro smiled. It wasn't the foal she was interested in; it was Robert McKay. "I would like that very much."

His easy smile returned. "Good, then I'll see you later this evening."

She nodded, watched him walk away. She shouldn't have agreed. He was a very handsome man and if she slipped away to meet him, he might think he could take liberties. Still, she was a grown woman and she could take care of herself.

"Robert's a good man," Emma said as if she read her thoughts. "And ye needn't worry. Ye'll be safe as a lamb with him."

"Thank you, Emma, I'm sure I will be." Beginning to tire of the heat in the kitchen, Caro took her pie plate over to the dry sink, washed it in a bucket of sudsy water, rinsed and dried it, then headed for the door.

As she walked out into the sunshine, she smiled, intrigued by the notion of spending an evening with Robert McKay.

The men went hunting again the next morning, and to keep the ladies entertained, the Wentzes planned a party that night. Along with their houseguests, a number of local residents had also been invited.

For much of the day, the women helped with the preparations, bringing flowers in from the garden and arranging them in cut-crystal vases, covering the tables with pretty lace tablecloths, helping the servants push the furniture back to allow for dancing.

The members of a three-piece orchestra arrived and set up at the end of the parlor. The guests, mostly local farmers and their wives, began to arrive, and Richard and Jacob Wentz made introductions.

As the evening progressed, Danielle danced with Richard, then with the merchant, Edmund Steigler, a lean man with black hair and thin features — rather enigmatic, Dani thought. She conversed with Sara Bookman, the judge's wife, who was interesting and funny and easy to like. Their hostess, Greta Wentz, was a sweet, kindly woman with a heavy German accent who wasn't afraid of hard work.

Dani thought that in time, she could become good friends with some of the ladies she had met in America. She liked the women's rugged spirit, the optimism with which they approached their lives.

Across the parlor, she caught a glimpse of Richard in conversation with Edmund Steigler and wondered if she would ever be able to form a true and lasting friendship with the man she was to wed. Several times during the evening she had gone in search of him, but he was always busy with one of his friends.

Or conversing with Rafael.

She saw Rafe just then and a little tremor went through her. Though she tried her best to ignore him, to pretend he wasn't there, time and again her unruly gaze went in search of him. More than once, she found him watching her, a troubled look on his face.

She wished she knew what he was thinking, wanted to ask him when he planned to return to England, but the right moment never seemed to come. As the evening wore on, she looked up to see him approaching from across the room, his long strides bearing down on her with purpose.

"I need to speak to you," he said simply. "I hoped to find a better time, but we'll all be leaving in the morning. It's important, Danielle."

"I don't know. . . . I don't think it's a good idea for us to —"

"I'll wait for you in the gazebo at the rear of the garden." He left her there in the parlor, halfway through the protest she had been about to make.

Angry that he'd left her no choice and more curious than she wanted to admit, she returned her attention momentarily to the guests. She danced again with Richard, then slipped quietly away when he began a conversation with Jacob Wentz about the high price of southern cotton, making her way outside into the garden.

Though several torches burned along the gravel paths, they were not well lit. Winding her way between the shadows, passing clusters of yellow pansies and tall purple iris, she headed for the gazebo, whose ornate spire marked its location some distance away at the back of the garden, near a bubbling brook.

She knew it was dangerous, this meeting with Rafael. Her reputation had been compromised once before. How would she explain her presence out here in the darkness with the handsome Duke of Sheffield? What would Richard's friends think if the two of them were found together?

A shiver of unease rippled through her. She would never forget the agony she had suffered that night five years ago, or the pain of the terrible weeks that followed. She'd been ostracized and humiliated. Worse yet, she had suffered the heartbreak of losing the man she loved.

She wasn't in love with Richard, as she had once been with Rafael, but the thought of enduring that sort of rebuke made her stomach roll with nausea.

Her eyes searched the darkness as she hurried along the path. Rafael must have recognized the danger and yet he had insisted on the meeting. She knew if she didn't appear, he would simply seek her out, perhaps under less private circumstances.

The gazebo loomed ahead, octagonal in design with ornate white-painted moldings, open sides and wooden seats that lined the raised interior. As she drew near, she could see the shadowy outline of Rafe's tall figure leaning against the railing inside. Glancing around to be certain no one was near, she lifted the hem of her sapphire silk gown up out of the way and took the first of three steep stairs.

Rafe caught her hand, helping her ascend to the platform beside him. "I was afraid you might not come."

She wouldn't have, if he had really given her a choice. "You said it was important."

"So I did."

He led her over to the bench along the rail and she sat down, though Rafe remained standing. He paced a moment, as if he searched for what to say, then turned to face her. In the dim light of a distant torch, she could see the blue of his eyes, read the uncertainty there. It was so out of character for Rafe, her heart set up a nervous clatter.

"What is it, Rafael?"

He took a deep breath, let it out slowly. "I'm not quite sure how to begin. I told you

I had discovered the truth of what happened that night five years ago."

"Yes . . ."

"I told you I wanted you to be happy, that I owed you that much."

"You said that, but —"

"I don't believe you will be happy with Richard Clemens."

She shot up off the bench. "It doesn't matter what you believe, Rafael. Richard and I will be married the end of next week."

"I've asked you twice if you loved him. This time I want an answer."

She squared her shoulders. "I'll give you the answer I gave you before. It's none of your business."

"You've never been one to mince words, Dani. If you loved him, you would say so. Therefore, I must assume that you do not. Since that is the case, I'm asking you to call off the wedding."

"Are you insane? I've crossed an entire ocean to marry Richard Clemens, and that is exactly what I intend to do."

Rafe gently caught her shoulders. "I realize things have changed between us . . . that you no longer hold me in the same regard you did before."

"I loved you once. Not anymore. Is that what you mean?"

"You may not love me, Danielle, but neither do you love Richard Clemens." He searched her face. "And I believe there is a difference."

"What difference is that?"

"When you look at me, there is something in your eyes, a spark of fire that isn't there when you look at Richard."

"You're mad."

"Am I? Why don't we see?"

Dani's breath caught as Rafe hauled her into his arms and his mouth came down over hers. For an instant, she fought him, pressing her hands against his chest, trying to push him away. But the heat was there, burning into her, the fire that should have died long ago. It was searing in its intensity, scorching through flesh and bone, turning her body soft and pliant.

Rafe deepened the kiss and her palms slid over the lapels of his coat, up, up, until her arms encircled his neck. For an instant, she was back in the apple orchard, kissing him with all her heart, with all of the love she felt for him.

Then her eyes filled with tears. This wasn't the apple orchard and she was no longer in love.

Danielle jerked away, trembling all over, loathing herself for what she'd let happen.

140

"I had to know," he said softly.

Dani backed away, trying to ignore the taste of him that lingered on her lips. "It meant nothing. Your kiss stirred old memories. It was nothing more than that."

"Perhaps."

"It's getting late. I have to go back in." She started to turn, but Rafe caught her arm.

"Listen to me, Danielle. There is still time to cancel the wedding. Instead of marrying Richard, I want you to marry me."

She just stood there, staring in disbelief. "You can't be serious."

"I am completely serious."

"That night at the ball . . . I saw you dancing with your betrothed, the Earl of Throckmorton's daughter."

"It was clear we didn't suit. I spoke to her father before I left England. He asked that the betrothal be ended."

Dani shook her head. "This can't happen, Rafael. Whatever existed between us is over. It ended five years ago."

"It isn't over, not until the record is set straight. Marry me and return to England as my duchess. All of London — all of England — will know it was I who wronged you, not the other way around."

"I don't care what people think — not anymore."

"You can go back to your home, return to your family and friends."

"I have very little family and even fewer friends. In time I'll have friends and family here."

Rafe's jaw hardened. In the flickering torchlight, his eyes appeared a deeper shade of blue. She knew that look, knew the determination it revealed, and a thread of uncertainty filtered through her.

"I had hoped I wouldn't have to resort to coercion to see this matter done, but you're leaving me no choice."

The color drained from her face. "What are you saying? Are you . . . are you threatening me?"

Rafael reached out and touched her cheek. "I'm trying to do what is right. I believe I can make you happy. I don't believe Richard Clemens ever will. Accept my offer of marriage."

Her gaze locked with his. "Or you'll do what, Rafael?"

He straightened to his full height, making him look even taller than he usually did. "I'll let word escape of The Scandal. People here will believe it's true, Richard's mother, his friends. You won't be able to prove your innocence here any more than you could in England."

She started shaking. "I told Richard about The Scandal before he ever proposed. Unlike you, he believed I was telling the truth."

"I was wrong. It doesn't change what needs to happen."

A lump began to thicken in her throat. "I can't believe you would do something like this, that you would hurt me this way again. I can't believe you would stoop so low." Tears welled in her eyes and she glanced away, refusing to let him see.

Rafe reached out and caught her chin, gently turning her to face him. "I'll make you happy, Danielle. I swear I will."

The tears in her eyes spilled over onto her cheeks. "If you force me to do this, I'll never forgive you, Rafael."

He brought her trembling hand to his lips and pressed a gentle kiss against the back. All the while his gaze remained on her face.

"That is a chance I have to take."

Ten

Danielle broke her engagement to Richard Clemens the day after she and Caro returned from the country, five days before her wedding. She had no choice, she told herself. She didn't doubt for a moment that Rafael would do exactly as he vowed. If she refused his offer of marriage, he would ruin her, just as he had before.

Dani loathed him for it.

And she didn't understand. Why was Rafe so insistent? Was his guilt so strong, his code of honor such that he believed marrying her was the only way he could redeem himself?

It was certainly possible.

At the news there would be no wedding, Richard had ranted and raved, begged and pleaded, tried every way he knew how to convince her to change her mind.

"What have I done, Danielle? Just tell me and I promise I'll make it up to you."

"It's nothing you've done, Richard. It is simply that we aren't . . . aren't well suited. I didn't realize that until now."

"We've made plans, Danielle. We were

144

going to share a future."

"I'm sorry, Richard, truly I am, but that is simply the way it is, the way it has to be."

His temper inched up. "You can't just walk away. What about my mother? She's spent a fortune on the wedding. What about my children . . . my friends? What will I say to them, how will I explain?"

"You would never have let me be a real mother to your children, and if they truly are your friends, they'll understand that sometimes these things happen."

Richard's face turned crimson. "Well, they don't happen to me!" He stomped out of the house and Danielle watched through the window as he stormed down the front porch steps, climbed into his carriage and slammed the door.

Her eyes burned, but the pain she'd expected to feel did not come. Turning away from the window, she sighed into the silence his departure had left in the parlor. Hoping to spare Richard's pride, she hadn't mentioned the duke, hadn't told Richard that she would be marrying another man, that she would be returning to England to become the Duchess of Sheffield.

She didn't tell him that Rafael was blackmailing her, that she had no choice but to break her engagement.

She felt like crying but couldn't seem to summon the tears. It bothered her that she wasn't more upset, that mostly she was angry — and afraid. What sort of future would she have with a ruthless man like Rafael, a man she no longer knew and did not trust?

It bothered her even more that it was only when she thought of Rafe that her emotions seemed to spin out of control.

Dear God, how had her life become so confused?

A warm August sun beat through the wavy glass panes two days later. After luncheon, she and Aunt Flora were going shopping, anything to get out of the house and away from her troubled thoughts, at least for a while.

Unfortunately, before it was time to leave, Rafe appeared on her doorstep, hat in hand, looking far too handsome to suit her.

"I received your note," he said as she led him into the parlor and closed the sliding doors. "I'm glad you acted so swiftly."

Dani cast him a glance. She had sent him a message telling him that she had broken her engagement. She hoped he could read the bitterness between the lines. "You gave me no choice. I acted swiftly, hoping to

146

make things less painful for Richard."

Danielle sat down in a high-backed Windsor chair and Rafe sat down on the rose velvet sofa in front of the hearth.

"The *Nimble* will be sailing for England the end of next week. I've booked passage for the two of us, as well as your aunt and your lady's maid, Miss Loon. I would like us to be married before we leave."

"What!" She practically leapt from her chair. "That's impossible! Why are you in such a hurry? Why can't we wait until we get back to England?"

She could tell by the stiffness that settled in his shoulders how greatly he was striving for control.

"We've waited five years already, Danielle. I want this matter settled once and for all, settled as it should have been then. Now that the decision has been made, I would see us wed, and soon. With your aunt's permission, I shall make arrangements for a small ceremony to take place here in the garden the day before we sail. We'll celebrate our marriage in a more proper manner once we're returned to London."

"But . . . but that is . . . is less than a week away. You can't possibly expect me to . . . to . . ."

"To what, Danielle?"

She took a deep breath, fighting to maintain her composure. "Our lives have changed. I don't know you anymore, Rafael. I need time to get used to the idea of . . . of sharing a bed with you. I can't just . . . just . . ."

The corner of his mouth edged up. "There was a time you were looking forward to sharing a bed with me."

Her cheeks went warm. She remembered that time all too well, remembered it even more clearly since the night he had kissed her in the garden. Still, she wasn't ready to take the steps that would lead to that kind of intimacy, wasn't ready to give him even more control over her than he had taken already.

She lifted her chin. "So far you've made all sorts of demands to which I have unwillingly agreed. Now I am asking for something in return. I want time, Rafael. Time to accept the fact that you are to be my husband."

There was something in his face. For an instant, he glanced away. "All right, that seems a fair-enough request. You want time. I am willing to give it to you. I won't make any husbandly demands on you until we are returned to England."

Fortified by the battle she had just won, she grew braver. "Perhaps it would be best if we kept it a marriage of convenience. We could both lead our own separate lives and —"

"Like bloody hell!" Rafe took a breath and clamped down on his temper. "You are smart enough to know that isn't going to happen. I've wanted you since the day I met you, Danielle. That is one thing that hasn't changed. I hope that in time, you may again feel that same desire for me."

Danielle didn't say more. Rafael Saunders was a strong, virile, potently attractive man. As a girl, she had lain awake at night wondering what it might be like for him to make love to her. As much as she wished it weren't so, part of her still did.

"Then I take it that we are agreed," she said.

"Though I shall regret it every day for the length of the voyage, we are agreed."

Caroline Loon stood in the alley behind the house on Arch Street. "Robert!"

He strode up to her, leaned over and gave her a swift kiss on the cheek. "My sweet Caroline."

Caro blushed. They had been back in the city for most of a week, seen each other every day since their return. Caro had been surprised to discover that the merchant, Edmund Steigler, lived right there in Philadelphia. Which meant Robert McKay lived there, too.

The night she had met him in the stable had been magical. When she had first arrived, he had guided her out to an open field next to the barn and pointed out a lovely little bay foal, cavorting next to its mother.

"His name is Dandy. Wentz's eldest daughter named him for the dandelions he loves to eat."

Caro laughed. "He's marvelous." They spent time with the horses, Robert showing her Jacob Wentz's blooded mares and stallions, showing a surprising knowledge of horses and obviously enjoying himself.

"One of my mother's cousins has an estate in the country and my mother often took me there to visit."

"What about your father?"

Robert shook his head. "I never knew him. He died before I was born."

As darkness fell, Robert led her up on a knoll overlooking the valley, guiding her over to the trunk of a fallen tree, where they each took a seat.

"The valley is lovely," she said, looking out over the rolling hills outlined by rays of silver moonlight. "Perhaps once we are settled in Mr. Clemens's house, I shall have a chance to draw it."

"You like to draw?"

"I paint watercolor landscapes, but only for fun. I am only mildly proficient."

"I'll wager you are a very good painter." He reached down and picked up a twig, twirled it absently in his hand. "I like to carve things. It helps to pass the time."

She looked at him in the moonlight, admiring the strong line of his jaw, thinking how handsome he was. "What sort of things do you carve?"

"Toys, mostly. Wooden horses, toy soldiers, miniature carriages, things like that." He smiled. "Perhaps someday we'll be able to make a trade — one of my wooden horses for one of your paintings."

Caro smiled back at him. "I would like that. I shall consider that we have struck a bargain."

She and Robert sat on the knoll in the moonlight, talking till well past midnight. Time seemed to fly as they laughed and talked, Caro speaking with an ease she had never felt with a man before.

She smiled to think of the days they'd spent since their return to the city, of the amazing number of things they had found in common. They both loved opera and poetry, both loved to read, both loved animals and children — Robert hoped to have a large family one day.

She told him about her childhood and how her family had been poor but so very happy. She told him about the summer five years ago when her parents had died and how she had grieved for them. All the while, Robert had held her hand and simply listened, truly listened.

And during those days, Caro had discovered a good deal about Robert McKay. Though the next four years of his life belonged to another man, Robert laughed often and sincerely. He seemed to keep a cheerful attitude no matter the circumstances.

No matter the abuse he took from the man who owned him.

"I'm his manservant," Robert once told her. "He could have given me any of a dozen different jobs, but he wanted me in service to him, personally. The man thrives on lording over others."

"How do you mean?"

"Steigler takes great pride in the fact I graduated from Cambridge and still have to scrape mud off his boots. I speak the King's English better than he does, and I'm far better read, but I still have to prepare his bath and mend his socks and shirts."

"Oh, Robert."

He smiled thinly. "He took a horse whip to me once in front of a group of his friends for correcting him about a Shakespearean play."

"Dear God, Robert — and you never tried to escape?"

He shrugged his wide shoulders, moving the fabric of his full-sleeved shirt. "Steigler's a powerful man in this country. He's made it clear he would have me hunted down. And the debt I owe him is real. I made a bargain with the devil. I have to live with it for the next four years."

Robert didn't seem to mind his circumstances, but Caro could hardly bear it.

In the short time since she had met him, Caro had fallen in love with Robert McKay.

At the sound of voices in the hallway, Danielle looked up from the book she was reading, Defoe's *Robinson Crusoe*, a novel she had brought with her from England. Framed in the doorway, Caro stood next to a handsome brown-haired man Danielle knew must be Robert McKay.

Since their return from the country, Caro had mentioned him a dozen times a day. It

153

was obvious she was enamored of McKay, though Robert was an indentured servant. Danielle worried the man might try to take advantage of a sweet, naive young woman like her friend.

Now that she saw how attractive he was, she was even more concerned.

Though Caro was a year older than Dani, she had little experience with men. Dani just hoped Caro's common sense and innate ability to judge people's character would be enough to guide her in matters of the heart.

"I am sorry to bother you, Danielle, but Robert stopped by for a moment and I was hoping you might have time to meet him."

"Of course I have time." Dani had been wanting to do just that since the first time Caro had mentioned him. She set her book down on the sofa beside her and came to her feet. "Please . . . both of you come in."

The couple walked into the parlor together, Robert's hand resting lightly on Caro's slim waist. They didn't really know each other well enough for that, but somehow, looking at them, it seemed perfectly natural.

"Danielle, I'd like you to meet my friend, Robert McKay, the man I've been telling you about."

Dani smiled. "Mr. McKay . . . it's a pleasure to meet you."

"The pleasure is mine, Miss Duval." He bowed over her hand as if he were a member of the nobility instead of an indentured servant and Dani cast him an assessing glance.

"You've quite impressed my friend Caro," she said.

Robert's smile widened. "As she has impressed me, Miss Duval." His gaze went to Caro and there was something so warm in his expression that some of Danielle's uncertainty eased.

They talked a while, about the weather, about the city, then Robert asked Danielle if she was enjoying the novel she was reading.

She arched a burnished brow. "You've read it?"

"Actually, I have. It's been some time ago, but I enjoyed it very much."

Aunt Flora walked in just then, ready to leave for their planned shopping excursion, only mildly surprised to see a handsome man standing in the parlor.

Another round of introductions were made, Aunt Flora seemingly unconcerned that she, a countess, was being introduced to a servant. But then, this was America. There was no royalty here and no one had a title. They were all growing used to the notion that here, men were treated, for the most part, as equals.

Still, it was clearly evident that Robert McKay was more than merely a servant.

"My lady," he said in his perfect, high-born English, bowing elaborately over Aunt Flora's hand.

"So this is the man who has been wooing our friend away from the house," Flora said, eyeing McKay from head to foot.

"Guilty, my lady, as charged. And I assure you, Miss Loon is extremely delightful company."

More polite conversation followed, McKay not the least intimidated by the fact that Flora Chamberlain was a high-ranking member of the aristocracy. Aunt Flora glanced shrewdly at Caro then back to their guest. "Perhaps you have time to join us for tea, Mr. McKay."

Robert seemed sincerely regretful. "I'm afraid I must decline. I've duties to fulfill and I've stayed longer than I should have already. Perhaps another time, my lady."

Aunt Flora smiled, pleased at the soft look he cast in Caro's direction. Robert bade them a pleasant farewell and Caro walked him to the door.

"You are lucky to have such friends," he said, still within earshot of Dani.

"I'm very lucky," Caro said.

Fabric rustled as he leaned closer, perhaps kissed her cheek. "I'm glad I met you, Caroline Loon."

Dani heard the door close behind him, then Caro walked back into the parlor, an expectant look on her face.

"Well . . . what did you think?"

"He's a handsome devil," Aunt Flora said. "Well educated and utterly charming." She shook her head, jiggling one of her several chins. "Why on earth is a man like that working as a servant?"

"It's a long story, Lady Wycombe."

She waved a blunt hand. "Yes, and none of my business. Still . . . it worries me."

"Well, I liked him very much," Dani said brightly. "And I believe he is as taken with you as you are with him."

A soft blush crept into Caro's cheeks. "Robert traded one of his carved wooden horses for a pair of tickets to a play. It's a comedy called *Life* and he has asked me to accompany him. He says Mr. Steigler has a business meeting and won't be home until late."

From the gossip Dani had heard, that was probably a polite way of saying Steigler was spending the night with his mistress.

Caro gazed out the window, watching

Robert walk off down the street. As he disappeared round the corner, the smile on her face slid away. Caro had believed she would be staying in America. Now Dani was returning to England with Rafael. Aunt Flora would go with them and Caro would be forced to go, as well.

She knew no one in America. And even if Robert's intentions were honorable, he couldn't ask her to marry him for at least four more years.

Dani watched her friend leave the room and her heart ached for her. If only Rafael had stayed in London, in time Caro might have found a future with Robert. Dani didn't think it was going to happen now.

Another misfortune she blamed on Rafael.

Eleven

Rafe paced the floor of his suite at the William Penn Hotel, his mind on Danielle and his upcoming wedding. It was actually going to happen. He was going to marry Danielle Duval. He could still hardly believe it.

He paused for a moment in front of the window, looked down at the lantern burning next to the sign on the front of the hotel, then turned at the sound of a firm knock on his door.

Rafe walked over and pulled it open, only mildly surprised to see Max Bradley standing in the hall instead of appearing in the suite without warning as he usually did.

"Max! Come in. I thought, perhaps, you had gone back to England."

"Not yet. Though if things go the way I plan, I should be leaving very soon."

As they walked into the parlor and closed the door, Rafe noticed the worry lines digging into Max's forehead. His black hair was mussed, as if he had run his fingers through it.

"What is it, Max? What have you found out?"

"Not as much as I'd like. I came to ask for your help."

"Of course. Whatever you need." He had promised Colonel Pendleton his aid and he intended to keep his word.

Max nodded. "I know you're getting married. I believe we can get this bit of business finished and be back in plenty of time for your wedding."

"How did you know about . . . ? Never mind. You ought to start some sort of information service. You could make a fortune."

Max almost smiled. "I need you to go with me to Baltimore. If we press hard, we can make the journey in a couple of days, three at most. That'll give us time for the meeting I've arranged and you'll still be back in time to get married."

Rafe hoped Max was right. Though Danielle might prefer he didn't show up at all, being late for his own wedding certainly wouldn't be the best way to begin their future.

"When do we leave?" Rafe asked, thinking of the note he would need to send Danielle explaining his disappearance and that he would be back very soon.

"Early in the morning. The sooner we get there the sooner we can return."

And Rafe still had plenty to do once he

got back. He was about to become a married man. He wondered why he wasn't the least bit worried by the thought.

Baltimore was a town of a little more than twenty thousand people, Rafe discovered, a bustling seaport that traded with England, the Caribbean and South America, a city that seemed to be growing by leaps and bounds.

As usual, Max Bradley had done his job. He had engineered a meeting with a wealthy shipbuilder named Phineas Brand. The story Max concocted was that the Duke of Sheffield was considering a venture with the Marquess of Belford, owner of the Belford Enterprises shipping fleet, and several other wealthy Englishmen. The duke had heard of the fabulous new schooner called a Baltimore Clipper that Brand's company was building and thought the vessel might be suitable for hauling goods into smaller, less accessible ports.

Or at least that was their story.

The meeting was set to take place in the inner office of the Maryland Shipbuilding Company on the lower floor of a large brick warehouse near the harbor. As the discussion progressed, Phineas Brand rose from his chair, a short man with curly gray hair, patches of which were missing, and wooly gray sideburns. Small silver spectacles sat on his prominent nose.

"The *Windlass* has just been completed," Brand said, smiling proudly as they left the building and headed for the dock where the ship was moored. "Wait till you see her. She's unparalleled for speed and maneuverability, the fastest ship of her kind ever built."

Rafe made no comment, but he was anxious to see the ship for himself, to discover if such a vessel actually posed a threat to England.

"Of course, if you're seriously interested," Brand continued, "you'll have to act swiftly." He cast Rafe a glance. "As I told your man, Bradley, there are other interested parties. It's first come, first serve around here."

"We're talking about twenty ships, is that correct?"

Brand nodded. "Since each ship takes a great deal of time to build, it's a five-year project to completion. You understand the highest bidder will get the deal."

Rafe nodded. "Mr. Bradley informed me."

"Of course, you can always wait until the first fleet has been built."

"I don't think that's an option."

They reached the spot where the *Windlass* rocked softly against the dock, her lines creaking in the breeze. Rafe paused to study the low, sleek, graceful lines of the hull, the twin masts tilting slightly toward the stern. He had never seen such a design before, but he could imagine how it might increase the schooner's speed.

The hull itself was also unique, and he thought that, indeed, the builder had created a craft that would be nearly impossible to duplicate without the designer's plans.

Brand invited him aboard for a demonstration and Rafe accepted. The day was sunny and warm, with just enough wind to fill the unusual, triangular-shaped sails, which again were unlike any Rafe had seen. Though the boat wasn't designed to carry much cargo, she was fast — amazingly so, and incredibly easy to maneuver.

Should the ship be armed with men and cannon, she would be a force to be reckoned with against slower, larger, less maneuverable war ships, which could easily fall prey to such a vessel.

As the wind whipped the sails and the sleek craft sliced through the water, Rafe believed the rumors could very well be true, that Napoléon was, indeed, interested in purchasing a fleet of these clippers to use against English war ships, vessels that had defeated him so soundly at Trafalgar last year.

"I'm having a little get-together tonight, duke," Brand said as they returned to the dock. "We'd love to have you join us."

Rafe's smile felt wolfish. He needed to gather as much information as he could, particularly about a trader named Bartel Schrader whom Max believed was the man behind the deal with the French. Phineas Brand had just provided the perfect opportunity.

"I would be delighted, Mr. Brand."

It was late, well into the evening when Rafe arrived at Phineas Brand's three-story stone mansion on Front Street. He had come late on purpose. He didn't want Brand to guess how anxious he was to prevent a fleet of Baltimore Clippers from being sold to the French.

He wasn't sure if England would be willing to make a higher bid for the fleet, but he was certain that if the ships went to Napoléon, it was going to cost a lot of British sailors their lives.

Lights blazed through the windows of the house as he climbed the wide front porch steps. A liveried servant stood on each side of the carved wooden door to welcome guests, and he was quickly ushered inside.

Two hours later, he was headed back out the door.

The evening had progressed even better than he had hoped and he was anxious to be on his way. He had the information he had come for. Now all he had to do was get that information back to Max.

"How did it go?" Max stood up from his chair near the unlit hearth in Rafe's room, one of two he and Bradley had taken at the Seafarer's Inn, downtown near the harbor. He hadn't seen Max since early that morning.

"Pendleton was right to be concerned," Rafe said, shrugging out of his tailcoat and tossing it over the back of a chair.

"Yes . . . I followed you down to the harbor this afternoon. I saw her . . . the *Windlass*." Max walked over to the dresser and poured them both a glass of brandy from the bottle that rested on top. "An amazing bit of craftsmanship." He handed a glass to Rafe. "Armed, she could be deadly."

"My thoughts exactly."

"Was Schrader at the party?"

"He was there." Max had filled him in on the international trader they called the Dutchman. Schrader made large sums of money by finding buyers and putting them together with sellers. The merchandise might vary, but if the deal went through, Schrader got paid a percentage for his efforts. According to Max, there was a very good chance he was working for the French.

"Sandy hair?" Max confirmed. "Blue-gray eyes? Perhaps late thirties?"

"That's him." Rafe took a sip of his drink, grateful for the ease it gave the muscles in his shoulders, thinking of the brief conversation he'd had with the man Phineas Brand had introduced him to at the house party.

"Your Grace," Schrader had said with only the slightest accent. He was Dutch, after all, and obviously a man of the world.

"A pleasure, Mr. Schrader."

"Our host tells me you enjoyed a brief sail aboard the *Windlass* today," the Dutchman said. "Quite a vessel, isn't she?"

"Indeed, she is."

"I've heard you may have an interest beyond that of simple curiosity."

"Have you? I've heard the same of you."

That seemed to surprise him. "Really? So I'll assume my information is correct."

"The ship is intriguing in some ways, but hardly designed for cargo. Which means its uses are limited."

"True enough."

"What about you, Mr. Schrader? What use might your client have for such a fleet?"

The Dutchman just smiled. "I'm really not at liberty to say. My job is simply to broker the sale, should my client decide he is ready to make the purchase."

Phineas Brand returned just then, putting an end to the conversation. But Rafe had already discovered what he wanted to know and now it was time to find Max.

Or more aptly, wait for Max to find him.

"Schrader has elegant tastes," Rafe continued. "He dresses in expensive clothes, wears shoes of fine Spanish leather." Schrader's black stock, Rafe recalled, was perfectly tied, his sandy hair immaculately groomed.

"That's the Dutchman, all right. He makes a lot of money and spends most of it on himself."

Rafe relayed their conversation, knowing Max would want to hear every word.

Bradley swirled the brandy in his glass, then took a drink. "I presume you assured Mr. Brand of your continued interest in buying his fleet."

"He's rubbing his hands together at the prospect of a higher bid."

"Then our job here is finished. We can

leave for Philadelphia first thing in the morning."

Rafe felt a sweep of relief. They were going back and in plenty of time for the wedding.

"Once we get there," Bradley continued, "I'll take the first ship bound for England. I need to inform the necessary parties what we've learned." Max smiled, not a common occurrence. "And in the meantime, you, my friend, can get yourself properly leg shackled."

Rafe just nodded. As he watched Max leave the room, an image of Danielle appeared in his mind, her flame-red hair swept up, her smooth skin glowing like pearls in the flickering light of the candles.

His groin tightened. He rarely allowed himself to feel the desire she could arouse with the slightest glance. In the past, a ripple of laughter could bring him fully erect, or a single soft smile. Now as he loosened his stock and shrugged out of his waistcoat, just the memory of her face made him hard.

He remembered the exact shape of her breasts, the ripe feel of them in his hands that day in the apple orchard behind Sheffield Hall, the small nipples that stiffened into tight little buds beneath his palms.

He shouldn't have taken liberties, but

their wedding was so near, and soon she would be his wife. He remembered how badly he had wanted her back then and realized he wanted her even more now.

His erection pulsed and he went achingly hard. He wanted her and soon she would be his.

As he stripped off his shirt and prepared himself for bed, Rafe suddenly felt uneasy at how eager he was for that to happen.

It was Thursday, the day before the wedding. The *Nimble* was set to sail early Saturday morning for the lengthy voyage back to England.

In the bedroom of her aunt's rented row house, Dani sat on a tapestry stool in front of her dresser, cursing Rafael, trying to think of a means of untangling herself from the awful web Rafe had dragged her unwillingly into.

She was only half-dressed, sitting there in a thin lawn chemise that barely came down mid-thigh, her hair not yet combed, when Aunt Flora knocked, then walked hurriedly into the bedchamber.

"Oh, dear, you are not yet dressed. The duke is here, my dear. He is just arrived downstairs."

"The duke? What does he want?"

"To discuss the wedding, I imagine. His Grace says all is set for tomorrow. You must hurry. He is waiting for you in the parlor."

"Let him wait," Dani said stubbornly. "He can wait till the devil sprouts a halo for all I care."

Aunt Flora nervously smoothed the skirt of her high-waisted morning dress, a soft pearl gray trimmed with rows of black lace beneath her substantial bosom. "I know this is not what you planned, but the duke came all the way to America to set matters straight between you. Perhaps marrying him is the right thing to do."

Dani got up from the stool, paced over to the window, then returned and sank down on the edge of the canopied bed. The white eyelet ruffle on top danced over her head.

"How can I marry a man I don't trust, Aunt Flora? He ruined me before. He would have done it again if I hadn't ended my engagement to Richard. Rafael will do anything to get what he wants, no matter who gets hurt."

"Perhaps he wants only what is best for you. If you marry him, you will be living in England, instead of thousands of miles away. It may be selfish, but I cannot be sorry."

Dani looked at her aunt, saw the gleam of

tears in the older woman's eyes. She stood up from the bed and the women embraced.

"You're right," Dani said, "that is something. At least we can be together." She sighed as she eased away, her gaze returning to the window. In the garden below, Caro had set up her watercolor easel and was painting a row of bright purple iris. She was such a sweet young woman. There was something about Caro Loon, a subtle elegance that most people didn't seem to see.

Dani turned away from the window. "With Richard, I would have had children," she said wistfully.

"Those two never would have been truly yours, no matter how hard you tried to make it so. Richard and his mother wouldn't have allowed it."

Danielle turned away from the window to look at her aunt. "There is always a chance Rafael will find out about the accident. What will happen then?"

Aunt Flora merely grunted. "Sheffield wronged you and he owes you his name. You were meant to be a duchess. Now you will be."

She hadn't told Rafe about the riding accident she had suffered during her years of banishment at Wycombe Park. Aunt Flora was convinced it didn't matter, that Rafe owed Danielle the protection of his name.

Dani wandered toward the dresser, catching a glimpse of herself in the mirror. Her hair was still slightly tousled and she wore only her chemise, stockings and garters. "I came here to marry Richard."

"It was a marriage of convenience. Be honest enough with yourself to admit it."

"At least it was my decision — not Rafael's."

Aunt Flora walked over and caught her hand. "Give it some time, dearest. Things have a way of working out." She turned toward the door. "I'll tell the duke you will be down as soon as you are ready."

Dani crossed her arms and stubbornly sat back down on the stool in front of the dresser. As far as she was concerned, Rafael could wait forever.

Rafe got up from the sofa in the parlor and began to pace back and forth across the rug. A grandfather clock in the corner marked the time, which seemed to be standing still.

After twenty minutes, he pulled his gold watch fob out of the pocket of his white piqué waistcoat, flipped open the lid of his watch and checked to be sure the big clock was working properly. Grumbling, he snapped the timepiece firmly closed and returned it to his pocket.

After thirty minutes, his temper began to heat. She knew he was here. She was avoiding him on purpose!

Forty-five minutes from the time of his arrival, he turned and walked out of the parlor. As he crossed the wide plank floors in the entry, he spotted Dani's friend, Caroline Loon, coming out of a bedchamber upstairs. Halfway down the staircase, she squeaked in surprise as she saw him coming up.

"Danielle is not yet dressed, Your Grace."

"That is her problem. I have given her plenty of time to do so." He climbed the next several stairs.

"Wait! You . . . you cannot just walk in there!"

Rafe gave her a wolfish smile. "Can't I?" Brushing past her, he continued toward the top of the staircase, Miss Loon's wide-eyed blue gaze following his every step. When he reached the landing, he strode down the hall, paused at the door he had seen Miss Loon come out of, knocked brusquely, opened the door and walked in.

"Rafael!" Danielle jumped up from the tapestry stool she perched on in front of her dresser. The book she had been reading tumbled to the floor at her feet.

Lovely feet, he noticed, encased in a pair of sheer white stockings; slender, feminine feet, gracefully arched. Her ankles were lovely, too, trim and elegant. The stockings fit over nicely shaped calves, held in place by pretty lace garters.

"How dare you come barging in here!"

His gaze moved up to her breasts, which had always been full, *plump,* he recalled, in his hand. Desire hit him like a fist and his groin tightened.

"You refused to come down," he said reasonably. "I had no choice but to come up."

She grabbed a green silk wrapper off the padded bench at the foot of the bed and pulled it on over her chemise. Lifting her long, softly curling red hair out of the way, she snugged the sash of the robe around her waist. "What is it you want?"

"I came to be certain you had not run away like a scared rabbit — or secretly married that idiot, Richard Clemens."

"How dare you!"

"I believe you've already said that. Be assured, sweeting, I will dare far more if you do not live up to our bargain."

She made a low, growling sound in her throat. "You are . . . insufferable. You're . . . domineering and . . . and obstinate . . . and . . . and . . ."

174

"Determined?" he supplied, one of his dark eyebrows arching up.

"Yes . . . maddeningly so."

"And you, my dear Danielle, are quite fetching, even when you're in a temper. I had forgotten what a terror you could be when you're angry." He smiled. "At least being married to you will not be dull."

Dani crossed her arms over her breasts, but it did nothing to erase the memory of small, pert nipples pressing against her thin chemise, nothing to ease the persistent throbbing in his groin. Now that he knew the truth of her innocence that night, knew she would soon belong to him as she should have before, he wanted her with a need that bordered on pain.

"I came to tell you that all is in readiness for tomorrow. I've arranged for a minister to perform the ceremony. He'll arrive at one o'clock tomorrow afternoon. As soon as we're married, we'll collect our things and board the ship. The *Nimble* sails with the tide first thing Saturday morning."

Max had already sailed. He'd sent a note relaying his regret that he would have to miss the wedding, then left aboard the first ship out of the harbor bound for England. Rafe hoped Max would be able to convince the prime minister that the threat posed by the Baltimore Clippers should not be ignored.

Danielle still stood there, her arms crossed over her very lovely breasts. She cast him a glance, eyeing him from beneath a row of thick burnished lashes. "I don't believe I remember you being quite so dictatorial."

His mouth faintly curved. "Perhaps there wasn't a need."

"Or perhaps you were merely younger, not so set in your ways."

"Undoubtedly." He moved toward her, just to see if she would move away. He thought of Mary Rose and imagined her trembling.

Dani stood her ground, looking up at him with fire in her pretty green eyes. "May I remind you, sir, we are not yet wed?"

"And even if we were, I would be forbidden by my vow to do what I am thinking about right now." He stood directly in front of her, so close he could smell her perfume, sweetly floral, stirring a memory of apple blossoms. He remembered she had worn it that night in the gazebo when he had kissed her.

His shaft filled, turned thick and heavy, pressed uncomfortably against the front of his breeches.

"You gave me your word."

"And I intend to keep it. But there are things I am not forbidden to do." He lifted a deep red curl off her shoulder, bent and pressed his mouth against the spot where the heavy coil had lain, heard her swift intake of breath. Beneath her silk robe, he saw that her nipples had tightened.

"There is hope for us, I think," he said softly, for he didn't believe she had ever responded to Richard Clemens as she did to him.

Danielle stepped away. "You needn't fear. Our bargain is struck. I won't run away."

"I suppose, deep down, I knew that you would not. I once doubted your word, but I have never doubted your courage."

He reached into his pocket and pulled out a red satin pouch. "I brought you something. It's a wedding gift." He still couldn't believe he had brought the necklace with him all the way to America, wouldn't have, except that Grace had insisted. Perhaps she knew even before he did that he would give the lovely pearl-and-diamond necklace to Danielle.

He took the necklace from the pouch and moved behind her, the pearls cool and smooth in his palm. Draping the ancient necklace around her slender throat, he fastened the diamond clasp. "It would please

177

me if you wore these tomorrow."

Danielle's fingers came up to the necklace, testing the weight and shape of each perfect pearl. Between each one, a single diamond glittered in the sunlight slanting in through the window.

She gazed in the mirror at her reflection. "They're beautiful. They're the most beautiful pearls I've ever seen."

"It's called the Bride's Necklace. It's extremely old, thirteenth century, a gift from Lord Fallon to his future bride, Lady Ariana of Merrick. There is a legend about it. I'll tell you sometime."

But there wasn't time today. He looked up to see Lady Wycombe standing very solidly in the doorway.

"This is highly inappropriate, Your Grace. You are not yet Danielle's husband."

Rafe made her an extravagant bow. "I beg your pardon, my lady. I was just leaving." He moved away from Danielle toward the door, walked past her aunt and stepped out into the hallway. "I look forward to seeing you both tomorrow afternoon."

His eyes found Dani's one last time. Her gaze looked troubled, as they hadn't until he'd walked in.

His faint smile slid away. He told himself

he would make things right between them, win at least her affection if not her love.

But something deep inside him warned it would not be easy.

Twelve

It was her wedding day. After the awful scandal five years ago, Danielle had never thought to marry. In the past two weeks, she had twice been engaged.

Today Rafael Saunders would become her husband, the last man on earth she wished to wed.

Danielle sighed as she moved restlessly around the bedchamber. Her wedding gown, pale topaz silk trimmed with bands of forest-green satin, lay on the bed. Caro had woven the same dark green ribbon into the heavy red curls she had pinned atop Dani's head. Matching kid slippers sat on the floor next to the bed, waiting to be slid on over her cream silk stockings.

Dani told herself it was time to finish dressing, to summon her courage and accept the future fate had forced upon her. Instead, she gazed out the window into the garden, watching the birds wind their way through the leaves on the sycamore, feeling lethargic and utterly depressed.

She barely heard the sound of the door

opening behind her, the light footsteps that signaled Caro had come into the room.

For a moment Caro said nothing. Then she sighed. "I knew I shouldn't have left you. Dear Lord, you have not yet finished getting dressed."

But Dani had needed some time alone, time to come to grips with a future as Rafael's wife.

"Everyone is waiting," Caro said. "You know what the duke did the last time you refused to come downstairs."

Dani's head came up. Rafe would haul her down in her chemise if she didn't obey his dictates. When had he become so demanding? How difficult would it be to live with such a man? And why did the thought of becoming his wife make her heart squeeze oddly inside her?

"All right, you win. Help me put this on."

She was ready, except for her gown and slippers. It didn't take long to do up the small pearl buttons at the back of the dress and slide her stockinged feet into her shoes. She took a last look at herself in the mirror, tried to smooth the worry lines from between her russet eyebrows, then turned toward the door.

"Wait! Your necklace!" Caro raced for the jewelry box on the bureau and pulled out

181

the beautiful pearl-and-diamond necklace that had been Rafe's wedding gift. She held the necklace up to examine it in the sunlight. "It is so very lovely . . . I've never seen anything quite like it."

"Rafe says it's very old. He says there is a legend about it."

"A legend? I wonder what it is." Caro urged her down on the stool in front of the mirror, and Dani sat while Caro settled the pearls around her neck and fastened the diamond clasp.

"You should see the way the light glints on the diamonds," Caro said. "It is almost as if they are lit from within."

Dani's fingers ran over the multifaceted stones. "I know what you mean. There is something very special about it . . . something . . . I can't exactly figure out what it is. I wonder where he got it."

"Why don't you ask him . . . after the wedding!" Caro hauled her up from the stool and tugged her toward the door. "I've got to go to the parlor and take my seat." She glanced up. "Remember, if you don't come down —"

"You needn't worry. I've finally accepted my fate." Though she resented Rafe for it. She had wanted to choose her own life, her own future, not have it forced upon her.

Caro leaned over and gave her a sympathetic hug. "You loved him once. Perhaps you can learn to love him again."

Unexpected tears sprang into Dani's eyes. "I won't let that happen — not ever. As long as I don't love him, he can't hurt me again."

Caro's eyes misted. Her gaze held a trace of pity. "Everything is going to be all right. I know it in here." Caro placed a hand over her heart. Then she turned and hurried out of the bedchamber.

With a slow, steadying breath, Dani turned to face the door and her uncertain future. She prayed with all her heart that Caro's words would prove true.

But thinking of the man Rafe had become, a hard man determined to get his way no matter the cost, she didn't really believe it.

Hoping his nervousness didn't show, Rafe waited at the bottom of the staircase, his legs braced a little apart, hands crossed in front of him.

The wedding guests were few, just Lady Wycombe and Caroline Loon; the minister, Reverend Dobbs, and his wife, Mary Ann. Danielle deserved far more than the simple ceremony that would make them man and wife. Rafe vowed that once they reached

London, he would see that she got the finest wedding money could provide.

He looked toward the top of the staircase, saw Caroline Loon descending the stairs in a flutter of pale blue skirts. She was Danielle's lady's maid and yet he had learned she was far more than that.

Lady Wycombe had explained the girl's circumstances, that she was the daughter of a vicar and his wife, a gently reared young woman left orphaned and penniless when her parents suddenly died. Lady Wycombe had hired her to work as Dani's maid, but soon the two had become fast friends. Caro had helped Danielle through the most difficult ordeal of her life — the scandal Rafe had unwittingly brought down upon her.

And for Caro's unflagging loyalty to Dani, she had won Rafe's lifelong gratitude.

"Miss Loon," he said, making her a bow as she reached the bottom of the staircase.

She looked anxiously back toward the top. "There's no need for you to go up, Your Grace. Danielle will be right down."

He almost smiled. She would be down, all right. She knew he would haul her down over his shoulder if he had to. Glancing up at the landing, he saw her bedchamber door open a second time, and Danielle stepped into the hall.

Rafe's pulse quickened. She was wearing a topaz silk gown banded with dark green satin, her flame-red hair laced with ribbons of the same dark green. She looked pale and fragile, and as lovely as he had ever seen her.

She descended the stairs, head held high, every inch the duchess that she would soon become, and her eyes caught his. He could read the turbulence there and his chest squeezed. Soon she would be his, as fate seemed to have decreed, and yet he wondered if she ever truly would be. If she could ever trust him again, ever come to care for him again.

He watched her walking toward him and wondered at the future he had forced upon her, wondered if he could find a way through the coil of events that had brought them to this place and time.

He met her at the bottom of the stairs, took her gloved hand and brought it to his lips. "You look beautiful," he said, and thought how inadequate the words. She was utterly enchanting, achingly lovely, completely divine.

"Thank you, Your Grace."

"Rafael," he softly corrected, wishing she had said his name, said something that would ease his troubled mind.

He couldn't miss the worry in her eyes,

the faint traces of uncertainty that must have kept her awake long into the night. He wished he'd had more time, a chance to woo her instead of coerce her into the marriage. Still, he was convinced that as a husband for Danielle, he was far better suited than Richard Clemens.

He took her hand, placed it on the sleeve of his dark blue tailcoat and felt her tremble. He wished he knew how to reassure her, but only time could do that. He owed her his name and he meant to see it done, but he wanted more than simply to right a wrong. He wanted to make her happy.

Time, he told himself.

Patience, his mind whispered, and he prayed that with patience, in time he would succeed.

"You wore the necklace," he said, feeling oddly pleased. "It suits you."

"You asked me to wear it."

His mouth edged up. "I told you there was a legend."

A hint of curiosity entered her expression. "Yes . . ."

"The legend says that whoever shall own the necklace shall know great happiness or great tragedy, depending upon whether or not his heart is pure."

She looked up at him, the green of her

eyes enhanced by the dark green ribbons in her hair. "And you believe my heart is pure?"

"I doubted it once. I never will again."

She glanced away.

In the silence that fell, Lady Wycombe bustled nervously up to where they stood. "The minister is waiting. Is everything all right?"

Rafe looked at Dani and prayed that it was. "Everything is fine."

"Come, then," Lady Wycombe said. "It is time to begin the ceremony."

Danielle had no father to escort her down the aisle, no close male friend to do the honors. Instead, she walked beside Rafe, out into the garden, her hand trembling on the sleeve of his coat. They paused beneath a white-painted arch covered with alabaster roses that had been set at one end of the terrace.

Reverend Dobbs stood behind a pedestal draped with a cloth of white satin, a Bible sitting open on top. A few feet away, his petite wife stood next to Lady Wycombe and Caroline Loon, who each held a small floral nosegay.

"If you are ready," the minister said, a stout little man with a shock of gray hair and spectacles, "we may proceed."

Rafe looked at Dani and hoped she could read the care in his eyes, the determination to make their marriage work. "Are you ready, love?"

Moisture collected in her eyes. She wasn't ready at all, he thought, but it made him no less determined. Dani took a deep breath and nodded, ready to face whatever lay ahead. Caroline Loon hurried forward and placed a nosegay of white roses laced with green ribbon into her hands, then returned to her place next to Lady Wycombe.

"You may begin, Reverend Dobbs," Rafe said, wishing, for Dani's sake, the ceremony was already over.

The minister surveyed the small group standing in the garden. "Dearly beloved . . . we are gathered here today to join in holy matrimony this man, Rafael Saunders, and this woman, Danielle Duval. If there is anyone here who can show cause why this man and woman should not be joined, let him speak now or forever hold his peace."

For an instant, Rafe's heart slowed to a dull rhythm that pulsed almost painfully inside his chest. When no one spoke up, when no other man dared to claim her, Rafe began, for the very first time, to believe that Danielle would finally become his wife.

The ceremony continued, though Dani barely heard the words. She thought that she responded in the appropriate places and prayed it would soon be over. Her mind kept wandering. She forced herself to concentrate.

The minister spoke to the groom. "Do you, Rafael, take this woman, Danielle, to be your lawful wedded wife? Do you promise to love her in sickness and in health, for richer, for poorer, for better or for worse and forsaking all others, so long as you both shall live?"

"I do," Rafe said strongly.

Reverend Dobbs asked the question of Danielle.

"I . . . do," she said softly.

"Do you have the ring?" the minister asked Rafe, and for a wild instant, Dani thought that surely there hadn't been time for him to buy one, and without a ring perhaps the ceremony could not go on.

But Rafe reached into the pocket of his waistcoat and withdrew a glittering gold band inset with diamonds.

The minister spoke the vow and Rafe repeated the words.

"With this ring, I thee wed." Reaching out, he caught her trembling hand and slipped the ring on her finger. Rafe captured her fingers with his and gave them a gentle squeeze.

With the ceremony over at last, Reverend Dobbs relaxed and a warm smile lit his face. "By the authority vested in me by the State of Pennsylvania, I now pronounce you man and wife. You may kiss your bride," Dobbs said to Rafael.

Danielle closed her eyes as his arm slid around her waist, easing her closer. If she had expected a sweet, gentlemanly kiss, she was surprised to find herself swept solidly against his chest and kissed very soundly, indeed.

His lips took firm possession, telling her in no uncertain terms that she was his. Her heart stuttered, began a galloping rhythm, and for an instant she gave in to the kiss. She could feel his hunger, his barely leashed control, and desire stirred inside her.

For the span of several heartbeats, she kissed him back, her lips parting under his, beginning to tremble as she breathed him in. Rafe ended the kiss and both of them broke away.

He looked down at her, his eyes so incredibly blue, and she saw the heat there, the white-hot, scorching desire. Then his gaze grew shuttered and he glanced away, leaving her light-headed, fighting the wild urge to run from the room. His hand remained possessively at the small of her back, lending her support, and for once she was grateful.

Dear God, how could she have forgotten the power he exuded? The heady rush of desire he could stir with a single glance? Had she really believed her dislike of him would protect her from the magnetic attraction she had always felt when he was near?

Trembling once more, she let him guide her over to a linen-draped table where bottles of champagne sat chilling in silver buckets. Servants scurried about, filling crystal goblets and delivering them on silver trays, others arriving with platters overflowing with an array of mouthwatering foods: roasted goose, beefsteak, creamed peas and buttered carrots, cold meats and pasties, candied fruits and custards, which were set down on the table.

Apparently Rafael and Aunt Flora had conspired to make a celebration feast for the small group of wedding guests. Dani forced herself to smile and accept congratulations, prepared to eat at least some small portion of the food, though she feared her stomach might rebel.

Once she had yearned to become Rafe's wife. Now falling once more under his spell was the last thing Dani wanted.

She was a different woman than she had been before, an independent woman who knew the risks of loving a man like Rafael, a man who could destroy a life with the snap of his fingers. She vowed she would never let it happen again.

He bent down, spoke softly in her ear. "Soon it will be time to leave. I've asked Miss Loon to see to your final packing. Perhaps you should go up and change into something more serviceable for boarding the ship."

She nodded, eager for the chance to escape. "Yes, I believe that is a very good idea." Making her way out of the garden back inside the house, she headed for the stairs in the entry and hurried up to her room.

Caro was waiting when she walked in. "Here . . . Let me help you."

Dani turned so Caro could unfasten the buttons at the back of her topaz gown, then stepped out of the garment and kicked off her slippers. She sat down on the stool and let Caro pull the pretty green ribbons from her hair.

"Perhaps we should braid it," Caro suggested.

"Yes, I think that would be best." The pins came out one by one. In minutes her long red curls were gathered into plaits and pinned once more on top of her head.

"Can you unfasten the necklace?" Dani asked.

In the mirror, Dani caught Caro's stiff nod. There was something in her face, something dark and troubled that Danielle hadn't noticed before. As the diamond clasp came undone and the pearls fell into Caro's palm, Danielle turned on the stool and looked up at her.

"What is it, dearest? I can see that something is wrong. Tell me what it is."

Caro simply shook her head, moving the tight blond curls beside her ears. She pressed the pearls into Dani's hand, looking even more desolate than she had before.

"Dear God, Caro, tell me what has happened."

Her friend's blue eyes welled with tears. "It's Robert."

"Robert? What about Robert?"

More tears welled, began to roll down her cheeks. "Last night he came to see me. Robert told me he loved me, Dani. He said he has never met a woman like me. *A woman like me,* Danielle. As if I were someone special, someone worthy of his love. But Robert can't speak of marriage — not until he is free."

Dani caught Caro's shaking hands in both of her own. She knew the story of Robert's indenture, how he'd been accused of a crime he didn't commit and been forced to flee his homeland.

"Listen to me, dearest, there is no need to cry. I'll speak to Rafael, convince him to purchase Robert's indenture papers."

Caro pulled her hands away and more tears washed down her cheeks. "Edmund Steigler won't sell them, and even if he would there isn't time."

"We shall make time. We'll delay our journey until Rafael can speak to Mr. Steigler, then go home on a later ship."

Caro wiped her eyes. "You don't understand."

"Then you must tell me, make me understand."

Caro dragged in a shaky breath. "Just before the wedding, Robert came to see me. He had received a letter from his cousin in England, a man named Stephen Lawrence. According to the letter, Stephen has discovered the identity of the man who murdered Nigel Truman . . . that is the man Robert was falsely accused of killing."

"Go on."

"I have never seen Robert this way." Caro stared off toward the window, as if she were there again with Robert McKay. "I think until now he didn't believe he would ever find a way to prove his innocence. Now he is desperate to return to England and clear his name. He means to escape, Danielle."

"Dear God."

"He says once he proves his innocence, he'll find a way to send Steigler the money for his contract. I want to help him, but there is nothing I can do." Caro stared down at the necklace Dani held in her hand. "I actually thought of stealing it." The tears returned to her eyes. "I thought that I would give the necklace to Robert and you wouldn't find out until after we had sailed."

Caro looked at Danielle and began to weep. "I couldn't do it. I could never steal from you — not even for Robert — not after everything you've done for me." She cried harder, her slender body shaking with sobs. "I'm sorry, Danielle. I just . . . I love him so much."

Dani eased her friend into her arms. "It's all right, dearest. Somehow we'll figure this out. Everything is going to be all right."

Danielle mentally went over what Caro had told her and her mind raced. She trusted her best friend's instincts and her own opinion of Robert McKay, and she believed Robert had told the truth, that he was innocent of any wrongdoing. She knew what it was like to be accused of a crime you didn't commit, and her heart went out to both of them.

Caro pulled away from her and walked over to the window. She stared down into the garden, her narrow shoulders shaking with silent sobs, while Dani tried desperately to think what to do.

She could speak to Rafael, but she wasn't sure he would help. She didn't know the man he had become, and she didn't trust him. What if he went to Steigler, betrayed Robert's intentions to his master?

Rafe could be ruthless. She knew that firsthand.

She looked down at the necklace still clutched in her hand. She had very little money. Both her parents were dead. She had only the small monthly stipend her father had left her, not enough to help Robert find a way to clear his name. Until she married, she was mostly dependent upon her aunt and she refused to ask Aunt Flora to involve herself in what would surely be a crime.

The necklace felt warm in her palm, oddly comforting, as if it tried to soothe her, perhaps lend her strength. Walking over to where Caro stood, Dani took her friend's hand and draped the strand of pearls across her palm.

"Take it. Give it to Robert. Tell him to use

it to save himself, to return to England and clear his name."

Caro gazed up at her, a look of disbelief on her face. "You would do that for Robert?"

A lump rose in Dani's throat. "I would do it for *you,* Caro. You are the sister I never had, my best friend in the world." She folded Caro's slim fingers around the pearls. "Take the necklace to Robert. Do it now. Rafael will begin to wonder where we are. There isn't much time."

Caro's throat moved up and down. Tears rolled down her cheeks. "I'll find a way to repay you — I swear it. I don't know how, but —"

"You've repaid me with your friendship a thousand times over." Dani hugged her. Turning, she walked over to the dresser and took the red satin pouch out of her jewelry box. Reaching for the pearls, she slipped them into the pouch and handed it back to her friend. "Now go."

Caro hugged her one last time. Tucking the pouch into the pocket of her gown, Caro hurried out the door. As she headed off down the hall, Dani took a steadying breath.

Sooner or later Rafael would discover what she had done. He would be angry. Furious, she knew. She shivered, remembering the fury on his face when he had walked into her bedchamber and found Oliver Randall in her bed, thinking of the way he had destroyed her life.

Dani steeled herself. She would deal with Rafael when the time came. Until then, she prayed that Robert would be able to safely escape.

Thirteen

Rafe escorted the ladies up the gangway, onto the deck of the *Nimble*, a big, square-rigged, triple-masted sailing ship that carried a total of a hundred-seventy passengers in steerage, first and second classes; thirty-five hundred barrels of cargo and a thirty-six-man crew.

Though there were fewer people traveling from Philadelphia to England than the large number of emigrants who traveled to America in search of a new home, the vessel hummed with activity.

The captain, Hugo Burns, a great bearded bear of an Englishman with black hair and dark eyes, greeted them as they departed the gangway and stepped onto the deck.

"Welcome aboard the *Nimble*," he said, "one of the finest ships ever to sail the Atlantic. She be four-hundred tons, one-hundred-eighteen feet long, twenty-eight feet in the beam, and she'll carry ye safely back ta England."

Rafe had been lucky to find a British ship

and crew ready to make their return trip home. The *Nimble* wasn't one of Ethan's ships, but from what Rafe could discover, Captain Burns was one of the most respected seamen around.

Lady Wycombe smiled up at the big, burly man. "I'm sure we will be safe in your very capable hands, Captain Burns."

"Aye, that ye will be, Lady Wycombe."

The first mate, a lanky sailor named Pike with a tanned, weathered complexion and wearing a dark blue uniform jacket showed them to their quarters, the best accommodations Rafe could purchase aboard the vessel.

Pike led the small group to a ladder midship that led down to the first-class passengers' quarters on the upper deck. Cabin 6A would be shared by Lady Wycombe and Caroline Loon. Pike assured the women that a crewman would deliver their baggage, then waited while the ladies made their way inside the cabin and began to settle in.

The first mate continued down the passage, leading Rafe and Danielle farther along the corridor to their quarters in the stern, the largest first-class cabin aboard the *Nimble*. As Pike unlocked the door and stepped back out of the way, Danielle paused nervously outside, peering in with a frown on her face.

"Thank you, Mr. Pike," Rafe said, "that will be all."

She looked up at him as the first mate disappeared down the passage. "But surely you don't intend that the two of us should share the same cabin?"

His jaw firmed. "That is exactly what I intend."

"I remind you, sir, we had an agreement. You said —"

"I know what I said. I said I wouldn't make love to you until we reached England. That doesn't change the fact that we are wed." He shoved the door farther open. "We'll not only be sharing this cabin, but also this bed."

Color washed into Danielle's cheeks. He wasn't sure if it was anger or embarrassment or perhaps a little of both.

Lifting her chin, she walked past him into the cabin, staring at the wide single berth as if it might swallow her whole. "Caro and Aunt Flora have berths — one atop the other."

Rafe kept his expression carefully bland. "We're married, Danielle. We don't need separate berths." And in the days since he had agreed to forfeit his husbandly rights for the duration of the journey, he had come to a decision: he had agreed not to make love to her, a promise he meant to keep.

Which left him with infinite possibilities.

His groin thickened as several of those intriguing possibilities popped into his head. Whatever Danielle felt for him, she was not immune to him in a physical sense. The kiss he had claimed at the altar had been proof of that. He could still recall the feel of her soft lips parting under his, the way she had trembled. Danielle had always been a passionate young woman. It was obvious that had not changed.

His arousal strengthened. They were wed and yet she would not be completely his until the marriage had been consummated.

To insure that happened, Rafe intended to seduce her.

Setting the leather satchel he carried on the floor, he closed the cabin door and walked over to where Danielle stood. Her gaze remained fixed on the berth stretching out beneath the porthole and he wondered what sort of imaginings were going on in her head. Setting his hands gently on her shoulders, he slowly turned her to face him.

"We have plenty of time, love. I'm not going to rush you. But we're married, Danielle. You may as well learn to accept it."

She just looked at him, her eyes troubled

and filled with doubt. Rafe caught her chin and very gently kissed her. The faint, sweet scent of her perfume filled his senses. Her lips felt petal-soft under his.

His body tightened, forcing his already rigid arousal uncomfortably against the front of his breeches. He wanted to deepen the kiss, to explore the sweet valleys of her mouth. He wanted to lay her down and re-move her clothes, wanted to caress the lovely apple-round breasts that had haunted his dreams for the past five years.

He wanted to make love to her for hours on end.

Instead, he ended the kiss. "Give us a chance, Dani. That's all I ask."

Danielle said nothing. She simply turned away.

Rafe watched her retreat to a corner of the cabin and his resolve strengthened. Before he'd met Danielle, he had slept with very few women. On his eighteenth birthday, his best friend, Cord Easton, had gifted him with a night at Madame Fontaneau's House of Pleasure. A few months later, he had taken a mistress, then later kept company with a countess whose husband suffered a failing memory.

After he'd met Danielle, there had been no need for other women. He knew, once they were wed, that he would be content.

That terrible night five years ago had changed all of that. Determined to forget her, he had slept with countless women. From opera singers to the most sought-after courtesans, Rafe knew the power of seduction. In those five years, he had used it well and often. He would use it now to correct the wrong he had done to Danielle and in the hope of securing a future that included pleasure for both of them.

Danielle surveyed the roomy cabin, trying to decide her best course. She could refuse to share the accommodation, demand that Rafe locate another cabin for her use, but she could see by the fierce glint in his eyes that in this, he was determined.

She flicked a glance in his direction, saw him lounging negligently beside the cabin door, one shoulder propped against the wall, arms crossed over his chest, watching her every move. On the surface, he looked harmless enough, but under that bland facade lurked a potent, virile male who, sooner or later, intended to claim his husbandly rights.

Her heartbeat quickened. Rafe made no secret of his desire for her and yet he had given his word. Though she didn't believe he would break it, once they reached England he wouldn't waste a moment in taking possession of her body.

Dani inwardly sighed. At five-and-twenty, she knew more of what occurred between men and women than she had five years ago, but still her knowledge on the subject was sorely limited. Perhaps sharing such intimate quarters with Rafe would be a good way to extend the education she so obviously needed.

Dani couldn't quite ignore a trickle of interest. What would it be like to lie next to a man as potently male as Rafael? To sleep beside him? To awaken next to him in the morning?

Disturbed by the unwanted thoughts, she turned to survey the stateroom. With its elegant teakwood paneling, built-in teakwood dresser and writing desk, the cabin would be far more comfortable than the quarters she had shared with Caro and Aunt Flora on her previous ocean voyage. There was even a small hearth in the corner for use on a cold Atlantic night.

And the fact was, sooner or later she would have to share a bed with the man who was her husband. That she had been forced into the marriage didn't change the fact that she belonged to him, wholly and completely.

At least for the present, she would be safe from his advances.

The afternoon progressed, turned into evening. At dawn, they would sail for England and home. Danielle found herself dreading the night ahead.

Though Rafe had been charming to both Caro and Aunt Flora all through the supper they had enjoyed at the captain's table, Dani couldn't miss the heat in his eyes, the anticipation. She thought he would disguise it, maintain the polite-but-distant demeanor he had unfailingly assumed in the presence of her friend and her aunt, but he made not the slightest attempt.

You're my wife and I want you, his hot blue gaze said, and every time he looked at her, butterflies swarmed in her stomach. Already tense, her nerves grew more and more frayed.

They had dined in the elegant first-class salon, a low-ceilinged room paneled in teakwood and brightened with red flocked wallpaper. Ornate gilt lanterns with tiny crystal prisms hung over the long mahogany table, and gilt sconces fashioned to tip when the ship was under sail lined the walls.

Captain Burns seemed a competent man, more concerned with his ship and crew than conversing with the small group of first-class passengers gathered in the salon. He left them as soon as the meal was finished, anxious to tend to final preparations for their early-morning departure.

By the end of the evening, the group had become acquainted: a Virginia planter named Willard Longbow and his tiny wife, Sarah; Lord and Lady Pettigrew, whom Rafe had apparently met once in England; a Philadelphia couple named Mahler taking their two older children on an extended trip abroad; and an American of dubious social standing named Carlton Baker.

Something about Mr. Baker, a tall, attractive man in his forties, made Danielle uneasy. From what she overheard, he seemed to be a footloose sort, traveling from town to town whenever it took his fancy, with no obvious means of support, though from the clothes he wore, he was a gentleman of some stature.

Baker was friendly enough, but the man had a way of looking at her that seemed a bit too bold, a little too familiar. She wondered if Rafe had noticed Mr. Baker's interest, and remembered how wildly jealous he had been five years ago. He was a different man now, his emotions kept well under control. More likely, he no longer cared for her in the manner he had before.

Still, though she was friendly to Baker, she made a point of keeping her distance.

The long evening passed. The others chatted pleasantly, but Dani was too aware of Rafael to make much of an effort at socializing. He stood too near, spoke too softly, smiled at her too often.

She kept thinking of the cabin they would soon share, the bed where she would be forced to sleep beside him. Exhausted as she was by the long day's events, her nerves on edge and stretched near the breaking point, half of her yearned for sleep while the other half wished the evening would never end.

She felt Rafe's hand on her shoulder and a shiver of awareness slipped through her. "Come, love. The day has been long and tiring. It's time we bid our newly made friends good night."

Danielle merely nodded. Staying up till dawn wouldn't change what lay ahead. Rafael gave her a moment to make her farewells, then escorted her along the deck to the ladder midship leading down to their cabin.

The passage was narrow and dimly lit. She was tall for a woman, but he was far taller and she could feel the power of him, the utter male strength.

A little shiver ran through her. She didn't know the man Rafe had become, a man who would force her into a marriage she did not want. And she couldn't help wondering if a man like that would truly keep his word.

Rafe opened the door and she stepped into the cabin. Outside the porthole, torch-lights flickering on the dock reflected on the surface of the water, casting a pale yellow glow into the cabin. Though the interior had seemed roomy before, now, as Rafe stepped through the door behind her, his large frame filled the space between them and the cabin seemed small and confining.

He lit a whale-oil lantern, and in the flare of light as the wick caught fire, she glimpsed the outline of his profile, the faint dark shadow of beard along his jaw, the slight cleft in his chin. Her heart set up a clatter. Dear God, the man was handsome! Just looking at him made her breath catch, made her feel suddenly light-headed.

"Come, love, let me help you undress."

The words rumbled through her and her mouth went dry. She wanted to tell him she didn't need his help — not now, not ever — but she couldn't reach the buttons at the back of her gown, and she was so very tired.

As if in a dream, she stepped out of her shoes and moved toward him, then turned and presented her back. With expert skill, his long dark fingers worked the small covered buttons closing up the aqua silk gown she had worn to supper, and she wondered how many times he had accomplished the task.

"I realize you are not used to disrobing in front of a man," he said softly, "but in time you'll get used to it. Perhaps you will even come to enjoy it."

Enjoy removing her clothes in front of Rafael? The idea seemed utterly impossible . . . and yet, deep down the notion intrigued her.

His hand brushed the nape of her neck, skimmed across her shoulders, and gooseflesh rose over her skin. She closed her eyes against a wave of embarrassment as Rafe eased the gown off her shoulders, urged it down over her hips, into a pool on the floor.

She was left in her thin lawn chemise, stockings and garters, and she recalled he had seen her that way before. She felt the press of his mouth against her bare shoulder, but instead of embarrassment, something warm and liquid slipped into her stomach. Beneath the bodice of her chemise, her nipples tightened into firm little buds that rubbed against the thin cotton fabric.

Dear God!

Praying Rafe wouldn't notice, she stepped out of the gown at her feet, bent to retrieve it, careful to keep her back to him, and hung it in the space provided. "Thank you. I can do the rest myself."

"Are you certain?" There was a husky edge to his voice, along with a hint of challenge.

Unable to resist, trying not to think of the half-naked picture she presented, she turned to face him, holding her head high, determined not to cower in front of him, no matter how scantily she was dressed. She could feel Rafe's gaze running over her, assessing every barely hidden curve, the length of her legs, the narrow circumference of her waist and the fullness of her bosom.

"Why don't you sit down . . ." he said in that same rough-husky voice, "and I'll unpin your hair."

Her stomach contracted. Sweet heaven above! "I — I can do it myself. I don't . . . don't need your help."

He smiled and something melted in her stomach. "Surely you won't deny me that small pleasure. All evening, I've been imagining how silky it would feel in my hands."

She swallowed. Since she had no idea how to reply to such a statement, she sank down on the stool and simply turned her back to him. Rafe moved behind her, his tall frame coming into view in the mirror. One pin at a time, he released each heavy red curl, then combed his fingers through the strands.

"The color of fire . . ." He spread the heavy mass around her shoulders. "I used to imagine how good it would feel draped over my chest when we made love."

She started to tremble. Once in the summer before they were to wed, she had come upon him down at the pond sitting on a tree stump in the sunshine without his shirt. He had a magnificent chest, she remembered, broad and heavily muscled. Rafe was a staunch outdoorsman who enjoyed hunting and riding, an athlete who boxed at Gentleman Jackson's parlor when he was in the city.

He kept himself in excellent physical condition and it showed.

In the mirror, she watched in fascination as he bent his dark head and pressed his mouth against the side of her neck. He drew an earlobe between his teeth, gently bit down, then retreated, drawing slowly away.

It took a moment to realize she wasn't breathing. She sucked in a shaky breath and noticed her hands were trembling. Praying he wouldn't notice, she busied herself braiding the hair he had just unpinned.

Though Rafe had backed a few steps away, she could see him in the mirror, his eyes still fixed on her face.

"Do you need me to help you finish?" he asked.

Dani practically leapt from the stool. "No! I mean . . . no thank you. I am fine. I'll just step behind the screen so that I can put on my night rail."

Rafe just shook his head. "You'll stay right where you are. You're my wife, Danielle. I've agreed to certain of your demands, but not this."

She swallowed. "You . . . you intend for me to finish undressing in front of you? You wish to see me . . . naked?"

A corner of his mouth edged up. "That is exactly my wish. There'll be no secrets between us, Danielle."

"But —"

"We're merely getting used to each other, love, nothing more."

Her heart pounded, thumped like a battering ram against the inside of her chest. Rafe wished to see her naked. He made the demand as if it were his due. Worse yet, as he was her husband, perhaps it was.

"What if I refuse?"

He shrugged those wide shoulders. "You're welcome to sleep in your chemise, if

213

that is your wish. I believe, now that you suggest it, I would like that very much."

"You are insufferable!"

Something flashed in his eyes. "That is what you believe? What do you think Richard Clemens would demand of you on your wedding night?"

Her stomach constricted. If she had married Richard, he would have taken her virginity without a moment's hesitation. For reasons she couldn't explain, she thought that he wouldn't have been the least concerned with her feelings in the matter.

Still, marrying Rafael had not been by choice, and his arrogant demands didn't sit well at all. Turning away from him, she propped each foot on the stool in front of the dresser and, one at a time, removed her garters and rolled down her stockings. Keeping her back to him, she snatched her long white cotton night rail off the hook beside the door, dragged her chemise off over her head, and tossed it over the dressing screen.

For several seconds she fumbled with the nightgown, her entire backside bare to his view, and she cursed him for the rogue he was. An instant later, the cotton gown fell into place and she felt a wave of relief.

Trying to pretend her face wasn't on fire,

she lifted her chin and turned to where he stood leaning back against the wall, his arms crossed over his chest. His eyes were a scorching shade of blue and the muscles in his jaw looked iron hard.

He was fighting for control, she realized, immensely disturbed by the display he had just viewed. A sense of power swept through her, unlike anything she had known, and some evil little demon she had thought long dead reared its ugly head.

"I am ready for bed. What about you?"

Fourteen

Dani fixed her gaze on the tall man lounging across the room. At the challenge in her words, Rafe's whole body tightened. He came away from the wall like a panther on the prowl and she forced herself to remain where she stood, though every instinct urged her to run from the cabin.

"I had thought to spare your maidenly sensibilities and dress behind the screen — at least for the first few nights."

He was giving her the chance to back down. She should take it, she knew. "You said there would be no secrets between us."

A corner of his mouth edged up. The heat in his eyes seemed to go hotter. "As you wish."

Dani moistened her lips. Part of her feared she had just uncaged a very dangerous beast, while the other part watched in fascination. Aside from tending a sick child at the orphanage, and a quick glimpse of Oliver Randall's skinny backside as he had climbed out of her bed five years ago, she had never seen a naked man, certainly not a virile man like Rafe.

She watched as he began to undress, removing his coat, waistcoat and wide white stock, then shrugging out of his shirt, revealing the wide, powerful chest she remembered. A swatch of curly dark brown chest hair arrowed down a flat stomach as solid as the rest of him.

He slid off his shoes and stockings. Her eyes widened as he began to unfasten the buttons on the front of his snug fitting breeches. He shoved them down a pair of long, lean muscled legs and stepped out of them, leaving him in only his small clothes, which stretched like a second layer of skin over the lower half of his body, ending just above his knees.

"I don't know how much you know of a man's anatomy, my love, but if you have not already noticed, watching you has aroused me greatly."

Her eyes lit on the thick ridge rising up beneath his thin cotton undergarments, and a cry of alarm escaped. Her bravado instantly faded. Whirling away from him, she hurried over to the bed, drew back the covers and slid between the sheets, turning onto her side, away from him.

She heard Rafe's soft chuckle but paid him no heed. It was one thing to see a man without his clothing, another altogether to see him rampantly aroused. She knew enough of the male anatomy to know that heavy ridge was the masculine reproductive organ and she knew where it joined with her body. Now that she had some idea of its size, she couldn't imagine how it would ever fit.

Behind her, Rafe moved closer to the bed and she held her breath as the mattress dipped beneath his weight.

"For the present, I suppose I'll have to give up sleeping in the nude, but I promise you, love, it won't be for long."

She couldn't help herself. Astonished at his words, she rolled over to look at him. He was still wearing his small clothes, but his wide, furred chest was completely bare. "You don't sleep in a night rail?"

"As I said, I prefer to sleep in the nude. It's far more comfortable, as you will discover once you are over your maidenly nerves."

He slept without a stitch of clothing and expected her to do the same! For heaven's sake, what other depravities was the man capable of committing? And why did she find the idea so titillating?

Face burning, she turned her back to him again. She couldn't imagine sleeping naked with a man. She had always believed that a man lifted a woman's nightgown when he made love to her, then lowered it when he was finished. Apparently that wasn't the case. Why had no one told her?

She felt Rafe's weight on the bed as he moved beside her on the mattress. She needed to use the chamber pot behind the screen in the corner, but she would wait until he had fallen asleep.

Easing closer, he settled an arm around her waist and drew her body spoon-fashion against him. Even through her nightgown, she could feel the brush of his curly dark chest hair, the rough hair on his calves.

She squeezed her eyes shut at the feel of the hard male ridge pressing against her bottom and tried to move away, but Rafe's hold merely tightened.

"It's a natural occurrence, Dani, when a man wants a woman as much as I want you. On our journey, I'm afraid I'll be in this condition a good deal of the time . . . unless, of course, you would care to release me from my vow."

She wildly shook her head.

He pressed a light kiss against the side of her neck. "Then go to sleep, love. Tomorrow we sail for home."

A week slid past, then another. It was the

middle of September and even at sea, fall was in the air. The days had begun to grow shorter, the nights more chill. A heavier mist hung in the salty sea air.

As a newly married couple, it was expected that Danielle spend a great deal of time with her husband, and Rafe paid her a goodly amount of attention. During the day, they played cards or read, conversed with the other passengers, or strolled about the ship.

After supper each night, he led her up on deck to a secluded spot he had discovered where they might be private. At first she had been uneasy with the notion, for somehow he seemed different during the time they were there.

In the cabin, an air of tension existed between them, Danielle wary, Rafe carefully reserved, fearful, she imagined, that if he let down his guard in such intimate quarters his thin control might snap. Aside from the evening ritual of undressing in front of each other and the intimate contact of their bodies during the night, he maintained a guarded distance.

Dani was grateful. She needed time, needed these weeks to resign herself to a future as Rafael's wife.

He was reserved in their cabin, but out

here in the moonlight, the sea splashing frothy white foam against the hull, Rafe allowed himself certain liberties, and as his wife, Dani could hardly protest.

And in truth, she was beginning to look forward to his advances, the heated kisses, gentle those first few nights, then growing deeper and more passionate. Out here, she felt safe in a way she didn't in the cabin, where his tall, hard muscled frame curled against her on the mattress kept her awake late into the night.

She looked up at him tonight as they stood in the darkness of their private world, bathed in the glow of the moon and stars. The glitter of desire was there in his eyes, and the tightness in his jaw that marked the restraint he used to control it.

His hand brushed her cheek. "London is still so far away. . . ."

She knew he referred to the moment when he would take her, claim her as his wife and consummate their marriage, and a fine thread of wanting slipped through her. Framing her face between his hands, he bent his head and kissed her and a sweet warmth tugged low in her belly.

Unconsciously, she leaned toward him. He was her husband, after all, and though she feared where such a kiss might lead, the heat of desire had begun to burn in her, too.

Rafe deepened the kiss, coaxing her lips apart, taking her deeply with his tongue. He kissed her and kissed her, soft butterfly kisses, deep sensual kisses that stirred the same hot need she had felt so long ago, a need she never thought to feel again.

It frightened her. She knew the folly of trusting him, of needing him, and yet as the moments slipped past, she no longer cared. Instead, her arms went around his neck and she kissed him back with the same fierce passion she could feel vibrating through him. Her pulse quickened as his hands slid down her back and he cupped her bottom, settled her in the vee between his long legs.

He was hard where he pressed against her, amazingly so, and a fierce heat centered in her core.

"Can you feel it, Dani? Can you tell how much I want you?"

There was a time she would have been afraid. Tonight, she was more curious than frightened, dangerous thinking, she knew, and yet it was the truth.

Rafe kissed the side of her neck and began to caress her breasts, touching her as he hadn't allowed himself until tonight, molding them in his palms, kneading the fullness through the fabric of her high-waisted gown. She remembered the way he had touched her that day in the apple orchard, and a wave of heat tore through her.

Her breasts ached and swelled. Rafe cupped them, chafed the ends until they were hard and throbbing. All the while he kissed her — deep, drugging kisses that left her restless and longing, hot, sensual kisses that made her ache inside.

She knew she should stop him. There were weeks yet until they reached home, but her nipples felt swollen and raw, sensitive in a way they never had before, and liquid heat burned between her legs.

His large hand continued to caress her breast. "Tonight I'll put my mouth there," he promised in a voice gone rough. "It's time you slept without your nightclothes."

A jolt of desire tugged low inside her, so strong she was frightened. Trembling, she tore free of his embrace. Her whole body burned for his touch and yet she recognized the danger. She needed more time, needed to understand what he wanted from her, needed to trust him at least a little, with her body, if nothing more.

She pressed a hand against his chest, as if to keep him away. "I'm not . . . not ready for that, Rafael."

His eyes searched her face, dark blue in

the moonlight, yet so hot they seemed to glitter. "I think you are. I think your body is more than ready." As if to prove it, he cupped a breast and gently squeezed, and a flood of heat washed through her.

"Please, Rafael. It's been just . . . two weeks." Two weeks of sleeping next to him, two weeks of feeling the heat and hardness of his body, the strength of his nightly arousal.

Rafe captured her lips in a slow, thorough kiss. "All right. If that is the way you feel, I'll give you a little more time. We've hardly begun our journey."

He was right. They had hardly begun and already she craved him, craved his hot, lusty kisses, the feel of his hands on her body.

Ached to touch him in return.

The truth hit her like a blow. She wanted to touch him the way he touched her, wanted to know the texture of his skin, press her mouth against his bare chest, examine the heavy ridge she felt each night when they were in bed.

Dani turned away from him and stepped out of the private, secluded spot in the moonlight. Silently she made her way over to the railing and looked down into the sea rushing past the hull. Above her head, yards of white canvas sail strained into the wind and the rigging clanked and clattered.

Dani turned her face into the chill ocean breeze and let the wind cool the heat in her face, the hot race of her blood. She turned a little more, saw a man's shadow approaching from behind her and thought for a moment that Rafael had followed.

Instead, Carlton Baker stepped out of the darkness into the moonlight beside her.

"Pleasant evening for a stroll," he said. Pale blue eyes moved over her, taking in the heightened color in her cheeks.

"Yes . . . yes it is."

He was a large man, perhaps in his forties, his temples touched with silver, a well-built man and attractive. And yet there was something about him. . . .

"I don't see your husband. Perhaps you had a different escort tonight."

Her cheeks went warm. Surely he wasn't implying she was having an illicit rendezvous with another man.

"I had no other escort." She glanced around, hoping Rafael would appear when only moments ago she had hoped to escape his disturbing presence.

Baker's gaze sharpened. "Then you are alone?"

"No! I mean, no I —"

"There you are, love. I lost track of you for a moment." Rafe stepped out of the private spot that she had just fled and relief swept through her. "I won't make that mistake again."

Baker's smile looked false. "With a wife as lovely as yours, I'm sure you won't."

"Enjoying the evening, Mr. Baker?" Rafe's tone was polite but his eyes looked hard. Perhaps, just as she, he had also noticed something not quite correct in the American's demeanor.

"Indeed," he said. His eyes ran over Danielle. "As I'm sure you are."

"Actually, it's a bit damp out here and the air has begun to turn chill." Rafe rested a possessive hand at Dani's waist. "I think it's time we went in."

She nodded, eager to escape, yet she couldn't quite say why. As they walked off down the deck, Dani cast a last glance over her shoulder at Carlton Baker. Though she dreaded another restless night sleeping next to Rafael, she was anxious to get back to the cabin.

The following morning, Danielle met Caro for breakfast. She hadn't slept well. She didn't believe Rafe had, either. Sleeping beside him night after night while trying to guard her virtue was beginning to take its toll.

Dressed in a russet day dress trimmed with dark brown velvet, Dani spotted her friend at a small table at the rear of the salon and started toward her. As she drew near, it occurred to her that Caro's thin face carried the same hints of fatigue as her own.

Caro smiled in welcome. "We might need a larger table if the duke will be joining us."

"I think he has already eaten. He was gone from the cabin when I woke up."

"Lady Wycombe is still sleeping. I didn't want to wake her." Caro said no more as Dani sat down at the table across from her. A steward came to take their order of chocolate and sweet biscuits, then left them alone.

"You look tired," Caro said, assessing her. "I'll wager you aren't sleeping very well."

"I'll wager you aren't, either."

Caro sighed and shook her head. "I keep thinking of Robert. I am so worried, Danielle. Do you think by now he has tried to escape? Escaping from an indenture contract is a crime, Dani. What if Mr. Steigler catches him?"

Dani reached over and took her friend's hand. "You mustn't do that to yourself, Caro. You mustn't think the worst, only the best. Whatever Robert decided to do, I'm sure he planned very carefully. Perhaps he has successfully escaped and found a ship to take him home. Perhaps he will reach England shortly after we do."

Caro glanced away, tears welling in her eyes. "I don't know, Dani. Perhaps he never really intended to return. What if he was only using me? What if he cared nothing for me at all, but simply wanted me to help him find a way to escape? I'm a plain woman, Dani, and Robert is so very handsome. What if he simply made a fool of me?"

"I don't believe that — not for a moment. And you are not plain. You are a very attractive woman. You have an elegant sort of beauty that is different from other women. Robert saw it. He saw your inner beauty, as well. I believe he was telling the truth in all that he said."

The steward walked up just then with cups of hot chocolate and a plate of biscuits, which he set down on the small round table in front of them. Caro used the time to compose herself.

"I'm sorry," she said. "I want to believe in him the way I did before. But if he duped me and in my ignorance I took advantage of your generous nature, I will never forgive myself."

Dani squeezed Caro's hand. "Whatever happens, it is not your fault. I wanted to help. I believed in his innocence, just as you did. I still do."

Caro took a shaky breath. "He was so very grateful for your help. He said that he would be forever in your debt, that his life was yours to command."

"I know, dearest. And we must continue to believe in him and keep him in our prayers."

Caro just nodded.

"Now, let us enjoy our chocolate in peace and no longer dwell on thoughts of men."

Caro smiled and so did Dani, but Danielle's smile slipped away as she thought of Rafael and the days ahead and spending each night in his very disturbing company.

The morning passed and then another. Two weeks turned into three, pushed toward four. As the days slipped away, Rafe demanded more and more of her. More kissing, more touching, more intimate contact, and her traitorous body responded.

At night she dreamed of him caressing her breasts, pressing his mouth there, touching her thighs, her belly, dreamed of him soothing the ache he stirred in the place between her legs. She was sleeping even more poorly, tossing and turning, her body on fire with a need she didn't understand.

It was Wednesday, she thought, but she had begun to lose track of time. As the day passed into evening, she grew restless and edgy. At supper, she snapped at Caro for some imagined transgression and spoke abruptly to Aunt Flora.

Professing a headache she didn't really have, she declined Rafe's invitation for their usual walk on deck, desperate to be away from him, at least for a while.

"I think I'll go down early," she told him as they rose from the supper table. "Perhaps you could interest Mr. Baker or Mr. Longbow in a game of cards."

Rafe's blue gaze moved over her and she wondered if he could see through her flimsy excuse to escape him.

The edge of his mouth barely curved. "I think I'll join you. Perhaps I can find a way to ease your . . . headache . . . once we reach the cabin."

At the husky note in his voice, her whole body tightened. Something hot unfurled in the pit of her stomach and moved out through her limbs. Too tired to argue, she resigned herself to whatever he intended and let him lead her out of the dining room.

She said nothing as they walked along the passage, nothing as he opened the door then waited for her to precede him into the cabin. He followed her into the room and closed the door, and she saw that his eyes had turned a smoky shade of blue.

"I'll help you unfasten your gown," he said.

Though she had grown used to accepting his aid and was no longer intimidated by his presence in the cabin, there was something in his look tonight, something hot and seductive that warned her to beware.

Instead, her traitorous body responded to that fierce male glance, her nipples tightening, her stomach constricting, and her fatigue began to slip away. Wordlessly, she moved to the dressing table to pull the pins from her hair, then rose to remove her shoes and stockings, and Rafe unbuttoned her gown. She drew her chemise off over her head, momentarily leaving her naked, though she carefully kept her back to him. But when she reached for her night rail, he plucked it out of her hand.

"Not tonight."

She glanced at him over her shoulder, read his desire in the hard lines of his face, and a look of determination.

She started shaking. "You said you would give me time."

"And so I have."

"You gave me your word, Rafael."

He tossed the night rail over the back of the chair. "I haven't come close to breaking

231

my vow, nor will I tonight."

Dani steeled herself. A husband made demands and a wife was supposed to fulfill them. But in the weeks since she had boarded the ship, she had learned that a woman held certain powers of her own.

Naked, she turned to face him, exposing herself fully to his view. Nearly as surprised as she, he clenched his jaw and his eyes seemed to burn.

"You've been playing a game with me, have you not?" she asked. "I am beginning to understand that a woman can play the game, as well."

His gaze ran over her and beneath his scorching regard, her nipples tightened even more, began to ache almost painfully, and suddenly she wanted him to touch her more than anything on earth.

"Do I please you?" she taunted, turning so that he might better view her naked figure, amazingly unashamed, her tone carrying a bravado that she was astonished to feel.

"You please me greatly, Danielle." The low rumble of his voice rolled through her and, trancelike, she moved closer, stopping just in front of him.

Rafe held nothing back, letting her know by his lengthy perusal how much he wanted her, how pleased he was with what she had revealed.

"Come here . . ."

She forced her legs to move. She didn't know where the game would lead, but she was determined to have a say in the rules. Rafe drew her into his arms and began to kiss her, gently at first, and she could feel the tension in his body, the control he exerted. He deepened the kiss, his tongue sweeping in, and a wild yearning rose inside her. Suddenly she was kissing him back, kissing him with abandon, driving her tongue into his mouth as she slid his coat off his shoulders and shoved it onto the floor, beginning to work the buttons on his waistcoat.

Rafe made a low, growling sound in his throat, kicked off his shoes and began to tug at his stock. He helped her pull off his shirt, leaving him bare chested, then lifted her up and carried her over to the bed.

"Release me from my vow," he urged, but she only shook her head.

Rafe didn't hesitate, just started kissing her again, raining kisses along her throat and shoulders, taking her breasts into his mouth and biting the ends. A swift shot of pleasure-pain tore through her and she cried out his name.

"Release me from my vow," he softly demanded, but again she refused. She needed these weeks, needed to protect herself for as long as she possibly could.

Her eyes met his, filled with all of her fears, all of her longing. All of her doubts and uncertainties were there in her gaze, revealed to him in that moment, beseeching him to understand.

"You want me," he said gruffly. "At least admit that much."

She swallowed, gave him the truth. "I want you. . . ."

The words seemed to enflame him. She thought that surely he would take her, force her if he had to, but instead, he started kissing her again, ravaging her mouth, laving her naked breasts, caressing them, biting the ends, suckling until she was shaking all over.

An ache welled inside her and a burning need so strong she thought she would go insane. She shifted on the bed, barely conscious of the hand that moved down her body, unaware until his fingers slid between her legs.

With a will of its own, her body arched upward, pressing against his palm, desperately searching for something.

"Please . . ." she whispered. "Help me, Rafael. . . ."

He made a guttural sound in his throat

and his fingers parted her burning flesh, slid inside her, stroked her gently, then with growing determination. A wave of pleasure hit her, incredible white-hot need. Every touch, every caress sent her higher, closer to a horizon just out of reach.

Need clashed with fear. "Rafael . . . ?"

"Let me give this to you, Dani." His skillful hands moved over her, inside her. "Let me do this for you."

Her insides wound tighter, tighter, then seemed to snap. Something deep and erotic blossomed inside her, something that seemed to have no end. Dani cried out his name as wild spasms of pleasure shook her, great tremors, one after another. Sweet darkness engulfed her, and for seconds that seemed like hours, she basked in the joy pouring through her.

Time slipped past and she began to spiral down, the pleasure slowly fading. When she opened her eyes, she saw Rafe sitting on the edge of the bed beside her, his hand holding hers, his eyes on her face, such a deep, dark blue they looked almost black.

Dani blinked up at him. "What . . . what did you do?"

The edge of his mouth lifted faintly. "I gave you pleasure. It's my right as your husband."

"Was that . . . making love?"

He shook his head, dislodging a short dark curl of hair that fell across his forehead. "It was only a small measure of what you will feel when we make love."

A small measure? Limp and sated, her mind still fuzzy, she tried to imagine how there could possibly be more. It seemed unimaginable. Gazing up at him, for the first time, she noticed the tightness along his jaw, the rigid set of his shoulders, the expression on his face that bordered on pain.

A glance at the thick ridge in his breeches confirmed that Rafe was still fully aroused.

"I don't understand."

He reached over and touched her cheek. "Tonight was for you, love. There'll be other nights, a lifetime of pleasure for both of us."

Dani didn't say more. She was relaxed and sleepy as she hadn't been in days, every muscle limp and completely sated. Yet they had not made love and it was obvious Rafael wasn't feeling nearly as replete as she.

It occurred to her that he had kept his word, at what seemed considerable cost to himself. Dani clung to the thought as she drifted off to sleep.

Fifteen

The London day was chill, a brisk wind sweeping in off the Thames. As the carriage pulled up in front of Whitehall Palace, Ethan Sharpe opened the door and climbed down to the paving stones, on his way to a meeting with Colonel Howard Pendleton of the British War Office.

He started walking and saw Max Bradley step out of the shadows of the big gray stone building and begin moving toward him.

"Good to see you, Ethan." Max was tall and gaunt and several years older, a friend Ethan trusted as much as any man on earth.

"You, as well, Max." Their relationship had long ago progressed beyond formal address. When a man saved your life, it created a bond that erased social boundaries.

"Pendleton's note was fairly vague," Ethan said, "just that you had returned to England. Apparently he wants my opinion on something that has to do with information you brought back with you."

They stepped inside the building out of the wind. "You were one of the country's

237

most successful privateers," Max said. "Your opinion could be of great value to the colonel."

Ethan just nodded. "Any news of Rafe?"

Max's mouth faintly curved. "Last I heard of him he was about to get married. If he did, he likely won't be far behind me."

"So he found her."

"Aye, that he did."

"Apparently he didn't think Clemens was the right man for her."

"I gather he was extremely unimpressed."

Ethan wondered what sort of man would impress Rafe enough to get him to stand by and permit the fellow to marry a woman who should have been his. He wasn't surprised Rafe hadn't let that happen. Ethan smiled as they continued down the hall, their boots ringing on the marble floors.

"I have a hunch Rafe meant to marry her the day he left London — though I don't think he knew it at the time." Ethan knocked, then pushed through the door leading into the colonel's office.

Max followed him into the sparsely furnished room that held only the colonel's scarred wooden desk, the two chairs in front of it, a bookcase and two tables covered with maps and charts.

Pendleton came to his feet as Ethan

walked in. "Thank you for coming, my lord."

"What can I do for you, Hal?" Pendleton was another man Ethan considered a very good friend, another man who had helped save his life.

The colonel smiled. He was silver-haired, very dignified, one of the most honest, most hardworking men in the service. "I think it would be best if Max explained what he has discovered. Then perhaps you can give me your thoughts as to where we should go from here."

For the next few minutes, Bradley explained about the Baltimore Clipper schooners the Americans were building, about the Dutchman, Bartel Schrader, and the deal the man appeared to be brokering with Napoléon and the French.

"These ships are unlike any I've ever seen," Max said. "Light, fast and extremely maneuverable. Fully armed, they could be devastating to the British fleet."

Sitting in front of the colonel's desk, Ethan stretched one long leg out in front of him. An old war injury had left him with a slight limp and occasionally it throbbed if he sat in one position too long.

"If I'm reading you correctly," Ethan said, "you're thinking the government should preempt the sale and make an offer of its own so the French can't get their hands on them."

Max nodded. "That's right. Sheffield sent a letter, which I carried back with me. The colonel has already seen it. In the duke's opinion, as well as mine, the threat these ships pose could be very grave, indeed."

The colonel placed a rolled-up sheet of paper on the top of his worn wooden desk and smoothed it open so that Ethan could see.

"This is a sketch Max made of a schooner called the *Windlass.*"

"The plans themselves were extremely well guarded," Max said. "I'm not much of an artist, but at least this will give you an idea why the damned things are so fast and easy to handle."

Ethan studied the drawing, noting the unique slope of the double masts, the low, sleek lines of the hull. It appeared that even his own ship, the *Sea Devil*, wouldn't be a match for the vessel, once it was under sail and cutting through the ocean.

Old feelings stirred to life. As content as he was in his new role as husband and father, he felt an itch to stand behind the wheel of such a ship. He fixed his gaze on the colonel.

"Neither Max nor Rafe would be worried

without good cause. If Max's drawing is anywhere near accurate — and I'm certain it is — I wouldn't waste any time in taking this to the highest authority."

Pendleton rolled up the drawing. "I was afraid that's what you'd say." He rounded the desk and walked toward them. "I'll move forward on this as quickly as I can, though there are no guarantees what will happen."

"With the war progressing as it is and Napoléon pressing for any sort of victory, I hope they listen."

But of course, as the colonel said, there was no way to know what the government would do.

Ethan bade both men farewell and returned to the carriage, his thoughts mulling over the meeting he'd just had and the information Max had relayed about Rafe. Ethan couldn't help wondering if Rafe was even now aboard a ship on its way back to London.

And if Rafael was now a married man.

A storm blew up. Heavy October winds swept across the decks and waves plunged over the bow. They were less than two weeks out of London, less than two weeks till Rafe would arrive home with his bride.

They had been at sea six long weeks and still his marriage had not been consummated.

He sighed as he sat in the salon and tried to concentrate on the hand of whist he played with Carlton Baker. In concession to the heavy seas, the fire had been put out and most of the passengers were stashed away in their cabins.

"Your turn, Your Grace."

Rafe studied his hand. He didn't much like Baker, but Danielle was downstairs in their cabin, embroidering with her aunt and Caroline Loon, staying as warm and dry as possible in such wet weather. With the terrible pounding seas, Lady Wycombe was suffering a bout of *mal de mer,* and he hoped Danielle did not also succumb.

He thought of her and felt a familiar rush of desire. Since the night he had brought her to fulfillment, he had stayed mostly away from her, his grand scheme of seduction utterly destroyed by the beseeching look in her eyes. He had read the fear, the doubt, seen the mistrust of him she still carried, and he simply could not go through with it.

Rafe remembered her tempting curves and the way she had responded, and his groin tightened. He wanted her with agonizing force. Still, he wouldn't alter his decision.

He laid down his cards and picked up the small pile of coins in the middle of the table, the gaming aboard ship gentlemanly and rarely very large.

"It seems luck is with you, Your Grace," Baker said. "But then, considering what a lovely bride you've acquired, that has already proved to be the case."

Rafe cast him a glance. "I'm an extremely lucky man." If he hadn't been so bored, he would have refused Baker's invitation to play. From the start, the American had seemed overly interested in Danielle. Then again, as beautiful as she was, Rafe could scarcely blame him.

His mind returned to Dani and the decision he had made.

He had betrayed her trust five years ago. In forcing her into a marriage she didn't want, he had betrayed her again.

He refused to do it a third time.

Rafe had promised to give Danielle the time she needed. After the night he had nearly seduced her, he had worked to see it done. In the days that followed, he had left the cabin each morning before she awakened, and though he spent time with her during the day and escorted her in to supper each evening, he had not taken her to their private place again; had, in fact, stayed away from the cabin at night until she was already asleep.

Barely conscious of Baker's muttered curse as he lost another hand, Rafe leaned back in his chair. In less than two weeks, they would be back on English soil and his painful celibacy would come to an end.

Danielle would have had the time he had promised her and — he fervently hoped — he would have gained some measure of her trust.

Danielle checked her appearance in the glass above the dresser. Yesterday's storm had passed. The seas were relatively calm, Aunt Flora's bout of *mal de mer* ended. Dani had braided her hair and pinned it up, and wore a light blue woolen gown in preparation for her trip to the main salon, where she and her aunt planned to meet for a cup of tea, as had become their habit each afternoon.

Dani shook her head, her gaze still fixed on the image in the mirror. The shadows had returned to her eyes and her features looked drawn. She knew Rafael and her uncertain future were partly to blame, but equally disturbing were thoughts of her return to London.

Once they arrived, her life would undergo

a drastic change. She would be the Duchess of Sheffield, no longer a pariah in society, and yet when she looked into the eyes of the people who had shunned her, friends who had turned away from her in her hour of need, how would she be able to forget?

Along with her misgivings about reentering society, there was Rafael. Since the morning after he had touched her so intimately, he had been inexplicably distant. She knew that he had been attempting to seduce her into making love and that night had nearly succeeded.

Dani believed he had seen the quiet desperation in her eyes that night, the awful, desperate need to keep herself apart from him until she could come to terms with the marriage he had forced upon her. Although they still shared a bed, he had not touched her again, had not kissed her as he had done each night before.

Dani told herself she was grateful, that this was what she wanted. But deep down, she was no longer sure.

She might not trust Rafe with her heart, but her treacherous body burned for him. At night she lay awake thinking about him, longing to reach over and touch him, to press her mouth against the spot above his heart.

With a sigh of frustration, Dani left the cabin Rafe had abandoned at first light and headed for the main salon, hurrying along the passage in an effort to make up for lost time. As she descended the ladder and entered the wood-paneled room, she spotted her aunt, who waved a plump hand, signaling Dani to join her.

Aunt Flora gazed up at her with a hint of concern in her eyes. "You are rarely late, my dear. I hope nothing untoward has happened."

"I am fine. I was woolgathering, I suppose. Somehow time slipped away."

Aunt Flora's silver eyebrows drew together. "I've a notion it's a bit more than that."

Dan sighed as she took a seat across from her aunt. "I don't know, Aunt Flora. I'm worried about what will happen when we are returned, and lately I have just been so . . . restless."

Aunt Flora reached over and caught her hand. "I realize you are now a married woman and it is scarcely my place to be giving you advice but . . ."

"I always appreciate your counsel, Aunt Flora."

"All right, then, I shall speak what is on my mind. First, let me say that I was once a married woman myself, which gives me some measure of authority on the subject."

"Of course."

"Several days before you were wed, you told me the duke agreed not to claim his husbandly rights until the two of you were returned to England."

"He made that pledge, yes."

"I may not know a great deal about the opposite sex, but I am certain of at least one thing. A strong, virile man like your husband does not sleep for weeks next to a woman he desires without paying a terrible price. Now, looking at you, I am beginning to believe you are also paying a price."

"I need time to get to know him. Surely you can understand that."

Her aunt sat back in her chair, her bulky frame filling it completely, studying Danielle as the steward arrived with cups and a pot of tea. He poured for them both, leaving behind the cream and sugar, which they applied themselves as the young man departed the table.

Aunt Flora daintily took a sip of tea, eyeing Dani over the rim of her cup. "If you had married Richard Clemens, he would never have agreed to such a pledge and you would, by now, be a wife in truth."

Dani glanced away, her cheeks coloring,

though she knew her aunt was right.

"You and I have been together for more than five years, Danielle. In that time, I have come to know you, perhaps even better than you know yourself."

"What are you saying, Aunt Flora?"

"The Duke of Sheffield is a handsome, magnetic man and it is obvious you feel a powerful attraction to him. It is there in your eyes whenever you look at him. It is equally obvious the duke feels an even stronger attraction to you."

She didn't bother to deny it. Though Rafe had returned to the polite distance he had once maintained, the heat in his eyes remained. "What are you suggesting, Aunt?"

"Release your husband from his vow. Let him make love to you."

Her cheeks went scarlet. It was hardly a subject she wished to discuss with her aunt . . . yet the thought had preyed on her mind for days. "We are nearly home. Once we are in London —"

"Once we are arrived, you will find yourself even more uncertain than you are now. Sharing a cabin as you have, you and your husband have reached a certain level of comfort with each other. That is important in matters between a husband and wife. If you wait, it will all seem new again and unfamiliar, and the intimacy you have shared on this voyage will be forgotten."

Flora set her teacup down and reached for Dani's hand. "Follow your instincts, my dear. Be a wife to your husband."

Dani said nothing. Memories assailed her: the soirée where they had first met, the way he had sought her out among all of the other women, the way he had looked at her, as if there were no one else in the room. Unlike the young ladies who buzzed about him, awed by his lofty status and swooning at his every word, Dani had always felt his equal. He was only a man, after all, not the godlike creature women seemed to believe.

She'd enjoyed his company from the start, conversing easily, discovering how much they had in common. She remembered the stolen moment on the terrace when Rafe had first held her hand, how her heart had flooded with an emotion so strong she felt dizzy.

Aunt Flora's words settled softly inside her. Whatever she felt for Rafael, she wanted him. She had admitted as much.

"Thank you, Aunt Flora. I'll think about what you have said."

Her aunt's round, powdered face creased into a smile. "I'm sure you will make the right decision, dear heart."

But deep down, Dani's decision had just been made. From this moment forward, it was only a question of time before she released Rafael from his pledge.

Sixteen

Dani needed to find her husband. It was getting late, well past midnight, and he had not yet returned to the cabin. After supper, he had escorted her back to their room, then abruptly departed. Dani hadn't seen him since.

She paced the cabin. The skirt of the burgundy velvet gown she had worn for Rafe brushed her ankles with every turn. She should have stopped him from leaving the cabin, spoken to him frankly, said the words that would have ended the torture that gripped them both in the long hours of the night.

She could wait for his arrival, but each night he had returned even later than before, the celibacy she had demanded racking his body and turning him more and more remote.

At supper he had been distant and brooding. Danielle believed if she released him from his vow, all of that would change. She wasn't sure where the intimacy would lead or exactly what to expect. There would be pain, she knew, but every woman endured it, and she knew it would only be painful the first time.

She glanced at the ship's clock over the tiny hearth in the corner where a small fire burned to keep away the chill. There was only a fingernail moon tonight, but the seas were mild, and she refused to wait any longer.

She had taken down her hair in anticipation of what would happen this night, leaving the heavy mass in soft curls down her back. She grabbed her woolen cloak off the hook beside the door, whirled it around her shoulders and pulled the hood up to cover her bright curls. The latch on the door lifted easily and Dani stepped out into the corridor.

It was highly improper to go on deck unescorted, but the hour was late and aside from a group of sailors singing sea chanteys up near the bow, no one seemed to be about.

She headed for the salon, but once she reached it, she could peer inside enough to discern that Rafe wasn't there. He had always been a man who needed physical activity and she imagined he was probably striding around the deck.

She pulled her cloak a little tighter against the breeze filling the sails, and an odd thought struck. Turning toward the private spot he had taken her to the first few weeks of their voyage, she started in that direction, rounding the deckhouse toward the stern, disappearing into the shadows.

She had almost reached her destination when a tall figure stepped out in front of her, blocking the faint rays of moonlight. She smiled, thinking that she had found Rafael.

"Well, isn't this a coincidence?" The voice of Carlton Baker drifted toward her, and she froze where she stood. "It would seem you and I both favor this part of the ship."

She swallowed. She disliked the American even more now than she had when she had first met him. "I am looking for my husband. I thought he might be here."

In the glow of a lantern hanging from the ratlines some distance away, she caught the odd gleam in Baker's pale eyes.

"I see. In that case, why don't I escort you in your search?"

Being in Baker's company was the last thing she wanted. "Thank you, but there is no need for that. If you will excuse me, I'll just be on my way." She started to brush past him, but Baker caught her arm.

"Why don't you stay, keep me company for a while?"

She looked up at him, a large man, nearly

as tall as her husband. "I hardly think that would be proper. Now, please let me pass."

But Baker had no such intention. For weeks, he had been watching her, or at least she thought he had been. Lately she had grown more and more wary. Moving closer, he held her arm in an unyielding grip and hauled her against him, shoving her backward and forcing her up against the wall of the deckhouse. The hood of her cloak fell back as Baker's head descended and he tried to kiss her, but Dani jerked away.

"Let me go!"

His long body pinned her. His hand brushed her cheek. "Come, now, is that really what you want? I've seen the way you look at me. I know what you are thinking. All you women are the same."

A wave of repulsion hit her. Dani struggled, becoming truly afraid. "I said, let me go!"

He tried to kiss her again and when she turned her face away, when she tried to scream, he covered her mouth with his hand. She felt him reaching beneath the hem of her gown, working to shove the fabric up her legs. He was strong and he used his strength to pin her against the wall.

"I'll have you," he said. "And you're going to like it." He might have said more, but an instant later, his body jerked away from her as if he were a puppet on a string.

Rafe whirled him around and hit him, once, then again, knocking him backward, slamming him into the rail. Baker recovered, charged forward, swung a hard blow that creased Rafe's jaw. Rafe stepped back and punched him, jabbing once, twice, then throwing a blow hard enough that Baker crashed into the deckhouse.

Another blow rained down on him, then another. Blood spurted from Baker's nose and a crimson stain blossomed on the front of his shirt. Rafe hauled the man up by the lapels of his coat and hit him so hard his head cracked against the wall. Baker slid onto the deck and this time he didn't get up.

Now that Rafe had won the fight, Dani stood there trembling. When he turned toward her, she saw that his eyes were blazing.

"Are you all right?" The question came out tightly, barely forced out between clenched teeth.

She only nodded, completely unable to speak. Leaving Baker in a crumpled heap on the deck, he slid his arm around her waist and urged her forward, and Dani let him guide her along the deck back toward their cabin. Her heart beat erratically, a new fear clogging her throat.

She knew what Rafe was thinking, recognized the look she had seen in his eyes that night five years ago, knew that he believed that she had encouraged Carlton Baker's advances, and though she was innocent of any wrongdoing, she knew that her husband would not believe her.

A soft sob caught in her throat as they descended the ladder leading to their cabin. Rafe opened the door and led her inside, and her eyes filled with tears.

"I didn't . . . I didn't encourage him," she said. "I know you won't believe it, but I swear that I did not." The tears in her eyes slipped onto her cheeks.

The hardness in Rafe's jaw turned into an expression of horror. "That is what you think? That I believe you were at fault in this?"

She started crying then, and Rafe swept her into his arms. He was trembling, she realized, though she couldn't imagine why.

Cupping the back of her head in his hand, he pressed her cheek to his and held her tightly against him. "Listen to me, Dani. Carlton Baker is a villain of the very worst sort. When I saw him accosting you, I wanted to kill him. I wanted to end his life with my own two hands. I would have called him out but a ship is hardly the place. I didn't think you would want that, and I didn't want to make matters worse."

He eased away to look at her. "I never believed you had any part in what happened, Danielle. Not for an instant."

Her tears turned into sobs and he drew her back into his arms. Five years ago, he hadn't believed her. She never truly imagined that would change.

"Don't cry," he said softly. "Not over him."

She sniffed and looked up at him, and he used his finger to wipe the tears from her cheek.

"I was looking for you," she said. "I needed to talk to you."

"I'm here now. Tell me what is so important you felt you had to go in search of me in the middle of the night."

Dani glanced away. Earlier, she had practiced the words she would say. After what had happened, Rafe's knuckles still swollen and bruised from the battle he had fought, the time no longer seemed right.

"It doesn't matter. Not now."

She tried to turn away but Rafe caught her arm, refusing to let her escape. "Tell me. Let me be the judge of whether or not it is important."

As usual, he left her no choice. Dani summoned her courage. "I wanted to tell you . . . that I wish to release you from your vow."

His blue eyes darkened for the space of a heartbeat, then turned hot and fierce. "You don't think that is important? Those are the most important words I have heard in the past five years."

And then he kissed her.

Dani leaned toward him. Rafe kissed her and kissed her, his big hands wound into her hair, holding her in place for his tender assault, gentling her, easing her fears.

"We'll take things slowly," he said. "I won't press you for more than you're ready to give." But as his mouth moved along her throat, as he nipped an earlobe, then claimed her lips for an even deeper, more thorough kiss, she thought that she could handle whatever he had in store for her.

He had believed her. He had trusted that she was telling him the truth. Her heart clutched, and something sweet unfurled inside her.

Rafe started removing her clothes, wasting little time, dispensed of them swiftly and efficiently, until both of them were naked. Though she had grown used to disrobing in his presence, this was the first time she had seen Rafe in a complete state of undress. He was fully, rampantly aroused, and she found herself fascinated by the sight.

"Don't be afraid," he said, noting the direction of her gaze.

"I'm not afraid," she told him, lying only a little. She trembled as he started kissing her again, deep, penetrating kisses that melted her insides. His lips trailed along her throat, over her shoulders and down to her breasts. He captured one erect nipple and then the other, tugging and suckling, sending a swirl of fire into the place between her legs.

They stood beside the bed, Rafe relentlessly teasing and caressing, nipping and tasting, until her legs felt too weak to hold her up. As if he knew, he lifted her up and settled her in the middle of the bed, then came down beside her.

Rising above her, he leaned over and kissed her, the weight of his body pressing her into the mattress. She could feel the rasp of his curly dark chest hair against her sensitive nipples, and desire flared inside her. She shifted beneath him, more and more restless, pressing herself against his long, hard frame, feeling the strength of his arousal.

Heavy and hot, it pulsed with each beat of his heart, and her own heartbeat quickened.

Oh, how she wanted him!

Dani kissed him fiercely, sliding her tongue into his mouth, arching upward, urging him to take her.

Rafe groaned.

"I don't want to rush you," he said gruffly, "but I am not sure how much longer I can last."

"I don't want you to wait any longer. Please, Rafael . . ."

Rafe made a low, growling sound in his throat, then came up over her, spreading her legs with his knee. "I'll try not to hurt you."

She didn't reply, just shifted restlessly, desperate to get closer, to feel that part of him that would claim her as his wife. His hard length probed the entrance to her passage, then he kissed her, long and deep, and drove himself home.

Time seemed to still. For an instant, her body stiffened and she bit back a cry of pain.

Rafe's body went tense. "I tried not to hurt you. Are you all right?"

She managed a nod, sensing the effort it took for him to hold back. His muscles were so taut they quivered as he gave her a chance to adjust to the length and size of him.

"The worst is past, love. Just let yourself relax."

He was a big man and he filled her completely, a sensation different from anything she had imagined. And yet it was not unpleasant. In fact . . . The pain was gone, she realized, replaced by a growing urgency that seemed to increase each moment.

"I like the way you feel inside me. . . ." She arched slightly upward, testing the position, taking even more of him.

Rafe hissed in a breath. His body tightened as he fought for control, then his taut leash, stretched to the limit, seemed to finally snap. Driving into her, he took her hard and fast, pounding against her as if he had no other choice.

For an instant, the sheer power of him frightened her, then the pleasure she had felt before began to spiral through her, grew and grew, until time and place slipped away. Her body tightened into a fine thread of need, then flew apart, sending her to a place of sweetness and joy where she had never been before.

She cried out Rafe's name and clung to him, her arms locked around his neck.

Eventually, the room came back into focus and she began to spiral down. Rafe lifted himself away from her and settled himself at her side. He eased her into the crook of his arm and she curled against him.

Rafe kissed her forehead. "Sleep well, love."

Exhausted and strangely content, she drifted off to sleep.

In the middle of the night she stirred. Sensing Rafe there beside her, she reached out to touch him, and realized he was once more aroused. Her gaze flew to his face and she saw that he was awake and watching her.

Dani leaned toward him, her body coming to life as she remembered the pleasure he had brought her. She pressed her lips against his bare chest, and Rafe's arms came around her. Like a lion claiming his mate, he rose above her, slid inside with far less resistance than before.

They made love slowly, allowing the pleasure to build, then afterward he nestled her against his side and drifted off to sleep.

Dani watched the rise and fall of his chest, his even breathing. He was her husband and her body craved him. But she had loved him once before and that love had nearly destroyed her.

For minutes that stretched into hours, Dani stared up at the ceiling, determined that whatever pleasure she received from Rafe's body, she would not fall in love with him again.

Seventeen

It was their last evening at sea. Tomorrow they would reach landfall, sail up the Thames to the London docks and depart the ship. By tomorrow, the *Nimble* would be only a memory.

In light of the passengers' impending departure, the captain planned a special farewell supper. Downstairs in their cabin, Rafe watched Danielle finish dressing in a high-waisted dark green velvet gown decorated with tiny seed pearls. With its slightly low décolletage, the dress was one of his favorites, setting off the green of her eyes and the ruby glints in her hair.

At first, she had declined to wear the garment, since it was the sort a man would particularly admire and Carlton Baker would be present, eyeing Dani sullenly and Rafe with open hostility, but Rafe refused to let Baker sully their evening and he thought that secretly Dani had wanted very much to wear the lovely gown.

He studied her from a few feet away, admiring her slender curves, feeling a rush of heat to his loins he forced himself to ignore. Since the night he had consummated their marriage, their relationship had changed. At the same time, it had not.

Though Danielle trusted him now with her body, she yet remained wary, and careful to guard her heart. In a way, Rafael was grateful. In the years they were apart, he had constructed a protective wall of his own. He remembered all too clearly the pain of loving someone, knew only too well its vicious, destructive force. He never wanted to suffer that kind of pain again.

Better to keep his careful control in place, guard his emotions and keep them under close rein. Which he managed to do most of the time, except when they were in bed.

Under different circumstances, Rafe might have smiled. When they made love, the desire he felt for Danielle burned as hot and fevered as it had five years ago, driving him mad with lust and destroying his prized self-control. Still, in the light of day, he protected his emotions as carefully as she, and he thought that it was better — safer — if they continued in that vein.

Rafe glanced at the ship's clock above the hearth in the cabin. He was dressed and ready for the evening, wearing a dark gray tailcoat over a burgundy brocade waistcoat, his white stock neatly tied. Danielle also appeared ready, save for the small pearl earbobs she threaded through her ears as she sat in front of the teakwood dresser.

It occurred to him how perfectly his gift, the Bride's Necklace, would look with her elegant costume tonight.

Moving behind her in the mirror, he settled his hands on her shoulders. "You haven't worn the necklace I gave you since we left Philadelphia. I presume you have packed it away somewhere safe for the journey."

In the mirror, as she finished attaching the second earbob, he noticed the faint tremor in her hand. The color in her face seemed to pale and his senses went on alert.

"If you have given it into the captain's care for safekeeping, I would be glad to retrieve it for you."

He saw the wariness creep into her lovely green eyes, along with something else he couldn't read. She turned away from the mirror and slowly rose to her feet.

Almost imperceptibly, her chin inched up. "The necklace is not in safekeeping with Captain Burns. In truth, it is not aboard the ship at all."

He tried to make sense of her words. "What are you saying?"

"I'm sorry, Rafael, but the necklace was stolen the day we boarded the ship. It must have happened right after the wedding. I didn't discover it was missing until we were already at sea."

"Why didn't you tell me?"

"I wanted to." For an instant, she glanced away. "I was frightened, afraid of what you would say." She refused to meet his gaze and it bothered him. He had come to trust her and yet . . .

"Do you have any idea who might have stolen the necklace?" he asked, careful to keep his voice even.

"I can't think who would do such a thing. I can only guess it was one of the household servants. I am sorry, Rafael, truly I am. It was a lovely piece of jewelry. The gift meant a great deal to me."

But not enough that she would come forward and inform him of the theft. Then again, they had been estranged for years and she had only begun to know him again. Perhaps as she said, she was afraid of his reaction.

"Once we're home, I'll send word to the American authorities, offer a substantial reward. Perhaps the pearls will be found and returned."

She clasped her hands together in her lap.

266

"Yes . . . perhaps they will. As I said, the necklace was exceedingly lovely."

Incredible, in fact. He couldn't help thinking of the legend that accompanied the ancient string of pearls. He wondered if there were any truth to it, and if so, what consequences might befall the person responsible for stealing the valuable piece of jewelry.

He studied his wife's nervous posture, her troubled expression, but told himself to ignore it. "At any rate, there is nothing we can do about it tonight. We won't let it spoil our evening."

Dani said nothing, but he thought that she was vaguely surprised by his words. Did she really believe he would blame her for the loss?

"You thought I would be angry, I gather."

"I . . . Yes. I thought you would lose your temper. I imagined that you would be furious that the necklace was missing."

A thin smile curved his lips. "I rarely lose my temper these days. I've gone to great lengths to ensure it doesn't happen . . . aside from encounters with Carlton Baker, of course."

Her gaze met his and he knew she was thinking of the beating he had given the American, which he didn't regret in the least.

"Yes . . . aside from Mr. Baker." Danielle moved away from the bureau. Rafe offered his arm and she rested her fingers on the sleeve of his coat. In her sumptuous green velvet gown, she looked as stunning as he had ever seen her.

And yet as they departed the cabin, he could feel the loss of the pearls and her furtiveness in the matter like a haunting specter between them.

Captain Gregory Latimer of the *Laurel*, the ship he sailed from Baltimore to Liverpool, stood before the small fire in his cabin. Draped across his palm was the most magnificent piece of jewelry he had ever seen. He held the necklace up in the flickering firelight, a fabulous string of pearls interspersed with diamonds.

Greg had taken the necklace as collateral, which, the passenger promised, would be exchanged for money — twice the normal fare — once he reached England. It was a bargain he couldn't resist.

Greg studied the pearls, examining the perfect roundness, the incredibly creamy hue, feeling the almost irresistible pull of the necklace. He wanted to own it as he had never wanted anything in his life. He couldn't afford to buy it. The piece had to be worth a small fortune, and even if he had that much money, he didn't believe the owner would sell it.

He would have to steal it, then dispense with its owner — a thought so appalling he couldn't believe it had crossed his mind.

And yet the necklace tempted him, drew him, compelled him toward the dark side of his soul.

Greg smiled and shook his head. He might not be a saint, but he was not a thief, nor a murderer. He slipped the necklace back into its red satin pouch and returned it to the safe in the wall of his cabin. They belonged to the man who called himself Robert McCabe, though Greg didn't believe for an instant that was his actual name.

Perhaps McCabe would be unable to raise the funds he needed within the three days after they arrived that he had been allotted. If so, the necklace would no longer be his and Greg could claim possession of the fabulous string of diamonds and pearls.

He sighed into the quiet inside his cabin. It wasn't going to happen. There wasn't a moneylender alive who would refuse a loan against such an exquisite piece of jewelry. He would have to be satisfied with the extra money he would earn from McCabe for the delayed payment of his passage.

Greg closed the safe, locking the necklace safely inside, and tried to ignore the odd feeling of loss once the jewelry had disappeared out of his sight.

Dani had been back in London two days, barely long enough to unpack her things, with Caro's help, in the duchess's suite adjoining that of the duke.

Just two days, and her safe world had already begun to fall apart.

First Rafe's mother had appeared, marching in from the dowager's apartments in a separate building on the east side of Sheffield House, a look of fury on her face. She found her son and daughter-in-law in the two-story library that served as Rafe's study and stormed in his direction, stopping directly in front of him.

She planted her hands on her hips. "I cannot believe you didn't tell me!" She shook a finger in Rafael's face, completely unruffled by the slight stiffening of the considerable breadth of his shoulders. "You could have said something before you simply hied off to America, leaving nothing but a very brief note! If it hadn't been for your friends, Lord and Lady Belford, I might have been taken completely unawares when you returned with the bride you abandoned five years ago!"

Rafe had the grace to flush. He made his mother an extravagant bow. "I apologize, Mother. At the time, things seemed to spiral rather rapidly out of control. I'm grateful Ethan and Grace came to see you."

"As am I. You can't imagine how worried I was. Then Ethan explained about Jonas McPhee and how the man had discovered the truth of what happened that night with Oliver Randall."

Rafe's jaw tightened. "Randall has been dealt with."

"I am aware of that, as well, thanks to Cord and Victoria."

"Then you know all there is to know of the affair and that Danielle was completely innocent of any misconduct that night."

The duchess sniffed. "I scarcely know all. I will expect a full accounting of what took place once you reached Philadelphia. Considering that it was known Danielle was to wed another man, I imagine the story will be quite entertaining."

Rafe looked uncomfortable but made no reply, and Dani thought he would probably tell his mother very little of what transpired.

"At any rate," the dowager said, "I suppose knowing the truth of Danielle's innocence is all that matters."

Rafe settled an arm protectively at Dani's waist. "Exactly. And even more important is the fact I am returned with a wife. Soon we'll have our nursery filled, as is your greatest wish."

The dowager smiled brilliantly, but the unexpected words hit Dani like a blow. For weeks, she had refused to think of the lie by omission she had told, the secret she should have revealed but didn't. At the time, it seemed rightful punishment for the pain Rafael had inflicted.

Five years ago, the man had discarded her as if she were a piece of rubbish. He had forced her to live in exile with a broken heart that took years to mend and never gave it a second thought. When he had coerced her into a marriage she did not want, she'd felt he was getting no more than he deserved.

Now that she was returned to England, guilt assailed her. Rafael was a duke and as his wife it was her responsibility to provide him with an heir. It wasn't going to happen, and dear God, she was terrified of what he would do if he ever discovered her deceit.

Dear Lord, the fall she had suffered at Wycombe Park had left her unable to bear him a child. Sooner or later, the fact she was barren was bound to surface. She had hoped that after years of her failing to conceive, Rafe would simply believe that something was wrong between them and accept what could not be.

Her stomach was squeezing even as the duchess finished the lecture she directed at her son.

"You are completely right, of course," she conceded. "You are wed and that is the only thing of importance." She turned the warmth of her smile on Dani. "Welcome to our family, my dear. After what happened, I never thought to say it, but I am extremely glad the past has been set to rights and things have turned out as they have."

Dani received a brief hug that she returned. "Thank you, Your Grace."

Her mother-in-law's smile went even wider. "Now that you both are home at last, as soon as you are settled in, we shall have a gala — a lavish ball to celebrate your marriage."

Rafe had asked if Dani wished to be married again once they reached England, a large, very proper wedding to announce to the world that she was his duchess, but Danielle had firmly declined. She wasn't all that certain about her return to society, and slowly easing into the stream of things seemed a far better approach.

A ball didn't really appeal to her, either,

but she could see by the look on her mother-in-law's face that the woman was determined, and perhaps it was necessary, a means of putting the record straight once and for all.

"I think that's a fine idea, Mother," Rafe said. "I'll leave the details to you . . . if that is agreeable with my wife."

"Of course." Having never been much for society, not even before The Scandal, Danielle was relieved. "I've been away so long I wouldn't know where to begin."

"Then it's settled," the dowager said. "Just leave everything to me."

Dani made it through that first day in her palatial new home, but she was exhausted by the time she retired upstairs to the big four-poster bed in the duchess's suite. Rafael did not join her and she was surprised to discover that she missed his presence beside her. She missed his passionate lovemaking, which she had grown accustomed to each night.

More visitors arrived at the house the following day, three women in a flurry of winter gowns and fur-lined cloaks. It was the first day of November, the days growing shorter and colder, a damp morning mist filling the air.

Danielle had met Rafe's best friends

during their betrothal five years ago: Cord Easton, Earl of Brant and Captain Ethan Sharpe, now the Marquess of Belford. The women who arrived at her doorstep were Cord's and Ethan's wives, Victoria Easton and Grace Sharpe, along with Claire Chezwick, Victoria's sister.

Grace was auburn-haired, a slender, spirited young woman with a warm, sincere smile. Victoria was shorter, with chestnut hair and a slightly more voluptuous figure. Claire was . . . well, Claire was unlike anyone Dani had ever met. With her long, silver-blond hair and cornflower-blue eyes, she was stunningly beautiful, and yet she didn't seem to know it.

"We are all so happy to meet you at last!" Grace said, coming forward and enveloping her in a hug she didn't expect. "I knew the moment I saw you that you were the perfect woman for Rafael."

Dani's russet eyebrows went up. "How could you possibly know that?"

Grace just smiled. "Because I have never seen the duke look at a woman the way he looked at you. For an instant, I thought he might end up a pile of cinders."

Dani laughed. She couldn't help it. Whatever other problems they faced, in the marriage bed they burned.

"I think I am going to like you, Grace Sharpe."

"We're going to be great friends — all of us. Just wait and see."

Dani hoped so. She liked Victoria Easton — Tory, she called herself, and with her sweet naïveté, there wasn't a person alive who could dislike Claire.

They were enjoying tea and biscuits in the China Room, a high-ceilinged chamber with great columns of black-and-gold marble. With its thick Persian carpets, cinnabar vases and Oriental-style gilt-and-lacquer furnishings, it was the most elegant room in the house.

Tory took a sip from her gold-rimmed porcelain teacup and set it back down in its saucer. "Rafe's mother says she is going to host a ball — a very lavish ball — in celebration of your wedding. She has asked for our help in planning it. She wants us to make certain she doesn't leave out any of your friends."

The smile on Dani's face slid away. "I'm afraid I don't have many friends . . . not after The Scandal. Even if they are willing to claim me now that I am married to the duke, I am no longer interested in claiming them."

"I don't blame you," Tory said, sitting a little straighter on the sofa. "There is a difference between a true friend and an acquaintance. We will include your acquaintances and make them wish they had been wise enough to appreciate the friendship they so easily discarded."

Claire's amazing blue eyes widened. "Oh, dear — what about your husbands? They didn't believe Danielle, either."

Both Grace and Tory looked at each other and Tory bit back a grin. "Leave it to my sister to baldly tell the truth."

"They are both extremely sorry, Danielle," Grace said. "They just felt so awful for Rafael. He suffered terribly, you know. According to Ethan, it changed him completely."

He *was* different. But Danielle did not believe for a moment it had anything to do with her. "He is older, that is all. A bit more reserved." She didn't believe Rafe had suffered. If he had cared for her in the least, he would have read her letters, would have listened when she tried to explain.

"If the earl and marquess are sorry," Claire continued, picking up her train of thought, "perhaps other of your friends will feel the same."

"Claire is right," Grace said. "Perhaps you should consider forgiving them, as you did Rafael."

But she hadn't truly forgiven Rafe. Not completely. He had said back then that he loved her. If that had been true, he would have believed in her innocence, would have defended her against her accusers.

She did not, however, say that to her newly made friends.

"There is no need to consider any of that now," Tory said gently. "At the moment, Danielle needs a chance to get used to being Rafael's wife."

"It is rather daunting," Dani admitted. "Now that we're back in London, I am expected to play the role of duchess. There was a time I was prepared, but that is no longer true."

"Things will fall into place," Grace assured her. "It is only a matter of time."

"And I'm sure you have a great deal to do," Tory said, setting her teacup and saucer down on the black lacquered table in front of her. "Which is our cue, ladies, to leave."

Grace and Claire both rose from their seats. "There is just one last thing. . . ." Grace said.

"Yes . . . ?"

"We were wondering . . . You see, once a week, the three of us meet at my house to do a bit of stargazing. We were hoping you might join us. I have the most marvelous telescope for viewing the heavens, a recent gift from Ethan, and another that is smaller but also very good. Studying the stars is a longtime hobby of mine."

"Grace has been teaching us the names of the constellations," Claire said brightly, "and the ancient Greek myths that go with them. You can't believe how beautiful the sky is through Grace's wondrous lens."

"You don't have to feel obligated," Grace hurriedly added. "We just thought . . . well, we hoped you might be interested."

Dani felt a curl of warmth spread out inside her. As she had said, since The Scandal, she had very few friends. "I should love to join you. Thank you so much for asking me."

"We are meeting Thursday next," Grace said. "Quite often, the men come as well, though they usually spirit themselves off to Ethan's study for a brandy or two. Rafe is more than welcome to come with you."

"Thank you. I'll tell him."

The women left the house, and at last Danielle was alone. It seemed her life was gaining some semblance of normality. Perhaps in time, things would work out.

At least so she thought until three weeks later — the day Cord Easton showed up at the house carrying her wedding gift in one of his big hands.

The dazzling string of diamonds and pearls called the Bride's Necklace.

Eighteen

A fire burned in the dark green marble hearth in the corner of the big two-story library that also served as Rafe's study. Rafe had been standing with his back to the blaze when his silver-haired butler, Wooster, arrived to announce a visitor, and Cord had walked into the room.

His friend had joined him in front of the fire and both men stood there now, warming themselves against the chill outside the house, Rafe holding the incredible strand of pearls interspersed with diamonds Cord had draped across his palm.

"I never thought I'd see it again," Rafe said, admiring the perfection of the exquisite piece of jewelry.

"Amazing, isn't it?"

"Incredible. Tell me again how you found it."

"I didn't find it. It found me. A money-lender in Liverpool sent me a message. As you know, from time to time, I collect exceptional items, mostly art and sculpture, but occasionally a piece of jewelry, something I think Victoria might like. I've made purchases from this particular dealer before. He has a very good reputation in the antiquities trade."

Rafe kept a tight rein on the emotions rolling through him, the doubts that kept creeping in. "So he sent you a note describing the necklace."

Cord nodded. "It wasn't actually for sale. The man who borrowed against it would, of course, have thirty days in which to redeem his merchandise, but the dealer didn't really believe he would be back. You'd told me the piece was stolen, so my interest was piqued. As I had some business dealings in that part of the country, I traveled there last week."

"And the dealer was willing to sell?"

"Once I convinced him the necklace was stolen property, he was happy to take the very large sum that I paid him for it. I knew you would want it, no matter the cost."

"I'll have my solicitor send you a bank draft."

"Which I'll gladly accept as I've already purchased the damned thing two times before."

Recalling the journey on which the necklace had led his friend, and the wife Cord had acquired because of it, Rafe almost smiled. Instead, he continued to stare at the necklace, watching the way it seemed to glow with an odd light in the blaze of the fire.

"Danielle believed the thief stole it the day we left Philadelphia. She thought it must have been one of the servants in the house where she and her aunt were living. But if you found it in Liverpool, it must have disappeared after she boarded the ship."

"Perhaps one of the crewmen took it from Danielle's baggage before it reached your cabin."

His fingers smoothed over the pearls. "If that is so, how did it wind up in Liverpool when the ship docked in London?" He glanced up. "Did the antiquities dealer give you a description of the man?"

Cord drew a folded piece of paper from the pocket of his waistcoat. "I figured you'd want to know. I wrote down what he said."

Rafe opened the paper and read the description aloud. "Brown hair, brown eyes, slightly taller than average." He glanced up. "It says here that by the way the man was dressed and his manner of speaking, the dealer believed he was a member of the upper classes."

"That's what he said."

"Not a crewman, then."

"Apparently not." Cord looked uncomfortable.

"Now tell me what you have left out."

Cord muttered something beneath his breath. They'd been friends too long to try to keep secrets. "The shopkeeper said his female employees were in a dither over the fellow. Apparently he was extremely good-looking."

Rafe fought to ignore a thread of doubt and an unwelcome surge of jealousy. His long fingers closed around the pearls. "I want this man found. I want to know how he got hold of the necklace and I want him punished for stealing it."

"Then I take it you intend to hire McPhee."

He nodded. "If anyone can find him, Jonas can." Rafe walked over and sat down behind his desk.

Replacing the pearls in their satin pouch, he set them down gently on the polished surface, then pulled out a piece of foolscap. Reaching for the white-plumed pen, he dipped it in the crystal inkwell and scratched out a note to Jonas, dried it with the help of the sand shaker, then sealed it with a drop of wax.

"I'll have one of the footmen deliver it," he said, holding up the note as he returned to where Cord stood by the fire. "I want McPhee to get started as soon as possible."

"What will Danielle say?" Cord asked.

Rafe felt a tightening in his chest. "I'm not telling her just yet. Not until I know how all of this came about."

Having had his own marital problems in the past, Cord made no reply.

Rafe just prayed his instincts were wrong and Danielle had told him the truth. But uncertainty gnawed at his insides as he carried the note out of the study, and his worry continued to build.

A chill December wind whipped the naked branches on the trees and stirred dry leaves against the plaster walls of the whitewashed cottage. Beneath the heavy thatched roof, a fire crackled in the hearth, warming the cozy, low-ceilinged interior.

Seated in a comfortable chair not far from the blaze, Robert McKay sipped a glass of whisky. On the sofa across from him, his cousin, Stephen Lawrence, finished his drink and stood up to retrieve another.

"Shall I freshen yours, as well?"

Robert shook his head. He swirled the amber liquid in his glass. "I still can't believe it. It's so entirely incredible."

Stephen refilled his drink, replaced the

stopper on the bottle and returned to his seat. He was five years older than Robert, average in height with a solid, compact body. He had the same brown hair, but the hazel eyes were a legacy of his mother, Robert's aunt.

"Incredible, but true," Stephen said. "It took a year after you left the country for my mother to come forward. Once she did, eventually it all became clear."

"In your letter, you said a man named Clifford Nash murdered the Earl of Leighton — the man I was supposed to have killed."

"That's right."

"And you believe the earl was my father."

"Not just your father, my friend. Your *legitimate* father. Nigel Truman married your mother in old St. Margaret's Church in the village of Fenwick-on-Hand, six months before you were born. My mother stood witness to the event. According to her, Nigel and Joan had been seeing each other for several years, whenever he spent time at his father's country estate. They fell in love and when he got her with child, he married her. Of course, his father was still alive, so he wasn't yet earl at the time."

"My mother was always so secretive about my father. She told me his name was also Robert McKay and that he was dead, killed in the war. She said his family sent the money we lived on, that they paid for my education. I never met any of them, though. My mother said they hadn't approved of her marriage."

"Robert McKay, the man you were named for, was a former suitor who remained your mother's friend even after she wed the earl, a marriage which was recognized only briefly. The earl and countess were extremely unhappy with their son's choice of bride, your mother being a commoner, so they paid her to keep silent in the matter."

"I never thought of my mother as particularly interested in money."

"According to what *my* mother said, it wasn't just the money. Any number of threats were made against her, including your possible disappearance, I gather. The Earl of Leighton was an extremely powerful man. He forced his son to return to London, and eventually he married a woman acceptable to the family."

"But according to Aunt Charlotte, they never had children."

"Correct. Which, as long as you remained out of the picture, put Clifford Nash, a distant cousin, in line for the title."

"Which clearly explains his motive in the

murder and also the reason he wanted it to appear as if I were the one who killed the earl."

"Exactly so," Stephen said. "As I recall, you received a note, supposedly from Molly Jameson, the widow you had been seeing."

"That's right."

"I don't know what part Molly played in the affair, but it is now apparent Clifford Nash was behind the note."

Robert remembered the intended rendezvous only too well. He had received a message from the young widow he had been involved with for nearly a year, asking him to meet her at a coaching inn called the Boar and Hen on the road to London. It was farther away than the usual places she chose for their assignations, but he figured perhaps she had been in the city and was staying there on her way home.

Even after he opened the door to the chamber above the taproom that should have been hers and heard the sound of a pistol being fired, it didn't occur to him that he would be accused of murder.

The dead man — who turned out to be the Earl of Leighton — had clutched his bloody chest and crumpled at Robert's feet.

"What the hell . . . ?" Robert had stared dumbfounded, the acrid smell of gunpowder burning his nose. He looked up to see a man emerging from the shadows, felt the butt of the still-smoking pistol pressed into his hand. The man turned and fled through the window, out onto the roof, and a dozen people surged up the outside stairs.

Robert stood dazed as the door flew open and a big, bearded man rushed in.

"Look! The bastard's murdered the earl!"

Robert dropped the gun.

"Get him!" yelled a smaller man wielding a knife.

There was bloodlust in their eyes and Robert did the only thing he could think of — bolted for the window and disappeared over the rooftop, just as the killer had done.

In the chaos that followed, he was able to retrieve his horse, swing himself up on the animal's back and ride like a madman off into the darkness.

His only possessions were the few shillings in his pocket and the horse beneath him. If they caught him, he was certain to hang. Robert headed for London, desperate to find a means of escape.

Now, sitting in front of the fire, he shifted in his seat and the memory faded. He took a swallow of his brandy. "So Nash killed the earl for his title and fortune. How do you suppose he found out about me?"

"I'm not quite certain. The vicar and his wife have both passed away. My mother knew the truth, of course, but she had also received money from Lord Leighton and been threatened if she should speak. My guess is that your father told Nash."

Robert set up a little straighter in his chair. "Why would he do that?"

"I imagine because Nash believed he was the heir. Perhaps Leighton felt he owed the man the truth."

"An unfortunate move, it would seem."

"Indeed. I think there is a very good chance the earl was on his way to find you when he was killed."

Robert snorted a laugh. "And he had waited but twenty-seven years."

"He was married to the daughter of a peer, an illegal marriage to be sure, but one he apparently felt obliged to uphold. From what I could discover, Elizabeth Truman died four years ago. I think that is the reason the earl decided to find you."

Robert mulled over his cousin's words. Stephen had been a friend to him in his youth. Over the years, that friendship had slipped away, but after the murder, after Robert had arrived safely in America, he had written to his cousin, explaining what had happened, professing his innocence and asking him for help.

Stephen had immediately set to work. Once his mother came forward, he began to turn up other bits of information that had finally led to the truth of Robert's birth and the reason for Clifford Nash's attempt to see him hanged.

"It would have all been so neat and tidy," Stephen said, "if you had not escaped from the inn that night. You would have been hanged for certain, and there would have been no chance of the fact ever coming to light that you were the earl's rightful heir."

I am an earl. And not just any earl, but the powerful Earl of Leighton. "If they find me, I may yet hang."

"You must be careful, Robert."

"You're certain there is proof I'm the earl's legitimate son?"

"My mother is still alive and apparently the records at St. Margaret's still exist. I don't think Nash knows where the marriage took place, or by now they would probably have disappeared."

Robert stretched his long legs out in front of him. He was an earl, not merely a solicitor working for wealthy squires who owned property near Guildford, where he had lived. As the Earl of Leighton, he would have plenty of money — more than enough to pay off his indenture contract and the debt he owed on the necklace.

Even if he couldn't retrieve the valuable pearls from the moneylender within the grace period, he could buy them from whoever might purchase them. He could return the necklace to the duchess with his head held high.

And he could see Caro again.

The thought filled him with a painful longing. Robert had known any number of women. He liked them, felt comfortable with them. But he had never known a woman with the sweet, gentle nature he had discovered in Caroline Loon. From the start, she had compelled him to confide in her, then sincerely believed in his innocence.

Caro had a way of seeing inside a man, of uncovering the person he really was. Her goodness spilled onto the people around her, touched them as it had touched him. He had missed her more than he could have imagined and he desperately wanted to see her again.

He glanced over at his cousin, whose hazel eyes reflected the light of the fire. "So how do we prove Clifford Nash is the man who killed the earl?"

Stephen peered at him over his whisky

glass. "Nash or whomever he hired. And finding proof won't be easy."

"You said Nash is living in London. Perhaps I should travel there —"

"You must stay away from the city at all costs, Robert. You've been gone three years. Nash must continue to believe you have either died or left the country. If he has the slightest suspicion that you are in England, that you have even an inkling of what he has done, you are truly a dead man."

Robert's jaw tightened. He wasn't a fool. He didn't want to die, but Caro was in London. If he could just see her one more time . . . Perhaps he would discover he was wrong, that she was no different from any other woman, that his feelings for her had changed.

Even if he tried, Robert couldn't make himself believe it.

"Are you hearing me, Robert? In this, you must heed my words. Let me continue my efforts, see what more I can find out. Stay here, Robert, where you are safe."

Robert nodded, knowing his cousin was right. But it was difficult to sit and do nothing. He wasn't sure how much longer he could continue.

Danielle sat before the dresser in her bedchamber, trying to work up the courage for another tedious supper with Rafael, who would politely withdraw to his study the moment the meal was over. For the past two weeks, he had been so distant, so strangely remote. It was as if they had never spent those weeks together aboard the ship.

Danielle sighed. It bothered her, and yet part of her was glad. As long as Rafe remained aloof, her heart was not in danger.

Which was exactly the way she wanted it — wasn't it?

She glanced up at a light knock on her door. Caro hurried in as she always did, filling the room with her bright presence.

"It is getting late, past time you dressed for supper. Have you decided what you wish to wear?"

"How about something in black? That will certainly match my mood." Though she and Rafael were now man and wife, of late, she rarely saw him. He had come to her bed only a very few times, and even when they made love, he remained strangely withdrawn.

"It is the duke, is it not?" Caro's voice broke into her thoughts. "He has been terribly remote of late."

"That is putting it kindly. He is as he was the night I first saw him at the Widows and

Orphans ball. I remember thinking that he had become the politely bored, aloof sort of man who wouldn't attract me a'tall."

"He has certainly been acting peculiar. I feel as if I am walking in a tiger's cage whenever I pass by him. On the surface he seems calm, but underneath he is a big cat crouched and ready to spring."

It was true, and Danielle had the most ridiculous urge to prod him into losing his tight control. She looked over her shoulder at the armoire in the corner.

"I think, perhaps, I would like to wear the emerald satin, the one with the very low décolletage." After her return to London, at the dowager's insistence, she had been fitted with an entire new wardrobe.

"You are the Duchess of Sheffield," her mother-in-law had said. "It is time you dressed the part."

Except for the tiresome fittings, wearing the lovely new morning dresses, day dresses and evening gowns she had acquired was scarcely a hardship.

Walking over to the armoire, Caro retrieved the gown and laid it out on the amber counterpane on top of the big four poster bed. The furnishings were ivory and gilt, the draperies a very soft gold. It was a lovely, feminine room that Rafe's mother had refurbished for the woman who would one day become his bride.

Caro looked down at the gown, surveyed the daring décolletage, and one of her pale blond eyebrows arched up. "If you wear this, I hope the dowager will not be joining the two of you for supper."

Dani went over to examine the gown. The satin bodice was designed to drape low over her breasts, exposing a great deal of her bosom. The narrow satin skirt was split nearly to the knee and trimmed with fine gold embroidery in a Grecian design.

"The duchess has plans for the evening," Dani said, her fingers running over the slick texture of the satin. "Let us see if Rafael can maintain his annoying distance while I am wearing this."

Caro laughed. She busied herself fetching the rest of Danielle's garments, her chemise, stockings and garters, a pair of emerald kid slippers, but as the minutes ticked past, her expression began to change.

Dani had seen that unhappy look far too often lately. "What is it, dearest?" But she already knew the answer.

Caro sank down on the four-poster bed, her narrow shoulders slumping. "It's Robert. I can't stop thinking about him, Dani. First I worry if he is safe, then I think that perhaps it was all a lie and he never cared a whit for me, that he only pretended to love me so that I would help him get the money he wanted."

She flashed Danielle an agonized glance and tears welled in her eyes. "I gave him your beautiful necklace. If he wanted money, he succeeded far better than he ever could have planned."

Danielle's heart went out to her friend. There was no way to know the truth. Dani couldn't help wondering if Caro would ever see the man she loved again.

"You mustn't give up hope. You had faith in him once, and you are no fool."

Caro wiped her eyes, dragged in a shaky breath. "You are right, of course." As if to push aside the painful thoughts, she tossed her head, ruffling her pale blond curls. "I'm sorry. I know it is foolish, but I miss him so very much."

Dani took her friend's fine-boned hand. "You mustn't fret, dearest. In time, it will all work out."

Caro just nodded. Her gaze returned to the emerald satin gown and she smiled. "In the meantime, perhaps one of us can improve her wretched mood."

Moving closer to the bed, Dani picked up the daringly low-cut gown she had purchased on a whim when she was being fitted for her new wardrobe.

"I think I shall leave my hair down," Dani said, reaching up to remove one of the pins holding it in place.

Caro rolled her eyes. "I wish I could be a fly on the wall."

Dani stared down at the dress, watching the way the lamplight flickered over the lustrous satin, shimmered on the Grecian designs sewn in fine gold thread. "Perhaps tonight will prove a bit more interesting than the past week has been."

Caro looked at Dani, and both of them grinned.

Nineteen

Dressed in a burgundy tailcoat and dove-gray breeches, Rafe waited till the last possible moment before descending the wide marble staircase on his way to supper. As per his request, the meal would be served in the sumptuous State Dining Room, where he and Danielle would be seated at a long, inlaid rosewood table lined with twenty-four chairs.

The moldings overhead were gilt and ornately carved. Three crystal chandeliers hung over the table, and a fire burned in the huge gilt-and-marble fireplace set into one wall.

Though Rafe generally preferred the more intimate atmosphere of the Yellow Salon where they could eat more casually, after Cord's visit he had ordered their meals be served in here.

Though he hadn't gone as far as to seat Danielle at the opposite end of the table, the room itself had a way of keeping things formal, less personal, and until he knew the truth of what had happened to the necklace, he refused to become any more deeply involved with her than he was already.

Rafe stood at the bottom of the stairs, awaiting Danielle's appearance so that he might escort her into the dining room, trying not to think of the necklace and what its disappearance might mean. Though he didn't blame his wife for the loss, he wished she had come to him, had trusted him enough to confide in him.

And deep down, he was fairly certain the story she had told him was not entirely the truth.

As he checked the time on the ornate grandfather clock in the entry, Rafael sighed. Danielle wasn't the naive young woman he had fallen in love with five years ago. She was a different person now, one he didn't really know. He wasn't about to let down his guard and risk himself until he knew the truth about the necklace.

The soft sound of footfalls on the carpet drew his attention to the top of the landing. He looked up to see Danielle beginning her descent down the sweeping marble stairs.

For an instant, he simply stared. In an elegant gown of emerald satin, she looked a vision, a goddess fallen to earth. Desire hit him hard, and his groin tightened with painful force. His shaft sprang to life, and though he clamped down on the need spreading through him, as she drew closer, it was all he could do not to climb the stairs, sweep her into his arms and carry her off to his bed.

Instead he stood statue-still in the entry, staring at her like a callow schoolboy. She had worn her hair loose tonight, as she rarely did, clipping it back on the sides with inlaid pearl combs, leaving a heavy mass of deep red curls to tumble down her back. He remembered the silky feel of those curls against his skin when they made love, and heat sank into his loins.

Danielle reached his side and smiled up at him. "I am exceedingly hungry tonight. How about you?"

His mouth went dry. His eyes raked her, came to rest on the lush swells of her bosom, revealed far too clearly beneath the low-cut bodice of her gown. "Of a sudden, I am feeling an incredible hunger myself."

The soft satin molded to the plump mounds and the shadowy valley between them, and he wanted to rip the gown off her shoulders, to reveal those luscious breasts and take them into his mouth.

"Shall we go into supper?" he asked mildly.

"Oh, yes, please." She took his arm and in

the process pressed one of those luscious breasts against his arm. The muscles across his belly contracted and he barely suppressed a groan.

In the dining room, he seated her to his right, then took his place at the head of the table. Though he had chosen this very room so that he could keep his distance, she now seemed too far away.

"I spoke to Cook earlier," Dani said. "I believe tonight we are having roast goose."

Rafe looked at her, felt a sharp jolt of lust and thought that indeed his goose was cooked tonight. Danielle had always been a temptation he couldn't resist, and there was no way he could resist her this evening. In truth, if it weren't for the footmen stationed against the wall to serve the meal, he would shove the damnable dishes onto the floor and take her in the middle of the table.

She flipped a lock of flame-red hair over her shoulder and leaned forward to settle herself more comfortably in the high-backed chair. For an instant, the gown draped open and he thought that he glimpsed the rosy crest of a nipple. Surely not, he told himself, but it didn't really matter. The image had arisen and it remained, seared like a fiery brand into his brain.

"I think I should like a glass of wine," she said, and one of the footmen rushed forward to fill her heavy crystal goblet. As the young man poured the wine, Danielle drew her napkin from its ornate gold ring and moved to place it across her lap. The footman's furtive glance strayed to her lovely bosom, and Rafe nearly came out of his chair.

He wanted to toss the youth bodily out of the dining room, wanted to haul him up by his blue satin livery and punch him in the face.

Rafe forced himself to take a breath and release it slowly. The lad was only human, for God's sake. And Rafe wasn't a fool. He remembered only too well where his overwhelming jealousy had led him the last time. If he hadn't been so passionately in love with Danielle, so wildly jealous, he would have listened to her that night, instead of destroying five years of their lives.

It was a mistake he would never make again and the reason he worked so hard to contain his emotions, nearly an impossible task when it came to Danielle.

The meal continued, each course more delectable than the last. It all tasted like sawdust to Rafe, who couldn't get his mind off Danielle and what he might do to her once the damnable, lengthy meal was over.

"How is the ball progressing?" he asked

blandly, careful to keep his tone even.

"Your mother has set the date for a week from Friday. Parliament will not yet be reconvened, so there won't be as many people in town as there would be after the first of the year, but she is eager to see us returned to society."

"My mother likes you very much. She always has."

"She loathed me for more than five years."

He shrugged his shoulders. "She is a mother, protective of her only son."

"She believed I had hurt you. Did I?"

His chest tightened as the awful memories swept in. "Gravely."

Dani looked away and he thought that she might not believe him. Perhaps it was better that way.

They turned to safer subjects, talked about the bitterly cold December weather, spoke of some inane article in the morning paper, made bland, boring conversation when what he wanted to do was drag her out of her chair and haul her into his bed. Every time he shifted in his chair, his arousal pressed painfully against the front of his breeches, and inwardly he cursed.

A footman arrived just then and they turned their attention to the cherry tarts the young man set on the table in front of them. A single, stemmed cherry perched in a pile of creamy custard in the center of each tart.

Danielle took the stem daintily between her fingers and lifted the cherry from its nest. Tilting her head back, she licked off the drop of custard that clung to the bottom.

Rafe's spoon paused in midair.

Danielle used her tongue to lick the cherry again, then slowly slid the fruit between her full, ruby lips.

Rafe's spoon clattered back down on his dish and he shoved back his chair. "I believe, madam, we are finished with dessert."

Eyes wide, Danielle looked up at him. "What are you talking about?"

Rafe caught her hand and hauled her to her feet. "You want dessert — I believe I have just the thing." Sliding an arm beneath her knees, he lifted her against his chest and started striding toward the door of the dining room, leaving a stunned pair of footmen in his wake.

Danielle slid her arms around his neck to steady herself. "What . . . what on earth are you doing?"

"I think you know. If you don't, I'll be happy to show you as soon as we reach my bed."

Her hold on his neck went tighter, but he didn't think she was afraid. A sharp jolt of lust sank into his groin, and he thought that perhaps she should be.

Danielle tightened her hold on Rafe's neck. She bit back a squeak of alarm as he opened his bedchamber door, carried her inside, then kicked the door closed with his foot.

Just inside the door, he set her on her feet, bent his head, and his mouth crushed down over hers. For an instant, her mind spun.

Dear God, I have unleashed a tiger, she thought. *Now what should I do?*

But she couldn't seem to think with Rafe kissing her senseless, with his tongue in her mouth, and his hard body molded against her. And there was all of this heat rushing through her, sending rational thought right out the window.

Easing her backward against the door, he skillfully popped several buttons at the back of her gown, which gaped open, giving him access to her breasts. He dipped his head, and she felt his mouth there, felt the scrape of his teeth against her nipple. A surge of heat dropped into her stomach and unconsciously, she arched toward him.

Rafe caught the hem of her emerald-satin

gown and he began to slide his hand up her skirt. The satin felt cool and slick against her skin and she started to tremble.

"I want you," he said against the side of her neck. "Right here. Right now." For an instant, his gaze caught hers, locked and held. His expression was no longer cool, no longer remote. The heat of desire glittered in those very blue eyes and his jaw was set with determination.

Dani gasped as Rafe's mouth claimed hers in a deep, scorching kiss that sent hot shivers down her spine. He bunched the gown around her waist, and beneath the lacy edge of her chemise his fingers found her softness, began to stroke her.

She was wet and hot and trembling. This was what she wanted, she realized, the reason she had purchased the nearly indecent gown. She had no use for Rafe's cool indifference; she wanted him hard and needy, pulsing with desire for her.

As she pulsed for him.

He settled one long leg between both of hers and lifted her a little. For a moment she rode his thigh, the rough material of his breeches rubbing sensually against her feminine flesh. Heat tore through her, settled in her core.

She reached toward him, began to unfasten the buttons on the front of his breeches, heard Rafe groan. He finished the job for her, freed himself, and she wrapped her fingers around him. He was a big man, thick and hard, fiercely aroused. Dani whimpered as he eased her legs apart, lifted her and drove himself home.

The pleasure swept through her, sank into her, filtered out through her limbs.

Rafe's big hands cupped her bottom, holding her in place to receive his penetrating thrusts, and a powerful scorching need curled inside her. One of his hands fisted in her hair and he kissed her deeply, even as he continued the heavy strokes that pleasured them both.

"Let yourself go," he commanded in that deep voice of his, and her body obeyed, bursting free, soaring, soaring. . . .

A few minutes later, Rafe followed her to release, his muscles tightening, a growl caught low in his throat.

Seconds ticked past and they remained as they were, Rafe's hard length inside her, her arms entwined around his neck.

Then he eased himself from her and stepped away, drew the skirt of her satin gown down over her hips.

"I didn't hurt you, did I?"

She shook her head. "No, you didn't hurt

me." Hardly. Her entire body still hummed with pleasure.

Rafe looked away. He had lost control and it was obvious he wasn't pleased about it. He fastened the buttons of the front of his breeches, one by one. "It's early yet," he said calmly. "I think I'll pay a visit to my club."

It was scarcely what she expected after such a fierce round of lovemaking. Fighting an urge to ask him to stay, Dani forced herself to reply in the same unaffected manner.

"I'm enjoying a very good book. I think I shall read for a while before I go to sleep."

They sounded so urbane, so civilized, when only moments ago they were both in the wild throes of passion.

Rafe made a polite nod of his head. "Good night, then."

"Good night." She watched him walk out of the bedchamber and wanted to scream. She wanted to throw something, wanted to shout, wanted to rail at him, and she didn't really understand why.

Instead she took a deep breath, turned and walked through the connecting door into her suite. Heading for the bell pull, she rang for a bath, hoping the hot water would soothe her nerves as, for a while, her husband's lovemaking had done.

Wishing Rafael had not decided to leave.

★ ★ ★

Final planning for the ball went into high gear. Everyone helped, even Aunt Flora, who had decided to remain in London for the next several weeks instead of returning to her home in the country.

"Even if Caro traveled with me," her aunt had said, "it would be lonely without you, my dear. And if I stay, I can continue my work with the orphanage."

"It would be wonderful if you stayed, Aunt Flora. And I would love to help with the children." A cause that had become Danielle's, as well.

She and Aunt Flora visited the orphanage at least twice a week, and for Christmastide, planned to give each child a gift. Unlike other institutions in the city, children of the Widows and Orphans Society wore decent clothing and always had enough to eat.

Maida Ann and little Terry had become especially dear, though each time she held them, Dani felt a pang of regret that she would never have a child of her own. She wished she could speak to Rafael about them, convince him to let her bring them home with her for good, but Rafe was expecting children of his own and the fear that he might discover her dark secret kept her from broaching the subject.

At last, the night of the ball arrived.

Sheffield House, one of the largest, most palatial homes in London, had a magnificent ballroom that covered the entire third story of the east wing of the house. The floor-to-ceiling mirrored walls reflected the glow of hundreds of beeswax candles burning in silver candelabras, and huge crystal chandeliers glittered overhead.

The guests were soon to arrive, and Danielle's nerves had begun to build. Gossip about the Duke of Sheffield's marriage to the woman he had jilted was on every wagging tongue in London, but fortunately, with their return so recent, the two of them had not often been out in society. After the ball, all of that would change.

Danielle prowled the bedchamber, watching the ormolu clock on the white-and-gold marble mantel, secretly wishing she didn't have to leave the protection of her room. When a knock came at her door, she thought that it must be Caro come to check on her one last time. Instead when she opened the door, the dowager duchess stood in the hallway.

"May I come in?"

"Why, yes, of course, Your Grace." She stepped back out of the way as her dark-haired mother-in-law swept into the bedchamber. Miriam Saunders wore a gown of burgundy silk studded with brilliants. More stones had been woven into the sleek coronet of braids atop her head and they sparkled against the fine streaks of silver in her hair.

Her gaze took in Dani's appearance. "You look lovely, my dear. Every inch the duchess you are."

It was a grand compliment coming from Rafe's mother. "Thank you."

"Rafael is waiting for us. I simply wanted you to know how very happy I am to have you in the family."

She knew she should say how happy she was to be married to Rafe, but the words stuck in her throat. Since the night she had worn the daring emerald satin gown and they had made such passionate love, Rafe had not come to her room. Most nights he went to his club and didn't return until the early hours of the morning.

"Thank you," she replied lamely, pasting a smile on her face.

"There is another reason I came to see you."

"Yes . . . ?"

"The two of you have been married several months now. I thought that perhaps . . . I was hoping there was a chance you might be with child."

A knot squeezed in Dani's chest. She just stood there staring, unable to believe her mother-in-law had broached such a delicate subject.

"I suppose I shouldn't have asked. I'm sure you would have said something yourself. It is just so very important that Rafe have a son."

Dani glanced off toward the window. Having a child had once been her fondest dream, but it wasn't going to happen. She felt the unexpected burn of tears but quickly blinked them away before the dowager could see.

"The answer is no. We've been married several months but . . . much of that time we were simply . . . getting reacquainted." She hoped the woman didn't notice the color creeping into her cheeks. The intimacy she shared with Rafe was hardly a subject she wished to discuss with her mother-in-law.

The duchess merely nodded. "I see. . . . Well, I hope you won't mention my meddling to Rafael. He would not appreciate my interference in his affairs."

Dani wasn't in favor of it, either. At least in this it seemed they were agreed. "I would never repeat what is said in confidence between us, Your Grace."

The dowager nodded, satisfied, it seemed.

"I suppose we had better go downstairs." She flicked Danielle a glance. "And you mustn't worry, dear. I'm sure, in time, everything will all turn out as it should."

But of course it was never going to turn out as it should. She would never bear Rafe a son and his mother would never forgive her.

Danielle ignored a feeling of despair and followed the dark-haired woman out the door. They passed along the corridor beneath the flickering light of a half-dozen gilt sconces and made their way to the head of the stairs.

Rafe paced impatiently at the foot of the stairs. The guests had begun to arrive, and as far as he was concerned, the sooner they got the damned affair under way, the sooner it would be over.

He glanced toward the top of the landing, saw his mother and his wife begin their descent down the sweeping marble staircase. Tonight Danielle wore an elegant sapphire velvet gown, beautifully fitted to her tall, slender frame. A feather plume waved from the fiery red curls pinned up on her head, and her arms were encased in long white gloves.

Though she was dressed not nearly so

provocatively as she had been the night they'd made love, Rafe's heartbeat quickened. The woman drove him mad with lust. No matter how hard he fought it, the desire he felt for her never seemed to wane.

Only the note he had received yesterday afternoon from Jonas McPhee had kept him from her bed last night, as it would again tonight, no matter how much he wanted her.

According to the message, McPhee had found the man who had stolen the Bride's Necklace. He had traveled from America aboard a ship called the *Laurel*, which had docked in Liverpool, where the pearls had been discovered. According to the note, the man had been apprehended.

Late on the morrow, McPhee would have returned to London. He had requested a meeting tomorrow night and Rafe was eager to hear what the man had to say. Though there was little information in the note, the tone seemed ominous to Rafe. He couldn't relax until he knew what had transpired those final days in America before they'd set sail for home.

He looked up to see Danielle walking up beside him and buried the worrisome thoughts.

"You look stunning tonight, Danielle."

He made a very formal bow over her white-gloved hand.

"And you look extraordinarily handsome, Your Grace."

His eyes found hers and he prayed they held no secrets from him, that the feelings for her that continued to grow would not bring him more pain.

"The guests are beginning to arrive," he said. "I suppose it's time we took our places."

She nodded and smiled, but he thought that her smile looked tight. He imagined how difficult it must be to face the people who had treated her so badly five years ago — thanks to him — and his protective instincts took over.

He brushed a light kiss over her lips, then whispered in her ear, "You mustn't worry, love. You're the Duchess of Sheffield — as you should have been five years ago. After tonight, all of London will accept the fact."

She swallowed and looked up at him, and he caught the glimmer of tears the instant before she glanced away.

His resolve strengthened. "I'm right here, sweeting. I'm not going to leave you." *Not ever again* were the words that popped into his head, and in that moment he realized how deeply enamored he was becoming. It frightened him and yet he saw no avenue of escape.

Rafe took a deep breath and braced himself for the long evening ahead.

Twenty

Dani rested her hand on the sleeve of Rafe's dark blue, velvet-collared tailcoat, and his fingers covered hers. He looked so very handsome tonight, his dark hair perfectly combed, his eyes such a vibrant shade of blue. He looked strong, powerful, fearless. But then, he always did.

Ignoring a tremor of awareness as she stood beside him in the receiving line next to the dowager duchess, Danielle squared her shoulders and prepared to face the line of guests streaming into the entry. Halfway down the velvet runner leading up the wide front steps, she spotted Rafe's two best friends and their wives.

A few minutes later, the couples arrived in the huge, marble-floored entry. A massive stained-glass dome rose overhead. Victoria surveyed the guests from a row of ancient Roman busts perched along the wall.

Tory Easton reached over and caught her hand. "I'm so happy for you both."

"Thank you," said Dani.

Ethan and Grace walked in behind them

and repeated the congratulations they had made when they had first heard the news.

"You look wonderful, Danielle," Grace said. "After tonight, you'll be the envy of every woman in London."

"That is kind of you to say," Danielle replied, though she thought more likely her appearance as Rafael's wife would simply be fuel for more gossip.

Grace just smiled. "I can see you don't believe me, but it's true."

She didn't want to be envied. She just wanted to be happy. She looked up at Rafe, saw the bland smile he wore to disguise whatever he was thinking, and bit back an unladylike curse.

"We are meeting again on Thursday night for stargazing," Grace said. "I hope you will join us."

"I had a wonderful time last week. I shall make my very best effort." It had been a marvelous experience and she felt good to be included among Rafe's friends, to feel as if they were becoming her own.

"Your mother has outdone herself," the marquess said to Rafe, his ice-blue eyes surveying the potted topiary cut in the shape of a heart that greeted arrivals in the entry. "This should set the *ton* on its ear."

The receiving rooms of the house and

ballroom had been done to mimic a giant conservatory, with miniature lemon trees, begonias, geraniums and an occasional branch of exotic, white-and-purple orchids. Huge pots of bright pink camellias added more color, and in the ballroom, there was even a small reflecting pool, complete with lily pads and goldfish.

Danielle spoke a moment more to Grace and Victoria, and though Rafe seemed to take it for granted, Danielle was warmed by their friendship and continued support. As the foursome headed up to the ballroom, another handsome couple arrived, the woman blond and fair, the man dark-haired and handsome, and Rafe introduced her to Ethan's sister, Sarah, and her husband, Jonathan Randall, Viscount Aimes.

The stream of guests continued past and Danielle recognized Lord and Lady Percy Chezwick, Victoria's sister and husband, who greeted them warmly then also made their way upstairs.

The minutes had begun to drag by the time Aunt Flora arrived. "I was afraid you had decided not to come," Danielle said, her spirits lifting at the sight of her. "I know you've been feeling a bit under the weather."

"Nonsense. A few aches and pains could

scarcely keep me away from my only niece's wedding celebration." Aunt Flora cast Rafe a glance. "Especially not one so long overdue."

Faint color rose beneath the bones in Rafe's cheeks. "Much too long overdue," he admitted, bowing over her aunt's gloved hand.

It was an elegant gathering that included members of the *ton* who had traveled back to town especially for the occasion. In the ballroom upstairs, an eight-piece orchestra, dressed in Sheffield light blue livery and wearing powdered wigs, began to play, and partygoers drifted in that direction.

Some of the men set off for a game of whist, hazard, or loo, while others made their way into the sumptuous black-and-gilt China Room, where the aroma of roasted meat and fowl, along with a lavish array of exotic foods, drifted in from linen-draped tables.

Dani had to admit Rafe's mother had done an outstanding job. She and Rafe joined guests in the ballroom, and little by little, she began to relax. Dancing first with Rafe, she also danced with Ethan and Cord, then began accepting invitations from other of the men. As good as his word, Rafe stayed close at hand, and his presence made it easier to ignore the occasional whispers, or the faintly raised eyebrow of a matron who glanced her way.

She was dancing with Lord Percy when she saw Rafe disappear from the ballroom with a man dressed in the scarlet uniform of an officer of the British Army.

"Good evening, Your Grace." Colonel Howard Pendleton, a late arrival, walked up to where Rafe stood near the dance floor.

"I'm glad you could make it, Hal."

The colonel sighed. "I needed a bit of a break. It's been a long day."

Rafe arched a dark eyebrow. "Anything to do with the Baltimore Clippers?"

"Everything to do with the bloody damn ships," Hal said, and since he rarely cursed, Rafe knew the news must be bad.

"I'd like to hear it. How about a brandy downstairs in my study?"

"I could certainly use one."

"I'd like Ethan to hear what you have to say."

"Good idea. I think Lord Brant may be interested, as well."

All three men had worked with Pendleton before. Rafe knew Ethan had been made privy to information about the impressive American-built clippers and what might happen if a fleet of them were acquired by the French. Rafe and Cord had also discussed the subject.

Glancing over to where Danielle danced with Percival Chezwick, knowing she was safe in the younger man's hands, he led the way out of the ballroom, pausing only long enough to collect his two friends.

Once they reached his library-study downstairs, Rafe walked straight to the sideboard to pour the colonel a drink.

"Either of you two need a refill?" he asked his friends.

Both men shook their heads, content with the glass each held in his hand. Rafe added a dash of brandy to his own crystal tumbler, then walked over and sat down with the group in front of the fire.

"All right, Colonel, let's hear it," Rafe said.

Pendleton took a sip of his drink. "Simply put, the War Office turned down the proposal. They say there is no ship built that poses that strong a threat to His Majesty's fleet."

Rafe swore softly.

Ethan got up and paced over to the fire, the slight limp from his days as a privateer barely noticeable. "They're making a costly mistake — I can tell you that firsthand. When I captained the *Sea Witch*, we were able to outrun our enemies time and again — and sink a goodly number. *Sea Witch* was fast and incredibly maneuverable, which gave us a distinct advantage. From the drawings I've seen, the design of the Baltimore Clippers would result in even greater speed and mobility."

"So what can we do to convince them?" Cord asked, leaning back in a dark green leather chair.

"I wish I knew," said Pendleton. "The American shipbuilders won't wait much longer to make a deal. They'll expect an answer from you, Your Grace. When they don't receive one, they'll take the offer made by the French — and line the Dutchman's already-bulging pockets with even more money."

"What if we bought them ourselves?" Cord suggested. "Separately, none of us could afford that kind of capital outlay, but if we could put together a group of investors, perhaps we could come up with the money we would need."

"Unfortunately, the best use of those ships is for military purposes," Ethan said. "They don't hold enough cargo to make them profitable for shipping."

"Buying them ourselves doesn't really seem feasible," Rafe agreed, "but perhaps we can stall the Americans a little while longer, time enough to convince our government how important these vessels are."

"We need them," Ethan said, "if for no other reason than to keep them out of the hands of the French."

The colonel sipped his brandy. "It will take two months for a message to reach Baltimore. Let's keep dangling the carrot in front of them. Suggest a higher dollar amount and tell them we are trying to raise the capital."

"As you say, it might give us a bit more time," Cord agreed.

"Yesterday, I spoke to Max Bradley," the colonel continued. "Bradley says the Dutchman must have sailed not long after you, Rafael. Schrader was recently spotted in France, undoubtedly there trying to conclude his transaction."

Rafe got up from his chair. "I'll pen a letter to Phineas Brand tonight."

Cord and the colonel rose as well and Ethan walked away from the fire to join them.

"Belford Enterprises has a ship sailing for America this week," Ethan said. "I'll have the captain carry your message directly to Baltimore and personally see it delivered to Phineas Brand."

For the first time Pendleton smiled. "Very good. Indeed, if there's one thing I've learned it's that the battle isn't over till it's over."

"Here, here!" Cord said.

And each man lifted his glass and took a drink.

"Here comes Rafael." The dowager duchess's gaze swung toward the door leading into the ballroom, and Danielle's gaze followed hers. Rafe had only been gone a few minutes, yet as Danielle watched him approach, she felt a trickle of relief that he had returned.

"Sorry," he said. "I hope my presence wasn't missed."

But she *had* missed him standing there beside the dance floor, watching her so protectively, and it frightened her to think how easily she might fall under his spell again.

"Business?" Dani asked, keeping her tone mild.

"The king's business." He studied her face. "Weathering the storm all right?"

"Better than I thought."

"She's been marvelous," the dowager said. "A real trouper. And seeing the two of you together . . . such a handsome couple. By the morrow, the gossips will be convinced it was a love match."

A love match. Once it would have been, Dani thought.

"And they'll be crucifying Oliver Randall," her mother-in-law finished, "for the pain he caused you both."

Dani's stomach constricted. Just the mention of the man's name brought a rush of hurtful memories she had tried for years to forget.

"Whatever they say about Oliver is nothing less than he deserves," Rafe said.

"The man should have been drawn and quartered," said the dowager, never one to mince words. She gave Danielle a smile, then her gaze moved off toward the blond man sauntering their way a bit unsteadily, the drink in his hand sloshing over the rim of his glass.

The dowager's smile slid away. "Don't look now, but your cousin, Arthur, is on his way over."

"I'm surprised you invited him," Rafe said.

"I didn't," said the dowager.

"I don't believe I've heard you speak of a cousin named Arthur," Dani said.

A muscle in Rafe's jaw tightened. "It's Arthur Bartholomew. And I speak of him as little as possible."

Rafe's mother pasted on an artificial smile and turned just as the man walked up. "Well, Artie, dear, what a surprise."

"I'm sure it is." He was perhaps a few years younger than Rafe, exceedingly handsome, with the Sheffield cleft in his chin and the family blue eyes, though with his pale complexion and wheat-blond hair, they were not nearly so remarkable as Rafe's.

Arthur made the duchess a rather sloppy bow, spilling several more drops of his drink, and Dani realized he wasn't just slightly drunk, he was completely foxed.

"Hello, Artie," Rafe said, and she noticed the harsh note in his voice.

"Ah, Rafael . . . back from your trip to the wild American colonies. And this must be your lovely bride." He bowed deeply over her hand, and she held her breath that he didn't topple squarely on his face. But Arthur seemed used to his precarious state of inebriation and stood unsteadily upright. "It's a pleasure to meet you, duchess."

"You, as well, Mr. Bartholomew."

"Please . . . you must call me Artie. We're all family now." His smile remained in place, but there was an insolence in his eyes Dani didn't like. His pale blue gaze raked her as if she were a piece of meat, and a corner of his mouth curled up.

"A fine choice, cousin," he said to Rafe. "A sturdy pair of hips wide enough for child-bearing, and certainly pleasing enough to the eye to keep a man interested long after she conceives. Very well done, old chap."

Rafe's big hand shot to the front of Arthur's coat, and he yanked the man up off his feet. "You weren't invited here, Arthur. By your vulgarity, you have again proved exactly the reason. Now get out — before I personally toss you out on your ear."

Rafe let go of Arthur's coat so abruptly the blond man staggered and nearly fell. Rafe signaled to a footman near the door, and he shouldered his way over to where the group stood.

"Show Mr. Bartholomew to the door, Mr. Cooney, will you?"

"Of course, Your Grace." The footman was large and he glowered at Arthur Bartholomew in a manner that warned what would happen if he failed to leave the ball-room.

Arthur straightened his tailcoat and combed back his blond hair. "Have a good evening, all." Turning, he weaved his way toward the door, the footman close behind him. They disappeared out into the hallway, and the tightness in Rafael's jaw slowly eased.

329

"I apologize for my cousin. He can be quite a nuisance when he is drunk — which he is most of the time."

The dowager sighed and shook her head. "I can't abide that man. Not only is he a drunk, in two years' time, he has squandered every cent of his inheritance. He gambles in excess, and even fritters away the generous monthly stipend he receives. Even the remote possibility that fool might become the next Duke of Sheffield is more than I can bear."

Dani blinked and looked up at Rafe's mother. "You are not saying that Arthur Bartholomew is in line for the Sheffield title?"

The dowager let out a sigh. "I am extremely aggrieved to say that is so. Until Rafael has a son to carry on the family name, our fortunes are not safe."

Dani's chest squeezed. She suddenly felt light-headed. Her face, she knew, must have turned the color of chalk.

She heard Rafe's voice in her ear. "You needn't look so worried. I realize I have been remiss in my duties of late, but you may be certain that will change. I intend to keep you well pleasured, madam, and in return, there is every likelihood you will give me a houseful of sons and daughters."

Dani couldn't manage to speak. For the first time she realized the gravity of what she had done. As long as Rafe was married to her, he would have no legitimate heir. If an accident were to befall him, if he grew ill unexpectedly and died — God forbid — Arthur Bartholomew would inherit the dukedom.

"Are you all right, love? You're looking awfully pale."

"I — I am fine." She tried to muster a smile. "It's been a long evening. I think I am beginning to tire."

"As am I," Rafe said, though he didn't look tired in the least. "Mother, I'm afraid you're going to have to make our excuses. Danielle is feeling unwell."

The duchess eyed her shrewdly. "Yes, I can see that." She smiled up at Rafe. "You must put your wife to bed immediately." *And, of course, you must join her* were the unspoken words. *The sooner you get her with child, the safer our family will be.*

"Come, love." Rafe's hand settled at her waist.

"Good night, Your Grace," Dani said to his mother as they walked away, but when they reached her room, he didn't join her, just rang for Caro to help her undress and retired to his own room to sleep.

The following morning, a note came for Rafe from Jonas McPhee. It confirmed his return to London and asked for an appointment with Rafael at Sheffield House that night.

Declining to sup with Danielle, worried about what news Jonas might be bringing, Rafe was at work in his study when the butler appeared to announce the Bow Street runner's arrival.

"Show him in," Rafe commanded, and a few minutes later, McPhee walked into the study, stout, balding, one of his knotted hands shoved into the pocket of his worn woolen coat.

"I'm sorry I couldn't get here sooner, Your Grace. The weather turned inclement and the damnable muddy roads were nearly impossible to traverse."

"Your note said you found the thief who stole my wife's necklace."

Jonas seemed to carefully choose his words. "I found the man you were seeking. Apparently, he used the necklace as collateral for a loan to pay for his passage from America. He was living in a small cottage that belongs to a man named Stephen Lawrence. As you requested, the authorities were contacted and the man arrested. Mr.

Lawrence was out of town at the time."

"What is this man's name?"

"He calls himself Robert McCabe, though I am not at all certain that is his true identity."

"Where is McCabe now?"

"He's being transported by wagon to Newgate prison. I imagine he will arrive there sometime tomorrow."

"How did you find him?"

"Actually, that wasn't as difficult as I had imagined. As it turns out, this McCabe is quite a handsome fellow. He is an educated man, the sort to charm the ladies. One of the shopkeepers' wives remembered him very well. Apparently, he asked her for directions to Evesham. I headed for the village, and once I got there, a tavern maid remembered seeing him. She said she thought he was staying somewhere nearby. I started asking around, and I found him at the cottage."

"I see."

The runner's face betrayed his nervousness. Rafe steepled his fingers as he leaned back in the deep leather chair behind his desk. "You have always been a diplomatic sort, Jonas. What is it you are wishing you didn't have to tell me?"

Jonas ran a hand over his bald head and sighed. "McCabe never denied he was the man who brought the necklace to the moneylender in Liverpool. But he vehemently denied being a thief. He said he hadn't sold the jewelry outright because he hoped to buy it back. He said the necklace was a gift, one he hoped to return one day to its rightful owner."

"Finish it, Jonas."

"McCabe said the Duchess of Sheffield gave him the necklace so that he would have the money to return to England."

A long silence ensued.

Rafe's stomach felt tied in a knot. "I take it you believe this man's story."

"I'm afraid I do. I could be wrong, of course, but —"

"Your instincts have never failed you, Jonas. I imagine they will hold you in good stead this time, as well." Rafe rose from his chair, fighting to control the jealousy boiling through him, the fury growing with every breath he took. "I'll proceed with the information you've provided. As always, thank you for your hard work."

Jonas rose to his feet. "You intend to speak to McCabe?"

"As soon as he arrives at the prison." He didn't say that in the meantime, he would be speaking at length to his wife.

"Good night, Your Grace."

334

"Good night, Jonas." The runner walked to the door and disappeared out into the corridor, and Rafe went over and poured himself a drink. The brandy burned down his throat, but it did nothing to calm the fury scorching through him. He downed the drink, poured himself another and took a hefty swallow.

All the while, his mind kept returning to the fact his wife had given his wedding gift to another man — a handsome, charming, educated man who appealed greatly to the ladies.

Of course, as McPhee had said, it might not be true. The man might have simply made up the tale in an effort to save his own skin. Whatever had happened, the man had not seduced her. Danielle had, after all, been a virgin when Rafe took her.

He thought of how he had accused her unfairly before and how wrong he had been, and the price they had both paid because of it. It was a mistake he refused to make again.

And yet, from the start, he had sensed Danielle was lying to him about the necklace.

Rafe tossed back the last of his drink, set the brandy glass down on the table and walked over to the safe built into the wall of his study. Reaching inside, he took out the red satin pouch and closed the heavy iron door.

Rafe tucked the bag into his pocket and strode out of the study.

Twenty-One

"I wish I knew what to do, Caro. I tell myself it is better that he remain distant, that it is safer for me that way, but Rafael is my husband and part of me wishes it could be different, that at least we could be friends."

Caro flicked her a glance, and Dani flushed where she sat on the stool in front of the mirror. She and Rafe might not be friends, but they were passionate lovers. Or at least for a while they had been.

"The duke has not been himself since well before the ball," Caro said, pulling the brush through Dani's hair. "Perhaps if you could discover what is amiss, matters would improve between you."

Dressed for bed in a white cotton night rail, her hair not yet braided for sleeping, she started to reply, but a sharp rap on the door ended the conversation with her friend.

"I'll get it," Caro said, heading toward the sound, assuming it was one of the chambermaids, but before she reached the door, it swung open and Rafael strode into the room.

His eyes were a glittering shade of blue and there was steel in his jaw. "If you will excuse us, Miss Loon."

Dani's heartbeat sputtered into gear.

Caro cast her a worried glance and practically bolted for the door. "Good night, Your Grace." The door closed firmly behind her.

Rafe's gaze swept over Danielle, his expression one of burning intensity. A muscle jumped in his cheek.

"You are dressed for bed. . . ." he said as if it didn't happen every night.

"Why, yes, I . . . I didn't expect you would join me. I — I mean, you haven't in some time, and I thought that . . ." She was babbling, she knew, but couldn't seem to stop.

"Yes . . . ?" The anger remained in his eyes, but now she saw something more, the heat of desire that always seemed to burn between them.

"Well, as I said, it has been some time."

"Too long a time." He moved toward her, hauled her up from the stool and straight into his arms.

Rafe's mouth crushed down over hers and for an instant she was simply too stunned to speak. She knew he was angry, knew he hadn't come to her room to make love. But now, as he kissed her, it was clear his intentions had changed. His long frame pressed against her and she could feel his rigid arousal. He tasted faintly of brandy and the virility that was Rafe. When he deepened the kiss, when his tongue slid into her mouth, the fire between them kindled to life and whatever he had come for no longer mattered.

Dani slipped her arms around his neck and kissed him back, slid her tongue over his and heard him groan. His hands found her breasts and he began to caress them, molding them through the soft cotton fabric, plucking the crests into hard little buds. Unconsciously, she arched toward him, pressing the fullness into his hands, rubbing her stiff nipples against his palms like a cat seeking attention.

"You like this."

A little mew seeped from her throat and a sliver of heat ran through her.

"I remember the first time I touched you this way," he said, "that day in the apple orchard. If I close my eyes, I can still feel the way you trembled, just as you are now."

Rafe kissed her again and raw need poured through her. She felt his hands sliding over her bottom, cupping her and pulling her against the hardness at the front of his breeches. He was fiercely aroused, and so was she. No matter what happened, she wanted this, wanted him.

The hands on her hips turned her to face the mirror and seeing the two of them together, knowing that soon they would be joined, made her loins tighten with need.

He reached toward her, pulled the ribbon at the neck of her night rail and slid the gown off her shoulders. He eased it down over her hips, into a puddle at her feet.

"Put your palms on the stool," he commanded, his fingers circling her wrists, easing her forward. In the mirror, he stood behind her, tall and dark, his eyes so very blue, and there was something incredibly erotic about being completely naked while he remained fully clothed.

"I've never had you this way," he said, "but I've wanted to." His gaze held hers in the mirror, mesmerized her as his hand stroked over her bottom. "Part your legs for me."

Her body pulsed, tightened. The look in his eyes promised pleasure and she trusted him to give her that. Still, the hard set of his jaw betrayed the anger that lay beneath his surface calm.

"I don't think —"

"Do it."

Her heartbeat quickened at the deep, masculine tone of authority. Heat collected between her legs, and desire burned through her blood. She did as he commanded, felt his hands running over her bottom, sliding between her legs, then he began to stroke her.

Desire melted into her stomach, slipped out through her limbs, and her loins throbbed. When she felt his heavy length probing for entrance, when he slid his hardness deep into her she arched her back and her eyes locked with his in the mirror.

Rafe gripped her hips, holding her in place to receive his deep thrusts, taking her roughly, pounding into her again and again. Her own need swelled and her body tightened around him. Her eyes slid closed as release shook her, but Rafe did not stop. Not until she peaked again, then he let himself go, taking his own release, a low groan coming from his throat.

They spiraled down together, Rafe still standing behind her. She felt him withdraw, and in the mirror, the rigid set of his features returned.

He plucked her blue quilted wrapper off the bench at the foot of her bed and handed it over as he refastened the front of his breeches and straightened his clothes. Dani slipped on the robe and firmly tied the sash.

Rafe glanced off toward the window. "I didn't mean for that to happen." His expression betrayed his regret. He had lost control. Rafe hated for that to happen, but Dani wasn't sorry. She despised his oh-so-precious control.

"If not to make love, then why did you come?"

Reaching into the pocket of his burgundy tailcoat, he drew out a red satin pouch. "I believe these belong to you."

Dani recognized the pouch. Dear God, the pearls! She started to tremble, opened her mouth to speak, but her mouth was so dry she could barely form the words. "The necklace."

"You look surprised to see it." He took the pearls out of the satin pouch, let them dangle from his long, dark fingers.

"Of . . . of course I'm surprised."

"Because they were stolen?"

"Why, yes . . ."

"Then again, perhaps it is something else. Perhaps the pearls weren't stolen at all and you are surprised because the man you gave them to must have returned to England, and yet he has not contacted you."

Her mind refused to function. What was he saying? What on earth was he talking about? "I don't . . . don't know what you mean."

"So he *has* contacted you."

"No!" He was talking about Robert. Dear God, he had somehow discovered her role in Robert's escape and come up with some wild reasoning that wasn't the least bit true. Her pulse jerked into an even faster pace. "I — I can only imagine what you must be thinking, but it isn't the way it seems."

"Isn't it?"

"I admit I gave Robert the necklace, but only because he had no one else to help him."

"Robert? That is how you address him? You and he must be very familiar, indeed."

"No! Oh, God . . ." She turned away from his rigid stance, fighting back tears, desperately trying to think of what to say. "How . . . how long have you known?"

"Cord brought me the pearls several weeks ago." He slipped them back into the pouch and set the pouch down on the dresser. "Your friend *Robert* had borrowed against them through a moneylender in Liverpool. The dealer thought Cord might be interested in buying them."

She shook her head. "You were acting so strangely. . . . I knew something was wrong, but —"

His fist slammed down on the dresser. "What the bloody hell is going on between you and this man, Robert McCabe?"

343

"Nothing is going on! Robert is . . . Robert is Caro's friend, not mine. She is desperately in love with him. Robert was in trouble and badly in need of money. Caro had no funds and we were sailing for England that day. I — I couldn't think of any other way to help him so I gave him the pearls."

For several seconds, Rafe just stared at her. He clamped down hard on his jaw, working to rein in his temper. "If you needed help, why didn't you come to me?"

"I wanted to. But we had only been married a few hours. I was afraid of what you would say, of what might happen to Robert."

She looked up at him, an awful thought striking. "What have you done to him?"

The edge of his mouth barely curved. "Your friend, McCabe, is on his way to Newgate prison."

The news hit her so hard her knees went weak. "Dear God . . ."

Rafe's hand shot out to steady her. "Damnation!" Easing her down on a nearby chair, he walked over to the porcelain pitcher and poured her a glass of water, then returned and pressed it into her hand. She dutifully took a sip, then set the glass down on the table with a trembling hand.

"I — I realize you have no reason to believe me, but I am telling you the truth."

"As you should have done before," Rafe said simply.

She blinked. "You . . . you believe me?"

"I am doing my best. Now, start at the beginning. I expect the truth this time and nothing less, and don't leave anything out."

Dani's heart constricted. Rafael was listening. She had been so sure he would not. She took a steadying breath and prayed she could find the right words.

"It all started in Philadelphia." Frightened for Robert and worried about Caro, she told Rafe how her friend had introduced her to Robert at Aunt Flora's house. She described the sort of man Caro believed Robert to be, how she had come to that same conclusion, and how Caro had fallen in love with him.

"Is McCabe his real name?"

She hesitated an instant too long.

"Dammit, Dani, when are you going to realize that I am your friend, not your enemy?"

Danielle took a breath. "I'm sorry. His name is McKay, not McCabe. But if the authorities discover Robert's true identity, they will hang him. Losing him would break Caro's heart."

345

"For God's sake, what has the fellow done?"

"That is the crux of the matter. He is accused of murder, but he is innocent. Since I know how it feels to be accused of a crime I didn't commit, I simply had to help him."

Rafe studied her for several long moments. Then he amazed her by reaching out and drawing her into his arms. "You are a handful, duchess."

Dani's throat closed up. Held snugly against him, she felt a mixture of worry and relief.

"I'll speak to your friend Robert. I'll do what I can to help him."

The tightness swelled until her throat ached painfully. Rafe would help her, help Robert. "Thank you."

"In return, I want your promise that from this day forward you will never lie to me again."

She nodded. She hadn't wanted to lie to him in the first place. And now, each day, she trusted him a little more.

"Say it. I want your word."

"I promise." But with the vow came the sharp sting of tears. By omitting the truth of her dark secret she was lying to him again. If he ever found out how she had duped him

— dear God, Dani didn't know if she would be able to bear it.

Rafe made his way through the musty, dank corridors of Newgate prison. Water dripped from the rough-hewn planks above his head, and slick moss covered the cold stone walls. The smell of unwashed bodies and human waste filled his nostrils, and one of the prisoners whimpered pitifully somewhere down the long, dimly lit hall.

"This way, Yer Grace." A fat, foul-smelling guard led him to a cell at the rear of the prison. The man shoved an iron key into the lock. The rusty mechanism screeched, then the heavy wooden door swung open and the guard stepped out of the way so that Rafe could walk into the cell.

"Just call out when yer ready to leave."

"Thank you." He hoped it wouldn't be long.

The guard's footfalls echoed down the corridor, and Rafe turned his attention to the man sitting in the wet straw on the floor, leaning back against the wall. In the faint lantern light outside the cell, Rafe couldn't tell exactly what he looked like, but his jacket and shirt were torn and covered with dirt and dried blood.

"Who are you?" the prisoner asked,

347

straightening a little but not getting up from where he sat.

"Sheffield. I believe you know the name."

He struggled then, tried to get up, and Rafe rested a hand on his shoulder, urging him to remain where he was. "Take it easy. You don't look very well. How badly are you injured?"

"Bastards beat the bloody hell out of me."

"The guard said you resisted arrest."

McKay made no reply.

"I spoke to my wife about you. The duchess says you're not a thief. She says she gave you the necklace." Rafe read the man's surprise in the faint tightening of the muscles across his shoulders.

"You seem surprised."

"I wasn't sure what the lady would say."

"Yes, well, unfortunately for you that is not what she said the day we sailed for home."

"I hope you understand she was only trying to help me. She's an incredible woman, your wife."

"Yes, she is. What about Caroline Loon?"

The prisoner's head fell back against the wall. "I didn't mention her because I didn't want to get her into trouble."

Moving closer to where the man leaned against the wall, Rafe crouched next to him in the dirty straw. He was close enough now to see the swollen eye and the bruises on McKay's face.

"Tell me the rest of it. Tell me about the murder you are accused of and why I should believe, as my wife and your friend Miss Loon do, that you are innocent of the crime."

McKay hesitated only a moment, then quietly began to tell his tale. It was half an hour later that Rafe called out for the guard to open the cell.

"Get some rest, McKay. I'll arrange for your release as quickly as I can. We need to do this quietly. So far no one knows who you really are and we need to keep it that way. It may take a few days. I'll leave a little money with the guards should you need anything and send a carriage to pick you up."

"Thank you, Your Grace."

"I'm trusting your word, Robert, as they did, trusting that you are telling me the truth. If you are, I'll do everything in my power to help you. If you are not, you will likely find yourself swinging from the end of a rope."

Biting back a hiss of pain, McKay shoved unsteadily to his feet, then leaned against the wall for support. "Every word I have spoken is true."

Rafe said nothing.

"I am in your debt, Your Grace. I shall never forget you or your lady wife for what you have done."

"Since I am the man who ordered your arrest, which resulted in the beating you received, you might wish to amend that."

In the faint light, he thought that he caught the edge of a smile.

"I'll see you soon, Robert."

"I won't disappoint you, Your Grace."

Rafe left the prison trying to decide if all of them had been duped or if the man was telling the truth. If he was, Robert McKay was the true Earl of Leighton.

Proving it, however, was an entirely different matter. Rafe couldn't help wondering, should the man, by some miracle of fate, actually became a powerful earl, a high ranking member of the aristocracy, what would happen to Caroline Loon?

Twenty-Two

Dani sat in front of the dresser in her bed-chamber while Caro perched on the gold velvet bench at the foot of the four poster bed. For the past half hour, they had been discussing Robert McKay.

"But the duke is certain that Robert will soon be released from prison?" Caro asked, not for the first time.

"He thought that it might take a day or two, but, yes, Rafael has promised to see it done. He didn't want to press the matter too hard for fear it might alert someone in authority."

"But you said Robert is injured. If that is so, he needs someone to take care of him, see that his wounds are tended."

Dani straightened on the stool, where she had been sitting while Caro put the finishing touches on her upswept red hair. Tonight, she and Rafe were going to a comic opera in Drury Lane called *Virginia*. Afterward, they would be stopping by a soirée being held in honor of the mayor's birthday. Her life as the wife of a duke had finally begun and Dani was determined to fulfill her duties.

"Listen to me, Caro. I know you are worried, but we must proceed with caution. Rafe says Robert's injuries are not life threatening, and he will be out of prison very soon."

But Robert had also told a wild tale of being the true Earl of Leighton, the only portion of the story Danielle had not revealed to her friend. She had left that bit of news for Robert to tell, unsure, should it prove true, how it would affect their relationship.

At present, Robert's biggest problem was proving his innocence. Until that happened, he would remain in very grave danger. Of course, she didn't say that to Caro.

A familiar knock sounded, and recognizing it as belonging to Rafael, Dani quickly checked her appearance in the mirror.

"Oh, dear, I forgot the pearls." Turning, she hurried over to the dresser, pulled the red satin pouch out of her jewelry box and spilled the necklace into her hand.

She turned to her friend as she hurried to open the door. "You mustn't worry, dearest. In a couple of days you'll see your Robert again."

Caro nodded and Dani caught the

glimmer of tears in her eyes. "You and the duke have been so very kind to both of us."

"Nonsense!" said a deep voice from the doorway. "You are a cherished friend, Caro. People help their friends."

Rafe walked into the room and Dani went over and kissed his cheek, seeing, as she often did now, traces of the old Rafael, who had always been so kind to others. Caro quietly slipped out of the bedchamber, and Dani handed the pearls to Rafe.

"Would you mind helping me put these on?"

Rafe smiled as he took the pearls, draped them around her neck and fastened the diamond clasp. He stepped back to survey the effect. "The pearls are magnificent and so are you."

She smiled. "Thank you."

"I've never told you about them. Would you like to hear the story?"

"Oh, yes." She could feel the comforting weight of the pearls, the way they seemed to fit so perfectly around her neck, just as they had when she had worn them all those weeks ago. "I should love to hear the tale."

"I warn you, it is not for the squeamish."

One of her eyebrows arched up. "Now you have piqued my curiosity."

Rafe reached up and briefly touched the

pearls. "As I told you, the necklace was designed in medieval times, commissioned by the powerful Lord Fallon. The earl chose each diamond and pearl himself. It was a wedding gift for his bride, the lady Ariana of Merrick. She was wearing the necklace that day as she waited for her groom to arrive at Castle Merrick. As the story goes, it was a love match unparalleled by any other in its day. Unfortunately, on his way to the castle, the earl and his men were set upon by brigands and murdered to a man."

"Oh, dear God."

"When Lady Ariana heard the news, she was so distraught she climbed to the top of the castle parapet and jumped to her death, still wearing the pearls. It was later discovered that she was carrying Lord Fallon's child."

A lump rose in Dani's throat. She reached up and touched the pearls, which seemed to warm beneath her fingers. The Bride's Necklace, it was called, and now she understood why.

She thought of the young mother who lost her true love and the child she would have born him. She tried not to think of the child she and Rafe would never have, but the thought hovered there in her heart.

She didn't realize she was crying until

Rafe reached out and brushed a tear from her cheek.

"If I had thought it would upset you, I never would have told you."

She tried to smile. "It is just so terribly sad."

"It happened a long time ago, love."

Her fingers ran over the pearls, testing the smoothness, the shape of each perfectly faceted diamond. "I knew there was something special about it, but I . . ." She looked up at him. "I won't let anything happen to it again. I'll keep it safe for her."

He bent his head and brushed her mouth with a kiss. "I know you will."

She took a deep breath and glanced toward the door. "I suppose we should go." But she didn't really want to leave. She was Rafael's wife, but there were those who had yet to believe in her innocence, some who believed instead that she had somehow duped him into marriage.

Rafe took her hand. "We don't want to keep Cord and the others waiting."

"No, of course not." But as she left the bedchamber on Rafael's arm, she couldn't stop thinking of the pearls and the tragic tale of Ariana and her beloved, and the child who had died with them. It haunted her well into the evening.

★ ★ ★

A determined rain beat down on the mullioned windows outside the yellow Cotswold stone of Leighton Hall. The rolling fields of the two-thousand-acre country estate turned muddy, and a harsh wind howled over the low stone fences.

In his wood-paneled study, Clifford Nash, fifth Earl of Leighton, lounged in an expensive leather chair in front of the hearth. He was a man of forty-two, with dark hair and dark brown eyes. Handsome, he had always thought himself, though the years had rounded him a bit.

And now that he was rich as Croesus, there was nothing Clifford wanted that he could not have.

Across from him, his estate manager, Burton Webster, sat forward in his seat. "So what do you think we should do?" Web had arrived at the house half an hour ago, barging in unannounced, obviously worried.

Clifford swirled the brandy in his glass. "How can you be sure the man is McKay?"

"I tell you it's him. He was in Evesham with his cousin, Stephen Lawrence. Surely you remember. Lawrence was the chap who started nosing about for information a year or so after the old earl's death. He was

356

bound and determined to prove McKay innocent of the crime."

"Yes, yes, I recall the fellow. Came up with nothing, I also recall. Since that was over a year ago, I thought we'd heard the last of him." They were drinking Clifford's finest brandy and smoking expensive cigars, but Webster was too nervous to enjoy them. Damnable waste of money.

"I'm not quite sure what happened with Lawrence," Web continued. "All I know is that the lass, Molly Jameson, sent me a note that McKay was back in England. Apparently, she received a message from him. McKay wanted to talk to her about the rendezvous they were supposed to have had that night at the inn."

"Did she see him?"

"No. He didn't show up for the meeting. But she believes McKay left the country after the murder, just as we thought. She says he is back in England, and Evesham is likely where he would go. She is the one who mentioned the cousin, Stephen Lawrence."

"So go to Evesham and take care of McKay."

Web sighed. He was a big man, muscularly built, with thick fingers and a nose that had been broken more than once. He had been in Nash's employ for the past five years. He was loyal to a fault, and in those years had become nearly indispensable to Clifford.

"I'm afraid that's the rub. I've been to Evesham. McKay is no longer there."

"Did you speak to the cousin?"

"Lawrence is gone, as well. According to the neighbors, his mother fell ill and he traveled north to take care of her."

Clifford puffed on the cigar and released the smoke into the air, giving himself time to think. "Start with Lawrence. Find out where he went and go after him, make him tell you the truth about McKay and find out where he is."

"If I find him, what should I do?"

"In the beginning, hanging for Leighton's murder would have neatly tied things up, but now I don't want the whole affair needlessly stirred up again. Just make him disappear."

"Kill him?"

Webster was valuable in many ways, but there were times Clifford wondered about the size of his brain. "Yes, kill him — or, if you prefer, hire it done as you did before. I just want him gone for good."

"Yes, my lord."

At least the fool had remembered to use Clifford's title, though it had taken him longer than it should have to get used to it. Clifford got up from his chair and Web did the same.

"Keep me posted on your progress."

"Yes, my lord."

The burly man left the study and Clifford sat back down to enjoy the rest of his cigar. He wasn't really worried. McKay was a wanted man. If Webster failed to deal with him, Clifford would simply call in the authorities. It would be far more trouble, but the result would be the same.

Either way, Robert McKay was a dead man.

As soon as the production of *Virginia* was over, Danielle and Rafe left for the mayor's birthday party. Grace and Ethan were traveling with them in the duke's impressive black coach-and-four with the fancy ducal crest emblazoned in gold on the doors. Cord and Victoria followed in the earl's sleek black carriage pulled by a pair of high-stepping bays.

The soirée was well in progress by the time the three couples arrived. The party was being held at the Duke of Tarrington's palatial home, which Cord and Victoria seemed particularly fond of.

"Quite a place the old boy has here," Cord

drawled, casting what could only be called a lascivious glance at his wife. "It brings back some very fond memories."

Victoria blushed, but her husband just smiled. "Perhaps later," he said to her softly, "we might revisit some of those times."

Tory's blush deepened, but she couldn't stop a grin. "I believe I may hold you to that, my lord."

Cord laughed, but there was a wicked gleam in his unusual golden-brown eyes.

"I'm afraid to guess what that was about," Rafe whispered in Dani's ear. "God knows when it comes to his wife, the man is insatiable."

Dani smiled. "And you, Your Grace?"

He looked at her, and his eyes turned the scorching shade of blue that signaled where his thoughts had gone.

"Touché," he said, adding, "though I hope I've enough strength of will to wait until we get home."

Danielle thought of the iron control he so prized and she so hated, and vowed that sometime in the very near future, she would take that as a challenge.

Not tonight, however. She had just begun to enter into society as the Duchess of Sheffield and she refused to do anything that might arouse the slightest gossip. Instead, she let Rafael lead her among the guests, making polite greetings to one after another, the Marquess of This and the Earl of That, the Baroness Something-or-other. There were several Sir Someones and their wives, and enough viscounts and viscountesses that she soon lost track.

The music floated toward them. There was dancing in one of the larger drawing rooms and Rafe urged her in that direction. The orchestra played a country dance and Rafe partnered her, then, when the dance was over, led her to the edge of the dance floor.

"I suppose I shall have to let you dance with some of these other fellows," he grumbled.

"If you don't, they might think you are jealous of my attentions. You certainly wouldn't want that."

"I *am* jealous of your attentions. But on that score, I've learned my lesson." He surveyed the crowded room, the crush of people gowned in satins and silks, and Dani caught his frown.

"What is it?"

"Carlton Baker is here."

Her stomach knotted as she remembered their awful encounter aboard ship. "Baker? I would have thought by now he would be on his way back to Philadelphia."

But instead, he walked toward them, tall and attractive, his dark hair, lightly silvered at the temples, cut short and combed forward in the popular Brutus style.

"Well, Duke, we meet again." Baker smiled, but there wasn't the least bit of warmth in his eyes. "I figured we would run into each other eventually."

"Yes, more's the pity."

Baker's mouth tightened. "Just so you know . . . I haven't forgotten the beating you handed me for no good reason, nor do I intend to."

"I had every reason, and you know it. Furthermore, if you ever bother my wife again, you will think the pounding I gave you that night was child's play."

Baker's whole body went rigid. "You dare to threaten me?"

Rafe shrugged his shoulders. "It is merely a warning."

"Then I have a warning for you. What goes around, comes around, Duke. You've had your turn. Sooner or later, I'll have mine."

As Baker walked away, Rafe unconsciously clenched his fists.

"You made a fool of him, is all," Dani said. "Now he is trying to salve his wounded pride."

Rafe's tension seemed to ease. "You're right. The man is a fool, but he isn't completely insane."

"Meaning?"

"Meaning, should Baker step out of line, I will gladly take up where I left off that night, and I think Baker knows it."

Dani didn't say more. Rafe was protective of her as no man ever had been. If Carlton Baker so much as looked at her wrong . . . She shivered, thinking of what had happened to Oliver Randall and hoping Carlton Baker would soon be returning to America.

The evening progressed. All three couples wandered into the gaming room and Cord sat down at one of the green baize tables to try his hand at whist. Rafe and Ethan soon joined in the play, and the women used the time for a trip to the ladies' retiring room.

They were on their way to rejoin the men when a woman's voice rang from behind them.

"Well, if it isn't the little tart who tricked the duke into marrying her."

A cold chill swept down Dani's spine. Turning, she came face-to-face with a woman she hadn't seen in years but certainly hadn't forgotten. The Marchioness of Caverly, Oliver Randall's mother. Through the buzzing in her ears, she heard Grace's

363

voice coming from beside her.

"Well, if it isn't the mother of that rotten, good-for-nothing swine whose abominable scheming nearly destroyed two innocent lives."

Dani gasped. "Grace!"

"Well, it's true," Victoria chimed in, then she, too, turned her wrath on Lady Caverly. "Your son's jealousy brought him to the end he has suffered. He has no one to blame but himself, and neither do you."

Danielle just stood there, scarcely able to believe what her two friends had just done. Still, their courage bolstered hers. Lifting her head, she spoke directly to the marchioness.

"I am sorry, Lady Caverly, for what your family has suffered, but it was Oliver's doing, not mine."

"How dare you! After the lies you have told, you aren't good enough to speak my son's name!"

"I told the truth. Perhaps one day your son will have the courage to do the same."

"This is your fault. Oliver would never —"

"That is enough, Margaret." The Marquess of Caverly walked up beside his wife. "There are better ways to handle matters than a public display in front of half the *ton*." A tall man with iron-gray hair, the marquess had an arrogance about him that made clear his position as a high-ranking member of the peerage. "Come, my dear. I believe it is time we went home."

Dani said nothing more, and the marquess led his wife off down the hall. Dani started walking, praying the weak knees beneath her gown would continue to hold her up.

Victoria hurried ahead, said something to Rafe as he strode toward them.

"Victoria told me what happened." He captured her hands, a worried look on his face. "I'm sorry, love. I didn't know they would be here. I thought they were still in residence in the country."

"I would have run into them sooner or later. Perhaps it is better it happened now."

"Are you sure you're all right?"

"I am fine." And thinking of Grace and Victoria, who had come to her defense like a pair of young tigresses, she discovered she actually was.

"I think it is time we went home," Rafe said, but Dani shook her head.

"We have weathered the worst of the storm. I refuse to run for cover now." She flicked a glance at the gaming tables. "Anyone for cards?"

Rafe smiled, and she saw the pride in his

eyes. "That sounds like a splendid notion . . . *Your Grace.*"

There was something in the way he said it,
something that warmed her insides.

Placing her hand on the sleeve of his coat,
she let him guide her across the Persian
carpet toward the row of green baize tables.

Twenty-Three

Two days passed. Robert McKay was released from prison, and as Rafe had promised, a carriage waited out in front to return him to Sheffield House.

Robert never appeared.

When the coachman checked on the man's whereabouts, he discovered McKay had left Newgate more than an hour earlier. He was gone, nowhere to be seen. Not quite certain what to do, the driver, a heavyset man named Mullens, drove the carriage back to Sheffield House.

"I'm sorry, Yer Grace," Michael Mullens said. "The bloke never showed up. They released 'im, though. I checked with the guards to be sure."

"Thank you, Mr. Mullens." Clamping down on a surge of anger, Rafe turned toward the two women standing anxiously behind him in the entry.

"You heard what the coachman said. McKay left the prison but he didn't return here as we had planned. There isn't much more I can say."

Caro started crying, turned and raced up the stairs.

Dani just stood there. "I can't believe Robert lied to all of us — even you."

"Either the man is the best actor in London or there is more to the story. I think we should wait a bit longer before we jump to conclusions."

"Yes . . . of course, you are right." But Rafe could see she was upset. In that moment, if he had known where to find Robert McKay, he would have hauled the fellow up by the lapels of his ragged coat and given him a beating far worse than the one the guards had dished out.

Instead, he glanced up the stairs and watched Caro run down the hall. "Perhaps you should speak to her."

Danielle's gaze followed his and she sighed. "I only wish I knew what to say."

"Tell her I plan to wait another day, give McKay one last chance to prove himself before I go to the authorities."

"I'll tell her." Lifting her skirt out of the way, Dani climbed the stairs.

Rafe watched her disappear down the upstairs hall and thought of the pain he had seen in Caro's eyes when McKay had not arrived as she so hoped he would.

Then again, the man had never actually

agreed to the arrangement, only adamantly sworn his innocence in the murder of the earl.

Recalling his conversation with McKay and how convincing the man had been, Rafe was only mildly surprised when an hour later, the footman, Mr. Cooney, arrived at the door of his study with a pair of notes, one addressed to the Duke of Sheffield, the other to Miss Caroline Loon.

"Thank you, Cooney," Rafe said, taking the notes from the footman's blunt fingers. "Did you see the man who delivered these?"

"Yes, sir. Come to the back door. Nice-lookin' chap 'cept his eye was all swolled up and his face was black-and-blue."

"Brown hair, brown eyes?"

"That'd be him, sir."

Rafe broke the wax seal and skimmed the message.

Your Grace,
I could not allow you, your wife or Miss Loon to involve yourselves any deeper in my problems. Please believe I have told you the truth and am determined to prove my innocence. I thank you for the funds you left for me at the prison. I hope in time I shall be able to repay your kind-

ness and generosity.

> Your servant,
> Robert McKay

After reading the note a second time and for reasons he couldn't explain, Rafe believed as he had before that McKay was telling the truth. Still, it was just as likely the man was a complete and utter fraud.

With a sigh, he set the message down next to the one that had been penned to Caroline Loon.

"Ask Miss Loon and the duchess to come down to my study, will you Mr. Cooney?"

"Yes, sir, Yer Grace."

The women appeared a few minutes later, and he could see faint traces of tears on Caro's cheeks.

"What's happened?" she asked, unable to maintain her usual reticence. "Have you heard from Robert?"

"I did, indeed. Your friend has sent us both a message." He handed the note to Caro, then turned the one he had received over to his wife.

Caro's eyes briefly closed as she finished reading the message. She clutched the paper fiercely against her breast. "He didn't run away. He is trying to prove his innocence."

"I realize the note is addressed to you, but

I should like to read it, if you don't mind."

Only a bit reluctantly, Caro handed it over, faint color rising in her cheeks.

My dearest Caro,
No day has passed since our parting that my mind has not been filled with thoughts of you. I pray that you have thought of me, as well. Still, I dare not seek you out, as I ache to do, until this matter is resolved. I must prove my innocence. To do that, there are questions I must ask, answers I need to find. Until such time as this is over, I will carry the memory of your beautiful smile in my heart.

Yours faithfully,
Robert

Rafe finished reading the message and handed it back, trying to ignore the dampness in Caro's eyes.

"I'll send a message to Jonas McPhee. If anyone can discover the truth of the murder, Jonas can."

Caro came forward and caught his hand. "Thank you so much, Your Grace. I will never forget what you have done."

"I give you a word of caution, sweeting. If McPhee discovers your friend is guilty of murder, I'll have no choice but to inform the authorities."

"I know that."

"He is innocent, Caro," Dani said firmly. "He would not have sent the notes if he were guilty. He would simply have run away."

But of course he might have done it just to stall for time, and all of them knew it.

"Is there anything else, Your Grace?" Caro asked.

"Actually, there is. I've been thinking for some time now that you have hidden yourself away long enough. You are a gently reared young woman who fell on hard times, but you are also Danielle's friend, and through your loyalty to her have become my friend, as well. There are any number of social functions you might enjoy and I think it is long past time that you did so."

Caro's eyes rounded. Danielle smiled up at him so brightly something tightened in his chest.

"She would need an entirely new wardrobe," Dani said.

"Without question." A corner of his mouth edged up. "I imagine the two of you are up to the task."

Caro just stood there, too stunned to speak. Then she shook her head. "I am sorry, Your Grace. I know you have nothing but the very best intentions, but I simply cannot accept your generous offer. I have always paid my own way. It is a vow I made to my mother before she died, and that is how it must remain. If you cannot accept me as I am, then I must leave your household."

Dani's face fell. "Rafael did not mean to insult you, dearest. As he said, you are our friend."

Caro managed a smile. "I am happy as I am. But I want you to know that I cherish, above all things, the friendship the two of you have given me."

Rafe cast Danielle a glance. It was clear Caro wouldn't change her mind. An offer of marriage from Robert McKay would alter the situation, of course, but so far McKay had not voiced his intentions. For Caro's sake, Rafe hoped they were honorable. Then again, if, indeed, the man were an earl and Caro but a lady's maid . . .

"The offer stands open," Rafe said. "If you change your mind —"

"I will not."

Rafe just nodded. He couldn't help admiring the girl. And he thought that any man would be lucky to have Caroline Loon for a wife.

Even an earl.

Still, there was every chance McKay was

nothing more than the murderer he was accused of being.

Time would tell.

Time and Jonas McPhee.

The Christmas holidays passed. Rafe's mother left her apartments and traveled to the country to spend the next several weeks at Sheffield Hall, the family estate in Buckinghamshire. Danielle and her husband spent a good deal of time in society, which, little by little, had begun to welcome her into its esteemed company.

The days marched steadily forward, but no word came from Robert McKay. Dani knew the runner, Jonas McPhee, was working hard to discover the truth of the murder but so far had found little of use.

People who knew McKay liked him. Before the murder, he had been a solicitor in the town of Guildford, a respected member of the community. They were reluctant to give up information that might cause him harm.

It was the ninth of January. The weather had been abominable, cold and windy with a chilling frost over the ground that refused to melt before noon. But yesterday the sun had shone and warmed the air, and Dani's spirits had brightened.

She and Aunt Flora decided to visit the orphanage, which they did as often as they could, bringing the children toys or a small gift of sweets. Dani was especially looking forward to seeing Maida Ann and Terry, who had become her favorites. It had been too long since her last visit, not since before the Twelve Days.

As her personal carriage, smaller than the ducal coach but carrying the distinctive Sheffield crest, rolled up in front of the red-brick building that housed the orphanage, Dani spotted two familiar heads racing ahead of the other children — little Maida, blond and grinning, Terry's red hair sticking up in tufts on his head.

Dani's heart squeezed at the sight of them. Kneeling on the walkway, she gathered them into her arms.

"I am so happy to see you!"

Maida Ann hugged Dani's neck. "I was so hoping you would come. Every day I said a prayer and now you are here."

Dani hugged her again. "I promise I won't stay away so long the next time." A slight tug on her skirt and she looked down to see little Terrance gazing up at her with big brown, hopeful eyes.

"Did you bring us a sweet?" the boy asked.

Dani laughed. "Of course, I did." She handed him several pieces of hard sugar candy, then gave the same amount to Maida Ann.

"There is enough for everyone." Aunt Flora spoke up from behind them, passing Terry a small cloth sack. "Take these round and pass them out to all of the other children."

"Thank you, milady, ever so much." Terry grinned and Dani saw that he was missing a tooth. He held his own candies as if they were pieces of gold, then raced off to distribute the precious gifts to his friends.

Maida Ann clung to Dani's hand. "You're so pretty."

"So are you, sweetheart," Dani said, meaning it, and little Maida, in her dress of coarse brown wool, blushed and shyly smiled.

Dani gave her a last hard hug and rose to her feet, holding on to Maida's hand. Dear God, how she wished she could take the children home with her! Her heart ached for the child she would never have, but it was too soon to speak of adoption. Rafe might grow suspicious, and if he did, if he somehow discovered she was barren and that she had known before they were wed . . .

She swallowed, unable to finish the thought.

The women stayed for a while with the children, Dani promising Mrs. Gibbons, the head mistress, to speak to the duke about the money for new spring clothing, then she and Aunt Flora left the orphanage.

The carriage rolled through the crowded streets, Aunt Flora's short, bulky figure perched on the opposite seat, complaining, which she rarely did.

"Thank God the sun is shining at last." Flora pulled her heavy fur lap robe more securely over her plump knees. "I thought I should never see it again."

"Yes, it's amazing how a bright day can lift one's spirits."

"I'm afraid it makes me yearn for home, my dear."

Dani's gaze sharpened on her aunt. "You're not thinking of leaving?"

"I have decided to leave, and soon. London is abysmal this time of year. I cannot manage another week."

"Are you sure the roads are dry enough to travel?"

"Dry enough to get me there. You and the duke seem to be rubbing on well enough. My presence is no longer needed, and at any rate, it is past time I returned."

Dani studied her aunt's kindly face. She thought of Rafael and how the two of them were now man and wife, as her aunt had once believed they should be. Dani couldn't help wondering how much of what had transpired had been engineered by the older woman.

Aunt Flora sighed. "It will be so good to be home."

Whatever the truth, Dani hated to see her go, but Aunt Flora missed the open spaces and clean country air, and Dani couldn't blame her for wanting to escape the dark skies, sooty fog and dirty streets of the city in winter.

That night at supper she relayed her aunt's decision to Rafe, who surprised her by suggesting they see her aunt home.

"It's not all that far and we could use a bit of time away ourselves. McPhee has gone north to speak to Robert's cousin, Stephen Lawrence. While we're waiting for news, perhaps a journey to the country will take Caro's mind off Robert McKay."

It was such a marvelous notion that Dani couldn't help a smile of warmth that Rafe would be so thoughtful. It had happened a great deal lately, which made it harder and harder for her to keep her distance, to hang on to her resolve not to place her trust in him as she had before.

Harder and harder not to love him.

The notion worried her greatly. What would happen when he realized she wouldn't be able to give him a child? When he discovered that he would never have a son? At least not with her?

She couldn't help thinking of Arthur Bartholomew, Rafe's wastrel cousin, and how desperately his family needed an heir.

Divorce was rare, nearly unheard of, but occasionally it happened. The scandal lingered for years. But Rafe needed a son to carry on his name, and divorce would be his only option. Dani shivered to think of facing the terrible gossip, the ostracism that she had suffered before.

And losing Rafael a second time . . . She didn't think she could survive it.

A jolt of pain tore into her heart at the thought of Rafe sharing his life with another woman, and in that moment she knew the awful truth.

I'm in love with him!

It was too late to save herself, too late to protect her heart. She had fallen in love with him — just as she had before.

Fear shook her. The road ahead was fraught with danger, a landscape of pain that could destroy her.

God in heaven, how could she have let it happen?

Preparations for the journey began. Caro helped Dani pack for the weeklong trip, but instead of being excited, Danielle's worry continued to build.

She loved Rafael — she knew that now, knew, as well, the more time she spent with him, the deeper that love would grow. And the awful truth was, there was every chance she would lose him.

At the time of the wedding, she had never considered it. Aunt Flora had believed Rafe owed her marriage, but neither she nor her aunt had any idea how desperately his family needed an heir. Neither of them had ever imagined that Rafe might consider divorce.

She was thinking about the grim possibility when Rafael called her into his study the day before their departure.

Though he smiled at her as he rose from behind his desk, her heart beat with uncertainty. "You wished to see me?"

"I'm sorry, love, something's come up and it looks as if I'm going to have to change my plans."

"What's happened?"

"I've just received a note from Colonel

Pendleton. Hal has requested a meeting, and as it is a matter of some importance, I am obliged to attend."

Rafe wasn't going with them! Dani felt a dizzying wave of relief. She could travel to the country with Caro and her aunt, escape her husband's powerful presence at least for the next several days, long enough to collect her scattered thoughts.

"I understand completely. Of course you must stay."

"Unless there is something more I'll need to do, I can leave the day after the meeting and join you."

It was a long day's journey, but no more. If Rafael left in the morning, he would be in Wycombe before dark.

Dani bit her lip. She needed this time apart from him, no matter how brief it was. "We only planned to be gone for a week. If you recall, you also have a meeting with your solicitor next Friday. It seems a lot of trouble to go to when you can stay but such a short time."

Rafael frowned. "Are you certain? I was rather looking forward to getting out of the damnable fog."

Dani glanced away. Her chest was squeezing. She was already missing him and she hadn't even left. Given her uncertain future, it was terrifying.

"Actually, I would enjoy having a bit of time alone with my aunt . . . I mean, now that the opportunity has arisen."

Rafe didn't look happy, and she felt a tug at her heart. He had loved her once. Perhaps, as she had, he was beginning to love her again.

Even if some miracle occurred and his feelings for her returned, there was the matter of a child and Rafe's duty to his family.

Guilt gnawed at her. Dear God, what had she done?

Dani smiled at him a little too brightly. "I'll only stay till the end of the week. I'll come back on Thursday, just as we planned."

He made a curt nod of his head. "If that is your wish. You can travel with your aunt and I'll send my carriage to fetch you home."

Dani just nodded. Blinking against the sudden sting of tears, she rounded the desk and kissed his cheek. "Thank you." She turned and crossed to the study door without looking his way again.

All the way up to her room, Dani thought of Rafe and the days she would spend without him. By the time she opened the door to her suite, she had begun to regret her decision.

★ ★ ★

His wife was gone. It was quiet this afternoon and Rafe found himself prowling aimlessly about the house. There was a time he'd been quite comfortable in the big empty rooms and long marble hallways. Now he missed the feminine sound of Dani's laughter, missed sharing supper with her and discussing the day's events, missed spending his nights in her bed and the pleasure he took from her body.

It was amazing how fast he'd grown accustomed to being married.

To fill the days, he kept himself busy, looking over Sheffield property ledgers, auditing estate managers' reports, searching for new investments. As time slipped past, he found himself looking forward to his meeting with Howard Pendleton, a welcome break in the dull routine of waiting for his wife's return.

It was ridiculous, he told himself. He was behaving like a green lad just out of the schoolroom, becoming as enamored of Danielle as he had been before.

The notion sobered him.

He cared for her, yes. He enjoyed her company, her intelligence, perhaps just as much as the passion they shared. But he was not in love with her. Would not allow himself to fall in love with her again.

That night, he took himself off to his gentlemen's club as he did each night thereafter. Danielle had a place in his life, but he wasn't about to let her into his heart.

Instead, he steeled himself against the emotions she stirred and sank even deeper into his legendary reserve.

By the time the day of his meeting arrived, Rafe climbed into his carriage with a single thought on his mind: had the colonel been able to convince the prime minister and his cabinet how important it was to purchase the Baltimore Clippers?

He was pondering the answer as he climbed the steps in front of Whitehall on his way to the War Office and spotted Cord and Ethan walking toward him.

"I figured I'd see the two of you here," Rafe said.

"Any idea what's happening with the purchase of the fleet?" Ethan asked.

Rafe shook his head.

Cord pulled open the heavy front door. "I imagine we're about to find out."

Three sets of boots echoed in the corridor leading to the colonel's office. The men walked into the Spartan room and the colonel rose from behind his desk. As usual, his scarlet uniform jacket was spotless, his silver hair cut very short and neatly combed.

"Have a seat, gentlemen."

The men sat down in straight-backed chairs on the opposite side of his desk.

"I might as well get to the point. I called you here to tell you Bartel Schrader, the man they call the Dutchman, has been spotted here in London. I'm not certain of his purpose, but he is here."

"Interesting," Rafe said, remembering the sandy-haired man he had briefly met in Philadelphia.

"Since Schrader is under the impression that you, Your Grace, are his chief competitor in the purchase of the Baltimore Clippers, I thought it was important that you know."

"Yes," Cord said, "and it is likely he'll believe Ethan is also involved, as the two of you are known to be friends and Ethan is heavily involved in the shipping trade."

"My thoughts exactly," said the colonel. "And that applies to you, Lord Brant, as well, since the three of you have invested in a number of business dealings together."

"I suppose that makes sense," Cord agreed.

"The man has a dangerous reputation," the colonel continued, "and there is a great deal of money at stake. You may cross paths with him. If you do, I need to be informed. And until we discover what he's up to, I advise you all to be careful."

Rafe just nodded.

"We'll let you know if we hear the whisper of his name," Cord said.

"I'll put the word out among a few of my friends in the shipping business," Ethan volunteered, "see what they might be able to learn."

The meeting concluded and the three friends walked together out of Pendleton's office, their thoughts moving away from the business they had just discussed, turning in a different direction.

"Your wife still out of town?" Ethan asked casually.

"Unfortunately," Rafe said darkly.

Cord grinned. "I'm happy to say my wife is at home awaiting my return, and I am extremely glad. I have plans for her this afternoon that should keep both of us entertained."

The gleam in Cord's golden eyes made his meaning clear, and Ethan laughed. "Now that you suggest it, that is not a bad notion."

Rafe swore softly. "I think you have both lost your minds."

"Love will do that to you, my friend," Ethan said with a smile.

"Exactly why I refuse to fall into such a state."

Cord and Ethan cast each other a glance. "I'm not certain we had any say in the matter," Cord said.

Rafe ignored the remark. He wasn't about to let it happen to him. Not again.

Still, he would be damned glad when Danielle returned.

The edge of his mouth faintly curved. Perhaps his two friends were not so far off the mark. He had plans for Danielle, as well. On Thursday when she returned, he intended to make very thorough love to her. Afterward, she would be surprised to discover, she would no longer be sleeping in her own bed, but spending her nights in his.

His shaft turned to steel at the thought. Damn, he would be glad when she got home.

Twenty-Four

Rafe's big black traveling coach, pulled by a team of four matched grays, rumbled down the road toward London. The coachman, Mr. Mullens, capably handled the reins, and at Rafe's insistence, two footmen rode at the back of the conveyance for protection in case of trouble along the way.

The weather had once more turned chill, but as yet it hadn't rained, which meant the roads were deeply rutted but not muddy. Inside the coach, Dani and Caro sat across from each other, each warmed by a thick fur lap robe.

"I enjoyed the time in the country," Dani said with a sigh, "but I will be glad to get home."

"As will I." Caro smoothed a tight blond curl back into the bun at the back of her head, her gaze fixed out the window. "Perhaps there will be news of Robert."

"Yes, perhaps there will." Dani hoped so, though she was worried. No word had come from McKay save for the notes they had received the day he left prison. Jonas McPhee had been off somewhere digging for information, but his results, so far, had been thin at best.

"Or perhaps Mr. McPhee will have discovered something," Caro added.

"Rafael says he is very good at his job."

"I am certain that he is. I hold high hopes that he will discover the proof Robert needs."

They spoke little more as the coach rumbled along toward home, the jarring, jostling ride tiring, and both of their minds on the men they had left behind. Dani had missed Rafael far more than she liked, and she knew Caro pined for Robert McKay.

The ride and the cold exhausted them and they slept for a while. The rattle of hooves over a wooden bridge as they neared the outskirts of London brought Dani awake and she glanced out the window at the barren winter landscape. The month of January was cold, the ground frozen, the trees leafless and barren. The wheels of the coach rumbled over the bridge and she saw the frothy white water of the stream rushing over the rocks below.

They were halfway across, the coachman urging the team a little faster as he neared the end of his journey, when she heard a loud clap that sounded like thunder, then the sound of grinding wood.

Caro screamed as the front axle cracked loudly, whined, then tore completely in two.

"Hang on!" Dani shouted, groping madly for something to cling to, the carriage tilting wildly, then tipping sideways and rolling completely over. For an instant, it seemed to hang suspended in the air, the body of the coach ripping loose from the horses, careening off the bridge into space.

A sharp jolt and more rending wood, her heart pounding fiercely. Dani saw the floor of the carriage above her, the ceiling at her feet, then the floor was beneath her once more.

Something tore loose inside the coach, struck her hard in the stomach and pain shot through her. A chunk of wood slammed into the side of her head, and she felt another brutal shot of pain. The last thing she remembered was the chill of the freezing water surging through the wrecked carriage floor, soaking into her skirts and weighing her down, then her eyes slid closed and she tumbled into darkness.

By six o'clock, Rafe began to pace the floor of his study. The carriage should have returned by now. Still, they might have got a late start or a wheel might have broken.

Surely they would be home soon.

By eight o'clock, he was beyond worried. Perhaps highwaymen had attacked the coach. Perhaps there had been some kind of an accident. He thought to saddle his horse and ride off for the road he was certain they traveled, but he feared the coach had already entered the city and in the maze of streets, he would miss them.

By ten o'clock he was frantic. He had sent two mounted riders in search of the coach, but they had not returned. If they didn't reach the house in the next thirty minutes, he would go in search of the vehicle himself.

At ten-fifteen, a commotion in the entry had him bolting from his study at a run. He recognized the coachman, Mr. Mullens, who spoke rapidly to the butler and stood there wringing his hands. His duster was torn and covered with mud, his face battered and bloody, and Rafe's stomach viciously contracted.

"What is it, Mullen? What's happened?"

The man looked up at him through swollen, bloodshot eyes. "There were an accident, Yer Grace. Front axle broke while we was goin' over a bridge."

"Where is the duchess?"

"She and her maid were injured, sir, and one of the footmen. Coach turned over, went into the stream. We got 'em out. Some folks come along and helped us get 'em to an inn called the Oxbow, and the owner sent for a doctor. I left 'em there and come straight away to fetch you."

Rafe clamped down on his fear. "How badly were the women hurt?"

"The maid were mostly scuffed up. The duchess . . . hard to say. She were still unconscious when I left."

The knot in Rafe's stomach went tighter. Dani was injured. He didn't know how badly. He had to get to her as quickly as he could.

"Let's go." Rafe started walking. His horse was already saddled, a big black stallion named Thor. He had ordered it done half an hour ago. It was by sheer force of will that he hadn't yet left the house. Now he was glad he had held on to his senses and made himself wait for word.

"How far is the inn?" he asked as he strode out the door to the stable behind the house, Michael Mullens hurrying along in his wake. The man looked exhausted. Rafe didn't care. If he found out the coachman was responsible for the accident, he was going to look much worse.

"Not far, Yer Grace. We had nearly reached the edge of the city."

Ignoring the fear gripping his insides,

Rafe ordered one of the grooms to saddle a second horse, and as soon as the task was completed, the men mounted up.

Rafe turned to his head groom. "There's an inn called the Oxbow on the road leading to Wycombe. We'll need a carriage to transport the women home. And have Wooster get word to Neil McCauley. Tell him to meet us at the inn."

McCauley, once a surgeon in the navy, was one of Rafe's best friends. McCauley had left the service, but not the practice of medicine. He was no longer a surgeon, but now one of London's most highly respected physicians. The man had delivered both Grace's and Victoria's babes, and Rafe trusted him completely.

The groom rapidly nodded his head. "I'll see to it, meself, Yer Grace." Turning, he began shouting orders to the rest of the grooms.

In minutes, Rafe and Mullens were riding over the cobbles at a breakneck pace, heading for the inn, Rafe doing his best not to let his worry overwhelm him.

She'll be all right, he told himself.

She has to be.

And he said a silent prayer that it was true.

Dani awakened in a haze of pain. There

was a man in the room she didn't know and he stood next to her bed.

"Take it easy, Duchess, you've been hurt pretty badly. My name is Neil McCauley. I'm a friend of your husband's, and I am a physician."

Danielle moistened her lips, which felt cotton dry. "Is . . . Rafael here?"

He stepped forward then, and she realized he had been standing in the shadows. His dark hair was mussed, faint smudges darkened the area beneath his blue eyes, and the shadow of a beard lined his jaw.

"I'm right here, love." He took hold of her hand, bent and placed a soft kiss on her forehead.

"The duke came as soon as he heard," the doctor said. "He's been pacing the floor for the past half hour, worried sick about you."

"What . . . happened?"

Rafe squeezed her hand. "There was a carriage accident. The coach broke an axle and went into the river."

She tried to remember the events but her mind refused to function. "What . . . what about Caro . . . and the others?"

"Your maid is pretty well battered," the doctor told her, "but she wasn't seriously injured. One of the footmen broke an arm, but the bone has been set and in time he should heal."

Thank God none of them were seriously hurt. Dani looked at Rafe and saw the worry in his eyes. During the week she had been gone, she had missed him so much, and dear God, she loved him.

Her eyes slid closed. She was so very tired.

"I've given you some laudanum to help you rest," the doctor said. "In the morning, you'll feel better. Once you do, your husband can take you home."

She forced her eyelids to open and looked at the two men standing beside the bed, Rafe tall and handsome even in his wrinkled, mud-spattered clothes, the brown-haired doctor a little shorter, and in his own way attractive. She felt the comforting warmth of Rafe's hand enclosing hers.

"Everything's going to be all right," he said gently.

Dani tried to smile but her eyelids drooped closed. Her entire body felt bruised, and she ached from head to foot. On top of that, there was this dull ache throbbing below her stomach. The laudanum helped, but it made her unbearably sleepy.

"Get some rest, love." Rafe's mouth brushed lightly over hers. He let go of her hand and turned to leave, his footfalls muffled on the carpet. She tried to stay awake a little longer, but her body refused to cooperate and she drifted into a heavy sleep.

She dreamed of Rafe and home, though later she didn't recall.

As soon as the door was closed, Rafe turned to McCauley. "Is she going to be all right? I want the truth, Neil."

They stood in an upstairs hallway of the Oxbow Inn. Neil didn't want to move Danielle until she had regained a little more of her strength.

The doctor set his satchel on the chair beside the door. "As I said, she took one helluva beating when the coach went off the bridge, but nothing seems to be broken."

"So you're saying she'll be fine."

"For the most part, yes."

Rafe straightened. "What does that mean?"

"It means there are a few complications."

Rafe's pulse kicked up. "What sort of complications?"

McCauley's face looked grim. "When I went in to see her the first time, she was bleeding from the womb. I examined her and discovered she had reopened an old injury that she had suffered before."

Rafe frowned. "What kind of injury was it?"

"I'm not sure exactly how it happened. Some sort of fall, I would guess. Whatever occurred, there was damage to her female organs. The carriage accident tore something loose again."

He fought a moment of nausea. "Tell me she'll be all right."

"Odds are good she'll heal without a problem as she did before. But there is something I must tell you, Rafael."

Rafe looked into Neil McCauley's face, saw the pity, and steeled himself for whatever the man had to say. "Go on."

"I'm afraid your wife will never have children. Her womb was severely damaged the first time. This has only made matters worse."

Rafe glanced away, trying to make sense of Neil's words. No children when they had once planned to have half a dozen? Danielle would be devastated.

"I don't know what to say, how I'm going to tell her."

"I'm sure she already knows. The initial injury occurred at least several years back. There would have been changes in her monthly cycle. The doctor would have explained her situation at the time."

Rafe shook his head. "It isn't possible. She would have said something. She must not have known."

McCauley looked away. "Perhaps not." But it was obvious the man didn't believe it.

Rafe's mind spun. Danielle couldn't have known she was barren. If she had known, she would have told him before they were wed. She knew he needed an heir, knew how crucial it was she bear him a son.

His thoughts slid back to the journey she had made to America. She had planned to marry a widower, a man who already had two children of his own.

I would have had a family, she had once said.

God's blood, she had known from the start she was barren!

Rafe's stomach tightened into a painful knot. He looked at Neil McCauley. "You're sure she'll be all right."

"As sure as I can be under the circumstances. She's a healthy young woman. Mostly she needs to rest and regain her strength."

Rafe just nodded. There was a thickness in his throat that made it hard to speak. "Thank you for coming, Neil."

McCauley gripped Rafe's shoulder. "I'm sorry, Rafael."

Rafe made no reply. But instead of returning to Dani's room as he had planned, he swung around and walked off down the hall.

Twenty-Five

Danielle was rapidly recovering. It had been a week since the accident and she was home and out of bed and fast regaining her usual robust constitution. In the mornings, though the January weather remained chill, she and Caro walked together in the garden.

"I am determined to get back on my feet as soon as possible," Dani said. "A week in bed is quite long enough."

"You need your rest," Caro argued. "Dr. McCauley said so."

"He also said that a bit of exercise is good for me." And she did feel better after a brisk morning stroll. Her body was healing nicely. It was her heart that was in trouble.

From the day they had wed, whenever a problem arose, Rafael had grown distant and remote. Since the accident, he had withdrawn once more, retreating even deeper behind his infuriating reserve than ever before.

Danielle ached to talk to him, to try to discover what was wrong. But each time she worked up the courage, she thought of what he might say and her resolve seeped away. Instead, she kept to herself just as he did, allowing her body to mend while her heart ached more and more.

At least Caro was recovered, though in truth her spirits were not much higher than Danielle's. During the day, the slender blonde moved restlessly around the house, her mind burdened with thoughts of Robert McKay. At night, Dani could hear her wandering about in the room next door, unable to sleep, even in the late hours of the night.

At present, Caro was downstairs in the Wedgwood Room, working on her embroidery, making little progress, Dani suspected. Danielle was worried about her. She wished word would come of Robert McKay.

Sitting in one of the smaller drawing rooms at the rear of the house, trying to concentrate on her embroidery and having little success, Caro looked up just as Wooster appeared in the open doorway.

"I am sorry to interrupt, Miss, but His Grace requests your presence in the library."

Caro's heart jerked into a faster motion. Perhaps, at last, Robert had come! "Thank you, Mr. Wooster. I shall go there straightaway." Her knees trembled as she set aside her work and rose hastily from the sofa. Taking a steadying breath, she collected herself, smoothed the front of her pale blue woolen gown, and started for the door, following the butler out of the drawing room.

Her hands were trembling as she waited for Wooster to turn the silver knob on the door, then step back out of the way so that she might walk past him into the study. But as her gaze searched the room, it wasn't Robert, but the Bow Street runner, Jonas McPhee, who stood in front of the massive rosewood desk across from the duke.

"Come in, my dear," Sheffield said. "I believe you've heard me speak of Mr. McPhee."

"Why, yes . . . Good afternoon, Mr. McPhee."

"A pleasure to meet you, Miss Loon." He was short and stout, wearing tiny spectacles, his head balding, but there was something in the thickness of his shoulders, the lines of his face that said he was a man who could hold his own.

The duke indicated she should take a seat next to the runner, and she sat down on the edge of the dark green leather chair, so nervous she had to concentrate to breathe.

"I asked you here because Mr. McPhee has brought news of Robert McKay, and I thought you would wish to hear."

"Oh, yes, very much. Thank you, Your Grace."

"Jonas, why don't you tell Miss Loon what you've just told me?"

McPhee nodded his balding head, then turned a little toward her. "To begin with, Miss Loon, much of what your friend has said has been verified as the truth."

Her body went so weak she thought she might slide right out of her chair.

"Are you all right, Caro?" the duke asked worriedly.

"I am fine." She braced herself, settling her hands once more in her lap. "Please continue, Mr. McPhee."

"Recently I traveled north to a small village near York, where I spoke to a man named Stephen Lawrence, who is Mr. McKay's cousin. Though it took a bit of persuasion, when he discovered I was working on Mr. McKay's behalf, Mr. Lawrence proved extremely helpful. You see, his mother is Robert's aunt. Apparently, she was in attendance when Nigel Truman, eldest son of the Earl of Leighton, married Robert's mother at St. Margaret's Church."

Caro frowned. "I'm afraid I don't understand."

Seated behind his desk, the duke leaned

toward them. "Although you know a great deal of Robert's story, Caro, there is a bit more to the tale. You see, Robert's cousin discovered Robert was Truman's legitimate son, which made him heir to the Leighton earldom. Apparently, that is the reason he was made suspect for the murder. With his father dead and Robert hanged for the crime, Clifford Nash, the late earl's distant cousin, was next in line for the Leighton title and lands."

Her mind spun. "Are you . . . are you saying it was this man, Clifford Nash, who murdered the earl?"

"Nash or someone he hired," McPhee answered. "We are not yet certain how Nash discovered Robert's existence. Stephen Lawrence believes the late earl may have told the man himself."

"A very poor decision, it would seem," said the duke.

The runner sighed. "At any rate, the problem comes in finding the proof."

"But if you know for certain that Robert is . . . is the legitimate earl —" she broke off for a moment, not quite able to grasp the notion "— then you have found the motive for the murder."

"That is correct, but as I said, the trouble lies in proving it."

"How will you go about it?"

"I'm afraid you will have to leave that to me."

Caro glanced from McPhee to the duke. "Do you know where Robert is now?"

Sheffield shook his head. "Not at present, but in time Mr. McPhee is certain to come across him."

"I see."

"Is there anything else you wish to know, Caro?" the duke asked kindly.

But even if she had other questions, her mind had gone completely blank. "Not at present."

"Then you may leave us."

Caro rose unsteadily from her chair and made her way toward the door of the library. Her mind was churning, her heart aching. All she could think of was that Robert was an earl and she was naught but a lady's maid.

Why was life so unfair?

Before she'd had time to reach the solitude of her bedchamber, Caro started to weep.

The last days of January approached. Dani and Caro were sitting in the Wedgwood Room, Caro making a fresh attempt at her embroidery while Danielle listened to the rain against the window and perused a text of Elizabeth Bentley poems.

Glancing over to the chair next to the sofa, Dani saw Caro's slim hand poised above her needlework while she stared into the flames in the hearth. Since her friend had learned the truth of Robert's birth, she had been practically inconsolable.

Caro's eyes met Dani's. "Even if Robert's innocence can be proved, it is over between us." She jabbed the needle a little too firmly into the fabric inside her embroidery hoop. "I am naught but the daughter of a vicar, a commoner, while Robert . . . Robert is the son of an earl."

"Perhaps it won't matter," Dani said, praying it was true. But Robert had never spoken of marriage and as the days slipped past with no word, it seemed clear it was not his intention.

"I wish I had stayed in America. I wish Robert had stayed. I would have waited for him to serve his indenture. I would have waited for him forever, if he had but asked."

"Nothing has been settled. We don't even know where Robert is. Perhaps in time this will all work out."

But Caro didn't believe it and neither did Dani. She said nothing more, just set her book aside and left the drawing room, her own mood equally grim.

She was well healed now, feeling completely herself again, and yet Rafael had not come to her bed.

At supper he watched her through hooded, heavy-lidded eyes, making only the meagerest attempts at conversation. Dani wanted to shout at him, demand he speak up and tell her what was wrong. She couldn't help thinking of the night she had worn the emerald satin gown with the indecent décolletage and actually considered wearing it again.

Instead, after another dull evening that ended with Rafe leaving the dining room immediately after supper and squirreling himself away in his library-study, she retired upstairs to her room next to his and began to pace the floor, angrier by the minute.

But with the anger came uncertainty.

Dear God, even his desire for her had waned. Since the accident, she saw none of the hot desire that had always shone in his eyes when he looked at her, none of the barely leashed passion that always simmered between them.

He didn't want her. The knowledge was devastating.

More and more he was spending the evenings at his club, returning only in the late hours of the morning. Dani believed that unless she broke through the barrier he had erected between them, it was only a matter of time before he sought the company of other women.

She was still wide-awake when she heard him enter his bedchamber. She could hear him wandering around and imagined him removing his clothes, saw in her mind his tall, lean frame, the indentation of the muscles over his ribs, the hard slabs of muscle on his chest. A little shiver of desire slipped through her.

Sweet God, the man was her husband. It was time he remembered it.

Her decision made, she hurried over to her dresser and pulled out a white satin nightgown. It felt like liquid silver as she drew it over her head and let it glide down over her hips. The nightgown was high-waisted, the bosom covered only by sheer white lace. When she looked into the mirror, she could see her nipples, dark rose circles that made her recall the feel of Rafe's hands on them, the way he made them peak and distend.

She touched herself there, felt the need burn through her, and realized how badly she wanted him to make love to her. It seemed forever since she had lain with him, not since before she had left with her aunt for the country.

Pulling the brush through her long red curls then arranging them around her shoulders, Dani drew in a breath and started for the door between their two rooms.

It was late, past the hour of midnight. Deciding not to ring for his valet, Rafe pulled the knot on his wide white stock and slid the long strip of cloth from around his neck. He draped his coat and waistcoat over a chair and pulled his thin lawn shirt off over his head, leaving him naked to the waist.

He was about to remove his shoes when he heard a faint knock at the door leading in from the duchess's suite. Surprised, he started in that direction, but before he got there, the silver knob turned and Danielle stepped into the room.

"Good evening, Your Grace." Her words came out softly, a little breathlessly, and his pulse took a leap.

She was dressed in a clingy white satin nightgown that revealed every luscious curve, and his loins tightened. His gaze took in the sheer lace top that barely disguised the twin rose circles crowning her breasts, and as he watched, they began to stiffen into small, erotic buds. His shaft lengthened and swelled, began to grow thick and heavy.

"Is there something you want?" he forced himself to ask.

Her eyes met his, bright green into blue. "Yes . . . and I believe you know what it is."

His body tightened and his arousal strengthened. She looked as beautiful as he had ever seen her, tall and regal, incredibly feminine, and he hadn't had her since before the accident.

The word struck sharply, reminding him of her treachery and renewing his resolve to keep himself apart from her. She had lied to him, betrayed him in an even more heinous fashion than he had wrongly accused her of before. He had promised himself he would take his ease with another woman, that it no longer mattered that he cleave only to her, since there would be no children from their union.

But each night as he lay in bed, it was Danielle he ached for, Danielle he wanted.

Now she was here, standing in his bedchamber, just a few feet away. In the flickering lamplight, he could see the pearly smoothness of her skin, the fiery hue of her long red hair. He could smell the faint, sweet scent of her perfume that reminded him of apple blossoms.

His groin tightened and yet he did not move. "You have been ill," he said blandly, though he could barely make himself utter the words. "You should rest and recover your strength."

"I am no longer ill, Rafael . . . except with wanting you."

He hissed in a breath, took an unconscious step toward her, then made himself stop and remain where he stood. He clenched his jaw. "Perhaps some other night."

She started walking toward him, her movements so graceful the nightgown flowed around her lithe figure as if she were gowned in clouds.

She stopped directly in front of him, rested a hand on his bare chest, and he could feel the heat of her slender fingers, the warmth of her breath against his skin.

"It's been far too long already." Her fingers sifted though the swath of dark hair on his chest, moved down to his waist, then over the heavy bulge pressing against the fly of his breeches.

His heart thundered. His arousal strained toward her hand.

"You want me," she said with what sounded like relief, lightly squeezing him through the cloth.

Rafe grit his jaw against the hot desire flooding through him, but when Danielle looked up at him, when she moistened her full ruby lips, his careful control stretched thin, then violently snapped.

With a growl low in his throat, he reached for her, slid an arm around her waist and hauled her hard against him, crushed his mouth down savagely over hers. He kissed her deeply, his tongue plunging in, taking what she offered, unable to resist a moment more. Dani slid her arms around his neck and kissed him back, her lips softening under his, her breasts pressing into his chest and making him groan.

He deepened the kiss, inhaling the familiar scent of her, tasting the sweet femininity that was hers alone, aching with want of her. Dani clung to him, kissing him back, using every erotic trick he had ever taught her, making his shaft grow painfully hard.

He reached out to cup a breast, tried to slide the straps of the white satin gown off her shoulders, but Dani stepped away.

"Not yet. First, I would help you undress."

He watched in fascination as she knelt in front of him to remove each of his shoes and stockings, then began to unfasten the buttons at the front of his breeches. Each brush of her fingers fired an agony of awareness, a blood lust that urged him to lift her up and strip away her gown, to spread her long, shapely legs and bury himself inside her.

And yet he did none of those things. Instead, he let her lead the way, refusing to rush her, absorbing each touch as if his body were dying of thirst and she were the first drops of rain.

Even when she had stripped away his clothes, leaving him naked, he did not move, just stood there in front of her, soaking up her presence, one of his hands skimming over the silk of her hair.

"I've missed you," he said softly, the admission torn from him against his will. She looked up at him and he told himself the glint in her eyes could not be tears.

She placed her mouth against his chest in the spot above his heart, then knelt once more in front of him. Reaching up, she captured his hardness, then took him into her mouth.

For an instant, Rafe stood frozen, certain he must be dreaming, yet praying he would not awaken as Danielle kissed and caressed him, used her lips and her tongue to give him the sort of pleasure a wife did not give to her husband.

But Danielle was no ordinary wife, and

this he had known from the start. When he couldn't bear the pleasure any longer, when the exquisite torture began to overwhelm him, he fisted a hand in her heavy red hair and drew her back to her feet.

He caught her chin between his fingers and lifted her mouth to his, tasting his essence, drawing her very breath into his lungs.

His eyes found hers as he lifted her into his arms and carried her over to his big four-poster bed, set her down atop the clean white sheets and drew the satin nightgown over her head, baring her to his hungry gaze. She waited for him to join her in the deep feather mattress, and he lay down at her side. Her eyes widened as he lifted her and set her astride him.

Her body was slender and supple. Her hair fanned out around her shoulders, brushed the tips of her breasts. When she leaned forward, the heavy mass slid like silk over his bare chest, moved like satin fire over his skin.

"So beautiful. . . ." he said. "Not like any other woman."

Her hand touched his cheek. Danielle leaned closer and he took the soft swell of her breast into his mouth. He suckled her there while his hand found the place between her legs. She was wet and slick, ready for him, and he entered her slowly, filling the beautiful, slender body that fit him so perfectly.

He told himself it was only that he was a man and she a woman and he had been without a woman too long.

But he knew it was a lie, and as he brought her to fulfillment and spent himself inside her, his heart cried out at another, even more hurtful lie.

One that Danielle had told without saying a single word.

Twenty-Six

Dani awakened in her husband's big bed. She felt pleasantly battered and completely sated. Last night, they had made the most splendid love.

A dreamy smile blossomed on her face as she recalled the pleasure they had shared, the joining of their bodies, which had happened more than once. Then she glanced at the empty place in bed where Rafe's hard-muscled frame should have lain and her smile slipped away.

He was gone as if he had never been there, as if they had never made love. Danielle slumped back against the feather pillow, suddenly tired again.

It was nearly an hour later that she dragged herself from beneath the covers and returned to her own suite of rooms. Walking over to the bell pull, she rang for a bath, hoping it would wash away her dismal mood. By the time she had finished, Caro had arrived to help her dress for the day, braid and pin up her hair.

For a while, she wandered the empty

rooms of the house, wondering where her husband might have gone, yearning to see him. As the morning waned, she and Caro walked the gravel paths of the winter garden, pretty, though stark, with its animal topiary and the first green shoots of the earliest spring bulbs pushing up through the soil.

By late afternoon, she began to worry. Was he angry at her brazen behavior last night? He had seemed so pleased at the time, but perhaps on reflection he had found her actions too forward. She hadn't planned for their lovemaking to unfold as it had. But Rafe was just so incredibly handsome, so entirely male, and she had wanted him so badly. Now she worried that perhaps she had displeased him.

Dani sighed. It was difficult to know where one stood with a man like Rafe, who kept so much to himself.

She was thinking about him as she returned to the duchess's suite, wondering if they would make love again tonight or if he would withdraw once more into his shell, when she received a note from him, requesting that she join him that evening for supper in the State Dining Room.

Dani's hand shook as she refolded the message and set the piece of paper down on top of her dresser. The occasion seemed entirely too formal to be anything but bad news. She paced the bedchamber, waiting with trepidation for the hours to pass, then sitting in silence until Caro arrived to help her change and re-dress her hair.

"Well, we had better get started," her friend said, taking charge of the situation, bustling about the room as she always did. "What would you like to wear? And don't you dare say black, though I can tell by the way your shoulders are slumped that you are in a dismal humor."

Dani felt the pull of a smile. "All right, no black." She sighed. She had shown Caro the note when it had first arrived. "I cannot imagine what he might want. He has been so odd of late. I am so worried."

"Perhaps you are worrying for no good cause. Perhaps he has some good fortune he wishes to impart."

Dani brightened. "Do you think so?"

"It is possible, is it not?"

"I suppose." But he had left this morning without a word and been gone from the house all day. Clamping down on a fresh jolt of fear, she joined Caro in front of the ivory-and-gilt armoire and pulled open the door, turning her attention to the task at hand.

"It is a formal invitation, so let us choose

something formal." Rifling through several different garments, a burgundy silk, a dark green velvet, a gown of cream and lace, she settled on an elegant dress of heavy amethyst silk, its bodice of the same rich color shot with gold. "This should do well enough."

"The gown is lovely. The duke won't be able to keep his eyes off you."

Caro spread the garment out on the bed and Dani sat down on the stool in front of the dresser. While Danielle fidgeted nervously, Caro went to work on her hair, brushing the heavy mass and pinning it up, then lacing gold ribbon into the upswept curls. When the task was complete, Dani slid her feet into soft gold slippers.

"Just this one last thing." Caro walked over to the bureau and took the red satin pouch out of Dani's ornately carved jewelry box. She returned and draped the Bride's Necklace around her neck and fastened the clasp. "It looks beautiful," Caro said. "Perfect with the gown."

Dani reached up and touched the elegant strand of pearls, her fingers moving over the sparkling diamonds between each perfect pearl. "I don't know why, but somehow wearing it always makes me feel better."

Caro stepped back to survey her handiwork, tipping her head from side to side to study each angle. "Well, you look as if you are ready to face the dragon in his lair."

Dani sighed as she rose from the stool. "I suppose I am." But inside, she was shaking. It was clear Rafael had something of importance to say, and from the way he had been behaving, she didn't think it was going to be good.

If only the day would come when there are no more secrets between us. When she would be able to look at him without guilt, without any sort of fear.

It wouldn't be this night, she was sure. "Wish me luck," she said. Lifting the hem of her gown, she crossed the carpet for the door, unconsciously raising her chin as she stepped out into the hallway.

When she reached the top of the marble staircase, she paused to look below. In his navy-blue tailcoat and dark gray breeches, his white stock perfectly tied, Rafael looked so handsome her heart squeezed hard inside her.

Head held high, she descended the stairs one by one, feeling his gaze upon her every step of the way. His eyes seemed even bluer than they usually did, or perhaps it was merely his somber expression that made them appear that way.

Whatever the reason, she caught herself studying him from beneath her lashes as he led her into the State Dining Room and seated her next to him at the end of the table.

"I've asked Cook to prepare a special meal in honor of the occasion," he said.

One of her eyebrows went up. "And what occasion might that be?"

"A thank-you for the pleasure you gave me last night."

Dani flicked him a glance. She wasn't sure she liked the idea of him paying her for making love to him, even in this small way. It made her feel a little like a scarlet woman.

Rafe, however, seemed unconcerned. Instead he conversed casually throughout the meal, his eyes drifting often to her breasts, displayed quite nicely in the amethyst gown, and she saw the heat there that had been missing for so long.

Perhaps last night hadn't been a fool's errand after all. Perhaps she had reached him in some way, as she had so desperately wanted to do.

The meal was served, half a dozen courses. Oysters in anchovy sauce, turtle soup, pickled salmon, roast suckling pig. Dani was so nervous she ate almost nothing and noticed Rafe ate less than usual, as well.

When they had finished their dessert, a molded custard covered with slivered almonds, one of the footmen poured them a last glass of wine and Rafe dismissed the servants from the dining room.

The moment the door closed behind them, he lifted his crystal goblet in toast. "To the future," he said, his eyes on her face.

"The future," she echoed hollowly, a fresh shot of worry slipping through her.

Rafe took a drink of his wine and so did Dani, perhaps a bit more than she should have.

He set his glass back down on the table, his eyes so very intense and locked on her face, his long fingers encircling the stem of the glass as he swirled the ruby liquid in the cut crystal bowl.

"Do you remember the promise you made to me not long ago?"

She swallowed. "The promise?"

"It was the night I asked you about the necklace, the night you confessed that you had given it to Robert McKay."

She moistened her lips, which had suddenly gone bone dry. "I . . . I remember."

"You promised me that night that you would never lie to me again."

"Yes . . ."

"But you have lied, haven't you, Dani?"

She trembled, wished she had drunk more wine. "What . . . what do you mean?"

"When did you plan to tell me you couldn't have my child?"

Danielle's heart simply stopped beating. It lay there in her chest, aching as if she were dying, as if no blood pumped through her veins.

"When, Danielle?"

She reached for her wineglass, but Rafe caught her hand.

"When were you going to tell me, Danielle!"

She looked up at him and tears filled her eyes. "Never . . ." she whispered, and then she started to weep.

Her chest constricted with the hot flood of her tears, not the soft weeping of a woman who had been caught in a falsehood, but the deep sobs of a barren woman who wept for the child she could never give the man she loved. She wept as if her heart were breaking, wept and wept and could not stop, and didn't even notice when Rafe drew her up from her chair and eased her into his arms.

"It's all right. . . . Everything is going to be all right."

"It will never be all right," she said, leaning into his embrace. "Not ever." She cried against his shoulder, felt the brush of his lips against her hair.

"Easy."

"I should . . . should have told you before we were wed. Dear God, I know I should have, but I . . ."

"You what . . . ?" he asked gently.

She drew in a ragged breath. "In the beginning I wanted to punish you. You were forcing me to marry you. I thought you were getting what you deserved."

"And later?"

"When we got . . . got back to London, your mother explained how urgent it was that you have an heir to carry on the Sheffield name. And then I met Arthur Bartholomew and saw how truly important it was." She looked up at him, tears rolling down her cheeks. "I'm so sorry, Rafael. So unbearably sorry." She started weeping again and Rafael tightened his hold.

"Don't cry, love."

But she couldn't seem to stop. "How did you . . . how did you find out?"

"Neil McCauley told me. He said you were injured before. What happened to you?"

She dragged in a ragged breath, tried to swallow past the ache in her throat. "I was . . . riding at Wycombe Park. After

424

you . . . ended our betrothal and I moved away from London, I took to riding quite often. It gave me a kind of ease I couldn't seem to find anywhere else."

"Go on."

"It had rained the night before and the fields . . . the fields were wet and muddy. Aunt Flora tried to convince me not to go. She thought it was too dangerous, but I . . . I wouldn't listen. My horse — her name was Blossom — she slipped as we approached a stone hedge and I went off over her head. I must have landed on something when I fell, or . . . I don't know, something just went wrong. When I didn't come home and Blossom came limping back into the stable, Aunt Flora sent the grooms in search of me."

She forced herself to look up at him. "It took a while, but eventually I recovered. Unfortunately, the doctor said I would never be able to have a child."

Dani brushed away the tears on her cheeks. Her heart squeezed painfully. "If I had told you, you never would have married me. You could have wed a woman who could give you a son."

Rafe gently caught her chin, forcing her to look him in the face. "Listen to me, Dani. I've had a great deal of time to think this

425

through, and I've come to understand something. I came to realize it doesn't matter. You're my wife, as you should have been five years ago. In truth, if I had believed you then as I should have done, you would have been living with me instead of your aunt. You wouldn't have been riding that day and you never would have been injured. In the end, the fault is mine and not yours."

Dani gazed into his beloved face. It was hard to speak past the thick lump in her throat. "Rafael . . ."

Her mouth trembled under his as he bent his dark head and kissed her. *I love you,* she wanted to say. *I love you so very much.*

But in the end she kept silent. She didn't know the feelings he carried for her, still wasn't certain of the future.

"Can you ever forgive me?" she asked.

"We shall have to forgive each other." He brushed her mouth with his. "No more secrets," he said.

"No. I swear it on my life."

Rafael kissed her so tenderly she thought she might weep once more.

"There is one thing more."

Worry slipped through her. "Yes?"

"From this night forward, you will be sleeping in my bed, not yours."

Dani's throat closed up. She managed a

nod, but inside her chest, her heart sang.

Caro stood outside the door of the duke's library-study. She had been passing by the open study door when she heard the sound of voices and caught a glimpse of the coachman, Michael Mullens, standing, hat in hand, in front of the duke's big rosewood desk.

She hadn't meant to eavesdrop, but then she realized that Mullens was talking about the carriage accident and he seemed abnormally upset.

"I tell ye, sir, it were no accident a'tall."

Caro flattened herself against the wall outside the door and strained to hear what the coachman said.

"While I was workin' on the axle, I happened ta notice the place where the wood broke apart had an odd look about it. I studied it closer and I seen it were sawed near in two."

The duke came out of his chair. "What are you saying? Are you telling me someone meant for that carriage to turn over?"

"Worse than that, sir. They meant for it ta happen just where it did. While I was studying the pieces of the axle, I noticed something buried in the wood."

Caro peered into the room long enough to

see the coachman reach into the pocket of his coarse brown jacket, pull something out and hand it to the duke.

"Someone must have been waiting fer us that day at the bridge, sir. Right before the accident, I heard a noise that sounded like a gunshot, but I never figured, till I dug out that lead ball, that someone might have been shootin' at us."

Caro ignored a chill as the duke held the round circle of lead up to examine it. "They were shooting at the axle. All it took was a little more pressure in just the right spot to make it snap."

"Yes, sir, that's the way I see it."

The duke's hand closed around the piece of lead. "If you don't mind, Mr. Mullens, I'll hang on to this. And thank you for coming to me with this information."

The coachman bowed and took his leave. Before he could reach the door, Caro lifted her skirt and dashed off down the hall. She had to find Danielle.

Sweet Jesus — someone had tried to kill them!

"I don't know what to say." Dani paced the floor of the Wedgwood Room, which was smaller than most of the other drawing rooms, overlooked the garden and had become her favorite. "Why would anyone want us dead?"

But an ugly thought kept rolling around in her head. In order to inherit the Sheffield dukedom, the rules of primogeniture demanded a son born in wedlock, a legitimate child of Rafe's blood. To make that happen, Rafe's only option would be divorce.

Unless, of course, she was dead and he could remarry.

She looked up at Caro and saw that her friend read her thoughts.

"No, do not even think it. I do not believe he would do such a thing — not for a moment. The duke is in love with you. You may not see it, but I do. He loves you and he would not hurt you."

Dani had no idea what Rafe's feelings for her might be, but even if Caro were correct and Rafe might be coming to love her again, sometimes loving someone wasn't enough. Rafe had a duty to his family, one he could not fulfill as long as she was his wife.

"We have to consider every possibility," Dani said, "no matter how painful it might be."

"But the duke didn't know until after the accident that you could not give him a child."

"Perhaps he did. There are other people

who know . . . the doctor who tended me in the country after my fall, servants in my aunt's household. Perhaps he somehow found out before Neil McCauley told him."

"I don't believe it."

"I don't want to, either, but whatever the truth, we must discover who is responsible — and why."

"I couldn't agree with you more."

Dani whirled at the sound of Rafe's voice, coming from the door leading into the drawing room. He walked into the intimate space and it suddenly seemed smaller than it had before.

"I've been looking for the two of you." His glance moved from one of them to the other. "Apparently you've heard what happened to the carriage."

Caro's narrow face reddened. "I didn't mean to eavesdrop, Your Grace, but I was passing down the hall and I heard you talking about the accident and —"

"It's all right. In this case, I'm glad you know. Since Jonas McPhee is currently in pursuit of information on the Earl of Leighton's murder, I've hired one of his associates, a man named Samuel Yarmouth, to look into the matter of the carriage accident."

Dani just nodded.

"What is it? I am beginning to recognize that look on your face."

"It's nothing, Your Grace," Caro answered for her. "She is just upset to think that someone might have tried to kill her."

"Yes, well, that is what I wished to speak to the two of you about. We need to discuss any enemies either of you might have."

Dani's head came up at Rafe's plain speaking. "Enemies? I can't imagine who might wish me harm. I can think of no one."

Rafe's eyes pinned her. "No one but me. That is what you are thinking."

"No, I . . . No, of course not." But the rose in her cheeks betrayed her earlier thoughts.

"I don't suppose professing my innocence would do a bit of good, but I'd like to point out that, one, I didn't know about your condition at the time of the accident, and two, I was supposed to be in that carriage, as well. My plans changed rather unexpectedly and only the day before we were scheduled to depart. If the villain had not been made aware of that circumstance, he might have gone forward exactly as he had planned."

The notion had merit. And the thought that Rafe might wish to do her harm was so repugnant she grasped onto the idea like a drowning woman thrown a rope. "Yes, I suppose that is true."

"And if I were the target and not you, there are a number of possibilities for who might wish me dead."

Her gaze sharpened on his face. "You are thinking of Oliver Randall."

"I am. Randall will not walk again and I am the man who made it so. As enemies go, I would put Lord Oliver at the top of my list."

Dani sat back in her chair. "After what happened, I'm not certain Oliver would have the courage to go against you."

"Perhaps not. Still, it merits looking into." He walked over to the window and stared out into the garden, clasping his hands behind his back. "There is also Carlton Baker. The American has made threats against me."

"Surely Mr. Baker wouldn't go as far as murder."

"When a man's pride has been injured, it is difficult to know what he might do." He turned to face her.

"And, of course, there is my cousin, Arthur Bartholomew. He is in debt up to his ears and in desperate need of money. Becoming the next Duke of Sheffield might well be worth committing murder."

Dani hadn't thought of that. It was a threat that would linger until Rafe had a son. Inside she shivered.

"Aside from those three, there is another possibility, a man named Bartel Schrader. I met him in America. They call him the Dutchman."

"Why would this man, Schrader, wish to kill you?"

"Schrader is involved in a shipping venture that would greatly aid the French, and I've done everything in my power to sabotage his efforts."

"Is that what you and Colonel Pendleton have been discussing?"

He nodded. "The Dutchman believes I'm his chief competitor in the purchase of a fleet of very unusual ships. With me out of the way, there is a chance he could finalize the sale and earn himself a great deal of money."

"I see." Dani bit her lip, beginning to worry about Rafe's involvement with the government, working on something that might get him killed. "Do you think this Mr. Yarmouth will be able to uncover the man responsible for what happened to the carriage?"

"That remains to be seen. In the meantime, we must all stay vigilant. I intend to speak to the staff, enlist their aid in keeping watch, though, in truth, one or more of them may be in league with the man or men who made the attempt."

"Surely not. Most of them have worked for your family for years."

"That's true, but still the possibility cannot be overlooked."

Just then the butler appeared at the door. "I'm sorry to disturb you, Your Grace, but Lords Brant and Belford are here."

Rafe nodded. "Good. Show them in." He turned his attention to Danielle. "I asked our friends to come. They're both powerful men and often out in society. I'm hoping they might turn up something useful."

Caro stood up from her chair. "I shall leave you, then."

"Stay," Rafael said. "You were in that carriage along with my wife. The matter concerns you, as well."

Caro made only a very slight nod and returned to her chair, but Dani could tell she was pleased to be included.

Wooster returned a few minutes later, leading the Earl of Brant and the Marquess of Belford into the drawing room.

"We came as quickly as we could," the earl said simply.

"Your note said it was important," the marquess added.

"And so it is," Rafe said, and for the next half hour, filled his friends in on the discovery the coachman, Mr. Mullens, had made.

"So it wasn't an accident after all," Ethan said darkly.

"Unfortunately, no."

"We'll start nosing around," Cord offered, "see what we can find out. With your permission, I'd like to tell Victoria. She has an amazing ability to enlist the aid of the people who work below stairs. They seem to have an underground system of communication that can be extremely useful."

"I'd like to tell Gracie, as well," Ethan said. "She'll want to help."

"I thought I would leave the women's involvement up to the two of you, since attempted murder is a rather unpleasant business. But we can certainly use all the help we can get."

"Anything else we should know?" the marquess asked.

Dani thought of Rafe and his mother, who would also benefit by her demise, but made no comment. Though it was oddly convenient that Rafe had been safely in London when the accident occurred, in her heart, she didn't believe her husband would do anything to harm her. And though the dowager would be beyond distressed to learn that Dani could not give Rafe an heir, she prayed that her mother-in-law was not the sort to commit murder.

The men left the house, and in the quiet after their departure, Rafe turned to Dani.

"I've a number of things to do in regard to this matter. I would prefer you and Caro stay at home for the next several days until we can iron this out."

Though Dani hated the idea of being a prisoner in her own home, she didn't argue. Outside it was cold and rainy. Perhaps staying safely inside was, indeed, the wiser course.

"As you wish — for now," she said, receiving a hard look from Rafe.

"Hear me, Danielle. I am not about to let you risk your life. In this you will do exactly as I say."

"And what of you? If you are right and you are the target, you are the one who should be staying at home."

The corner of his mouth edged up. "I'm glad you're concerned, and you may rest assured that I intend to be extremely careful."

Rafe took his leave from the drawing room, and following in his footsteps, Caro returned upstairs a few minutes later. Surely the grounds were part of the house, Dani thought, restless now and needing a breath of fresh air. Still, as Rafe intended to do, she would be careful.

One attempt on her life was more than enough as far as Danielle was concerned.

Twenty-Seven

A black night enveloped the city. Only a thin fingernail moon hung over the duke's big stone house in Hanover Square. Upstairs in her bedchamber, Caro lay staring at the ceiling above her bed, studying the ornate white moldings, counting the plaster oak leaves, trying in vain to fall asleep.

So much had happened in the months since she and Danielle had left Wycombe Park and returned to the city.

So much had changed.

They had traveled to America and back. Danielle was wed and Caro was handmaid now to a duchess.

Robert McKay had stumbled into her life. She had met him and fallen in love.

Caro's eyes welled with tears she quickly blinked away. She had cried enough for Robert McKay.

Though proof had been found that Robert had told the truth and was innocent of the murder, no word of his feelings for her had been spoken, and in the months since her return to England, not once had he come to see her. The reason was clear. Robert was an earl and she a maid. Of course he would not come. Even if he had once carried feelings for her, they would have changed when he discovered himself a member of the aristocracy.

Robert was lost to her now and the best she could do was accept the fact and content herself with the plain, unfettered life she had led before she met him.

But even as she said the words, Caro's heart lurched. Dear God, if she had known the pain of loving someone, she never would have gone with Robert to the stable that first night. She never would have kissed him or allowed him to kiss her.

Caro bit back a sob, determined to put thoughts of Robert McKay behind her. Still, she could not sleep. Instead, she listened to the whisper of the wind through the branches of the tree outside her window, the faint clop of hooves on the cobbled street and the whir of carriage wheels passing by down the block.

As the hours slowly passed, Caro slept off and on, then awakened again. It was the light tapping against the windowpane that caught her attention, an oddly rhythmical pattern that grew more persistent and had her climbing out of bed, padding across the carpet to peer out into the darkness.

Caro gasped at the sight of a man perched on the tiny wrought-iron railing outside the second-floor window. The man leaned closer, tapped again, and her heart leapt.

Robert!

Her hands shook as she lifted the latch and shoved the two halves of the window open. Silently, Robert climbed over the sill, jumped softly down on the carpet and closed the window against the cold. He turned toward her and just stood there staring, and it occurred to her what a fright she must look.

Dear Lord, she hadn't even braided her hair! She had left it curling wildly down her back and now a riot of pale blond hair stood out all over her head. She was wearing only a white cotton night rail, her bare feet peeping out from beneath the hem, and in the cold, her nipples stood out shamelessly against the fabric.

Caro blushed. "I . . . I am not dressed," she said lamely. "I know I look a fright. I —"

Whatever she might have said disappeared beneath the onslaught of his mouth crushing down over hers. Robert kissed her as he had never kissed her before, with a fierce, hot yearning that said all that she had ached to hear and more.

"I'm sorry," he said stepping away. "I didn't mean . . . I hope I didn't frighten you."

"You didn't frighten me." She touched her trembling, well-kissed lips. "I am so glad to see you, Robert."

"I had to come." He reached out to touch her cheek. "I couldn't stay away a moment longer."

"Robert . . ." Caro went back into his arms and knew a joy unlike anything she had known. "I've missed you so very much."

She felt his fingers sliding into her hair, gently cupping the back of her head as he lowered his head and kissed her again. When he had taken his fill, he eased away to look at her, standing there in the faint rays of moonlight streaming in through the window.

"I had forgotten how beautiful you are."

A fresh blush darkened her cheeks. "I am not beautiful at all."

"You are. You are like a flower in spring, your features so delicate, your skin so fair. Your hair is the color of palest gold and as fine as spun silver. You may not see it, but I do."

No one had ever spoken to her that way and inside she trembled with love for him. "Robert . . ." She leaned into his embrace.

"So much has happened."

Robert shook his head, released a frustrated sigh. "So much and not nearly enough. I am still a wanted man."

And also an earl, she thought but didn't say it. She refused to speak the words that might end this moment between them. Tonight was hers and hers alone and she would treasure every second she had with him.

"Tell me your news," she said, "and I will tell you mine."

"My news? I have traveled half of England and have yet to find what I am seeking. But I will relay what I've found." For the next half hour, they talked of all that had occurred, talked with the same ease they had shared from the moment they had first met. Caro told him about the duke and his investigator, Jonas McPhee, and how the runner had verified the truth of Robert's story.

"He is searching for proof of your innocence," she told him. "The duke believes he will find it."

Robert glanced away. "I had those same hopes myself. I spoke to the woman I was supposed to meet that night at the inn, but she was no help. She wept and said that a man gave her money to send me a note suggesting we rendezvous at the Boar and Hen, but she had no idea what was going to happen when I got there. She said she never saw the man who paid her, though I am not wholly sure I believe her."

They spoke a while longer. When all had been said of the murder, Robert kissed her again. "I came because I wanted to see you," he said, "not burden you further with my troubles."

"Your troubles have become my troubles, Robert. Surely you know that by now." Caro drew his mouth down to hers for another lingering kiss. At first he returned it, his tongue sweeping in as it had before, but as their passion heated and their breathing grew shallow, Robert pulled away.

"It is time for me to leave. I desire you greatly, my love, and I am not sure how long my control will last."

Her heartbeat quickened. *He wanted her!* It seemed almost a dream that he stood there beside her, looking at her with desire in his warm brown eyes. And as she thought of the obstacles between them and the lonely years she would have to face without him, she realized that she desired him, too.

"Don't go, Robert." She reached out to touch his cheek. "Stay here with me tonight."

His gaze ran over her and she saw the burning heat. "You're a maiden, Caro. I would not take your innocence from you. Not the way things stand."

"It doesn't matter. I want it to be you, Robert. You who makes me a woman. Say that you will stay."

He started to shake his head, but Caro leaned over and kissed him. She took his hand and placed it over her breast, felt the heat of his fingers curving over the fullness. "Say you will stay."

"We don't know the future. I yet may hang, love. What if there is a child?"

She looked at him, her heart in her eyes. "That would be the greatest gift you could give me, Robert."

A low sound came from his throat and he hauled her into his arms. "You are like no other woman." He kissed her gently, then more fiercely, kissed her until neither of them seemed capable of rational thought.

She didn't realize he had stripped off her night rail until she felt the coolness of the air against her skin as he lifted her into his arms and carried her over to the bed. Robert joined her there naked, his body strong and beautifully muscled in the faint beams of moonlight streaming into the room.

"I know this is wrong, but I have no will where you are concerned, when the sight of your sweet body so heats my blood."

"We'll take this night for ourselves," Caro said, "and no matter what happens, we will never regret it."

"Do you promise that?"

"On my word, I vow it."

"Then I will love you tonight and forever, Caroline Loon." And when he kissed her, when he touched her body with such tenderness, Caro almost believed him.

Clifford Nash, Earl of Leighton, sat back in a deep leather chair in front of the fire in his study at Leighton Hall. Outside, a cold February wind swept over the land. God's teeth, he would be glad for spring.

A light knock sounded at the door, and he beckoned Burton Webster into the study, big and hulking, a brute of a man, though intelligent enough, for all his coarse looks.

"So, is it done? Is McKay dead and out of my hair for good?"

Webster shook his shaggy head. "Not yet, but it shouldn't be much longer. I've finally found the man, though it took far longer than it ought."

"Where is he?"

"London. Perhaps the last place I would have thought to find him."

"What's he doing in London?"

"I'm not sure, but according to my

sources, he's staying in a garret above a tavern in the East End called the Dove. I've spoken to Sweeney —"

"Sweeney?"

"Albert Sweeney, the man I hired before. Sweeney has already left for London. He's been paid well to take care of McKay. I believe this is the last you'll hear of the fellow."

"Good. It is well past time the matter was ended once and for all."

Webster rose from his chair. "Is there anything else, my lord?"

"Just make sure it's done this time."

"It will be. I'm off to London myself. Once I'm sure the problem has been dealt with in a satisfactory manner, I'll send word."

At Clifford's nod of approval, Webster turned and walked out of the study. It would all be over soon.

As Clifford had said, it was well past time.

Caro knocked timidly at the door to the duke's library-study. She had sent a note requesting a meeting and a few minutes later, he had summoned her downstairs.

The duke bid her enter and she opened the door and walked in, hoping he couldn't hear the thunderous beating of her heart.

"You wished to see me?"

"Yes, Your Grace. I bring news of Robert McKay."

He set the sheet of paper he had been studying down on the top of his desk. "Sit down, Caro. Whatever you have to say, you needn't be afraid to say it."

She sank down in a chair across from him and looked up to see him rounding the desk and walking toward her. He sat down in the leather chair next to hers.

"Now, tell me this news you have brought of McKay."

Caro fiddled with a pleat in her skirt, careful to keep her mind off the intimacies she and Robert had shared. "Last night Robert came to see me."

The duke's dark eyebrows drew together. "He came to the house?"

"Yes, Your Grace. He climbed the tree next to my room and I let him in through the window."

His eyebrows pulled down ever farther. "How did he know which room was yours?"

"I don't know, but Robert is extremely clever."

"I'm sure he is."

"I told him about the man you hired, Mr. McPhee, and that you believe this man will find the proof to clear his name, but Robert doesn't believe it will happen. He says he

447

has tried every avenue and come up with nothing. He is very discouraged."

"Where is Robert now?"

She glanced away. "He asked me not to tell."

"But you love him and you wish to help him so you will tell me exactly where to find him."

She blinked and looked up at him. "Please, do not ask me."

"I'm not Robert's enemy, nor yours, Caro. Tell me so that I may give him the help he so very badly needs."

She had promised Robert and yet she knew that unless the duke found a way to prove his innocence, in the end he would hang. "He is staying in a room above an inn in the East End called the Dove."

"Thank you, Caro. I will not betray your trust, nor Robert's."

"I know that, Your Grace."

"Has he discovered anything new, anything that might be of help to him?"

"He mentioned a woman named Molly Jameson. He was supposed to meet her at the inn the night of the murder. Robert went to see her. He said she told him someone paid her money to get him to come to the inn that night, but she didn't know who it was. He said he wasn't sure he believed her."

Caro told him the rest of what Robert had said, hoping it might help in some way.

"Thank you for trusting me," the duke said. He reached over and took hold of her hand, gave it a reassuring squeeze. "It's obvious Robert cares for you a very great deal. Whatever happens, you must always remember that."

She knew what he was trying to say, knew that an earl didn't marry a maid, even if he loved her. But she already knew that, so she simply nodded. The duke stood up, ending the interview, and she left the study. She prayed he would find a way to help Robert before it was too late.

Danielle snuggled next to Rafael in his huge four-poster bed. The room that belonged to six generations of Sheffield dukes was masculine, if a little too dark, with heavy, ornately carved furniture and rich blue velvet draperies. Blue velvet bed-hangings hung from the carved wooden bedposts, protecting the bed from the cold winter chill.

It was a man's room and Rafael had made it his own, which was the reason Danielle liked it so much. His boots stood next to the armoire against the wall, and several bottles of his favorite colognes sat on the dresser next to his silver-etched comb. He liked to read, and a half-dozen books sat on the nightstand next to his side of the bed.

Danielle liked that he wanted her here in the big bed beside him, that he reached for her in the middle of the night and again before they rose in the mornings.

Their desire for each other never seemed to wane and yet dark shadows lay between them. Someone had tried to kill her. Or perhaps the target was meant to be Rafael, as he seemed to believe, and she and Caro were merely casualties of the intended crime.

As she lay in bed, Rafael asleep beside her, the questions whirled round in her head, but no answers came. She would be glad when Jonas McPhee returned to the city. Rafael had great faith in the runner and Danielle thought that they could certainly use his help.

As the minutes slipped past and the heat of Rafe's body warmed her, she finally fell asleep, but it was a restless, fitful slumber. When an odd smell filled her nostrils, beginning to slowly penetrate her consciousness, when her eyes began to burn, she jerked awake.

For an instant, she imagined that she still dreamed, that the flickering yellow light trailing along the fringe of carpet, the orange-and-yellow flames licking up the draperies, wasn't actually real.

Then she took a deep breath and started coughing and bolted upright in the bed. "Wake up, Rafael, the room is on fire!"

Madly, she tugged on his shoulder. "Rafe, wake up! We have to get out of here!"

He stirred groggily and she realized how deeply he had been asleep. If it weren't for her restlessness, likely both of them would have been overcome by the smoke and never awakened again.

"What is it?" He glanced round the room. "Sweet Jesus!" Wide-awake now, he leapt from the bed, tossed over her quilted wrapper, and pulled on his burgundy dressing gown. "We have to get out of here now!"

Taking her hand, he moved in front of her toward the door. Half of the carpet was on fire and the walls blazed steadily upward. Expecting to find the entire house engulfed in flames, she was stunned when he yanked open the door to see that the fire raged only in their bedchamber.

"Fire!" Rafe shouted down the hall. "Fire in the house!"

Third-floor doors burst open and servants began racing about, shouting and yelling orders, scrambling down the stairs to

451

the second floor. Two doors down from the duke's suite of rooms, in the bedchamber next to Danielle's, Caro raced out in her robe and slippers. Loose strands of her hair had come loose from her braid and curled round her face, and her blue eyes were round as platters.

"What is it?" She glanced past them through the open doorway, saw the orange-red lick of flames just before Rafe slammed the door. "Oh, my Lord!"

"Let's go!" Rafe commanded, urging both women toward the stairs. He hurried them down the staircase and out through the French doors leading into the garden. "You'll be safe out here. Stay here until this is over."

"Wait!" Dani called after him, but Rafe was already racing back to the house, shouting orders to the footmen to double the efforts of the bucket brigade, running back through the French doors out of sight.

"We have to help," Dani said, fear making her voice a little high.

"I can lift a bucket as well as anyone," Caro said, and both of them started running.

Wooden buckets were filled and passed hand over hand down a line of servants that disappeared inside the house. From where she stood in the garden, helping to pass the heavy buckets down the line, Dani could see the upper floors of the house, see the flames licking out the windowsills of the master's suite.

She gasped as several of the wavy glass panes shattered from the heat. An instant later, she recognized Rafe's tall figure standing inside the room, dousing the chamber with water, working next to Mr. Cooney, the footman, and Mr. Mullens, the coachman, and it looked as if they were making a good deal of progress.

Her back was aching, her quilted wrapper soggy and clinging to her body, which was naked beneath her robe, when Rafe walked back out into the garden. He was covered with soot, his face blackened, his hair mussed, several dark strands hanging over his forehead.

"It's out," he said to the group working at the fountain. "We managed to get the fire under control before it could spread through the rest of the house. Thank you all for your help."

Dani sagged with relief. "Thank God." Rafe's blue eyes zeroed in on her water-soaked apparel.

"I thought I told you to stay out of the way where you would be safe."

"I was scarcely in any danger out here. I am not an invalid, *Your Grace,* and I had every right to help save my own home."

Something moved across his features and his hard look softened. "I apologize. As you say, you have every right to help save your own home."

For an instant their eyes met and held. For all the dirt and soot, Dani thought the Duke of Sheffield was the handsomest man in England.

She glanced away, embarrassed by her thoughts. "What happened up there? Could you tell how the fire got started?"

Rafe's jaw tightened, deepening the cleft in his chin. "There was lamp oil on the carpet. It had also been poured on the draperies."

Her eyes widened. "The fire was started on purpose?"

"I'm sorry to say so, yes."

"Oh, dear God."

Caro made a funny sound in her throat. "He is trying to kill you both!"

"Come, let's go inside," Rafe said. "There is no need to overset the servants."

But the staff was already frantic and Dani's insides were churning. Twice someone had tried to kill her.

She flicked a glance at her husband. Tonight, Rafe had come even closer to death than she.

At least one thing was clear and her heart expanded with relief. Whoever had tried to kill her, she knew now for certain it was *not* her husband.

Twenty-Eight

Rafe escorted the women back inside the house. With his bedchamber destroyed, the hall carpets wet and muddy, and the smell of smoke pervading the air, there would be no sleeping in the west wing of the residence. He had ordered the entire wing closed down and the chambermaids set to work preparing adjoining rooms in the east wing for his and Danielle's use, as well as a bedchamber for Caro.

Eventually, the house grew quiet as everyone retired once more to bed. It was late, only a few more hours until dawn. Rafe lay next to Danielle, his mind running again and again over the list of people who might want him dead. Or perhaps, as Caro had said, might want both of them dead.

"How do you think the man who started the fire got into the house?" Danielle turned onto her side to look at him.

"I thought you were sleeping."

"I knew you were not. I don't think either of us is going to get any more sleep tonight."

"No, I don't suppose we are."

"So how do you think he got in?"

"I'm not sure. Perhaps he came in through a window, as Robert did the night he came to see Caro. More likely, someone let him in."

"That is what I was thinking. Several weeks ago, the housekeeper hired a new chambermaid. In fact, several new female employees have lately been added to the staff. Perhaps it is one of them."

"Why don't you speak to Mrs. Whitley, see what she can tell you about them?"

"That is a very good notion."

"In the meantime, there are several hours until dawn and both of us could use some sleep. I think I may know a way to make that happen." Rafe leaned over Danielle and kissed her. She had the sweetest, softest lips, and he loved the way they seemed to sink into his. Dani kissed him back and his body hardened.

In minutes, he was inside her, the two of them moving in perfect rhythm. They reached release together, a fierce climax that tightened every muscle in his body.

As he lay back down on the deep feather mattress, sated and content, he curled Danielle against his side. He listened as her breathing deepened and she drifted into an exhausted slumber.

Rafe wished he could rest as well, but even as tired as he was, he was too worried to sleep.

Danielle rose early the following morning. Her muscles ached from lifting the heavy buckets last night, and with all of the commotion, she had gotten only a few short hours of sleep before it was time to face the day ahead.

She dressed herself, hoping to give Caro a few badly needed hours of rest, clipped her hair back on the sides with tortoiseshell combs and headed out into the hall. A commotion in the entry drew her attention.

At the bottom of the stairs, she spotted the Dowager Duchess of Sheffield, tall, dark hair sprinkled with silver, and still extremely attractive. She was speaking rather loudly to her son.

"How could you not have sent word? Your wife is nearly killed in a carriage accident and you do not think to tell me?"

"I didn't want you to worry."

"And am I also not to worry when I arrive at your home and discover that someone has set your bedchamber on fire?"

He scowled. "How do you know about that?"

"To begin with, the entire place smells

dreadfully of smoke, and even if it didn't, there is little that happens in this household of which I am not aware. Where is Danielle?"

"I am here, Your Grace."

The dowager turned, surveyed her with shrewd blue eyes. "How are you feeling? And do not say you are fine. I don't imagine you got much rest last night. Instead of standing here talking, you should be upstairs in bed, getting some obviously needed sleep."

Dani wasn't sure if her mother-in-law was concerned for her health or just worried that her lack of rest might somehow affect her ability to produce an heir. "I promise to nap this afternoon. Aside from being a little sleepy, I truly am fine."

The dowager returned her attention to Rafe. "And you! You should be hiring men to protect you and your wife. Someone is making attempts on your lives and you have taken no steps to protect yourselves."

"Actually, I have, Mother. I've hired a man named Samuel Yarmouth to investigate the matter. Today, I'll ask Yarmouth to hire men he deems trustworthy to stand guard outside the house. I'll put them to work round the clock. There. Now do you feel better?"

She harrumphed. "It is probably that good-for-nothing cousin of yours, Artie Bartholomew. He would certainly have the most to gain from your demise."

Rafe frowned. He glanced up and down the hall to see who might be listening to their conversation. "I don't think we should be airing the family laundry here in the entry, Mother. Why don't we all go into the drawing room where we may be private?"

The duchess lifted her chin and marched ahead of them into the nearest drawing room, then waited for Rafe to close the heavy sliding doors. He walked over to where she sat on the brocade sofa while Dani sat down in a chair not far away.

"Whatever else you have to say, Mother, now is the time to say it. Once we are finished, I need to see Yarmouth and set plans into motion, and Danielle needs to interview the housekeeper, Mrs. Whitley, in regard to the newly hired help."

"Indeed," the dark-haired woman said. She flicked a surreptitious glance at Dani, then looked back at Rafe. "Perhaps you should go ahead and leave. Danielle and I can discuss the matter in greater detail and do a bit of catching up while you are gone."

Rafe just nodded. "All right. I'll leave you to it, then. I'll be back as soon as I can."

"Be careful, Rafael," Dani said, and received a tender smile for her concern.

"You do the same." And then he was gone and she was left alone with her mother-in-law. Dani knew exactly the topic the woman wished to discuss and dread swept through her.

She wasn't yet with child, and she never would be.

Dani pasted on a smile and turned to face the woman who, if she discovered the truth, would surely be among those who also might wish her dead.

It was the middle of the night. Rafe had been sleeping, though fitfully, when the butler's familiar sharp rap at the door awakened him. Worried at what might have occurred, he threw back the covers, grabbed his dressing gown and hurried for the door.

"What is it, Wooster?"

"I'm sorry to disturb you, Your Grace, but Mr. McPhee is downstairs. He is in company with two other men, one of whom is a rather unsavory-looking character. Mr. McPhee says it is urgent he speak to you as soon as possible."

Dani walked up behind him. "What is it, Rafael?"

"Jonas is here. I think he may have uncovered something important." Rafe hurriedly pulled on his breeches and a clean white shirt. "Stay here. I'll be back in a minute."

He left Danielle standing at the door of the bedchamber, but before he had reached his study, he spotted her racing toward him down the stairs. Whispering a silent curse and knowing he should have guessed she would disobey his wishes, he waited for her to catch up with him.

"Don't say a word, Rafael. This is my concern as well as yours."

He clamped down on his temper, as it was most certainly true. "Very well, then." Taking her arm, he led her down the hall in her simple dove-gray skirt and white cotton blouse. Her thick braid of hair swished against her back with every step and he caught a glimpse of her bare feet beneath the hem of her skirt. He almost smiled at how young she looked, how much like the red-haired girl, so long ago, that he had fallen in love with.

His chest tightened. He had loved her once. He would be a fool to risk his heart again.

They walked into the study together and he found McPhee standing over a man with his hands tied behind his back. The man standing next to them was none other than Robert McKay.

462

"Good evening, Your Graces," Jonas said. "I am sorry to disturb you, but this is a matter that cannot wait."

"I appreciate your coming."

"Good evening, Robert," Danielle said.

"A pleasure as always, Duchess. And it would seem I am once more in your and your husband's debt."

Rafe fixed him with a stare. "And how, exactly, is that?"

Robert cast a look at the runner. "If it weren't for your friend's timely arrival, there is every chance I would be dead."

Robert went on to explain how Jonas McPhee had come to his East End garret above the Dove and been watching his movements.

"Which was fortunate for Mr. McKay," Jonas added. He tipped his head toward the man whose hands were bound. "This man's name is Albert Sweeney. When I overheard him asking the tavern keep about McKay, paying the man to tell him which room McKay occupied, I followed him. He picked the lock and went inside, and when I stepped in behind him, it was obvious his intention was murder."

"And it wouldn't have been the first," Robert said.

"That is correct," Jonas confirmed. "After

the man was apprehended, McKay and I had a chat with him."

The sort of *chat* was more than apparent. One of Sweeney's eyes was nearly swollen shut, his lip split and bleeding, and his clothes spattered with blood.

"What sort of information did you uncover?" Rafe asked.

"Arthur Sweeney was paid to kill the Earl of Leighton," Jonas told him bluntly.

Dani's eyes widened. "He said that? He admitted to the murder?"

"It took a bit of persuasion," Jonas continued, "and a promise that the Duke of Sheffield would intercede on his behalf should he help us catch the men who hired him."

Rafe nodded his concurrence. "Who was it?"

"A fellow named Burton Webster. I'm hoping to prove Webster works for Clifford Nash."

Rafe could feel Dani's excitement as her fingers tightened around his arm. "This is wonderful news."

Sweeney swore an oath and McPhee slammed him up against the wall. "Keep a civil tongue in your head. You're in the presence of a lady."

"I'll talk to Webster," Robert said.

"Maybe he'll cooperate if he thinks it might go easier for him with the authorities."

"Let me handle it," McPhee said. "Webster was also the man who hired Sweeney to kill you. Which means Nash must know you're in England. As long as you're alive, you're a threat to him and your life is in danger."

"Jonas is right," Rafe said. "You need to let him handle it." He turned to the runner. "Is there anything you need me to do?"

"Not at the moment."

"Let me know if there is."

"Thank you, Your Grace. If that is all, I shall take my leave. I need to turn our friend, here, over to the authorities."

Jonas left the house, taking his prisoner with him, and Rafe turned his attention to Robert McKay. "You may stay here, Robert, until this matter is completely resolved."

Robert looked uncertain. "It might take a while. Even if Sweeney confesses, he may not be believed. My name won't be completely cleared until Webster and Nash are brought to justice."

"You're probably right. Still, you're far closer to gaining your freedom than you were before, and you are welcome to stay."

Robert nodded solemnly. "All right, then. I owe you both so much. I shall never be able to repay you."

"You owe us nothing, but there is a matter I would like to discuss."

Robert's head came up. "You are speaking of Caroline Loon."

"That is correct. It would seem that Miss Loon has developed certain feelings for you. It is unclear what feelings you carry for her."

"I love her," Robert said simply.

"That is all well and good, but should you win your freedom, you will also inherit an earldom. Miss Loon is only a lady's maid."

"I wouldn't care if she were a chimney sweep. I love her. I want to marry her."

Rafe could almost feel Dani's heart beating. She stepped forward and took hold of Robert's hand. "I was right about you, Robert McKay. I knew when I watched the two of you together that you saw the same beauty in Caro that I did."

"She is the best thing that has ever happened to me."

Dani smiled and let go of his hand, looking as happy as Rafe had ever seen her.

Robert glanced toward the door. "I know it's the middle of the night, but is there any chance I could —"

Just then the knob turned and the door burst open. "Robert!"

"God save us from eavesdropping

women," Rafe grumbled, but he couldn't keep from smiling as Robert strode toward the tall blond woman he loved and swept her into his arms.

For several long seconds he simply held her. Rafe made a motion to Dani that they should quietly leave, but before they had reached the door, Robert went down on one knee in front of Caro.

"I know this isn't the proper time or place, but I don't care. I love you desperately, Caroline Loon. Will you marry me?"

Caro's blue eyes rounded in shock. "What are you saying? You cannot marry me. You are an earl!"

"I may be an earl, but I'm still a man and I love you. Say yes, Caro. Do me the honor of becoming my wife."

Caro turned huge, uncertain blue eyes to Dani. "I can't marry him. It wouldn't be fair — would it?"

"It wouldn't be fair to leave him with a broken heart." Dani grinned. "And I think you would make a wonderful countess. Just think, you already know exactly the right clothes to wear."

Caro laughed through the tears spilling onto her cheeks and turned back to the man still kneeling on the floor. "I love you, too, Robert McKay, and if it is truly your wish, I would be honored to marry you."

Robert made a sound of sheer joy, rose and swept her into his arms.

Rafe led Dani out of the study and pretended not to notice that she was crying, too.

"I'm so happy for them," Dani said.

"This isn't over yet, you know. There are still some rough spots ahead and a chance that something yet might go wrong."

"I know. I only pray that it does not. Caro deserves to be happy and with Robert she will be." As they climbed the stairs to their bedchamber, an odd thought occurred. "You know, for a brief period of time, Robert owned the necklace. I gave it to him myself, remember?"

Rafe chuckled. "You don't believe they are together because of the necklace?"

"Well, I think his heart is very pure, don't you?"

"Yes, love. I do. And I am happy for them." But he didn't believe in legends or curses or strange, inexplicable powers. If he did, he wouldn't be worried about the man who was trying to kill them.

He wouldn't be afraid for Dani, or worried that the bastard might just succeed.

Twenty-Nine

It was nearly time for supper when Danielle went in search of her husband the following night, foraging through the downstairs drawing rooms, checking his library-study, but Rafe was nowhere to be found.

"Good evening, Wooster," she said to the white-haired butler. "Do you know where I might find the duke?"

"Certainly, Your Grace. He is upstairs preparing to go out for the evening."

The notion surprised her. Rafe hadn't mentioned going out, and ridiculously she had imagined him staying at home as long as the threat to his life remained. She should have known he would never be that sensible.

"Thank you, Wooster." Lifting her skirt up out of the way, she climbed the stairs and hurried down the hall of the east wing, to the adjoining rooms they were using until their rooms in the west wing could be refurbished.

Dani didn't bother to knock, just opened the door and walked in. Rafe paused in the act of tying his wide white stock.

"Good evening, love."

She ignored the little curl of warmth that came with the endearment and tried not to notice how good he looked in his evening clothes. He hadn't yet put on his tailcoat. His white shirt stretched nicely over a set of very wide, very solid shoulders, and his breeches fit so snugly she could see the outline of his maleness against the front.

A delicious little shiver went through her. Dani firmly reminded herself why she had come. "What are you doing, Rafael? You never said you would be going out for the evening."

Rafe went back to work on knotting his stock. He rarely made use of his valet and even less since they had moved into the east wing of the house. "There is a soirée at the Earl of Louden's town house. Rumor has it Bartel Schrader will be there. If he is, I want to have a word with him."

The Dutchman, an international trader who might benefit from Rafael's death. A chill swept down Dani's spine. "If you're going, then I am going with you."

He stopped tugging on the long white strip of cloth. "Not tonight. You're staying home where you will be safe."

Dani came forward and began to work on his stock. "Are you sure I'll be safer here by

470

myself than I will be if I am with you?"

Rafe's nearly black eyebrows pulled together. "You will scarcely be alone. The entire house is overflowing with servants and there are a half-dozen guards outside."

"There were footmen on the carriage as well, if you recall, to say nothing of the possibility that one of the servants is somehow involved." In fact, there was a very good chance, though she had interviewed Mrs. Whitley, the housekeeper, about the two newly hired chambermaids, spoken to the young women herself and was convinced they had nothing to do with setting the blaze that had destroyed a portion of the house.

Rafe's frown deepened. He took over the work on his stock and pulled the knot perfectly into place. "You are simply chafing at the confinement."

Dani gave him a sugary smile. "So you are certain, then, that I will be safer here."

Rafe cast her a glance that would have made the average man cower. He whispered a nearly silent curse. "You are a conniving little baggage. Get dressed. And don't you even think to leave my side for the duration of the evening."

Dani bit back a grin of triumph. "Of course not, darling." Hurrying away from him before he could change his mind, she scooted through the door between their two rooms and made her way toward the bell pull. She hadn't quite reached it when Caro came bustling into the bedchamber.

Dani arched a burnished brow. "How is it you always seem to know what I need even before I am certain I need it?"

Caro laughed. "In truth, I saw you looking for the duke. I heard Wooster telling you that your husband was going out for the evening. I knew you would wish to go with him."

Danielle walked over to the armoire in search of something to wear. "I'm hiring another maid as soon as I can find one. You're going to be a countess. It is highly improper for you to be waiting on me."

"We are friends and I enjoy helping you." Caro's lips curved into a dreamy smile. "I still can't believe it. Robert loves me. He is an earl and yet he wishes to marry me."

"He is lucky to have you and he knows it."

Caro looked over at Dani. "I'm afraid for Robert. Until all of this is settled, he could still be arrested."

"Robert is using the name *McCabe*. There is no reason for anyone to connect him with a crime that happened three years ago."

"I hope you're right." Caro began to dig

472

through the armoire, assessing one gown and then another. She pulled out a rose silk trimmed with bands of heavy black velvet. "How about this one? Or perhaps the forest-green with the overskirt of gold-shot lace would better suit."

Dani took the rose silk from Caro's hand. "This will do nicely." She waited while her friend unfastened the buttons on her day dress, hurriedly stepped out of the garment and drew the evening gown over her head.

Caro settled the dress in place and began to work the buttons. "Robert is anxious to wed." She looked at Dani and faint rose circles appeared in her cheeks. "He says he cannot bear living under the same roof with me and not being able to share my bed."

Dani grinned. "He loves you."

Caro sighed. "Now that it looks as if he may be able to clear his name, Robert is determined to play the gentleman. He says until we are man and wife, he will do nothing that might sully my reputation."

"I think you should be flattered."

"I suppose so, but I —" She broke off and glanced away.

"You what, dearest?"

"I want him to make love to me, Dani. The way he did the night he came into my room."

Dani clamped down on her surprise. Caro was in love. When Danielle had first fallen in love with Rafael, she would gladly have gifted him with her innocence.

Reaching out, she caught hold of her friend's pale hand. "Desire is only natural when you love someone." Turning thoughtful, she pursed her lips. "I suppose that is the reason Rafael was so determined to discover Robert's intentions. I think he must have guessed."

Caro blushed fiercely. "Surely not."

Dani just smiled. "It hardly matters now. Soon the two of you will be married and you can make love as often as you like."

Caro's cheeks went redder still, but she said nothing more on the subject and neither did Dani. They told each other most everything. Perhaps if Dani hadn't been so obsessed with her own set of problems, she would have guessed the depth of Robert and Caro's involvement.

As Dani finished dressing and left to join Rafael, she couldn't help feeling a twinge of envy. Robert loved Caro. Dani had no idea what Rafe felt for her.

Her heart squeezed a little as she made her way toward the staircase and spotted him waiting for her at the bottom. She tried to read his expression but, as always, he kept it carefully guarded. Rafe led her out to the carriage and settled her inside, then seated himself across from her.

Dani said nothing as the carriage rolled over the cobbles on its way to the earl's soirée.

It was well after dark, beyond ten o'clock, when Rafe and Danielle arrived at the three-story brick mansion in Cavendish Street. Lights blazed through the windows of the Earl of Louden's town house as Rafe and Dani descended the iron stairs of the fancy new ducal carriage Rafe had purchased after the old one was destroyed. A pair of armed footmen rode at the rear of the coach, and Michael Mullens, the driver, also carried a pistol.

Though no one knew Rafe intended to leave the house, he wasn't taking any chances.

Keeping an eye out for trouble, he led Danielle along the path and up the steps to the wide front porch. A liveried footman stood on each side of the door and politely ushered them inside.

The party was already well under way. Shouldering a path through the crush of people milling in the entry, Rafe led Danielle into one of the drawing rooms, pausing only long enough to lift a glass of champagne off a passing silver tray, along with a glass of brandy for himself.

He surveyed the throng, checking again for any possible threat, but saw nothing out of the ordinary.

"Look!" Dani motioned toward a handsome couple standing off to the right. "There's Cord and Victoria."

"So it is." He led her in that direction, grateful to see a friend, then spotted Ethan and Grace a little farther away. "And there is another pair of familiar faces."

Cord spotted him walking toward them and cast him a look of reproach. "I thought you were staying at home."

"I can hardly discover who is trying to kill me when I am locked away inside my house."

"What about Danielle?" Ethan asked. "Both of you should be staying out of harm's way."

Dani smiled. "I'm grateful for your concern, my lord, but surely you agree I am safer with Rafael than I am home by myself."

"Of course she is," Grace put in before Ethan could answer. "With Rafe to protect her, she is quite safe, indeed."

Cord rolled his eyes. "We were just on our

way to get something to eat," he said. "Why don't you join us?"

Rafe nodded, using the excuse to survey the guests in the drawing room. They made their way through the well-dressed crowd into a long gallery where refreshments were being served. A crystal punch bowl sat next to several silver trays overflowing with an array of treats: roasted fowl, a round of beef, pickled salmon, cheeses of every variety, freshly baked breads and an assortment of fruits and sweets.

The line was long and Rafe stood there with his friends, though he didn't plan to stay long enough to enjoy the meal.

"So why this particular affair?" Cord asked, his gaze wandering the gallery and the drawing room beyond.

Rafe's gaze followed his. "Rumor has it the Dutchman will be here tonight."

"Schrader?"

He nodded. "If he's here, I want to talk to him."

It was only a few minutes later that Rafe spotted the man, sandy hair, late thirties, in conversation with the earl himself. Schrader moved in upper-class circles with the ease of an aristocrat and Rafe wondered if perhaps his family was among the Dutch nobility.

"Will you look after Danielle for a moment?" he said to Ethan and Cord.

Both men nodded.

"Don't let her out of your sight."

"But surely, I'm in no danger here in —"

"We won't," promised Cord, and both men moved a little closer to the women, forming a shield around Danielle.

Rafe strode toward the Dutchman, intercepting the man as he finished his conversation and made his way toward the door.

"Excuse me, Mr. Schrader," Rafe said. "You may not remember, but we met in Philadelphia. My name is Rafael Saunders. I'd like a word with you, if you don't mind."

Schrader was lean and athletically built, his eyes an unusual shade of bluish-gray and amazingly discerning. "Your Grace." He made a slight bow of his head. "It is good to see you again."

"Is it?"

Schrader just smiled. "Ah, yes, I heard about your troubles."

"Is that so?" Rafe tipped his head toward the door, urging the man out of the drawing room, down the hall where they might be private.

The men stopped beneath a pair of gilded sconces and the Dutchman eyed him warily. "Surely you don't think that because we are competitors, I would wish to kill you?"

Rafe was only mildly surprised the man knew about the attempts being made on his life. He was, after all, in a business that required information.

"It's possible. Perhaps you believe my demise would clear the way for you to make the deal you've been working on so long."

"Perhaps. But even with you out of the way, there is always the chance your two friends would move forward with the acquisition in your stead."

"You amaze me, Schrader. You seem to know more about my business than I do."

The Dutchman shrugged. "That is my job."

"Since you're in England, it would appear you have not yet made the sale of the fleet to the French."

"I'm afraid I am not at liberty to discuss my client's business."

Rafe thought of Dani and the carriage accident, thought about the fire and how both of them might have died. "I don't give a damn about your clients, Schrader, but let me make one thing clear. Killing me will not solve your problems, and should something happen to my wife and I discover that you are the man responsible, there will be no place on earth where you will be able to hide."

Schrader merely laughed. "I am a businessman, nothing more. Look elsewhere for your villain, my friend."

Rafe studied the man a moment longer, then turned and started walking. Bartel Schrader was intelligent and extremely clever. Rafe was no more certain of the man's guilt or innocence than he had been before.

Wishing the interview had been more helpful, he strode back into the drawing room in search of his wife and friends and spotted the group near the corner.

Anthony Cushing, Viscount Kemble, had joined them. He was a rake of grand renown, handsome and wealthy, and he was staring with hot eyes at Dani. She laughed at something Kemble said, and a chafe of irritation crept up Rafe's spine.

He walked to where his friends stood guard over his wife, slid a proprietary arm around her waist and fixed his gaze on the viscount. "Nice to see you, Kemble."

"You, as well, Your Grace." The black-haired man smiled, rather wolfishly, Rafe thought. "I've just had the pleasure of meeting your very lovely wife. I discovered that she is quite charming."

"Indeed, she is," Rafe said through clenched teeth.

The viscount turned back to the others, his gaze lighting once more on Danielle. "If you will excuse me, I'm afraid I've got to run. It's been a pleasure, Your Grace." He bowed deeply over Dani's hand, and Rafe's jaw hardened. "Have a good evening."

Rafe didn't say a word. So he was a little jealous. It was only natural when a man had a wife as beautiful as Danielle. It had nothing to do with the depth of his feelings for her.

"Well . . . ?" Cord drawled, turning Rafe's thoughts back to his earlier conversation.

"Schrader denied any involvement in the incidents. My instinct is to believe him, but there is no way to know for sure." Rafe caught a final glimpse of the international trader as he crossed the entry toward the door.

"We'll keep our eyes and ears open where Schrader is concerned," Cord promised.

"Which reminds me . . ." Ethan said. "I was planning to stop by and see you in the morning. Carlton Baker has sailed for New York. His name showed up on the passenger list of a ship called the *Mariner*."

"You've been keeping track of him?"

Ethan shrugged. "I'm in the shipping business. It wasn't that difficult to do."

"When did he leave?"

"The *Mariner* sailed yesterday morning. If he's the man you are seeking, he's no longer a threat."

"You're probably right. Baker's the sort who would only enjoy my demise if he saw to it personally." Rafe managed a smile. "Thank you."

Cord clapped him on the shoulder. "We're all on the lookout for news. If we find out anything that might be useful we'll let you know."

Rafe just nodded. He had two of the best friends a man could have. Still, even with their help, he wasn't much closer to finding out who was trying to kill them than he had been before.

Rafe's hold tightened around Dani's waist. "Time to go, love . . . before your admirer reappears and I have to call him out."

Her big green eyes rounded and he actually smiled. "I'm jesting, love, though I wouldn't mind going a few rounds with the rogue the next time we're boxing at the club."

Dani just smiled. She'd been quiet all evening, distracted in a way he hadn't seen her. She was worried, he was sure, and he didn't blame her.

He kept her close by his side as he led her back to the carriage. In minutes, they were headed for home.

Several extra lamps had been lit, their yellow light glowing through the windows of the mansion when they arrived at his house in Hanover Square.

Rafe's senses went on alert as he helped Danielle down from the carriage and led her up the walkway to the door. Several guards stood their posts in various places around the mansion, and he relaxed a little when he saw them. Still, something was going on, and this late in the evening, it paid to be cautious.

Wooster pulled open the door and Rafe ushered Danielle into the domed, stained-glass entry.

"I realize it is late," the butler said, "but you have visitors, Your Grace. Mr. McPhee is here. I told him you had gone out for the evening and I wasn't sure when you would return, but he said he wished to wait. I showed him into your study. Mr. McCabe and Miss Loon are in there, as well."

"Thank you, Wooster."

"Dear God, I hope nothing bad has happened," Dani said. She hurried ahead of him down the hall and he held open the door for her as she swept into the study.

Near the fireplace, Robert, Caro and

Jonas McPhee all rose from their seats as they walked in.

Jonas spoke first. "Good news, Your Grace. I believe the matter of the Earl of Leighton's murder is about to come to an end."

"That is good news."

"Yes, and once that happens, Clifford Nash can be dealt with and the Leighton title and fortune can be returned to its rightful heir."

Robert grinned so broadly he looked boyish. Standing at his side, nearly as tall as he, Caro beamed.

"I take it you've spoken to Burton Webster," Rafe said to McPhee, guiding Dani over to the sofa. He sat down beside her and the others returned to their seats.

"It wasn't as difficult as we imagined," Jonas said. "Apparently Webster was afraid Nash's scheme would come to a very bad end, and the man had wisely taken steps to protect himself."

"Then you were able to persuade him to speak out against his employer," Dani said.

Jonas shrugged his thick shoulders. "It took a bit of persuasion, but apparently Clifford Nash had been lording it over Webster from the moment he assumed the role of earl and Webster was extremely unhappy about it."

"So Sweeney was telling the truth," Rafe said. "Webster was the man who paid him to murder the earl, but it was done at Clifford Nash's instruction."

"That is correct. To prove it, Webster kept every note Nash wrote to him, including several letters detailing Lord Leighton's movements. Apparently Nash had paid someone in the earl's employ to keep him informed. That is how Sweeney knew Leighton would be stopping that night at the Boar and Hen and was able to carry out the murder."

"Webster is willing to testify in exchange for leniency," Robert added, casting a soft smile at Caro. "I'm hoping his testimony, combined with the notes written in Nash's hand and Sweeney's confession, will be enough to prove my innocence."

"I don't think there is any question," Rafe said.

"And the marriage documents from the church of St. Margaret's will verify Mr. McKay's claim to the title," McPhee added.

Rafe leaned back in his chair. "Well, Robert, it looks as if you are very nearly a free man."

Robert squeezed Caro's hand. "Which means I will soon be a married man, as well."

Caro blushed.

"Congratulations," Rafe said.

"We are so happy for you both." Dani's eyes glistened with tears.

"I'm turning the details over to my associate, Mr. Yarmouth," Jonas said, "so that I may focus my attention on the matter of your safety, Your Grace, and of course that of the duchess."

Rafe just nodded, but in truth, he was damned glad to have McPhee back on the job. "Perhaps we can discuss the investigation in more detail in the morning."

"My thoughts exactly. I shall plan on seeing you then."

The runner left the study, followed by Caro and Robert, who had eyes only for each other.

Rafe ignored a twinge of envy. Once he and Dani had loved openly and freely as Caro and Robert did. Now both of them guarded their emotions, afraid of the pain they might suffer if they dared to love again.

Lately, Rafe had begun to wonder if living that way was truly what he wanted.

He shook his head. At present, his main concern was finding the man who was trying to kill them. Now was not the time to think about falling in love.

Thirty

Danielle wandered about the bedchamber she used next door to the one she shared with Rafe. It was early and yet the sun was up and it looked as if the cold February day might turn at least mildly warm. She walked over to the window. Through the wavy mullioned panes, she could see an empty bird's nest perched in a barren tree outside the house. Dear Lord, how she yearned for spring.

Dani turned at the sound of a soft knock on her door, and a moment later, Caro walked into the room. "You are already up and dressed."

"I spoke to one of the chambermaids. I asked her to act as my lady's maid until we could hire a permanent replacement." But so far, by Caro's standards, no one suitable had been found.

Caro sighed. "I keep trying to imagine myself as a countess, but it is not that easy to do. I want so badly to please Robert, but I'm afraid I'll disappoint him."

"Don't be silly. You aren't going to disappoint him. You were gently reared and well educated. You acted as my lady's maid for the last five years. You know a great deal about being a lady."

Caro turned away from her. "I pray you are right."

"Besides that, you love him and he loves you. That is all that matters."

The *only* thing that mattered, Dani now knew. She loved Rafael to the very depths of her soul. Her heart's greatest desire was that Rafe should love her in return.

Caro walked up beside Dani at the window. For the first time, Danielle noticed the worry on her face. "What is it, dearest? What's wrong?"

"There is something I must tell you . . . something Robert told me last night. I've been thinking about it all morning and I believe you ought to know. It concerns the American, Richard Clemens."

"Robert told you something about Richard?"

Caro exhaled a breath. "Robert said that Richard had a terrible reputation, that he was considered a dreadful rake. He said that everyone knew he kept a mistress, more than one, in fact. Apparently, Richard told Edmund Steigler, the man who owned Robert's indenture, that even after he married, he intended to continue his liaison with Madeleine Harris, the woman he kept in the country near his factory at Easton. Robert overheard them talking about it."

Danielle's face went pale. "Richard intended to be unfaithful even after we were wed?"

"That is what Robert believes. He thinks the duke discovered Richard's intentions and that is the reason he forced you to marry him."

Danielle stared out the window, her mind spinning. "Rafael said he believed marrying Richard would not make me happy."

"He knew you, Dani. He must have known you could never be happy with a man who was unfaithful."

For a moment, Dani couldn't speak. Rafe had married her to save her from a life of misery with Richard. He was doing his best to protect her. A painful swell of emotion swept through her. From the day Rafe had reappeared in her life, he had shown nothing but concern for her. In return, she had destroyed his chance of ever having a child of his own.

There would be no heir, and if something happened to Rafael, his family would be at the mercy of Artie Bartholomew — and it would be completely her fault.

"Thank you for telling me," she said softly.

"I know you love the duke. You haven't said so, but I can see it in your eyes whenever you look at him. I thought you would wish to know."

Danielle just nodded. Her throat was aching, her heart squeezing inside her chest. Caro loved Robert. She would never do anything to hurt him. Dani loved Rafe, more than she could have dreamed, but in leaving him childless, she was hurting him greatly.

Caro quietly left the room, closing the door softly behind her, and Dani stood staring out the window. Even now there was a very good chance that his cousin, Arthur Bartholomew, was plotting to kill him to gain the Sheffield fortune. His family was at risk and the fault was hers entirely.

Tears blurred her vision. She loved Rafael, had, in truth, never stopped loving him, not even in the years they had spent apart. After they had married, she had tried to convince herself that her barrenness did not matter. Aunt Flora believed it.

Even Rafe had said so.

But deep in her heart, Dani couldn't make herself believe it. She felt as if she were only half a woman, half a wife. She had married Rafael under false pretenses. If she had told him the truth from the start, Rafe never would have married her.

Danielle drew in a shaky breath. Her heart was aching, beating dully in her chest. She had lied to herself long enough. No matter how painful, no matter the cost to herself, Dani knew what she had to do.

Danielle had retired upstairs for the night, but Rafe wasn't ready to join her. Instead, as he had been doing of late, he made his way down the hall and went into his study. A fire burned there, one at each end of the two-story room, heating the interior against the February chill.

Absently, he moved toward the marble-manteled hearth, his mind on the carriage accident, the fire in his bedchamber and the man who might be responsible. As he passed one of the high-backed leather chairs, he caught the dim outline of a man, and his muscles tensed.

Then he recognized the tall, dark figure of his friend, Max Bradley.

"Dammit man, you have a knack for sneaking up on a fellow." Rafe dropped wearily down in the chair across from Max. "There are guards all around the house. How in bloody hell did you get in here?"

Max just shrugged. "One of the French

doors was unlocked. Not a good idea, considering someone wants you dead."

He wasn't surprised Max knew. There wasn't much that happened Max didn't know about.

Rafe sighed. "I wish to God I knew who it was."

"I can tell you who it isn't."

Rafe leaned forward in his chair. "Who?"

"Bartel Schrader."

"He's here in London. I spoke to him last night. How can you be sure he isn't the man?"

"Because the French made a decision not to purchase the Baltimore Clippers. That happened nearly two weeks ago — well before the fire in your bedchamber. We only just found out. Schrader is in England on a completely different matter and he is planning to leave at the end of the week."

Rafe ran a hand through his hair. "Christ."

"At least your list is one man shorter."

"Two. Carlton Baker has sailed for Philadelphia, though to be honest, I never really believed he was involved. Which means, unfortunately, the two prime suspects remain."

"Artie Bartholomew and Oliver Randall."

"Exactly. Jonas McPhee is keeping tabs

on Randall, while his associate, Mr. Yarmouth, watches dear ol' cousin Artie."

"I've put the word out for information. If I hear anything, I'll let you know."

"I'd appreciate that."

Max stood up from his chair. "Keep a sharp eye, my friend."

Rafe stood up, as well. "I'll walk you out. No use getting shot by one of my own men."

Max just smiled. Odds were the guards would never see him. Still, Rafe walked him to the door and opened it, making it clear to the men outside that he was an acquaintance. Max slipped quietly into the dark and disappeared.

With a sigh, Rafe closed the door and headed up the stairs to his bedchamber, though he doubted he would sleep. Still, with Danielle at his side, he would rest, and until all of this was over and he could be certain of her safety, it would have to be enough.

Darkness enclosed the house. Pleading a headache, Danielle had retired upstairs to the room she shared with Rafe. She needed time to herself, time to deal with the decision she had made.

She knew it was the right one, knew that her conscience could never allow her to stand in the way of Rafael's future. He needed children, needed a wife who could give them to him.

For weeks, she had been certain that once he knew the truth of her childless condition he would divorce her. Instead, he had taken the blame for the accident upon himself and said that her barrenness did not matter.

It wasn't true and both of them knew it.

After listening to Caro, all the uncertainties she had buried rose up from deep inside her. She had known the truth almost from the start, known that sooner or later she would have to give him up.

The door opened and Rafe walked quietly into the bedchamber. Danielle listened to the sound of his footsteps as he moved around the room, preparing himself for bed. Even in this wing of the house, she slept beside him, and she reveled in the closeness. He slept naked and she had learned to do the same, their shared body heat enough to keep them warm during the night.

All day, she had thought of him, thought of the conversation she'd had with Caro and how Rafael had tried so hard to make things right between them. He had been so determined to make her happy — and he had — more than she could have dreamed.

As she watched his quiet movements, her

heart swelled with love for him. He thought that she was sleeping, but instead she watched as he disrobed with a casual grace most men lacked. He discarded his stock, tailcoat and waistcoat, then pulled off his shirt, leaving him bare to the waist. He was all lean muscle and smooth dark skin, the bands of sinew across his ribs contracting as he bent to remove his shoes and stockings.

He slid off his breeches and small clothes, baring his broad back and round, muscular buttocks, and she thought how much she loved to touch him, to feel his muscles moving beneath her hands. Naked he padded across the carpet toward the opposite side of the bed, a virile man whose masculine anatomy was impressive even when he wasn't aroused.

Dani watched him and her heart constricted hard inside her. She had made her decision. She was leaving. She was setting him free, making things right, as she should have done long ago.

She felt his heavy weight settle on the bed beside her and ached to think this would be their last night together. He must have sensed that she was awake for he moved closer and gathered her into his arms.

"Trouble falling asleep?"

"I was waiting for you."

Rafe leaned down and very softly kissed her. "I'm glad."

Dani slid her arms around his neck and felt a wave of love for him. Desire quickly followed. She wanted him, more tonight than ever before. She wanted this last night with him, needed these last few hours, these final precious memories, to give her the courage to leave.

Dani blocked the sadness pouring through her and concentrated on his love-making, determined to enjoy these parting moments together. Rafe kissed her again, a deep, penetrating kiss that filled her senses and turned her insides to butter. She arched toward him, pressing her breasts into his chest, feeling the brush of his curly dark chest hair against her skin.

He lowered his head to her nipple, and a sob of pleasure caught in her throat. Another sob followed, this a cry of despair, though she couldn't let him know. Every time he touched her, every time his body joined with hers, she fell more deeply in love with him, and because she loved him so much, she wanted him to have the life he deserved.

She wanted him to be able to protect his family, to fulfill his duty to them, a duty that meant so much to him.

There was only one way for that to happen and tomorrow she meant to see it done. They had only this one night, this last brief moment in time. It would have to last her a lifetime.

Arching upward to give him better access, she felt a deep tug low in her belly as he took the fullness of her breast into his mouth. He spread her legs with his knee and came up over her, kissing her all the while, taking her deeply with his tongue even as he slid himself inside her.

Rafael . . . my dearest love, she silently cried out to him. But she didn't say the words and never would. She would take this night of pleasure, join with him this one last time. On the morrow, she would leave.

Danielle wrapped her arms around Rafe's neck and clung to him as he moved deep inside her. She matched her rhythm to his, arching upward to meet his thrusts, her face buried against the side of his neck as they climbed the pinnacle together. With each stroke, pleasure filled her, and a sad, sweet yearning for what could never be.

She closed her eyes against the heart-wrenching pain that rose each time their bodies came together and concentrated, instead, on the passion and the incredible love she felt for him.

They reached their peak together, Rafe's muscles tightening as he spilled his seed inside her. But there would be no child, not tonight, not for them. Not ever.

Dani bit back a cry of such despair her eyes filled with tears. She turned away so that Rafe would not see and let him settle her there on the mattress beside him.

"Sleep well, my love." He kissed her forehead before he lay back down and his head sank into the pillow.

But Dani would not sleep. Not tonight, nor most of the empty nights ahead of her. Tears leaked from beneath her lashes as she lay in the darkness listening to Rafe's deep breathing, memorizing the sound of it for the lonely years ahead.

It was late afternoon. Rafe hadn't seen Danielle since he had left her that morning in his bed. Last night, she had slept very little, and he was worried about her.

Even more so since he had received her note asking him to meet her at three o'clock in the afternoon in the China Room.

With its black-and-gold marble columns, black-lacquer-and-gold-brocade furniture, the room was mostly used for greeting guests or on special occasions, an extremely formal setting that made him wonder why his wife had summoned him there.

He walked in with the note in his hand and was surprised to find his mother sitting on one of the brocade sofas in a gown of dark blue silk, her silver-streaked hair perfectly coiffed, looking as puzzled as he.

"I received a message from Danielle," she explained, holding up a note that looked much like the one he had received. "She asked if I would meet her here at three."

"I received the same message."

"Do you have any idea why she has asked us to come?"

"None whatsoever." And for some odd reason, he had begun to grow uneasy.

"Perhaps I should ring for tea," his mother suggested, glancing toward the open doorway while he sat down in the chair across from her.

But just then Wooster appeared, announcing the duchess's arrival, and Rafael came to his feet.

"I'm sorry to interrupt your day," Danielle said, walking briskly into the room. "I hope I didn't inconvenience you."

"Not in the least," Rafe said. Behind them, Wooster busied himself closing the tall sliding doors, making them private, and Rafe used the moment to study his wife's drawn features. Her skin looked pale and faint smudges appeared beneath her eyes, increasing the worry he felt.

"Would you like me to get us some tea?" his mother asked, but Danielle just shook her head.

"This won't take long. I have something of importance to say and I wanted to say it to both of you."

Rafe flicked his mother a glance. She had begun to look as worried as he. "We're listening," he said, and seated himself once more.

Dani's gaze traveled to the woman on the sofa, then returned to Rafe. "I asked your mother to join us because I thought that if I couldn't make you understand, then perhaps she would be able to convince you."

Something moved inside him, something that shouted a warning. His heartbeat quickened, began a dull pounding in his chest.

Danielle fixed her attention on his mother. "There is something you must know, Your Grace, something I didn't tell Rafael until it was too late."

And suddenly he knew. "No," he said as he shot to his feet. "No!"

Danielle ignored him. "There was an accident during the years Rafael and I were apart. A riding accident. I was injured.

Somehow my insides were damaged in such a way that I can never have a child. I am barren, Your Grace."

"Stop it!" Rafe's heart was hammering now, threatening to pound its way through his chest. He strode toward his wife, caught hold of her shoulders. "This is our business —ours, ours and no other's!"

She didn't look at him, just started talking again. Beneath his hands he could feel her trembling. "I took advantage of him, Your Grace. I should have told him the truth, but I didn't. At the time, I suppose I wasn't thinking clearly, or I didn't . . . didn't realize how badly your family needed an heir."

He shook her. He couldn't let her go on, couldn't let her humble herself this way. "I forbid you to continue this, Danielle. You're my wife. My mother has no place in this discussion."

She turned to him and he caught the sheen of tears. He could see how much this cost her, see the pain in her eyes, and felt a surge of emotion so raw, so powerful for a moment he couldn't speak.

"She has a right to know the truth," Dani said softly. "A right to know that as long as I am married to you, her future is in jeopardy." She turned back to the dowager duchess. "There is only one way to solve the problem. Rafael must marry a woman who can bear him a child. To do that he must divorce me."

Terror gripped him like a fist around his heart. It spurred him to an even greater anger. "That is insane! There will be no divorce in this family! We are married. In the eyes of the law and those of God Almighty. That is *not* going to change."

The tears in her eyes slipped down her cheeks. "You must do this, Rafael. You have a duty —"

"No! My first duty is to you, Danielle, to you and no other." He hauled her into his arms and she trembled even harder. "I lost you once," he said against her hair. "I won't lose you again."

Her soft sob cut straight through him. His chest was squeezing, his heart aching. She drew away and turned to look at his mother. She sat there on the sofa, as pale as Rafe had ever seen her, and her light blue eyes slowly filled with tears.

"Make him understand . . ." Dani pleaded. "Make him see there is no other way."

His mother said nothing, just sat there staring at Danielle as if she were a creature his mother had never seen.

Rafe caught Dani's shoulders. "My

mother has no say in this. I'm your husband and I am not divorcing you — not now or ever!"

Danielle looked up at him. She blinked and the tears in her eyes rolled down her cheeks. "Then I am divorcing you, Rafael."

Jerking free of his hold, she started running, racing out the wide double doors and down the hall.

"Danielle!" Rafe bolted after her.

"Rafael!" The sharpness in his mother's voice stopped him.

Rafe turned toward her. "Do not waste your breath, Mother. Nothing that has happened is Danielle's fault — it is mine."

"But —"

"I'm sorry things didn't work out the way you planned. But I love her and I'm not going to let her go."

The words sprang forth from a well deep inside him and he knew the moment he said them they were true. He had tried not to love Danielle, done everything in his power to control his emotions where she was concerned, but in these past months, she had come to mean everything to him.

Everything.

Turning, he started once more for the door, striding out into the hall, heading for the stairs up to the rooms they shared on the second story.

Wooster stopped him just as he started climbing. "She is not up there, Your Grace."

"Where is she?"

"I'm afraid the duchess has left the house."

"What?"

"Before she went into the drawing room, she asked that her carriage be brought round. When she came out, she took her cloak and raced out the front door. That is the last I saw of her, sir."

It was all Rafe could do not to grab the old man by the front of his shirt and shake him for letting her go. There was a murderer out there somewhere. Danielle's life could be in danger.

But it wasn't the butler's fault, it was his own.

If he had told her that he loved her, made it clear to her that she was the most important thing in his life, his world, she would have understood that having his child no longer mattered. All he really cared about was her.

The coach was out of sight by the time he got to the door. Rafe turned and ran for the stables. He would find her, bring her home, tell her the way he felt. He only prayed it wasn't too late.

Rafe had almost reached the back door when Robert McKay and Caroline Loon caught up with him.

"What the devil's going on?" Robert asked.

"Where is Danielle?" Caro demanded. "One of the footmen said she took off in her carriage. He said she was crying. Why was she crying, Your Grace?"

Rafe's chest squeezed. "There's been a misunderstanding. I've got to find her, make her understand." He looked over at McKay. "There's a killer out there. She may be in very grave danger."

"I'll go with you." Robert clapped him on the shoulder. "Come on, let's go!"

They raced out to the stable, Caro right on their heels, both men pitching in to get their horses saddled and ready as quickly as possible.

While a pair of grooms tightened the cinches, Rafe spoke to Caro. "Do you have any idea where Danielle might be headed?"

"The only place I can think of is Wycombe Park. She has always felt safe there, and Lady Wycombe is in residence. But for the past several days, she has been acting strangely and I cannot say for certain what she might do."

505

"We'll head for Wycombe," Rafe said, "stop along the road and find out if anyone has seen the Duchess of Sheffield's carriage. It bears the crest. If she has traveled the road to Wycombe, someone will have seen the coach."

The men swung up on their flat leather saddles, Rafe on Thor, his big black stallion, Robert on a sleek bay gelding, both animals dancing, eager to be on their way.

Caro caught hold of Robert's leg. "Be careful." She looked over at Rafe. "Both of you."

Robert leaned down and very swiftly kissed her. "Speak to the servants. See if you can find out where the duchess might have gone."

Caro nodded, bobbing the thick blond curls around her face. "I'll find out what I can."

The men dug their heels into their horses' ribs and the animals leapt forward. In seconds, they were pounding over the cobbles, headed for the road leading to the village of Wycombe.

The hours dragged. The horses grew weary and a bone-chilling cold set in. They stopped at every inn and way station along the road, spoke to a dozen travelers and a half-dozen wagoneers, but no one had seen the Sheffield carriage.

It was dark by the time they drew their animals to a halt in the deeply rutted road for what must have been the fifteenth time.

"She isn't headed for Wycombe," Rafe said tiredly. "Of that we can now be sure."

"We need to get back to the city," Robert said. "Perhaps by now, Caro will have discovered the duchess's plans."

Both men turned their horses then bent forward into the wind. It was freezing and growing colder, their coats not nearly enough protection against the icy chill.

Rafe urged the stallion forward. "I was so certain she was headed for her aunt's."

"Perhaps she simply rode around for a while, then decided to go back home."

Rafe shook his head. "She was determined that we should divorce. She wouldn't have made such a serious decision without a good deal of thought. She is bound and determined to go through with it, and unless I can convince her otherwise, that is what she will do."

"She loves you, Rafael. Why would she want a divorce?"

Rafe sighed. "It's a long story. Suffice it to say if I had been as honest about my feelings as you were with Caro, this likely would not have happened."

Robert smiled. "Then there is nothing to worry about. As soon as you find her, you will tell her the way you feel and everything will be all right."

Rafe prayed Robert was right. But he was growing more and more worried. Once her mind was made up, Danielle could be nearly as stubborn as he, and she truly believed she was doing what was best for him.

Christ, what a muddle. He just prayed that wherever she was she was safe.

Thirty-One

The ransom note was waiting when Rafe arrived back at the house, weary to the bone, his clothes damp and covered with mud. Gravely, Wooster handed him the wax-sealed message, somehow sensing the note boded ill.

Standing next to Robert, Rafe popped the seal and scanned the words, certain even before he read them what they would say.

> We have your wife. If you want her to stay alive, you will follow these instructions. Come to Green Park at midnight. Take the path to the top of the knoll. Wait at the old oak tree. Come alone. Tell no one or your wife will die.

Green Park. It was a place he knew well — the place he had dueled with Oliver Randall.

"What does it say?" McKay asked, Caro clinging fearfully to his arm.

"They've taken Danielle."

"Who?"

"Oliver Randall. The note says I'm to go at midnight to the knoll in Green Park. That is the place we dueled. Randall was injured, very severely. Apparently, he is the man we've been seeking." He tapped the note. "McPhee was supposed to be watching him while Yarmouth kept an eye on my cousin. Something must have gone wrong."

Robert looked up at the grandfather clock in the entry. "You've got less than an hour to reach the park. We need to make some sort of plan." Robert started toward the study, but Rafe caught his arm.

"There isn't going to be any plan because you aren't going with me. The note said to come alone and that is what I intend to do."

"Don't be a fool. The man has tried to kill you twice before and nearly succeeded. Odds are he'll have hired men to help him, and this time he won't fail. If you go to the park by yourself, you're a dead man."

"I don't have any choice. I won't risk Dani's life. I appreciate your offer, but I can't take the chance."

"Dammit, man —"

Rafe shouted orders to a footman, telling him to have his phaeton readied and brought round to the front of the house, a vehicle to carry them home.

"I won't go unarmed," he told Robert.

"And I'm a damned good shot." Still, there were no guarantees. Rafe turned to Caro. "If something goes wrong, Dani will need you here when she gets home."

"I'll be here."

"Tell her I love her, will you? Tell her I wish I had told her just how much. Can you do that for me?"

Caro's blue eyes brimmed with tears. "I'll tell her."

He turned to McKay. "You're a good man, Robert. If anything happens to me, I trust you to look after both of them."

"Dammit, let me go with you. I'll stay in the darkness out of sight. I can cover you and they'll never know I'm there."

Rafe just started walking. He headed down the hall to his study, went in and pulled open the bottom drawer of his desk. A small pistol lay inside. Rafe took out the gun, shoved it into the pocket of his tailcoat and headed for the door leading out to the stables.

What happened to him didn't matter.

One way or another, the woman he loved was coming safely home.

Danielle sat rigidly in the carriage next to a bearded, foul-smelling man gripping a pistol in one of his dirty, hairy hands. Her own carriage sat abandoned on a darkened side street not more than ten blocks from Sheffield House. The driver, Michael Mullens, was bound and gagged, lying unconscious on the floor inside the coach.

Dear God, she had been a fool to leave! At the time, all she could think of was getting away from the house — away from Rafael. She was afraid that if she stayed, he would somehow convince her to abandon her plans, and in doing so, she would betray him.

She looked down at her hands, bound together in her lap. She hadn't really believed that she was in danger. It was Rafe who had enemies, not her. It had never occurred to her that the man who wanted him dead might use her as a weapon against him.

She had overheard them talking, knew they had sent him a note, or someone had, demanding a meeting. She shivered as the carriage rumbled along. She loved him so much. She had wanted to give him the one thing he truly wanted — a son to carry on his name.

Instead, she had put him in terrible danger.

Dear God, what if she wound up getting him killed?

She dragged in a shaky breath, forced a

note of calm into her voice. "Where are we going?" She stared out the isinglass window but the night was too dark to recognize anything familiar.

"Green Park," her captor said. Another man sat across from him, two of his bottom teeth missing, a bulbous nose spread across his ugly face.

"That is the place of the meeting?"

"We're hardly going there for a Sunday outin', luvie."

Green Park. It was the place Rafe had dueled with Oliver Randall. He had told her about it once and she had seen the scar on his arm.

So Randall was the man who wanted to kill him, just as Rafe had thought.

She glanced around the carriage, surveying the dark red velvet curtains, the polished brass lamps next to the windows, far too fine a vehicle for the likes of the two disreputable-looking characters sitting on the plush velvet seats. She imagined the rig must belong to Oliver and wondered if he planned to kill her as well as Rafe.

She said nothing as the pair of matched bay horses at the front of the carriage drew the coach through the darkened streets, but her mind whirled with plans, ways of helping Rafael. She discarded one after another, deciding she would have to wait and see how events unfolded. Whatever happened, she would not stand idly by and let these men murder her husband.

She would find a way to save him, no matter what it took.

Only a few more minutes passed before the carriage eased to a halt and the driver set the brake. He jumped down from his perch, a beefy man with thin gray hair and a hard set to his jaw.

Dani drew her cloak more tightly around her as he opened the door, and one of her captors prodded her with the barrel of his gun.

"Get out. And don't move too fast or I'll pull the trigger."

She ducked her head through the doorway and climbed down the iron stairs, the bearded man close behind her. The pistol prodded her ribs and she walked toward a path leading up the hill, the second man falling in behind them. All the way to the top, her mind whirled with ways she might elude them, ways she might escape and warn Rafael. But she had no idea where he was or which way he might enter the park.

She had no doubt he would come. Rafe

was a man of honor and he would come in defense of his wife, no matter what had passed between them. She had to wait until he got there, had to be ready to help him in whatever way she could.

"Up there." The pistol poked into her ribs and she moved forward, up the hill toward the top of the knoll. An ancient sycamore spread its boughs over the brown, dormant grass, and an icy wind swept over the darkened landscape. At the base of the tree, she paused, her gaze searching the darkness for the man she had once thought her friend, Oliver Randall.

Instead, another man stepped out of the darkness, a well-dressed figure wearing a great coat and tall beaver hat. He was perhaps in his late thirties, a handsome man she had never seen before. A second figure stepped forward and she froze at the unexpected sight of a woman.

"Well . . . here we are at last." She was dressed head to foot in black, with a fine black veil over the rim of her bonnet, which didn't quite cover her face. She was slightly shorter than Dani, more stoutly built, and she wore the cloak of authority as well as any man.

Danielle knew the woman as the Marchioness of Caverly, Oliver Randall's mother.

"So it was you, not your son."

"Thanks to your husband, my son is no longer the man he was before. In his stead, I am forced to do what he is now unable to accomplish."

"You think to kill Rafael?"

Her lips curled into an expression of disgust. "Before this night is over, I will see both of you dead."

A chill swept down Dani's spine. The old woman's hatred was nearly palpable. It was clear the marchioness wouldn't rest as long as either one of them was alive.

She glanced around the knoll, looking for something to use as a weapon, anything that might aid them, praying Rafe would not come.

Knowing with a certainty that reached deep inside her that he would.

Her heart twisted. She had only meant to spare him the lifelong pain of being childless, wed to a barren woman who could not give him the heir he so desperately needed. Instead, she had put him in the gravest of peril.

Footsteps sounded on the path, the long, familiar strides that belonged to Rafael.

Her pulse shot up, began a vicious pounding. She glanced wildly around the knoll, but the hill was as barren as she, and she saw no means of escape.

"Go back, Rafael! It's a trap!"

A fierce blow struck her across the cheek, sent her reeling back against the trunk of the tree.

"Shut up, ye bloody wench, or I'll shut yer bleedin' mouth meself."

She lay there shaking. She dragged a calming breath into her lungs and shoved herself unsteadily to her feet. The footsteps continued, though she knew Rafe had heard her warning, and a moment later, he appeared on the knoll. For an instant, his tall frame was outlined in a ray of moonlight that slipped through the clouds before the sky closed up again, and her heart trembled with love for him.

He stood no more than five feet away, and yet it might as well have been five miles. She wanted to reach out and touch him, to feel the beat of his heart, the swell of his chest as he drew breath into his lungs.

"I've come as you asked." His eyes left the well-dressed man and found her in the darkness. "Are you all right, my love?"

Her eyes welled with tears. "This is all my fault. I'm so terribly sorry."

His voice firmed. "This isn't your fault. Nothing that has ever happened has been your fault." He returned his attention to the well-dressed man. "I don't believe we've met."

"His name is Phillip Goddard." The marchioness's voice rose out of the darkness. She stepped from behind the tree and Rafe turned to her in surprise.

"Well, Lady Caverly . . . I must admit your involvement in this affair never occurred to me. The possibility of your husband seeking vengeance crossed my mind, but not you."

"Pity how often a man underestimates a woman."

Rafe's gaze found Danielle's and she saw something there she had never seen in his eyes before. It looked so much like love it made her want to weep. "Yes, it is."

"Mr. Goddard works for me. He is quite invaluable, as you have already discovered."

Rafe's fierce blue eyes swung to Phillip Goddard. "You set the fire."

"Arranged for it to be set."

"And the carriage accident?"

He shrugged. "Rather a nice bit of business, I thought. I'm surprised it didn't work as well as I planned."

"So what happens now?" Rafael asked.

The marchioness's stout figure moved slightly forward. "Now that you understand the reason you are here, you will die. Afterward, your bodies will be transported somewhere far away and you will simply disappear."

"You think you can murder the Duke and Duchess of Sheffield and no one will know that you are the one responsible?"

"You didn't figure it out. I'm an old woman, hardly a suspect. No one will ever be the wiser."

And Danielle thought that perhaps the old woman was right.

"Finish it," Lady Caverly said to Phillip Goddard.

Goddard tipped his head to the bearded man with the gun and he pointed the pistol at Rafe. Across from them, a pistol appeared in the hands of the toothless henchman, who pointed the weapon at Danielle, and everything happened at once.

Dani hurled herself at the man aiming at Rafe, slamming them both to the ground. His gun went off, the shot going wild, whizzing through the air. At the same instant, Rafe fired a shot from a pistol that must have been in the pocket of his coat and the man to his right went down. The henchman fired as he hit the grass, and Dani cried out at the burning pain that tore into her side.

"Danielle!"

Men seemed to appear out of nowhere. As she curled into a ball against the pain, she caught sight of the Earl of Brant's muscular figure racing toward them up the hill, running next to the Marquess of Belford, Ethan Sharpe. Robert McKay appeared on the opposite side of the knoll, a pistol pointed at Phillip Goddard.

Then Rafe was there, kneeling at her side, taking her hand and whispering her name.

"Danielle. Dear God, Danielle!"

The smell of gunpowder burned her eyes and the ache in her side swelled until she could barely breathe. Her eyelids felt heavy and darkness seemed to spread like a cloak around her. She forced her eyes open. "I'm so sorry."

"I am the one who is sorry. I love you, Danielle. I love you so very much."

Dani looked into his beloved face and saw the tears that spilled onto his cheeks. "I love you . . . too, Rafael. I never . . . really . . . stopped."

Then her eyes slid closed on a wave of pain and the darkness sucked her down.

Her final thought was of Rafael and that, at last, she would give him the gift of his freedom, the chance for a son he deserved so very much.

Thirty-Two

Neil McCauley stood next to Rafe in Danielle's bedchamber at Sheffield House. Her still figure lay limp and pale beneath the covers; her deep red hair fanned out around her pillow.

Since the night of the shooting, she had not awakened, and though he prayed her condition would change, it had not. He recalled that night and his chest tightened. According to the jumbled tale he had been told by his friends, Cord and Ethan had stopped by the house, worried about him and Dani, just minutes after his departure.

Robert had just been leaving, determined to follow Rafe to Green Park. The three men went together, which turned out to be a very good thing.

When the pistol shots quieted and the smell of gunpowder lifted, one of Philip Goddard's henchmen was dead, along with the Marchioness of Caverly, who was struck by a stray ball fired during the melee, though no one knew for certain which gun the shot had come from. Cord and Ethan had brought Goddard down, and Robert had taken down the other henchman.

With a bit of persuasion, the location of the abandoned carriage had been obtained and Mr. Mullens rescued.

Both Oliver Randall and the Marquess of Caverly were in mourning. The marquess himself had come to Sheffield House to speak to Rafael.

"It is over," he vowed. "Revenge has cost me a son and a wife. Oliver has confessed the truth of what happened that night five years ago. You have nothing more to fear from anyone in my family."

"I'm sorry for your loss," Rafe had said.

"I wish your wife a swift recovery," the marquess replied.

But so far that had not happened. Instead, Danielle lay near death and there was nothing that anyone seemed able to do.

Rafe looked down at the woman he loved and barely heard the doctor's words.

"I need to speak to you outside," McCauley said.

Rafe nodded dully. For the past five days he had been sitting with Danielle, holding on to her hand, telling her how much he loved her, that he couldn't live without her, saying the things he had been afraid to say before.

But Danielle had shown no signs of improvement, had made not the least response.

She simply lay there dying, and he felt as if his heart were being torn out of his chest.

He followed Neil out the door and closed it softly behind him.

"I'm sorry, Rafael. I wish I could tell you she is improving, but she is not."

His chest squeezed until it was hard to breathe. "You said she was young and strong, that there was a very good chance she would heal. You were able to remove the ball. You said that in time she should get better."

"I said those things, yes. I've seen far worse cases mend. But in this instance, there is something missing."

"What is it? What is missing?"

"The will to live. Little by little your wife is drifting away. She seems content to die. It is rare in someone so young. I really don't understand it."

The words burned like a hot coal in Rafe's stomach. Neil might not understand, but Rafe did. He remembered the afternoon Danielle had summoned him to the drawing room and told him that she wanted him to divorce her. She wanted to set him free so that he could remarry, so that he could have the heir he so badly needed.

There would be no divorce, Rafe had told her. Now dying had become her solution.

He raked a shaky hand through his hair, shoving it back from his forehead. He hadn't slept in days, hadn't eaten, couldn't summon the least bit of appetite.

"I don't know how to help her. I've talked to her, told her how much I love her, how much I need her. I can't seem to reach her." His voice broke on this last. "I don't know what to do."

"Perhaps there is nothing you can do."

The swish of a feminine skirt marked his mother's approach along the hall. She looked nearly as exhausted as he. "I don't believe that is true — not for a moment."

Rafe rubbed his weary eyes, wiping away a trace of wetness. "What are you saying?"

"You've done your best, Rafael. You've done everything you possibly could. Now it is my turn. I wish to speak to Danielle."

He eyed her warily. "Why?"

"Because I am a woman and perhaps the only one who can make her understand. I've had a great deal of time to think this through, and I believe, if anyone can reach her, I am the one who can." She pushed past them, opened the door and walked in.

Rafe watched her through the open door

as she sat down in the chair next to Dani's bed, reached over and took hold of her pale, limp hand. She cradled it carefully between both of her own.

"I want you to listen to me, Danielle. This is Rafael's mother speaking . . . your mother now, as well."

Danielle made no move.

His mother took a breath and released it slowly. "I've come to beg a favor, Danielle, a boon for me and my son. I am here to ask you to return to us, to make our lives whole again."

Rafe swallowed and glanced away.

"You know by now that Rafael loves you," his mother continued. "He has said so a thousand times since you have been lying here so gravely injured."

She pulled a handkerchief from the pocket of her skirt and dabbed it against her eyes. "But perhaps you don't know that without you, he is dying just as you are. Perhaps you don't understand that if you leave him, he will never recover. I know that it's true, because I saw what happened to him when he lost you before. Losing you nearly destroyed him. When you came back to him, you brought him back to life. You made him whole, Danielle, in a way he wasn't while he was without you."

The dowager sniffed, pressed the handkerchief beneath her nose. "I know you believe that if you go away, Rafael will remarry, that he will be able to have the son he needs to carry on his name. But I am here to tell you that is not what is most important. In these months since you married my son, I've learned any number of things. I've learned there are things more important than titles and money. Things like happiness. Like loving someone with all of your heart and being loved in return."

She wiped away more tears. "We are all of us Sheffields and we are survivors. We always have been. My sister and I, Rafael's cousins, if something happens and the title passes to Artie or somebody else, we might not have all of the things we have now, but we would not starve."

She raised Danielle's cold hand to her lips and kissed the back. "When you married Rafael, you gave my son back to me. You gave him the chance to be the man he was meant to be. He needs you, Danielle. He won't be that man without you. Please come back to us, darling girl. Come back to my son. He loves you so very, very much."

Rafe ignored the lump in his throat as his mother rose from beside Danielle's bed. As she walked past him out the door, he stopped her, then bent and kissed her cheek.

"Thank you, Mother."

She nodded. "It took a while for me to figure things out, but I see it all very clearly now." She wiped away a last unruly tear. "I only pray that she heard me and that she will return to us."

Rafe just nodded. Walking past her into the room, he returned to his place next to Dani's bed, reached over and took her hand.

"Return to me, my love," he said softly. "I don't want to live without you."

It wasn't until the following day, Rafe completely exhausted and utterly without hope, that Danielle opened her eyes and looked up at him.

"Rafael . . . ?"

"Danielle . . . dear God, I love you so much. Please don't leave me."

"Are you . . . sure?"

"Very, very sure."

Faint color seeped beneath the pale skin over her cheeks. "Then I'll stay with you . . . forever." And when she smiled at him, Rafe believed her and his heart soared.

Epilogue

Danielle stood at her bedchamber window, looking down on the garden below. It was a warm August day, the sun just beginning to sink below the horizon. There were children in the garden. Dani smiled as she watched little Maida Ann and Terry playing hide-and-seek along the gravel pathways, laughing as they darted in and out among the blooming flowers and leafy green foliage of the garden. Their nanny, Mrs. Higgins, watched over them from her perch on a wrought-iron bench near the fountain.

Maida held one of Robert's carved wooden horses tightly against her small chest, a treasure she prized above all the wonders she had received since she had become the adopted daughter of a duke.

Dani's heart squeezed as she watched them, the children who had made her house a home. Rafael had brought the little boy and girl to her bedside during the days of her recovery after the shooting, telling her that he remembered her talking about them and that Caro had explained that her fondest wish was to adopt them.

"Maida and Terry will be our first children, but not our last. We'll have as many as you want, my love, an entire houseful, if that is your wish."

She had wept when he told her, and silently vowed to make an even speedier recovery.

She was well now, back on her feet with little more than a scar in her side to remind her of the dark days back then. After all that had happened, she rarely thought of the bitter time before that night in Green Park, a time when she had believed that her husband would be better off without her.

Though Dani couldn't really remember the words Rafe's mother had spoken as she lay unconscious, somehow they had reached inside and called her back to the world she meant to leave behind.

She was needed, the dowager had said very firmly.

And she was loved.

And so these past six months, she had been happy, wildly, deliriously happy, and madly in love with her husband, who seemed to be equally in love with her.

They took long walks together, planned

Sunday outings in the country, took the children to Wycombe Park for a weeklong visit with Aunt Flora. They often spent time with Caro and Robert, who had repaid his indenture to Edmund Steigler and returned the money Rafe had spent to redeem the necklace.

At present, the earl and countess were staying at Robert's home, Leighton Hall, enjoying their time in the country, but they would soon return to the city.

Dani's life was filled with boundless joy, and yet as she rang for her lady's maid, a shy young woman named Mary Summers who had been with her since Caro's wedding, Dani could barely contain her excitement.

Something had happened. Something wonderful that she had discovered only this very day, a grand miracle that could not be and yet . . . And yet she knew deep inside, deep in the womanly recesses of her body, that the miracle was true.

She heard a light knock and hurried for the door, though it wasn't the timid knock she knew to be Mary Summers's. Instead, Rafael stepped into the opulent, refurbished duchess's suite, adjacent to the master's suite, where she slept each night with the duke.

"I ran into Mary. She was on her way up

to help you finish dressing, but I thought that I would help in her stead."

She blushed at the heat in the blue, blue eyes that skimmed over her body. She was gowned in emerald silk, dressed for an evening at the theater then a late supper with their best friends, Ethan and Grace, Cord and Victoria.

"I see you are nearly finished, much to my chagrin. I would rather have found you naked, but perhaps later on, we can take care of that. In the meantime, what can I do to help?"

She laughed as she turned her back to him, thinking that his plans exactly matched her own. "I just need you to do up the buttons and fasten my necklace."

She waited as he closed up the back of her gown, then set the pearls in the palm of his hand. Rafe draped the elegant strand around her neck and fastened the clasp. In the mirror, the glittering diamonds nestled between each perfect pearl sparkled in the light of the lamp. Rafe bent and pressed a kiss to the nape of her neck, then turned her to face him.

She was smiling so brightly his eyebrows went up. "You look extremely pleased with yourself. What is it?"

She reached up and touched the necklace,

felt its familiar, comforting warmth, and took a deep breath. "I've news, Your Grace. Very exciting news." She blinked, but couldn't keep the happy tears from brimming, then spilling onto her cheeks.

"You're crying."

She nodded. "I went to see Dr. McCauley today."

Worry crept into his features. "You're not ill? There is nothing —"

"No, it's nothing like that." Her smile went even wider. "A miracle has happened, Rafael. I don't know how or why. I know it isn't possible but it's happened just the same. I am going to have your child, my love. I'm going to have your baby."

For long moments, Rafe just stared. Then he swept her into his arms and crushed her against him. "Are you certain? Is the doctor sure?"

"He is very sure. I am more than four months gone with child. He says he doesn't understand how it could possibly have happened, but it has. And I know it is true. I can feel your child growing inside me."

Rafe simply held her and she felt faint tremors running through his tall, lean frame.

"I never thought . . . it was no longer important, but I . . . I am the happiest man in the world."

She laughed through her tears and clung to him and there were no words to describe the sheer joy bubbling inside her. She eased a little away, reached up and touched the pearls at her throat.

"It was the necklace," she said. "I know it." She thought that he would scoff, say that she was being foolish, that there had to be some other explanation.

Instead, he bent his head and very softly kissed her. "Perhaps. I suppose we shall never really know."

But Danielle knew. She had received the gift of great happiness the necklace promised. Caro and Robert had received that same gift, as had Victoria and Cord, Grace and Ethan.

Dani thought of Lady Ariana of Merrick and the great love she had shared with Lord Fallon.

Though it could never be proved and most people wouldn't believe it, deep in her heart, Dani knew the legend of the Bride's Necklace was true.

Author's Note

Rafe's concern over Napoléon's possible purchase of a fleet of Baltimore Clippers was not unfounded. The sleek-hulled sailing vessels were unique, fast and extremely maneuverable, far more so than the heavier, clumsier, full-rigged British ships of that time. In fact, just a few years later, during the War of 1812, American privateers, many of them sailing the amazing clippers, used them just as Rafe and his friends had feared, capturing or sinking more than 1,700 British merchant ships.

Fortunately, Napoléon's naval forces never commanded such a fleet.

I hope you all enjoyed Rafe and Dani's story, the final book in the *Necklace Trilogy*. If you haven't read *The Bride's Necklace* and *The Devil's Necklace*, I hope you will soon.

Till next time, happy reading!
All best wishes, Kat